SHADOW ENGINEER

BOOK ONE IN THE SCIQUEST LEGACY SERIES

SHADOW ENGINEER

AN ACTION-ADVENTURE TECHNO-THRILLER NOVEL

ERIC BOGATIN

LORI DEBOER

 Addie Rose Press

Published by
Addie Rose Press
www.AddieRosePress.com

ISBN-13: 978-0692571187 (paperback)

Cover design: Michael Molinet, Michael-Molinet.com
Interior layout: Veronica Yager, YellowStudiosOnline.com

Fourth Edition, December 2019
Printed in the United States of America

*This book has been a labor of love. We hope you enjoy
reading it as much as we enjoyed writing it.*

*Thanks to Susan and Michael, our patient spouses,
for giving us the support to finish.*

Lori also wants to thank Max for his enthusiasm and cheer.

*Much of this book was written, edited and re-written at the Starbucks in
Longmont, The Eagle Grill in Longmont and the Laughing Goat
in Boulder, Colorado.*

"SCIENCE FICTION IS to technology as romance novels are to marriage, propaganda."

—Jean Pontin, Technology Review, March 1, 2007

www.technologyreview.com/fromtheeditor/407393/on-science-fiction

1

I'M AN ENGINEER. My SEAL buddy, "Rusty" Steelanowski, once called me a ninjaneer because he said I'd grab a technical problem by the throat, throttle the life out of it, and grind its little face into the sand with my boot just to feel its eyeballs squish out. He knew that feeling well. That's what he said he did to bad guys. Okay, so he's a Navy SEAL. I'm not. I don't do violent stuff. I always felt there were alternatives. And so far, it had worked for me.

I can't resist pushing buttons or turning knobs. It's in my DNA. Flashing lights and shiny objects to me are like a fluttering bird to a cat. It's this obsession that got me into this mess.

My current client, Sciquest, has a plant in the brand new manufacturing district of Silicon Valley. Their production line was down because they had a plasma etcher laying on its back, feet up in the air, playing dead. I had until 6 am to breathe life back into it before two hundred operators showed up to work the line on Monday morning—nine and a half hours. I initially thought I would need ten hours. Piece of cake, my ninjaneer half was saying. My insecure half wasn't so sure.

I was ten blocks away, parallel to the fence line bordering the farms, on the western edge of Silicon Valley. With the ragtop down on my Jeep and the warm Santa Clara summer air blowing through my short curly hair, I could hear the wop, wop, wop of sprinklers in the distance and smell the earthy aroma of fresh tilled farms. My left arm rested on the window sill, the loose shirt sleeve of my white shirt flapping in the wind. Nine and a half hours. I could feel the cold sweat of fear dampening my brow. My insecure half was winning.

I was pushing it as fast as I thought safe. Less than five minutes out, I was turning on my ninjaneer sense, planning my attack. I was mentally listing the possible root causes of the problem and tests I'd run.

The manufacturing district was too new to have all the streetlights installed so many of the streets in the area were dark. A flicker at the end of the side street I just passed absently drew my gaze. I was thinking about monitoring the power draw during boot up to see if I could detect the inrush current when my foot slammed on the brakes.

It was purely unconscious. As my antilock brakes pulled me against my seat belt, I played back the after image recorded in my head.

I'd seen a fight. Down the end of the side street on the street parallel to me. Two large men, dragging a smaller man between them. I'd caught a glint from the smaller guy's glasses reflecting a distant streetlight.

I shifted into reverse, jammed the pedal to the floor. I was pulled against my seatbelt again. I stopped, straddling the cross street. It was only a block long to the end. The nearest streetlight was barely enough to give me a hint of the action.

It wasn't a fight. The short person was dwarfed by the two big guys. They each held an arm, dragging him kicking down the street.

I was momentarily torn. What could I do against two great big guys? It wasn't my fight. My life was going great. I had a lot to lose. And I was already late.

At least I could call the police.

I'd integrated a cell phone link in my visor with a DSP noise canceling interface. I pulled it down, activating the phone interface. "Phone, call 911," I said quietly. I knew the DSP circuit could pick up my voice.

"Cannot connect. Bluetooth secure. Static level at 13 dB above carrier. Trying alternative channels. Static level at 12 dB above carrier. Cannot lock. Excessive noise," responded the synthesized voice.

That couldn't be. I'd jacked the transmission power to an illegal eighteen watts and added an automatic gain control circuit in the receiver. I knew my car's phone interface was more sensitive than the cell phone in my pocket. With it, I could reach cell towers fifty miles away. I'd programmed in a few diagnostic responses. These indicated good local connections, but with too much outside interference. This was not the time for a glitch. And no time to debug the system.

I pushed the visor up and pulled it down again to reset it. "Phone, dial 911," I said more forcefully, as if that would help.

"Cannot connect. Bluetooth secure. Static level at 14 dB above carrier. Trying alternative channels. Static level at 15 dB above carrier. Cannot lock. Excessive noise," it responded again. The interference noise was even stronger now.

I stole quick glances down the street to watch the progress. The three were at the end of the street and the light was really bad. I could just see the struggle as vague shapes. The shorter guy wasn't being hit or anything, it was more like an abduction. He was being dragged. The two big wrestler types didn't seem to notice me. I wasn't feeling particularly brave right now. Maybe I could make it to the factory and call 911 from a land line.

And then I heard *her* scream.

2

THEY WERE ABDUCTING a woman. Her scream was like a catalyst. I felt something hard-wired in me was being turned on for the first time. The flood of adrenaline through my system gave me clarity. It took me all of a nanosecond to decide.

No phone service, couldn't call for help. It was up to me. What could I do?

I turned the wheel hard to the right and pointed my 3,500-pound Jeep at the end of the street. I clicked the high beams. I got a better look at the set up. Like Rusty used to say to me, "Leverage your strengths."

She was not going down quietly. I could make out her screams even a block away. "Help! Help me!"

They held her wrists between them, immobile, while her head and body twisted. I reacted without a clear plan. I'd just have to make it up as I went along. My right foot pushed the pedal to the floor and the Jeep accelerated toward them.

I flashed the high beams and honked my horn. It worked. I got their attention. One of the guys let her go, stepped away and turned to face me. He was big, so broad shouldered and his arms hung down away from his body. He was little more than a dark shadow even in my high beams in his black leather jacket and dark pants.

I was closing. It was his eyes that rattled me. They glowed back like a couple of LEDs. What man has eyes that reflect light like a cat? It didn't matter though—those eyes were going to be his undoing tonight. I used them like a beacon to home in.

Let's see how you do against 3,500 pounds of steel and carbon fiber composite, I thought. I was maybe twenty yards away, doing about thirty miles per hour, accelerating. I lined up on those eyes. I saw him smile, reach under his jacket, and pull out a gun.

In the one second before I was going to smash him against the building, my brain was working overtime. I thought it was a gun, but it was just a long barrel with a mirror shiny surface. I saw its large diameter, black hole facing me, getting larger. Was it a pipe he was going to throw at me?

The muscle-bound giant's fingers curled around the barrel but he held it level, pointing at me. I saw his fingers move along the barrel grip. Not to throw, but like he was going to fire. It looked like a flare gun. I wasn't too concerned. My windshield would deflect a flare. But his smile got broader, and with his teeth showing, it wasn't a pretty sight.

In the split second before I plowed into him, I noticed his really bad teeth. He was missing two on the bottom, and one upper incisor seemed to point outward. But he smiled. I was about to smash him against the wall. Why was he smiling? He looked more confident than someone holding just a flare gun. Could it be a grenade launcher? In the last microsecond I had to live, I thought I might have underestimated his weapon.

I was pinned by my seat belt. In a last-ditch effort, I slid to the right, as far down below the dash as I could. It was just in time. I heard a loud *poof*, and even with my eyes tightly shut, expecting to be blown into constituent atoms, sensed a flash just above and behind me. The Jeep bounced up when it hit the curb, jerking me back upright.

I was still alive, but engulfed in a cloud of smoke and charred debris from the headrest stuffing. I couldn't see much through the smoky haze, more felt the bump when the front of the car smashed into the stomach of the would-be kidnapper. I slammed the brakes and heard a loud clank on the hood. The smoke cleared enough for me to see his head disappear under the front of my Jeep. I came to a stop a good two feet from the building.

Wait a minute. I was looking through the still-intact windshield he had shot. My head rest was gone. I could feel the heat from its still smoldering remains against my neck.

A laser weapon? Who has a hand-held laser weapon? But what else could it be? Had I just entered the Twilight Zone?

Maybe she was screaming this whole time. I was too distracted to notice. With one threat down, I turned to the woman held by the other captor. I could hear her screaming at him now. "Let go, you big troll, You're hurting me!" He was saying something, but it sounded more like low grunts. He held her by the wrist. Her other hand was trying to pry open those sausage-like fingers. They didn't budge.

He had big shoulders like his buddy under this leather jacket. Thick neck. How to take him out? I was frantically working through one scenario after another. Like I said, I'm not good with violence and I'm not very strong.

I saw his free hand reaching under his jacket. I had to do something.

I shouted over to them, "Hey, let her go. I've got a gun. I'll shoot if you don't let her go."

He looked at me. Then he smiled back. What's with these guys? Bluffing always worked in the movies. His eyes never left me as he fumbled under his jacket.

I shoved the car door open and hopped out. And immediately let out a howl. I twisted my ankle on something. I glanced down. It was that silvery pipe. It had rolled under the car and I'd slipped on it.

I picked it up. Still holding the car door, favoring my twisted ankle, I pointed the pipe at the big guy and shouted again, "Let her go or I'll shoot." He paused, hand under his jacket. No more smile.

I couldn't risk looking at the pipe. I was too fixated on the big fellow in front of me. I was feeling around the end of the pipe with my fingers. Nothing, just a smooth surface. I couldn't even tell which end the beam came out. Was I pointing the business end at him or at me?

That broad smile came back. It must have been at me.

Either he was Cat-Eye's brother, or at least they shared the same dentist. He had gaps in the bottom row and one incisor that looked like it could rip a chunk off a raw leg of lamb. I saw this in an instant.

I was running out of options as fast as I was running out of time. I was too exposed, the woman was still in danger. I desperately needed a plan. His free hand apparently found what it was searching for under his jacket. I had a pretty good idea what it would be holding.

I'd run out of time.

3

THE WOMAN GAVE up trying to pry the fingers off her wrist. When her kidnapper was distracted toying with me, she stretched as far back as her pinned arm allowed and swung her leg around, going for the 100-yard field goal right into his balls. He let out a deep guttural growl.

He doubled over, moaning, but never let go of her. With his head down, she followed through with a sharp knee jab into his nose. As his bloodied face came up, she swung her free arm around like a tennis racquet into his exposed ear. I heard her scream in pain when her hand smashed into the guy's head. But it did the trick, she was free.

"Come on," I shouted. "Quick get in, I'll get you out of here."

She came around the front of the Jeep and I got back in the front seat. I slipped the laser weapon in the console between the seats. I saw her step on top of Mr. Cat Eyes who was still on the ground. She gave him an extra sharp stomp and said something that sounded like "God-damned Neanderthal." I thought that an apt description. I was soon to find out just how apt.

She came around the passenger side of the Jeep and fumbled with the door. "Unlock the door!" She was pushing the button and pulling the door but not making any progress, obviously not able to apply much strength. "Hurry." She was frantic.

Jeep doors are sometimes hard to open. "It's unlocked. Just push the button and pull." The tough guy, who had gotten up was staggering toward me.

"I can't. My hands are too sore. Open the God damn door!"

I turned toward her. "Hold on, I'll get it for you." Up close, all I saw were her wide, green eyes looking back at me. They were stunning. Her pupils were large, black holes from the dim light. They contrasted with her irises, yellow bands spreading radially outwards against a green background. Even through the pair of black, wide-framed glasses she wore, her eyes shone.

I forgot to mention, I'm attracted by bright, shiny objects and cute women with green eyes. But, they weren't really looking at me, they were focused behind me.

"He's coming! Move faster! Let me in."

I lost the lock on her eyes. In my twisted position, reaching for the passenger door, I had to strain to look over my left shoulder. The musclebound kidnapper was charging toward us.

Help her and he gets me. Back up and he gets her.

I was reacting in the worst possible way to my fear, freezing into inaction. I was the deer in the headlights. This was exactly the sort of situation I'd tried to avoid all my life.

Time slowed down. I lived between heartbeats. The stupidest details stood out to me. His head was bent toward me as he picked up steam. I noticed his hair, bristly, in tufts like crab grass growing in a lawn or like an antique stuffed buffalo I once saw.

"The door!" Her panicked shout pulled me out of my fatalistic trance.

I looked back at the woman, struggling to get in. Those green eyes decided it for me.

I reached over to the passenger door and unlatched the door for her. "Just pull the door straight back," I shouted to her. She finally yanked the door open and was sliding in. Too late. Her kidnapper was reaching for me through my window, almost on me. His nose was a bloody mess, flinging off blood as he shook his head in his rage.

I unlatched my door and kicked it wide open, the thick part of the door catching him in the stomach. His hands were inches from my neck. He doubled over, the window frame connected with his face making a delightful sound, like a sledgehammer hitting a watermelon. Blood spattered to either side of his face. He left a bloody smear on the door frame.

But it didn't stop him. He staggered back a few steps. His nose was crushed, almost flat against his face. Blood flowed down his face and dripped from his chin. He grabbed the door frame, bellowing at me like an animal, trying to rip the door off its hinges.

Jeeps have Kevlar hinges, stronger than steel, but he looked like he might be able test their limits. We were playing tug of war with the door and he was winning.

"I'm in. Go go go!" I heard beside me. I didn't need any more encouragement. I was completely exposed. I reached down, shifted into reverse and floored it.

He was running beside the door for the first ten feet, then lost his footing. He still held the door frame. From the way the Jeep tipped, my engineer brain estimated he weighed in at more than 350. I accelerated, he hung on.

I swung the Jeep around in an arc. The door was opened to its maximum. With his mass on the end of the swinging door, I felt for sure the Kevlar hinge was going to snap.

At the end of our ninety-degree arc, I shifted into drive and stepped on it. Buffalo hair was fast for his size. In that brief instant when I was reversing direction, he got back on his feet, still clutching the door frame with one arm. The door was wide open between us. Reaching out his free arm toward me, he looked like a ghoul that had just taken a bite out of a freshly killed body and wanted seconds from me.

I did the only thing I could; I floored it.

As I accelerated forward, he was dragged off balance again. He grabbed the car frame. The door tried to come back to its natural, resting state, closed, but his fingers were in the way. I heard over the revving engine the satisfying crunch of his fingers. With one final howl, he let go and fell to the road. I slammed the door shut and we accelerated away.

Out of my side mirror, I watched his prone shadow blend with the dark street. All I wanted to do was put distance between me and what must have been 700 collective pounds of bad guy.

Not too shabby a job, I was thinking. Two big, hairy tough guys down, one woman rescued, and I was still alive and mostly unharmed. My ankle was still little sore. My neck was irritated from what was left of the smoldering headrest. I was feeling more than okay; I was feeling great. But she was screaming something at me.

4

"**YOUR PHONE, GIVE** me your phone, I need to make a call right away."

I picked up the panic in her voice. "It's okay, you're safe now."

"You have no idea," she said to me, her voice teetering on hysteria. "We are not safe. We're never going to be safe again." Her hands were balling up into fists and she was shaking them.

She opened her fists and used one hand to rub the wrist of the other. "Damn, that hurts."

I paused. I didn't know how to react to her outburst. She looked over at me, fire in her eyes. "Are you the only guy in Silicon Valley without a phone?"

Two strands of light brown hair dangling on either side of her face, escapees from the shaking her ponytail had gone through. A broad black strap held her glasses in place. That was probably why she hadn't shaken them off in her struggles. The reflections from those glasses saved her life tonight.

My adrenaline rush was dying down. "I'll try again, but I wasn't able to get through a minute ago." I pulled down the visor, and said clearly, "Phone, dial 911."

"Cannot connect. Bluetooth secure. Static level at 17 dB above carrier. Trying alternative channels. Static level at 19 dB above carrier. Cannot lock. Excessive noise."

"What kind of phone do you have? It's got diagnostics built in." She sounded a little surprised.

"I've made some modifications to it," I said with more than a little pride. "Must be something wrong with the local cell towers." The interfering noise level was increasing.

"That's what I was afraid of. Turn right at the next corner." She was a little calmer now. Her tone was more commanding, less hysterical.

"What's going on?"

"I don't think there's much time. Just drive, faster."

I'd been flooring it, but even downhill with a strong tail wind, fast is not a term anyone would use to describe a Jeep.

"Where's your car? I can drop you off."

"My vehicle had problems. That's why I was on foot. My company has a branch office maybe a mile from here," she said. "We have to get there. They'll have a LAN hardline connection." She was speaking my language. Who was this woman?

"Wouldn't you rather we get you to a police station? You're hurt. I can get you to a hospital."

"My wrists are still sore from those brutes but I'm okay. It's more important I call in."

"What's going on? Who were those two guys? Were they just trolling the neighborhood around here? Most of these buildings are empty. Not sure what they would be looking for. How unlucky they just happened to find you?"

Wait a minute, that wasn't the most bizarre aspect of the evening. "Did you know they had laser hand weapons?"

"That's not important. The only important thing is I have to contact my boss. If these buildings are empty that rules out breaking in somewhere and accessing a land line," she mumbled mostly to herself. "My office is going to be the nearest phone. Turn left at the next block."

I was getting a little irritated at being given orders and not getting answers. Not even a thank you. I glanced over at her again. She looked to be about thirty, close to my age. She wore a plain, light tan tee shirt and dark brown shorts. Her ponytail was flapping a little in the growing wind of the slipstream. Those two wisps of hair on either side of her head were flying around her face. She tried to move one of them back in place behind her ear with her right hand. She was tucking it under her glasses' band.

I noticed the faint outline of a tattoo under her tee shirt on her left shoulder. It looked like a spider with legs curled around its central body. A bizarre figure like that must be some kind of gang tattoo. What had I gotten myself into?

"Cell phone's out," I said. "It's Sunday night. I only know of one building around here that might be occupied. There's still a lot of construction going on. Not too many companies have moved in yet."

I had to slow down around the last curb. I was just straightening out and accelerating.

"Can't you go any faster? You don't understand how important this is."

"Hey, I'm going as fast as I can and you're right, I don't understand how important this is. Don't you want to go someplace more public? More people, more cell phone options. It might be safer."

"No," she nearly shouted at me. "My building will be secure. Just keep down this street. I'll tell you when to turn."

I was getting a little fed up with her orders and I did not want to get involved in some sort of turf war. She knew a lot more than she was saying. If it wasn't for the anomaly of the laser hand weapons, I'd be very tempted to just drop her off at the curb and let her hoof it to her office. I did rescue her from those thugs, after all. I really didn't want to get sucked into something that was feeling to be more and more in the shadows of what was legal.

On the other hand, I really wanted to find out who had laser hand weapons.

"Tell me what's going on right now, or I pull over and let you off. You've got a good head start on your friends back there."

"Oh crap," she shouted. "Break left! NOW!"

It took me a fraction of a second before I reacted while I debated with myself. She won by a hair. I jerked the wheel to the left.

In the street to our right, where we would have been, a mushroom cloud of exploded asphalt, black, oily smoke and flame roiled upward. We left it in our wake. I glanced in my rearview mirror. "They're behind us!"

She hunched forward, looking at the passenger side mirror. "Ya think?" she shouted. "Right, slide right!"

I jerked the wheel, but wasn't fast enough.

There was a boom right next to my ear. It was like I was standing next to a 155 millimeter howitzer cannon. My ears rang from the explosion. Dense, black, smelly smoke like burning rubber washed into the front seat. We were both gagging for an instant. My eyes watered so much I was having a hard time seeing the road. I drove by feel, kept weaving back and forth as quickly as I dared until the smoke cleared a little with the slipstream.

Her quick thinking gained us a few more precious seconds. She was good. I rubbed my watery eyes on my shoulder to clear them and risked a quick glance in the rearview mirror. I was looking through a hole in the back spare tire, right between our heads. An instant of hesitation either way, and it would have been one of us with a hole.

We were the hunted. The only tool I had was my Jeep. How to leverage it? Fueled by fear, I was quickly running through my limited options. We couldn't outrun them. I had to outmaneuver them. What else could we do?

I turned a corner. Farther back, down the street we had just entered, a few blocks behind us, I could see a parking lot. It couldn't have been, but it looked like a small plane was sitting in the parking lot, its tail sticking partly out into the street. There were two jet engine pods in the rear in front of the tail fins. What was a jet doing in the middle of a parking lot in an industrial zone? Had I made a wrong turn into a separate reality somewhere?

I blinked away this anomaly. Much closer behind us, now finishing the same turn we just completed, was the white panel van, gaining on us. Sticking out the passenger window was an arm long enough to belong on a gorilla, holding a silvery pipe pointed at us. I slid left to block their passenger side from us.

"Take the next right," she interrupted my thoughts. "We have another few blocks farther on."

"Can't do rights. That'll put us broadside to their laser. We have to keep their passenger side away from us. Buckle up! It's going to be pretty rough."

"But my building is just a few blocks away."

I was swerving around, trying to be a little random, anything but a straight line. I was favoring the left side.

"We don't have a few blocks. We're sitting ducks out here."

To accent my point, there was another explosion. This time, the lamp post we'd just passed shot sparks to the other side of the street. It was severed almost in half. I was running out of street, already nearly hugging the curb.

"The mirrors!" she shouted.

I didn't need any more of a hint. Of course! I reached out and turned my side mirror as far out as it would go. I saw her do the same. I took one more glance in the rear view mirror over the dashboard. I saw the gorilla arm hanging out the window, struggling to reach around the front of the van to line up on us, now closer. For the second time tonight, I was staring down the open, black hole in the center of the barrel.

I tilted the mirror up to its limit and pulled my arm down. Just in time. The mirror frame and center support of the windshield exploded in a shower of molten metal and glass.

I heard her scream.

A few drops of molten goo had splashed on her arm, which she'd held up to protect her face. I knew exactly what that felt like. I had a few still-molten drops of hot glass searing their way into my arm. Even through my adrenaline fueled fever, I could feel their hot needles puncturing my skin. If I wasn't so scared, I'd have been screaming my head off too. The only thing I hated more than roller coaster rides was pain.

It could have been much worse. If she hadn't given me that hint, it would have been my head exploding in a shower of brain and bone droplets. Who was this woman?

"Are you okay?"

"Damn it hurts. Keep driving. We have to get away from them. Just go faster."

"We can't outrun them," I said. "We have to keep them turning." We were not going to make it much farther. Our luck was going to run out. I desperately needed a plan. How could we hide from a laser weapon?

"The parking garage! Turn right. Maybe we can lose them inside!" she said.

I saw it too and did a two-wheel turn into the garage. We just missed another blast that blew a hole in the cement pillar at the entrance of the garage. A cloud of dust and rocks blasted out behind us. But we were inside and had a head start.

The garage was empty. It looked like the building above wasn't even finished. No overhead lights installed yet. Our headlights cast shadows from the pillars every twenty feet.

"Where are they?" I shouted. My mirrors were out and I couldn't risk a look back. I was maneuvering around the pillars set up almost like an obstacle course.

"They just pulled up by the curb," she said, looking behind us.

I suddenly realized why they didn't follow us in. I saw cement walls everywhere I looked. The parking garage wasn't a pass through. It looked like there was only one entrance. And it was also the exit. We were trapped and they knew it. If I didn't do something fast, we'd be like a target in a shooting range.

The garage was partitioned into a large area and a more private area with a four-foot cement wall separating the regions. I turned the corner and used some of the wall to protect most of the Jeep. We could stretch our necks and peer over the wall to see the entrance.

She had the better view. "One of those goons just got out the passenger side," she said. "He's limping. I hope he's the one I kicked in the balls."

The one with the laser turned toward us. He locked his eyes on mine. There was no smile this time. He just held my eyes like a snake about to strike at a rat. I was the rat. The laser was leveled at me.

For the third time tonight, I found myself looking down the long silver barrel of a laser hand weapon. When I saw his fingers move along the back end, I knew exactly what to do.

"Duck!" I shouted. We both crouched in our seats below the level of the cement wall.

Three feet from us, another thunderous explosion and a cloud of dust and dirt blew outward from the other side of the wall. It didn't penetrate. One more blast in the same spot and it probably would.

We carefully raised our head above the wall. The laser armed gunman wasn't looking at us. He was looking down the street. I followed his gaze but couldn't see anything from my angle. "What's going on?" I whispered.

"There's a car coming. He's lining up," she said. "Holy crap, he just shot at them!"

I stood up in my seat to get a good look over the wall. I saw the car drive by. In the driver's seat, the head of the driver was just slumping over the steering wheel. Even from my position, at least twenty five yards away, I could see the hole clear through the poor man's head. There was no blood. Just a path wide enough to stick a fist through. I could just make out the window on the other side of the poor man's head, the background flickering though what once was his brain. That laser weapon made short work of skull and brains, cauterizing along the way.

The car logo read Carlyle Cleaning Services. He must have been cleaning up one of the buildings preparing to open in the morning. He was just an unlucky bystander tonight, in the wrong place at the wrong time. Kind of like me.

But they weren't finished with him yet. This wrestler with the long arms raised the laser and tracked the car as it appeared on the other side of the van and fired again. The driver was already dead.

Now he was going after the car. His shot hit the rear wheel. It exploded in a black, billowing oily cloud. We could hear the explosion echoing through the open cavern of the parking garage. The car swerved, bring its rear into a direct line to the laser.

He fired again and this time must have struck the gas tank. The back half of the car blew up. The fireball flipped it over. The whole car skidded a few feet and came to rest on its back, totally engulfed in flames. The whole attack took less than three seconds.

With the witness out of the way, he could bring his attention back to us.

The guy with the laser was raising his arm when his partner said something. I only heard it as an indistinct grunt from deep inside the garage. But he handed a small grey-colored ball out the window.

It looked about the size of a softball and had a small flashing blue light. Mr. Buffalo hair pushed twice on its surface and the flashing doubled in frequency. Then he smiled and tossed the ball into the parking lot. It rolled about two yards, stopped and then started up again, and rolled to the center of the garage. It was self-propelled.

Not good. I didn't need a demonstration to know this ball was going to be bad news for us. At this point, I was ready to believe it could have been some kind of black hole bomb that was going to suck the building into a singularity with us in it.

It was also between us and the only way out.

"Turn your headlights off!" It wasn't a request. She was screaming an order.

She'd gotten us into this trap, but she'd also saved our neck a few times tonight. I turned the headlights off.

A faint glow emerged from the darkness ahead.

"There, to the left. Drive. There may be a way out."

Now that she had pointed it out, I saw it too. Maybe we weren't trapped.

I screeched the tires on the slick cement floor. Sure enough, in another five yards, I saw down a passageway to the left. This wasn't a dead end. It was a private entrance, not quite finished yet, and not much wider than my Jeep.

It ended in a black plastic sheet held in place by two crossed wooden two by fours. In the otherwise pitch black corridor, there was a little light leaking through the edges of the black sheet. Was this covering another half a wall or an escape route? Did we have a choice? Take our chances with the flashing baseball or crash into a wall? I didn't really like either option but I'd run out of time. I turned down the passageway and floored it. I was too late.

The sphere in the middle of the parking garage exploded. The explosion rocked the Jeep, lifting the back up and bouncing us forward.

It wasn't a black hole bomb. Quite the opposite. As tiny as it was, it packed an explosion that started the ceiling collapsing.

We had bounced maybe only twice when the entire ceiling, with the rest of the building following, collapsed. Chunks fell around the car, like someone was pouring rubble from a giant cauldron. The cloud of rocks and fragments and dust billowed outward like a shock wave front through the open framework of the unfinished garage. It started in the center and the tsunami wave of cement fragments spread outward, right toward us.

"Get us out of here!" screamed my passenger.

We were rocketing down the short passageway when the shock front caught up with us. It lifted the rear wheels of the Jeep. Propelling us down the rest of the passage way like a bullet fired out of a rifle barrel, right through the wooden cross frame. The black plastic sheeting bulged outward and with our impact, burst like a balloon.

In the middle of the dense fog of dust and debris, I was blinded. The dust choked me. In an instant we popped through the plastic barrier and ten yards into the street, emerged beyond the dust front. I could breathe again. We ended up on the opposite side of the street from the parking garage entrance.

We coughed out the dust after we blasted into fresh air. Like a chain reaction, the entire building, right where we just left, collapsed in ruin.

"Oh my God," she said, her face pale and covered with dust.

I accelerated down the street, away from this disaster. "Who are these guys? Do you realize they just killed that poor man and literally blew up a building trying to take us out?" I shouted at her over the engine roar.

"I don't know who they are, but now you know how important it is for me to call in to my headquarters. I have to get to a phone right away."

I was driving as fast as I could. "I'll try the phone again." I pulled the visor down and said, "Phone, call 911."

All we had time for was the "Unable to connect," message before she screamed again in my ear. "They're still behind us. They just turned the corner. You have to do something. They're gaining."

I took the next left, driving over the curb to cut it close. With the mirror out, I turned my head back over my left shoulder to watch for the van. The killers had to slow to make the turn and their passenger side was blocked.

"Now you've done it!" she shouted over the roar of the engine, "We're trapped."

Still looking over my shoulder, I caught the sign mounted on the pole by the curb as we passed: Dead End.

5

THERE WAS A fence a half a block away, at the border to a soybean farm. I was thinking frantically, though my head had never been so clear. The proximity to death washed away absolutely every other thought except what I needed for my next move.

I was cursing myself for wishing for more excitement in my life. I didn't mean like this. But there was a small part of me that noticed the closer to death I came, the more alive I felt. I wanted a technical challenge on a deadline, well now I had one. What was my next move going to be?

Of course! How do you hide from a laser weapon? I pressed my foot to the floor and the Jeep screamed forward.

"You fool! You're going to kill us."

"No, this is perfect," I said.

"We'll get stuck in the field. Then we'll really be sitting ducks!"

I ignored her comments and just smiled to myself, thinking what Rusty would say about my plan. "You've never been in a Jeep before, have you?" I shouted in triumph. "Just hold on!"

We hit the curb and went airborne for at least five feet. The chain link fence was no match to the heavy Jeep traveling at forty miles an hour. The trampled fence was the perfect ramp to navigate us over the drainage ditch bordering the farm. Then we hit the plowed field.

With the engine revved near the red line, the wheels spun in the soft, sometimes damp earth, throwing up huge contrails of mud and pieces of soybean stems and leaves. I was having problems steering. The rear wheels slipped in and out of the furrows.

A strobe flash went off behind and above us with an instantaneous crack of thunder. Mud clods and leaves erupted in a steam explosion as the water inside them exploded like giant popcorn. The mud protected us from the laser blast. My plan was working.

I reached down with my right hand and engaged the four wheel drive. The front wheels bit into the ground. Much better, now that I could steer. We had four rooster tales of dirt and debris flying behind us. By shifting the wheel slightly, I could direct two of them for better coverage. We also picked up speed.

There were two more flashes and thunderous explosions as pieces of our mud shield exploded. But each was farther behind. Another explosion hit the field more than twenty yards to the left. Not even close.

"Look behind us," I told her. "What are they doing?"

"The van just entered the field. It's swerving all over. Looks like they're angling to get around your mud cloud. Veer right a little."

"We have to stick to the plowed tracks. Only thing we can do is put more distance between us."

"Turn your wheel to the right, now!" she shouted.

I followed her lead. The front wheel was spinning too fast to bite in and carry us over the plowed furrow, but the rooster tail of mud shot off to the side. A lightning strobe illuminated the Jeep and the explosive blast scattered dirt and mud into our hair. But the laser blast was absorbed by our shield. She was good.

"They're bouncing all around now, trying to cross the field. I don't think they can get in a clean shot."

There was another blast in the field behind us and off to our left. With them at this angle, my mud shield was useless, but between their bouncing and our distance, they couldn't get in a good shot. We made a beeline down the plowed path.

"This is not good," she said. "We're heading farther away from my branch office. I have to get back. Everything is at risk if I can't call in."

She was right. We were heading into the open field. Where could we go?

"Maybe we can lead them far enough into the field and then reverse back," I said. "At least they can't get a good shot at us while they're bouncing around."

"It's getting worse," she said. "It looks like they're heading toward the service road. If they make it, they can circle around the field and beat us in either direction."

They were still shooting wild. If they got to the service road, I was more worried they'd be stable enough to get in a lucky shot. I did not think I had enough Karma left in my Karma bank to cover more than another few minutes at this rate.

"I told you this was a bad idea," she said. "We have to get out of this field. If they call in reinforcements, we'll be trapped for sure."

"What are you talking about? What reinforcements? Do you know who these guys are? Are they in your gang or a rival gang?"

"My gang? What are you talking about?" She turned to me, looking perplexed. "Why would you think I was in a gang? Do I look like a gang member to you?"

"Your tattoo. Isn't that spider a gang symbol?"

"Spider? That's not a spider! That's the Andromeda Galaxy."

"It sure looks like a spider."

"You try finding a tattoo artist at one in the morning who knows what the Andromeda Galaxy looks like. We're wasting time and I don't have any to spare." She was scared and frustrated.

An Andromeda Galaxy tattoo? Who was this woman?

"They're going to get a lucky shot in and hit us for sure. You have to do something."

She was right, though. She was throwing the ball to my court. I was tired of being chased down by a pair of bullies. I don't tolerate bullies very well. Ready for plan B.

"Not if we get them first," I said.

6

WE WERE MAYBE a hundred yards away from the white van. I could see our pursuers highlighted against the dark field in the dimming twilight. But, how well could they see us? My green and brown Jeep, now mostly covered in mud, would blend in with the dark field. If those glowing eyes had the same features of a cat's, at least one of those guys could see better in the dark than I could. I turned off our headlights. No sense making it too easy for them. The last hit was in the field more than twenty feet away. I turned the Jeep so my driver side door was broadside to the van and came to a halt.

She was frantic. She grabbed my arm, pulled me around to face her. "What are you doing? I told you we'd get stuck. We're sitting here like an insect pinned to a board."

I shook off her grip and reached for the laser weapon I'd thrown between the seats. "We're not stuck. The only way we're getting out of here is if we can take them out with this, before they take us out."

I shook the silvery tube in emphasis. "It's time to go on the offensive. Either get out and run or calm down."

"You know I can't get far in this field on foot." Almost under her breath, she added, "I'm not so sure I'm better off now than I was before you came around."

That hurt. I got us this far against pretty long odds. I'd invested too much of my hard-earned Karma. All my chips were on the table.

Besides, I'd never tolerated bullies very well. Now I was in a position to do something about a pair of them and I didn't need a lot of negative energy around me.

"Don't give up on me yet." My bravado was more for me than her. "They're in a white van. We're so covered in mud, we're mostly camouflaged. I think I can see them better than they can see us. We can use that, and this," I held the laser in front of me.

"Do you know anything about this laser?" I asked. "Like how to fire it?"

"No," she said, glancing over. "This is the first time I've seen anything like it. Let me see it." She reached over to grab it.

I brushed her hand aside. Okay, she thought of the mirrors and she had an Andromeda tattoo on her shoulder, but if we were starting from the same level, I had more confidence in my ability to figure out how to fire the laser.

"I'm an astrophysicist," she said, reaching for it again, "I can figure it out."

"And I'm an engineer, I can make it work." I raised my elbow to block her hand. "You watch the van. Let me know if it stops."

She shut up and rested her hand on my shoulder to help her twist around and watch the van. "They're almost to the edge of the field. In a few seconds they're going to be on the service road." Her touch was distracting. But I was not going to ask her to remove it.

Concentrate. I looked at the laser tube carefully. One end was round like a hemispherical cap. The other end was squared off, with a hole. At the risk of doing something really stupid, I looked down in the hole, careful to not move my hand on the barrel. I still didn't know how to fire this thing.

Maybe an inch inside the opening was a solid membrane, probably the front surface mirror. The back end of the tube did not have any visible buttons. The vision of the big guy's hand with his fingers sliding over the grip just before he shot at me, three times, I reminded myself with a shudder, was still frozen in my mind's eye.

"They stopped. I think they saw us stop and are trying to line up a shot," she said quietly in my ear.

I held the laser out the side window. I focused in the distance and caught the white van silhouetted against the dark field. My hand carefully slid down my end of the barrel. I felt three small bubbles in the surface, two along the side, one on top. My exploration was rudely interrupted with another explosion just a few feet in front of my window. "Can you do this?" she breathed in my ear. "They're getting our range."

I looked over at her, leaning in close to me to stare over my shoulder. Those green eyes stared back at me, wide open. What an incentive. She was the carrot. Getting evaporated by the next laser blast was the stick.

Even if I wanted to, I didn't have the time now to start the Jeep up and get moving. Maybe she was right, were we stuck in the mud? It wouldn't be the first time for me.

Could I figure this out in time? I had maybe two seconds before they scored a direct hit. My insecure side was shouting at me. It was always like this as I approached a deadline with a project incomplete. I heard the voices: *I can't do it. It's too hard, I'll never figure it out. I'm going to fail this project. I'll never be able to find work in this town again. I'm a failure.* My stomach would churn, sweat would start to pour and I'd start shaking. With a looming deadline and pressure mounting, it was always harder to fight my inner demons. Except this time. Not so much my life, but another's life, in this case a very attractive woman with an Andromeda tattoo, held in the balance.

I always wondered how SEALs like Rusty did it. There was not an ounce of quit in his considerable body. Now I had a sense of what drove that level of determination. I would not allow a single nanogram of quit in me. As my childhood heroes at NASA once said, failure is not an option.

If ever I needed a deadline to be inspired, I couldn't have picked a bigger one. My arrogant side half-smiled at the unintended pun. We can do this, it was shouting down my insecure half. My inner Ninjaneer was already feeling eyeballs squirting out.

"Bet on it," I said to her and turned back to align the laser to the van.

"I am," I heard ever so faintly.

They were lining up for a better shot, too. Three buttons. I tried each one sequentially. Nothing. Another blast, this one right under my window. A geyser of mud and stems exploded from the ground. I spit out some of the dirt and ignored it.

This must be what it was like in an 18th century duel with pistols at twenty paces. Only I was still learning how to load my musket. Fortunately, there weren't many combinations to play with.

Big fingers, maybe you held the two buttons down first, then the third. An explosion erupted midway to the van. Now we were in business.

"Increase your elevation," she said.

"Ya think?" I replied, never taking my eye off the distant van.

I aimed down the barrel and lined up the van, holding the two buttons down with one hand and pressed the third button. A hit!

Sparks flew from the side of the rear door. I pressed the button again. Nothing! Was it out of power or was there a recharge period? My hit to their door threw off their next shot. It was wide by a good five feet.

I realigned to the lower rear of the van, took a deep breath, held the two side buttons and pushed the top button again.

I saw the flash, and a fraction of a second later, heard the double explosions. My shot penetrated the gas tank and the molten metal ignited the fumes. The explosion lit up the field, as the reflections of the flames danced on the hood of the Jeep.

I guess it was just a recharge period.

7

SHE'D BEEN QUIET, letting me take the shot, her hand resting on my shoulder as she sighted with me down the barrel. I heard her triumphant, "Yes!" in my ear simultaneous with the extra squeeze on my shoulder. The risk was totally worth it. I was never so thrilled to be alive.

Remorse at having just killed at least two people never even entered my mind. I don't tolerate bullies. If you threatened me, I felt that you'd give up any rights to my compassion. Besides. I had just taken out two really bad men who had killed one innocent bystander and leveled an entire building. And I rescued a woman who might have suffered a similar fate. Point to the good guys; extra point for doing it with the bad guys' own weapon. Yeah, I was feeling pretty good about our victory.

She turned around in her seat, facing forward, muttering to herself. I turned toward her. In the reflected flames, I could see her eyes darting around, her hands weaving patterns in front of her as she talked softly into the air. Had she cracked?

I thought we were doing pretty good as a team. I could take the mysterious part of this smart woman with the Andromeda tattoo, wasn't too thrilled with the bitchy, demanding version, but a crazy woman? I was beginning to regret getting involved. As the ringing in my ears died down, I could make out what she was saying.

"… hear you Fred. Move these files for immediate transmission to the server and patch in a secure link with Sciquest, this is urgent."

"My name's not Fred," I replied, "It's Bryan Postman. How did you know I was heading toward the Sciquest plant tonight?" I should have picked up the connection before. Where else could she have meant by her branch office. What else was open in their neighborhood this late? "Is that your branch office? Just who are you?"

With the danger gone, I was coming back down from my adrenaline high. By my nature, I do not like mysteries. I've conditioned myself to take them personally—it's how I channel my mojo. I absolutely believe there is always an explanation for everything, the trait that makes me a professional problem solver. But tonight mysteries were building up faster than they were being solved. I wanted some answers.

"I'm sorry," she said, turning toward me. "My name is Kathy, Kathy O'Neil. I wasn't talking to you."

My mouth opened to reply but stopped when she looked away, moving her hands again, ignoring me and spoke urgently into the air again. "Fred, upload these files and prepare these for decipher. Then search for any contact from Michael and get me connected to Andy right now."

"Kathy, what are you talking about? Who's Fred? How do you know about Sciquest?"

She looked over at me and said: "Fred's my PDA." She paused, as if responding to something I couldn't see. "It's about time!"

She immediately turned forward again, moving her hands together and then expanding them apart in front of her. The two seconds of attention she was willing to devote to me, now over. Seemingly as an afterthought, she gave me another bonus two seconds out of the side of her mouth, "I work for Sciquest. I'm finally in touch with the network."

"What's going on here?" I said with suspicion. "Who are you really and who were those guys?"

"Hang on, I'm back online." I only heard her side of the conversation, as she gazed straight ahead and spoke again.

"Andy, you have to look at the files I'm sending…"

She paused.

"I can't talk about the details right now, but the bottom line is, you were right. I think we found them…"

Silence for three seconds.

"Yes, I brought back one sample we can use to confirm. I hope these aren't the designers. We're in terrible danger…."

She shook her head, emphasizing her point. I heard the panic coming back to her tone as she talked into space. "No, all Earth is."

Another few seconds of silence and I saw her visibly relax. Whatever she heard calmed her down. I wish I could have listened in. I could have used those words earlier.

"Yes, I'm safe for now…"

"Okay, I'll meet you at the main plant. Wait," she paused and turned to look at me. It was like I had been invisible up to now.

"Can you take me to 101 and Moffat, where the main Sciquest building is?"

"Yes, but I want…" was all I was able to get out. She ignored me again, turning back to look straight ahead. Since she'd been online, I wasn't important anymore, relegated to second class status.

"Give me fifteen minutes and I'll fill you in, in person. In the meantime, check out the files."

"...right...Fred end."

After my abrupt dismissal, I pulled down the visor and said calmly, "Phone, dial 911."

This time I heard the expected dial tone and fast digital beeping of the connection being made. The familiar ringing was a comfort. Why did the phone line and her PDA suddenly open up after the van exploded? One obvious possibility came to mind.

"What do you think you're doing?" she said.

"I'm calling the police. What do you think I'm doing? Just what the hell is going on here?"

"911 emergency line. State the nature of your emergency," the visor speaker said.

"Look Bryan," she said in a low voice. Her hand rested on my arm, still sore from the few, scattered burns. She squeezed it gently, looking at me with those eyes, those wide open pleading, green eyes reflecting the flickering flames of the still-burning van behind me. I winced slightly from the pain of my burns. Looking into those green eyes, the feel of her touch overwhelmed the pain. She continued, "Cancel the call and I'll fill you in. Please. It's complicated."

Those eyes caught and pinned me, refusing to let me go. I couldn't look away to break their spell. No hint of a demand in her tone this time, just a request. I took a deep breath and made the second-most-important snap decision of the night, and, as it turned out, of my life.

"Never mind, 911" I said toward the visor. "Phone, hang up. Okay, now talk."

"Head over to the Sciquest headquarters building, and I'll tell you what I can on the way."

At the mention of Sciquest again, I suddenly remembered what I was supposed to be doing tonight. I glanced down at my watch for the first time. Oh crap! It was past 9 p.m. I had less than nine hours left in my deadline.

"Wait a minute, I'm already way late for my job at the Sciquest plant. I've got to get over there right now. I should at least call in." I reached up to pull down the visor again.

"You work for Sciquest?" Her eyebrows shot up. "I haven't heard your name before." She was looking at me, as though appraising me.

"I just consult periodically. I was supposed to start a new contract tonight. I told Reggie I'd be there more than an hour ago."

"Reggie Johansson? You work with Reggie?"

I nodded, my turn to be surprised. "You know Reggie?"

"Of course. I don't work with him, but I've been in some meetings with him."

What would Reggie have been doing in a meeting with an astrophysicist who has an Andromeda Galaxy tattoo? Tenuous threads were dangling in space with no visible connection yet. How did they fit together? She interrupted my thoughts. "Let me contact him. I need to check with him on something."

She did that staring ahead thing again. "Fred, you were following? Patch me through to Reggie."

"Hey, Reg, you know Bryan? …… Right. He's gonna be late, my fault….yeah…What's his deal?"

She looked over at me, listening to Reggie. I strained but I couldn't hear any of his side of the conversation. I couldn't even tell what she was listening on or talking into. Her expression changed suddenly. Her eyes opened wide, she actually smiled at me, really smiled, for the first time. I decided to star that note I'd made of how cute she was. She nodded her head, but it wasn't meant for me. I couldn't imagine Reggie had seen her nod.

"Your recommendation?" She only paused for two seconds before jumping in.

"Cancel my last comment. Bryan's not coming by tonight. He's just been reassigned to a special project reporting to Andy.... Sorry.... Like Michael says, find another way.... Don't know when.... Don't count on it.... Believe me, it is really important.... Put it on my tab. I'll be in touch. Out."

8

IT WAS A bumpy, muddy ride across the plowed field out to the service road. The van was a smoldering hulk, residual flames still licking up from the burning wheels, black smoke disappearing into the night sky. One glance told me that it was pointless to look for survivors. I couldn't think of anything we'd left behind that could point back to me. Still, we gave the wreckage a wide berth.

In minutes, we were back on paved streets, leaving a trail of mud patches behind us for the first hundred meters. As the Jeep sped up, the last remaining mud clumps were thrown off the wheels and the staccato rattle against the wheel well quieted below the engine noise and air whipping by. I had maybe ten minutes before we hit the Sciquest headquarters building.

"Now you can tell me. What's really going on here, Kathy?"

"I had a problem with my sh..." She hesitated a moment. "With my vehicle." She spoke softly, looking forward, head lowered. This was a much more subdued woman than I'd seen all evening. Her guard was down. "It was damaged. I couldn't make it to the headquarters building, so I diverted to the Sciquest plant down the street from where you found me. When my vehicle quit, I had to go on foot. My PDA wasn't able to sync up, and I couldn't connect to the cell phone network. Not sure why." She paused.

"I've been thinking about that," I said. "My cell phone and your PDA connected at the same time when the van blew up. There must have been a jammer in it. If they have laser hand weapons, I could believe they have jammers. So who were they?"

"I'm not sure. You'll have to ask Andy when you see him."

"Andy who?"

"Andy Rayburn, our CEO. I work directly for Andy. I know he'll want to talk with you."

Oh, that Andy, I thought. One of the most successful CEOs in a valley, and known worldwide for a string of high-tech success stories. The questions were still piling up faster than they were being answered.

She was quiet. Out of immediate danger, Kathy seemed tired. She picked at the mud in her hair and reaffixed the errant strands behind her ears. Her right elbow rested on the passenger window ledge.

I had to prompt her to continue her story. What was really going on here? "It's Sunday night. I know why I was out this late. What brought you out so late?"

Still looking at the freeway ahead, she said, "I was in the field on a special project, just returning. I really wanted to get back to the main building complex at Moffitt field, but like I said, my transportation broke down and I was close to our remote factory. I wanted to at least get in range and tie into our network."

I looked at the freeway, then back at her. "I'm pretty up on PDA technology. I don't see one with you. How were you planning to tie into your network? How were you talking to Fred? Is Fred like Siri?"

"Bryan," she said chuckling at me, "the PDA I have is a bit past what's available on the street. Fred is the PDA communications system built into my glasses."

I took my eyes off the freeway and stole a quick glance at her glasses, more carefully this time. "You have Google Glass? I've been thinking about getting a pair."

She laughed a soft, smug chuckle. "These are way beyond what you've ever seen before. Sciquest actually designed and produced the first generation of Google Glass over five years ago. What I have is more than four generations beyond that. Some of the features these have won't be on the street for at least another five years."

I took a longer look at her and her glasses. They were pretty ordinary, maybe a bit nerdy looking. The frames were black plastic with some sort of antiglare coating on the lenses. A strap hung around the back of her head, under her pony tail, attached to the frames. Once you knew to look, the nosepiece was a little larger than usual, but nothing else was really odd.

"Where's the ear piece?"

"Most folks use bone conduction from the frames. I had a cochlear implant surgically embedded just below the skin behind each ear with a wireless link to the frames. It's much better fidelity and after calibration, never needs adjusting."

"I always thought it was only a matter of time before people started to get Borg implants. But the rest of it sounds really cool. How do I get one of these PDA glasses with seamless voice input and output?"

She looked over at me, and smiled back. "I think that might be arranged if you get me to headquarters."

She stopped talking again. I waited a few moments for her to continue with her story. She just looked out the window. Finally, I said: "So, what's really going on?"

She took a deep breath. "Like I said, I had a serious problem with my transportation. I got as close as I could to the Sciquest plant. I thought I could make it the rest of the way on foot."

She paused, rubbing her wrists. Muscle memory seemed to be making her relive the terror of being grabbed. But I wasn't learning anything new. It was like she was stalling.

"It's not too late for me to call 911," I prompted.

She took a deep breath and breathed out loudly. Shaking her head, she continued. "Three blocks away from the plant, I thought I was safe," her voice was cracking. "Then that van came out of nowhere and pulled up in front of me. Those two monsters got out and I ran. They ran after me. I must have run for two blocks.

"They were right behind me. I was too tired to run very fast and they caught up. If you hadn't come on the scene, I'd be in that van and taken who knows where." She was almost in tears. I wasn't good with tears.

"Hey, you're safe now," I said softly. "Everything's going to be all right."

Kathy looked over at me again. This was a different woman. The scared girl was gone, replaced with an imperious, how -dare-you look. Her lips pursed to narrow lines. Lights from oncoming cars reflected like little fireworks shooting out of her eyes, directed at me. "Don't patronize me. You have no idea." She emphasized the word 'idea'. "Earth as we know it might be lost. We're all, all of us, in big trouble."

9

THIS WAS GETTING out of hand, I thought. Who was taking who for a ride here? The whole Earth was in trouble? What, a bigger threat than global warming? Even my naïve BS detector was going off with 'red alert, red alert.'

I had a woman in my Jeep with an Andromeda Galaxy tattoo, claiming to be an astrophysicist and affiliated with the most well-known tech company in Silicon Valley, used what she said was a voice interfaced advanced PDA, and had beautiful green eyes. Add to the mix powerful laser hand weapons used by big thugs who had small, high explosive, self-propelled spheres and powerful cell phone jammers and went around kidnapping women off the streets. And I had no clue what connected them. Yet.

I had gotten myself tangled up in a mystery, and like all puzzles and technical challenges, I felt events were teasing me, thumbing their noses at me as if telling me that I wasn't smart enough to connect the dots. The hook was set. I had risked too much now to let go of this mystery.

"Wait a minute, Kathy, if that's your real name. The deal was, I won't call the cops and you tell me the truth."

I was losing patience. My desire for answers to the puzzle pieces was trumping even those green eyes. Were they even her own? I had once dated a woman who changed her eye color to match her outfits. That relationship crashed and burned fast.

"I did my part," I continued. "I find it hard to believe much of your story." As it came out, my frustration fed on itself. I didn't pause for reaction, just continued firing at her, "Like, what do you do at Sciquest? Why were you out at night, heading to a factory that is shut down? Where did you get your PDA glasses, if that is really what they are? Who were those guys after you? I don't believe they just happened to find you. And where did they get laser hand weapons and self-propelled bombs? I'm real up on current technology so how come I haven't heard about any of this stuff? And what's this melodramatic crap about the end of the world as we know it?" I paused for breath, just coasting now from my initial roll.

My engineer side chimed in: "The only thing I do know is those were some really tough-looking guys going after you and they were loaded with some pretty high-tech gadgets. Between your PDA and their lasers, bombs and jammers, something is going on here." I paused, glance over at her and smiled. "And I want in."

Kathy was silent through my tirade. She just stared out the front window. My tone softened but my persistence remained. "Do you really work for the government? Are you some kind of agent? Are you one of the good guys or did I just help one of the bad guys?"

I let the last out more as a bargaining chip. If those ugly, overstuffed weightlifters who liked to kidnap women on deserted streets were the good guys and she was one of the bad guys, I'd consider switching sides.

"Bryan, everything I told you is true!" she cried. She was pumping her hands up and down in frustration. "I want to tell you more, but I just can't. I do special projects for Sciquest. That's all I can tell you."

Well, if she was some kind of secret agent, she wasn't a very good one. She should have had some sort of plausible cover story ready.

"Look," Kathy said, taking a deep breath, hands now back to her lap, "we're almost at the main building." I was pulling into the sprawling parking lot between the office building and their main assembly plant. "Go around to the back entrance. I'll talk to Andy and he can decide how much more to tell you."

"I want some straight answers now. It's after 9 p.m. on a Sunday night. You really think Andy is going to be here now? I'm not sticking around a couple of days for an appointment."

"I know he's here. I just talked to him. He's always on site when one of us is out in . . . ." She skipped a beat, "on a special trip."

"I have my doubts, but I'll let this play out." I'd find out soon enough. We were really close to the building. As I turned the corner into the side lot and circled around to the back, Kathy pointed to the back entrance of the huge, flat roofed, two story building. "Pull into that spot by the rear entrance."

I parked the Jeep, contemplating the questions I had for Andy. I hadn't met him yet, but I had certainly heard of the elusive and respected CEO.

I stepped out of the Jeep and straightened up. But before I closed the Jeep's door, I reached back in and grabbed the laser weapon I had thrown on the dash. At least now I knew how to fire this thing if I needed to again. I looked around the parking lot. Other than a few empty cars, we were alone.

My legs were a little stiff from the rough ride in the field. I walked around to the front of the Jeep, waiting for Kathy. I glanced down at the mud splatters on my white shirt and saw how they matched the speckled mud pattern on my Jeep.

I was pretty proud of what my little Jeep had done for us tonight, and not a little surprised we didn't get stuck in the mud. Its entire front and sides were sprinkled with thick, uneven splotches of hardened mud, even with some stems embedded.

What was left of my one and only sticker on the front bumper was barely visible. Hardly enough letters were readable to win a hangman's game. But I remembered what it said. "Space, the Final Frontier." That was about all I had left of my childhood dream. I was thinking that when I got the mud washed off, it was probably time to peel off the remaining pieces of this bumper sticker.

I remember putting on that bumper sticker eight years ago when I finished my PhD and started work at HP. My dream to fly space shuttles drifted farther and farther away during college and graduate school, but I never let it go entirely. At HP, I kept thinking I could come up with some excuse to conduct an experiment in space so complicated it would require a very experienced mission specialist to run it, me.

It was time to finally let go of my childish dreams of going into space and move on with real life. I was supposed to be an adult now. But maybe a new adventure awaited me after my chat with Andy.

When I flexed my arm, I could feel the small burns from the molten bits of glass. I absently picked a few of them out of my skin. The jabs of pain as I pulled a little skin off were a not-so-subtle reminder of how narrowly I'd escaped death more than once tonight. What had I gotten myself into, I thought? I should have been shaking in my boots after what I'd gone through, but I was too distracted with the mystery I had stumbled into and my need to solve it.

Once I set my mind on it, I am usually tenacious in resolving technical puzzles. They are like mosquito bites to me. They irritate me, demanding to be scratched. I scratch at them to the exclusion of anything else until solved. I just hoped this one wouldn't end up with me bleeding.

Kathy came around the front of the Jeep and saw the weapon in my hand. She reached out her hand for it. "I'll take that now."

"Hah!" I said, "In your dreams. When the time comes, I might consider sharing. It's mine now. I think I earned this tonight—the spoils of war."

She just shook her head and let it go. She stepped ahead of me and led me up the few stairs to the back entrance door.

There was an audible click of the door unlocking even before she reached it. She didn't appear to do anything special, it just swung open in front of her. Some hidden camera must recognize her.

My eyes roved around the outside of the building. A small cylindrical close-circuit TV camera, complete with cable sticking out the back, disappearing into the building's wall, was off to the right side of the entrance. *How old fashioned*, I thought. I would have used hidden wireless cameras and placed two, one on either side of the entrance to eliminate blind spots.

Sure enough, I looked to the left and there was a much smaller, black knob sticking out from the side of the building. No one would notice this one unless you were looking for it. A mix of new and legacy systems. They should have hired me to redo their security. I'd clean it up for them. I made a note to pitch this to Andy.

We entered the anteroom. There were just two chairs and a coffee table in front of them with a few technical journals causally placed. A single lamp in the corner bathed the room in a dim, soft glow, casting shadows against the walls. Another door was diagonally across from the entrance. A few paintings were on the walls. They looked like Renoirs. *Very tasteful*, I thought.

I'd recommend their security team add cameras in the two diagonal corners of the ceiling. I glanced over to the spots I'd pick. The position of the lampshade cast shadows in those corners. I stared hard. Yes, there were small black button cameras hidden there.

I surveyed the room more carefully. The paintings. I saw a slight texture variation in the frames. This place was loaded with miniature security cameras. As they were placed, there were no blind spots. Maybe I didn't have much to suggest to improve what they had. I was reaching. If security was so important, I'd recommend IR and acoustic emission sensors. But why would a commercial office building need such high level security? I squeezed the barrel in my hand for a moment's added comfort.

My distracting thoughts were interrupted by Kathy's mumble into the air, "It's okay, he's with me. Andy wants to talk to him." The door at the far end of the anteroom opened on its own for us.

This interior room was much larger. No windows. It was like a nexus into other parts of the building. Immediately to my left was a pair of large potted ficus trees with a wide double door between them. Three more doors arrayed around the empty room, two relatively close together and the third isolated on the wall to my right. A couch was placed directly against the wall opposite the third door, facing the entrance. I saw a foot-square panel on the side of this door. It could have been a palm print sensor. As I expected, two tiny cameras were placed in the corners above this door.

No such panels were near the other two doors. Three parallel cables wrapped around the door frames of the other two doors. I assumed it was part of an automated tracking system. I'd designed a few of those. Every employee probably carried an ID card with a smart chip or rf ID tag. When they walked through the door the antenna would interrogate the smart chip, track their comings and goings. I would have hidden the sensing antenna in the door frame. It was almost like the security systems were hastily added recently and weren't quite finished.

I took all this in at a glance.

"Bryan, have a seat on the couch. I need to talk to Andy, alone, first. Give us some time. I know he'll want to talk to you afterwards."

"I'll give you fifteen minutes, then I'm out of here and I really will call someone."

"Who will you call, the police?" she said with a small, smug smile. And what will you tell them, that you just blew up a van with a laser weapon?" She was calling my bluff. I hadn't thought through my next step. I just let her comment hang in the air. She continued, "Don't worry, I'll be back. I think it's in our best interests to have you on our side."

Maybe a few minutes to gather my thoughts would help me prepare for when I had the chance to question Andy.

I walked to the couch and sat back. Kathy walked to the isolated right hand door and it opened for her and as quickly, swung shut behind her. I caught a brief glimpse of a short corridor.

Sitting down and motionless for the first time in hours, I was suddenly very tired. I was prepared to work all night repairing the plasma etching system, but the emotional roller coaster of the last hour had left me drained. My hand, still holding the mirror smooth barrel, trembled slightly as the adrenaline finally drained from my body. I stared anxiously at the closed door, knowing my answers might be on the other side.

I'd actually been thinking about taking a little trip, like a drive up the coast to Bodega Bay. I had a small cabin there, built on stilts along the shore. It was my little retreat from the rat race in Silicon Valley. A glass of wine, a sunset, the lapping of the waves against the pillars under the cabin; it was sounding mighty nice right now. I really didn't like to fly, too much like roller coasters and I never felt in control, but a driving trip might add a little adventure. A real life game of deadly laser tag was not what I had in mind.

How did I end up here? I ran through each decision I made tonight. I couldn't have done anything except what I did. I'm no vigilante, but I don't tolerate bullies very well. I'm just not built that way. It was infused in my DNA when I was thirteen.

10

ALMOST TWENTY YEARS ago, in my tiny home town of Quincy, Illinois, I was the science nerd, the "space cadet," the jocks used to call me. They thought they were insulting me, but I was secretly proud of the name. They seemed to take particular delight in finding ways of terrorizing the only kid in our small school who showed any spark of interest in science. It probably helped them feel good about their ignorance of anything other than football.

I grew up during the start of the Space Shuttle launches. I had a model of the last shuttle built, the Endeavor. I had meticulously assembled it from a kit, memorizing each piece, where it went and what it did as I put it together. It lived on my bedroom dresser right in front of my window.

I would lay in my bed at night with my model of the shuttle outlined against the crisp night sky, speckled with stars. I'd fall asleep imagining I was in that shuttle flying through space to one of those stars. That's what being pickled in Star Trek juices did to a kid in those days. I could not care less about football or baseball or any other sport. The engineers who built the shuttles and the astronauts who flew them, they were my heroes.

The last week of eighth grade, I brought my precision model to school as part of my science project presentation. Big mistake.

One of the football players got wind of me and my model. To a typical Neanderthal brain, a nerd with a science toy was like waving a red flag to a bull.

I was on my way home after school. I made it less than fifty yards before I was tackled to the ground, held down by four of them while two others took turns stomping my shuttle to pieces as I was forced to watch. Jeffrey Roberts, the captain of the football team, the arrogant bastard, stood around giving the orders.

Even my rage didn't give me enough strength to overcome the 500 pounds of mouth-breathers pinning me down.

When they tired of grinding the tiny pieces of shuttle into the ground with their cleated shoes, they released their hold on me and let me up. My left hand was the first part of me free and I struck out in an uncontrolled rage. The insignificant single blow I landed on Frankie Wilson was the trigger they needed to give me the same treatment they gave my shuttle. I was left in a bloody heap, with a broken arm, a broken collar bone, three broken ribs, a swollen lip, bloody nose, and two black eyes.

I staggered home in the dark, holding my broken arm against my side to keep the jagged edges of the bones from scraping together. It was like pieces of broken glass rubbing inside my arm and through my shoulder with every slight jostle. They were accented by the red hot needles jabbing me in the side with every breath.

This was a rude awakening for a thirteen-year-old kid. Sweating from the pain pulsing through my body with each slow step home in the dark, the budding scientist part of me, growing in my forebrain, saw the symbolism of a group of ignorant bullies, wanting to force their beliefs on someone else, literally stomping my dreams to death.

See, their attack had a more chilling impact on my future than just my broken bones. I had brought my space shuttle model into class that day to illustrate the blastoff to splashdown stages in a shuttle launch. I chose that theme to present as my science project because I had already memorized each phase in preparation for my summer plans. I had been accepted to Space Camp at the Marshall Space Flight Center, in Huntsville, Alabama.

Five days after the end of school, I was starting a two-month summer program. I was going to walk in the footsteps of astronauts, sit in shuttle simulators, wear a real space suit, and go to an actual shuttle launch. It was going to be the launch of my fourteen-year plan to become an astronaut.

I had every year planned out and an entire course of study outlined and it started with Space Camp. MIT would be next, with maybe a masters or PhD at Stanford, ending when I was twenty-seven, accepted into the last NASA class of astronaut candidates for the shuttle program. I was determined to be on one of those space-planes. My lifetime dream was scheduled for liftoff in five days. But it had just exploded on the launch pad. Hell, I didn't even make it to the launch pad. I had crashed and burned just taxiing out.

I stumbled home, slow step by slow step. The pain I felt from my broken body was pushed into the background by the overwhelming pain of my disappointment. The entrance application was very specific. Expect to have your physical endurance tested. There would be centrifuges, three axis full motion simulators, survival training, and maybe a ride in the Vomit Comet, the brochures had teased. In other words, no broken bones allowed. Well, that ruled me out.

Everything started with Space Camp. More than five thousand kids my age applied for the hundred slots there. And I was one of the hundred. Missing this camp meant fourteen years from now, I was at best, going to be 101 in line to apply to the 15 slots for the last astronaut training class. One missed step in my plan and I was going to miss my one shot at being an astronaut.

On that bleak walk home, I had a long talk with myself. My immediate gratification side wanted me to go postal. While that fantasy brought a few seconds of momentary relief from my pains, I also knew it wasn't me. I didn't like violence. I didn't really want to shoot anyone. I didn't want to learn how to fight better and possibly get hurt worse. Me and pain don't go well together.

I cringed at that helpless feeling, being physically trapped and pinned by an overwhelming force, bigger and stronger. I vowed never again. I would never again allow myself to be forced physically against my will into anything. I knew this was not an overnight goal. It was going to take time. The same energy I devoted to planning to be an astronaut, I would devote to this goal.

On that disastrous night the only way I was able to put one foot in front of the other, knowing it would be more excruciating than the last, was by focusing on my new plan. I decided then and there I would bring science and engineering to my next fight. I was going to get a black belt in engineering. I was going to become a Ninjaneer.

The initiation task for embarking on my new path was retribution. I spent that summer with taped ribs and an arm in a cast plotting my revenge. I learned a little electronics. I learned a little entomology. I learned a little about air conditioning systems. I learned a little about lock picking. I learned how to access the school's blueprints.

That Fall, one week after football practice started and before school officially started, I waited until the team was out on the field. It was trivial to pick the lock to the empty locker room. I snuck in and found the air circulation vent right where I expected it. I pulled a chair underneath, climbed on top and unscrewed the vent screen. It hadn't been touched in at least twenty years and the screws were rusted tight.

Normally, this would have stopped anyone's plan right at the beginning. But I learned this summer the most important lesson in engineering. It's saved many of my projects to this day. I discovered that sometimes things can go wrong.

While prepping for my Space Camp application, I had read every book in our middle school library on space. It really wasn't that many. After all, Quincy, Illinois, was just a small rural town and not known for its science curriculum. One of the books I had read was about the first high gee rocket sled experiments. They weren't pleasant for the test pilots who experienced sometimes as much as twelve gees accelerating, and almost an equal amount in the deceleration phase when they hit the water brakes.

Even after reading about these sorts of experiences test pilots and future astronauts went through, I never really made the connection that it might be something I would have to go through. I don't even like roller coaster rides.

In the first rocket sled run ever, the test pilot was hooked up to dozens of sensors to check vital signs like blood pressure, heart rate, and muscle tension. I couldn't remember the name of the first test pilot, but, like a typical nerd kid, I did remember the name of the supervising engineer responsible for the sensors. Each sensor had two wires.

After the first bone-crushing run, the engineers looked at the recovered data. It was all blank. There were only two ways of connecting the wires into the panel, the right way and the reversed way, in which all the sensor values were shorted. The technician had connected each of the two wires in exactly the wrong way. It was Captain Edward Murphy, the engineer in charge, who, cursing the technician, said, "if there are only two ways of doing something, he would do it the wrong way."

I had taken careful note of this lesson. I knew that to become a Ninjaneer, I would also have to become an expert in Murphy's Law; that if something could go wrong, it would. The way to get around Murphy's Law was to anticipate everything that could go wrong and plan contingencies. I should always have a backup plan for my backup plan. This was the NASA way.

I had anticipated rusted over screws on the air duct vent and had brought a little dab of WD-40. I had expected the screen on the vent cover might have too fine a mesh for what I wanted. That was okay, I had also brought a backup cover in my backpack. It had openings plenty wide for what I needed. I anticipated I might break the head off a screw, so I brought wire to fasten the new screen back on. I was ready for any contingency, or so I thought.

I had placed my backpack on the bench next to the chair. I stepped down, opened it up, and pulled out a small, folded umbrella. It was easy to push it as far back in the duct as I could reach and expand it. Now the air conditioning duct was blocked. There was only one way out.

I placed a few pieces of paper towel at the back of the blocked duct. On this, I sprinkled an entire bottle of tea tree oil, a few drops of peppermint extract, and then a dozen cucumber slices. I had studied what would anger and repel hornets. This was the best I could come up with. Some of the peppermint oil got on my fingers. I wiped them as best I could on the paper towel.

I had scouted three hornet's nests in the park within a mile of my house. The night before, I had placed traps made from plastic gallon milk jugs. In the neck I placed a funnel. Inside the jug, I placed a little raw hamburger meat. This was one of the tricks I'd researched. I needed to recruit an Army, or in this case, an Air Force. I choose to go after the most vicious attack drones I could easily acquire, hornets. There was a reason the new Air Force fighter plane, the F-18, was nicknamed for them.

Hornets are attracted to the smell of rotting meat. The intense aroma of decaying protein was supposed to attract the most aggressive hornets, the ones most motivated to please the queen. They'd crawl into the funnel and wouldn't be able to find their way out. I had harvested more than a hundred angry, buzzing, killers from the three traps and placed everyone into their new home. Their furious buzzing was like a soothing lullaby to me. I tapped the box to stir them up a little, feeling from the increased vibrations in my hand, their trapped, potential energy.

My Plexiglas box, about the size of a shoe box, had a heavy, fine-mesh screen I had duct taped to the end, and a hinged trap door on the other end. I learned enough electronics to build a 15-minute timer using a 555 timer chip and a 32 bit counter. When it reached zero, it would energize a relay that unlatched the trap door. The counter-weighted door would plop open like the ramp of a ship, ready to release my warriors.

I set the Plexiglas box in the duct, open mesh toward the noxious smelling concoction, to a hornet, anyway. It was far enough back so there was plenty of room for the door to drop open. I could already hear the buzzing increase. That tea tree oil was irritating to a wasp and the peppermint was a stimulant. I soon had a box of pissed off hornets all of whom wanted to get as far away from the back of the air conditioning duct as they could. Maybe, I was hoping, some of them would think their queen was in danger. If I could have come up with an odorless attractant, I would have figured out some way of planting it on the towels in the locker room.

I checked my watch. It was 4:45. I was right on schedule. Practice ended about now. It would take another five minutes for them to swagger back to the locker room, then another five minutes to undress and get to the shower. I started my 15-minute countdown timer. The very faint red LED glowed in the dark tunnel of the duct like a one-eyed devil, ready to pounce from its cave. I shivered in anticipation. Everything was going according to my plan.

I replaced the front vent cover with my homemade grill, which had the wider mesh, allowing easy access to the humid locker room for my lethal drones. I dropped down off the chair, moved it back against the wall and admired my handiwork. No sign of any tampering.

I picked up my backpack and heard the back door to the field squeaking open. They were early.

This was not part of my plan. I was still on the wrong side of the locker room from my escape route. From victory to disaster in a microsecond. Damn, damn, damn! I needed a new plan, fast.

I could hear voices of the first few guys entering the convoluted hallway from the field to the locker room. I couldn't be found here. I had seconds. There were only two exits to the locker room, to the outside playing field and to the inside of the school building. I could see the entrance to the corridor leading into the school building, but with the sweaty, hyped up jocks just entering the locker room, it could have been a mile away and easier to get to.

Stooped with my head below the rows of lockers, I scrambled along the wall, keeping one row between me and the guys coming in. There was one gap between the last row of lockers and the beginning of the corridor. I had to get into that corridor. After two bends, it ended in the door to the inside building, and safety.

I needed a distraction, but this was one complication I had not anticipated. I mentally ran through the inventory of what I had brought with me. What could I use to draw attention away from the gap I was about to cross?

I couldn't think straight. I was reliving that moment less than three months ago. I was feeling the first tackle, then the whoosh of getting all the air in my lungs forced out when the second guy landed on top of me. I started shaking in fear. I was trapped. They'd catch me again and this time, it would be worse.

I forced myself to focus. I could do this. I wasn't caught yet.

I had a few tools, a roll of duct tape and some wire with me. I grabbed the roll of duct tape and threw it against the glass window of the coach's office, to the left of the corridor. I waited a second and used the loud thud as the trigger to launch myself through the gap into the hallway.

I heard some shouting, "What's that? Who's there? Is someone in the locker room?" I knew that voice. The last time I had heard it, he had called me a son of a bitch for trying to hit him. Everything after that was a blur of pain and fear. I didn't think I could have been more scared crouching in the locker room, but hearing that chilling voice sent me momentarily over the edge. I couldn't stop my trembling. It took all of my courage and my internal voice shouting at my insecure half to hold my panic. I tried to quietly tiptoe down the corridor. I felt for sure they could hear my heart thudding as loudly as it sounded to me.

Behind me, I heard the other voice I had come to dread, Jeffrey Roberts, the asshole Captain.

"Frankie, who did you see?" Roberts shouted.

"I didn't see nuthing. But I think there's someone in Coach's office."

"Well, get your butt over there and look around. If some kid snuck in here while we were at practice, we'll have some fun with him, won't we guys?"

"Yeah, like that nerd we beat the crap out of," another voice laughed. I really didn't need to hear that.

I finally reached the end of the corridor and what I desperately hoped would be escape from this nightmare. I pushed the paddle to unlatch the door. Security lay on the other side. It was locked.

"Billy and George, you look around the rest of the locker room." Roberts was still giving the orders. I wanted him to be the first victim of my vicious recruits.

Here I was, at the end of the too-short hallway, a locked door on one end, and around the corner, a room full of hyped up, fourteen- and fifteen-year old jocks. Ten more feet and they would see me. I fought my insecurity demons, battling for control. I wasn't giving up yet.

The door was locked, but I was familiar with this sort of lock. In addition to the curved tongue sticking out that latched the door closed, there was a small lever that slipped into the matching hole in the door frame. It was this lever that the key pulled aside, allowing the tongue to slip out of its hole. I knew I could pick the lock if I had time. But I had just seconds.

The sound of footsteps echoed down the corridor. They were up to the last corner.

Our school building was old and not kept up. In old buildings, the wooden framing shrinks, and settles. There was a gap between the door frame and the door. I could see the tongue and the latch through the gap. The metal guard that was supposed to protect the lock mechanism from tampering, didn't quite cover it. I took back every bad thought I had had about our town not supporting our school, except for the football team. Old and decrepit was going to save my butt.

My hands shook so much I couldn't get the clasp unfastened on my backpack. I had to will my fingers to work together. It felt like seconds but probably happened between heartbeats. I finally had the flap open and pulled out the strip of wire I'd brought as my backup plan to secure the grill. I bent the wire into a U shape. It took two tries with shaking hands to slip it through the gap, around the tongue and latch, the end coming back out to me.

The footsteps were louder. No lights in the corridor. Shadows danced on the wall next to me as the suspicious football jocks came down the hallway.

I said a silent prayer to Captain Murphy and pulled the two ends of the wire toward me as quickly as I could, catching the tongue and latch. The wire slipped under the levers and pulled them out and away from the socket. The door popped away from the frame.

I cringed at the slight click. Was I was the only one who had heard it? I pushed the door open enough to slip through and pulled it nearly closed behind me. Through the closing gap I caught sight of the swinging arm of Frankie turning the corner. I couldn't push the door closed completely or the latch would make a loud click. I'd be discovered for sure. Instead, I positioned the door barely closed, and held my breath. There were voices on the other side of the door. "Nuthin' back here either." I so wanted the owner of that voice to be my second victim. I could hear his footsteps moving away and finally disappear.

I was in the main corridor of the school building and so far, undiscovered. I leaned against the corridor wall, breathing hard. I must have been holding my breath through most of my escape. I took two more deep breaths deciding on my next move. The library was just down the hallway.

With my lock picking skills, there were no locked doors to me in my junior high school. If I was caught in the library, I could always say the door was unlocked. After all, in my school, who would purposefully try to break into the library?

My watch showed 5:03. The trapped door should have dropped down onto its cushioned support and my pissed-off commando force should have found the grill opening. I hoped they would find the locker room smelled so much better than the tea tree oil, peppermint, and cucumber stench in their former prison.

At 5:04, I heard the first scream. By 5:05, it sounded like a riot had broken out. At 5:06, the shouting got louder and I saw through the embedded wire mesh window in the library's door, five naked jocks, not acting so macho any more, screaming and running down the hallway. They flapped their hands around their heads.

Crouching under the glass window, I smelled some of the residual peppermint on my fingers. To this day, the scent of peppermint brings a moment of contentment and a satisfying smile.

Maybe I shouldn't have left that back door unlatched, I was thinking. I had inadvertently allowed these bullies another avenue of escape. But from their bellows, they had not escaped unscathed.

For one fleeting instant, I felt a twinge of guilt. I couldn't imagine the intense, burning pain of a hornet sting. But then I found myself absently scratching my arm, where the cast had just recently come off, and felt the still discernable throbbing of my healing ribs with each deep breath. And suddenly, I didn't feel so guilty. Vengeance really was intensely satisfying.

The next day, the first day of school, I did a damage assessment. I estimated a seventy percent effectiveness. There were maybe a hundred hornets in my box. There were twelve players. I counted an average of six huge welts per player, that I could see. I was already doing a post mortem in my head, thinking through strategies to increase my effectiveness, should a future need ever arise. Maybe being sure to lock the back door, fewer towels, more peppermint. Maybe I'd research that odorless attractant.

This experience taught me first-hand the power of engineering. I was pretty good at it and I knew I could get a lot better.

Over the years, and to stay in practice, I've learned to channel my aggression onto technical problems. I've come to look at a puzzle I've committed to solve as like a bully, trying to intimidate me, scare me away. I don't tolerate bullies. If I commit to solving a problem, I bring every ounce of my technical mojo to killing it, and I take no prisoners.

Of course, when it comes to human bullies, I don't usually waste my time paying attention to them if I can help it. It's much more effective for me to just walk away and let them battle for dominance between themselves.

But the problems I'd been dealing with in my consulting gigs just weren't enough of a challenge anymore. I'd finish a contract, get my check and still feel unsatisfied. The money was great, but it hardly meant anything to me. I needed more at risk to feel good about killing a problem dead. I needed a more worthy opponent, or more at stake. It was like I needed a bigger and bigger fix to feel satisfied. This was not going in a healthy direction.

To get my fix, I was artificially increasing my risk. I'd been subconsciously setting myself up for deadlines that were harder and harder to meet. It's not like I did anything really dangerous. No one was going to die if I was an hour late or even a day late in completing a project. But it was the only way I knew to scratch the growing itch.

I sat and stared at the Monet print hanging to the left of the door. I knew this one. It was the painter's village in Vetheuil, France. Two people casually rowed on a placid stretch of the Seine, passing through a beautiful, lush garden meadow. A picnic party was camped on the shore. The entire setting was so peaceful, except for the large, billowing, swirling clouds gathering behind them. Whether just a choice of paints or trying to capture a specific moment, the sky looked like an imminent storm approached.

11

A CLICK FROM the door brought me back to the present. I looked at my watch and was shocked to see it had been fifteen minutes. I'd been reliving my past and staring at the Monet all this time. Now it was time for answers.

I kicked myself that I hadn't used some of this time to examine the laser weapon in more detail. My left hand was still clenched around it, which had been forgotten. Too late.

The door opened and Kathy shuffled through. Her shoulders were a little hunched over, as though she didn't have the strength to stand upright.

My eyes locked on hers, one of my eyebrows slightly raised, looking for a response. She pulled back the two strands of hair that hung at the side of her face. She wrapped them behind her ears and looked up at me. She seemed to work hard to force a weak smile back. I stood up to greet her.

"It's about time," I said. Seeing her set my clock back in motion, freshly energized. I wanted answers; enough stalling.

"He wants to see you now," she said in a tired voice. She walked closer to me. I could see she still had a few patches of mud on her tee shirt and shorts where she had missed picking them off. Her face was only slightly cleaner and her ponytail was tight, except for those two strands, and she still wore a patch of mud in her hair. She must have missed that one. I tried not to stare at it, instead, looked into those beautiful green and yellow eyes. They were accented by small wrinkles in the corners.

"And Bryan, I didn't tell you before, but, thanks." She reached over, touched my arm and kissed me lightly on the cheek. Her smile looked less forced this time.

Still gently touching my arm, she continued, "You risked your life for me. You don't know yet how important your actions were, but I think you're going to find out." Her eyes smiled back at me, the little crinkles in their corners spreading outward.

She was disarming. Before I could embarrass myself with some corny response like, "Aw shucks, it was nothing," a recessed speaker spoke out in a smooth, calm, older woman's voice.

"Bryan, Andy will see you now. Please place your hand on the panel and proceed through the side door to your right."

"Maybe I'll see you later, then?" I said, heading to the marked door.

"Bet on it," she said over her shoulder and walked off through the door on the left.

I reached my hand to the flat panel on the wall by the doorway and pressed. I was curious why they wanted me to press my hand on the reader. I didn't think they had my prints. I was a consultant to Sciquest and had worked a few short jobs before, but I didn't recall giving them my prints. At least, they never asked for them.

The door opened into a corridor ending in three doors. Two doors were unmarked, but the right hand door, a fine-wood-grained door with a small plaque just displayed "Andy Rayburn" on the outside. I stood in front of the door. Reaching up to knock, I found myself suddenly as nervous as a fourteen-year-old boy meeting his date's father for the first time.

I'm not usually intimidated meeting CEOs. The best ones were always honest and upfront, make eye contact and sealing deals with a handshake. Some of them can be real jerks. But, this was bigger than interviewing for just another consulting gig. There was something going on and Andy was at the heart of it. With the high-tech gadgets I'd seen so far, and what I knew of Sciquest, I wanted in. A lot was riding on the next few minutes. I took a deep breath and knocked three times.

"Come," I heard from the other side. I opened the door into a spacious but Spartan office. Andy rose from behind his desk. He wore a pale blue polo shirt and black jeans. His attire was as featureless as his office. He didn't even wear a watch or any noticeable jewelry. I thought I heard him say the word 'execute' softly just before he took off his glasses. I walked over to him, glancing around briefly. He placed his glasses frames down on his desk. The black strap spread out in an open loop.

He was much older than I expected, at least fifty with some grey hairs around the temples. Given the focus of Sciquest on cool consumer electronics gadgets, I was expecting a "young," hip CEO, even though I knew this was at least his second company. His last was a wireless chip-set company that enabled cell towers to multiplex narrow beams and do seamless handshakes, increasing a tower's capacity more than tenfold. Five years ago, he made more than $500 M selling the chipset to Qualcomm. I had read in *Wired Magazine* that Sciquest sprouted from that seed money.

It only took a quick glance to check out what little there was of his office. The sparseness of it was startling. His desk was at one end, two chairs in front. A large oval conference table with a few chairs were on the other side of the office. The walls were white and featureless. That was it. It was too neat and where was the computer monitor or even laptop? His desk was a lightly stained oak, bare except for a pen and pencil set and now his glasses. They had the same look as Kathy's.

This was more of a minimalist version of an office than that of a CEO of a high-tech company. Behind his desk was a floor-to-ceiling bookcase filled with books of all sizes and colors. It provided the only color or texture in the entire office. Normally, I would have scanned the titles to get a feel for the owner's taste, but I was too intent on planning how I would manipulate the discussion to even think about doing this now. After this cursory glance, all my attention was now on Andy.

I caught a glimpse of him watching me as I walked over to his desk. I could see him shifting his gaze between the laser in my left hand and directly at me. He was really interested in the laser, but clearly wasn't ready to mention it. What was he going to offer me for it? I mentally upped its value.

I felt I had to respond to him watching me. I reached over his desk to shake hands, locking my eyes with his. I said, trying to be as casual as I could muster, "Nice office. Not much clutter."

He just smiled at me and said in a quiet voice. "Have a seat," I selected the chair closest to the door, directly across the desk. From here, I could see an alcove to my left behind the door entrance with a small coffee service. I was momentarily tempted to suggest some coffee. I noticed Andy still focusing on the laser weapon I clutched in my other hand. An eyebrow rose slightly, but he didn't ask about it.

Andy smiled politely. "Bryan, Kathy told me about your help tonight. I wanted to personally thank you for rescuing her. I don't know what we would have done without you. Your assistance has been immensely valuable. I know you are on contract with Sciquest. I've arranged for a significant bonus to your account."

I smiled a little at the acknowledgement, but that wasn't what I was looking for. "That's very generous of you, Andy, but I'd really like some answers." I almost added, "instead," but caught myself at the last minute. I'm not one to pass up a bonus.

"Bryan, I have ten minutes until a very important staff meeting. For your troubles, I'll grant you a little of my time. Ask away."

"This wasn't just a typical mugging was it?" I said.

Andy shrugged, "I'm not sure what happened tonight. A lot of new information has just come to my attention. I haven't had time to process all of it."

"That wasn't really my first question, Andy. I meant it as an observation. Let me rephrase it. This wasn't just a typical mugging. Who were those guys with laser hand weapons like this," I raised the barrel in the air for emphasis, "and wireless jammers? It was no coincidence they found Kathy on a deserted street in the new, empty warehouse district. And those aren't just a pair of glasses on your desk, are they?" I nodded my head toward his glasses on the desk. "What's really going on here?"

Andy stared back, a slow smile spreading. "Kathy warned me about you. She didn't think I could just get you out of here with a simple thank you and a bribe. You're a consultant. Give me your assessment of what you think is going on." He paused, then added, "What do you know about Sciquest?" He leaned back in his chair and motioned at me, giving me the floor.

I sat up a little straighter in my chair, getting into my zone. My client just asked for my opinion. I took a second to collect my thoughts, reviewing and internally accessing my immediate impressions.

"You are currently the leading consumer electronics manufacturer in the U.S. You're trying to bring back vertical integration to the U.S. electronics industry, doing the silicon design, chip fab, board fab and all the system design and assembly. You probably have half the Valley hoping you will succeed and the other half hoping you will fail, to justify their bad decisions."

As I said the words, realization suddenly crystallized. "You're a threat to China Inc. Is that what's going on? Is that why you have all the security around the building? Is there some Chinese company trying to shut you down, make you fail, to keep electronics manufacturing from starting back up in the U.S.?"

"If only that were the real threat, Bryan. We have our share of industrial spies. It's inevitable when you are threatening a large installed industrial base." He said this causally, as though it were no big deal. "We've learned how to deal with the overt and covert attempts at surveillance and disruption. You've already picked up on some of the security precautions we've implemented."

He leaned a little forward, the intensity picking up in his voice. "What you know about Sciquest is just what we want the world to know. But there is more, much more, going on. You have nine and a half minutes to convince me I should tell you anything else." He paused for an instant, glanced away and said into the air, "Computer, start a countdown timer until the staff meeting, update on the minute."

"Yes, Andy," I heard from speakers coming from somewhere among the books. It was the same voice that had asked me to put my hand on the palm reader.

I was taken aback, but just for a moment. Two could play this game. And I had at least one good card to play.

"I think you need me more right now than I need you."

"Why would you think that?" He smiled back at my challenge.

"You're awfully paranoid even for a high-tech company being threatened by industrial spies. You have cameras, overt and hidden, everywhere. You track movements of all your employees inside the building and you have palm prints, even of consultants, on file. And as paranoid as you are, you sent an astrophysicist out on some mission that put her in danger and didn't give her any preparation or backup."

I was just warming up.

"I don't think you're paranoid about the right things. You have a really cool voice interfaced pair of glasses that Kathy says is an advanced, sophisticated communications PDA, but whoever is after you has long range wireless jammers, miniature autonomous rolling high-explosive bombs and laser hand weapons." I said the last wiggling the laser.

"I've already demonstrated I can handle your opposition. But I can't help you if you don't let me in." Andy didn't look happy now. Had I pissed him off, or was I close to the truth? I thought I'd risk it and go all in.

"Nine minutes," the computer's voice said from the speaker.

"It's been a pleasure meeting you, Andy. I'll save you the rest of your nine minutes and head off now. With this laser as a starting place, I can do some investigating on my own. I'm still consulting for you. If I learn anything important, maybe I'll report back." I shifted my weight and put my hands on the arm rests, starting to get up.

Andy raised his hand in front of him, signaling me to stop.

"Hold on Bryan. You're right about a few things, but way off base about me knowingly putting Kathy in the kind of danger she encountered. I never had any inkling of what we might have just stumbled into. We're paranoid for a reason. And you're right, there is a new threat we've uncovered, to more than just our company."

He paused, resting his forehead in his hands and took a deep breath. He was silent, clearly trying to decide. I'd made my case. Then he looked up at me and said, "I only had a chance to glance at your file before you came in. I need to check one last thing."

Before I could respond, he spoke into the air, "Computer, what's the status on the watch list for Bryan Postman, consultant."

Now that I knew the voice was synthesized, I could pick up a few nuances suggesting it wasn't human. The r's were too soft and the s's weren't sharp enough. It had just a hint of gravely texture to suggest an older, matronly woman behind the voice. Even so, it was more refined than any computer voice I had ever heard.

"Bryan has been on the watch list for six months. Second stage initiated two months ago with hiring as consultant for the manufacturing division. Stage three scheduled for this week."

"Recommendations on file?" he responded.

"Reggie Johansson flagged for accelerated evaluation."

"Much better than I hoped." Andy looked back at me. "I don't need to check the rest of your resume. You wouldn't be on our list if it didn't already check out."

I was a little surprised they had been paying extra attention to me. I quickly thought over some of my discussions with Reggie, but couldn't recall a hint of any extra scrutiny other than a plant manager's concern for his line. I realized my value to Sciquest was higher than I had been led to believe. I made an instant decision to increase my rates and bill Sciquest for all my time tonight, starting with the moment I turned down the sidestreet and saw Kathy.

"I am in a difficult position, Bryan. My organization is in big trouble right now. What I just learned from Kathy has confirmed my worst fears and has me more scared that I've ever been. And right now, as we speak, one of my employees, a very dear friend, is still in danger." He paused, shaking his head slightly. "And I'm not sure what I can do about it." Andy folded his hands in front of him on the desk. He held my gaze, staring, unblinking at me, like he was trying to read my thoughts.

"You might be useful to us, but I don't know if I can trust you. Too much is at stake. Can I trust you?" He spoke with a steady, measured, calm voice now, laser focused on my eyes. If he was scared, he was keeping it out of his voice now. He was absolutely serious. It was very intimidating.

"I'm already bound by an NDA with Sciquest," I said. "I know how to keep corporate secrets."

"This goes way beyond company proprietary information. What's going on here is bigger than just our products or our company. It's got global impact. Give me a reason to trust you, Bryan." He gave me that intense stare.

Where was Andy going with this? Getting involved in a life and death laser duel was serious enough. Did I want to get myself in deeper with something possibly illegal or dangerous? Were they the good guys or the bad guys? I had to remind myself of the thugs going after Kathy, the beautiful astrophysicist with the Andromeda tattoo. Which side did I want to be on? That was a no brainer. But, did I want to join a side already involved in what could be a dangerous business? I knew the answer before I finished asking myself the question… if it mattered.

"Eight minutes," the computer said, interrupting me.

"I don't want to get involved if it's illegal. I'm not interested in helping you if you're running some sort of secret government sponsored espionage program. And if it's some rival company trying to steal your trade secrets, I can recommend a private security firm that can help you better than I can.

"But," I continued, "I don't like it when a bunch of bullies try to push the good guys around. Convince me you're the good guys and I'm in, committed, absolutely."

Now Andy sat up straighter in his chair. He scooted forward, closer to his desk. "Oh, we are definitely the good guys, as you put it, Bryan. I can assure you what we are doing here is not illegal, nor unethical, and has nothing to do with the government."

"So what's going on? I thought you just made advanced PDAs. Why was Kathy attacked and what organization has laser hand weapons like these?" I said the last twitching the laser.

He paused for five seconds, very serious. I could almost see the wheels spinning in his head, trying to decide.

He took a deep breath. "You win. You did something tonight to impress Kathy and she doesn't impress easily. She says we need you on our team."

I smiled at my small victory, also feeling pretty good that Kathy felt so strongly about me. Andy reacted to my smug smile. He raised his hand as though to stop my thoughts.

"Before you get overconfident, she also said she thought we were screwed whether you were on the team or not. I'm going to take a huge risk and bring you in. We usually put candidates through a yearlong evaluation. You've been on our watch list for half that time, and even in the best case, would be evaluated for another three months." He paused. "But these are desperate times."

I sat up in my chair, ears wide open. This was it, the moment of revelation.

"She wasn't exaggerating when she said she thought all Earth was in danger."

Why is everyone sounding so melodramatic tonight?

Andy leaned forward, folded his hands on his desk. His intense gaze pinned me. "Regardless of what we agree on tonight, I want your word you will keep this to yourself. It probably won't matter who you tell in a few days anyway, if we fail."

I looked back, unblinking and said, "Agreed." Finally, the answers. No more fairytales.

Andy leaned back again, glancing up toward the ceiling, like he was collecting his thoughts. Then he looked back at me. "Let me tell you a story."

"Seven minutes."

Andy hastened to add, "A short story. Four years ago, I started Sciquest. I knew exactly what I wanted to do. This company was founded, not to make money, but to make progress."

"In what?" I asked.

"In advancing science and technology to reach its full potential, in electronics, in energy, in bioengineering, in information science, and in the fundamental nature of space-time."

I sat dumbfounded. Where was he going? The clock was literally ticking. I bit my tongue to keep from interrupting and delaying him further.

"I spent the first year talking to the best minds around the world, trying to do my own assessment on where we were and where we could go and what was stopping us from getting there. I began to notice a few peculiarities. Most researchers spent more time scrambling for funding than doing research. Institutions, led by a few powerful people, had tremendous control over the direction of research, rather than individual scientists. This keeps the best scientists focused on mediocre fields that will get funding."

"DARPA comes closest to supporting high risk, high reward activities, but there always has to be an element of military value, and it's all compartmentalized. Anything space related seems to be carefully regulated. For the last fifteen years, it's almost as though our space technology has being purposefully slowed down or suppressed."

"Are you saying there is some master plan about the direction and progress of technology development? Who's the puppet master that's been pulling the strings?" I paused, thinking through the details. "What about the advances in iPhones, computers, video games and consumer electronics?"

"That is the one area where the demand forces are so strong, progress proceeds in spite of government regulation and barriers. If it soothes the masses with mind wasting activities, rapid technology advance seems to be acceptable."

"What about medicine and DNA research? It feels like it's advancing pretty fast."

"Bryan," he said giving me a patronizing look, "We are so far behind what is possible. If you knew how far some private groups are in DNA design and booting up new synthetic life forms you would be shocked at why so little of it has seen the light of day."

"Six minutes."

"Four years ago, I decided to create my own research organization, unrestricted by government regulation, funding constraints, or conventional wisdom. But, I was a little paranoid there was some other organization manipulating our technology advance, a puppet master, as you put it. So I decided to start my company in secret, hidden from view. Consumer electronics seemed to be the least restricted field for development, so I formed the public part of Sciquest around a consumer electronics company. We leak a tiny portion of our real research efforts into our consumer products division."

"A secret research organization?" I blurted out. "How can you keep that sort of thing secret in the Valley?"

"It's been done before. I modeled it on Howard Hughes' company and the Lockheed Skunk Works. I selected the best and the brightest in a few selected fields, gave them each a small personal fortune so they never had to worry about money again and provided the best laboratory facilities money could buy. The only condition was, they could not publish or talk about their activities outside of our team. Over the years, we've built up our secret group into eleven of the most creative scientists and engineers in the world, and a small support staff."

"So you created a secret company, in the shadow of a legitimate high tech company, to do basic research. What could eleven scientists do that the rest of the world's millions of scientists couldn't do?"

"Bryan, when you get a critical mass of brain power together and take off all the restrictions, you begin to make progress, fast. It's ironic you say we are in the shadows," he continued. "We often joke that we are the ones now beginning to see the light of a new dawn. We've gotten a glimpse of what is possible while everyone else still lives in the shadows. If we can implement half of what we've discovered, the last fifty years will be known as a dark age by comparison."

"Like what," I said challenging, still not sure how much of what I was hearing I could believe.

"Four discoveries in particular, have gotten us into this current mess we're in. We've learned how to shield an object from the Higg's field."

"What's the Higgs field? Is it related to the Higgs Boson?"

"The Higgs field permeates all space. Every particle that has mass gets its mass from how strongly it couples to the Higgs field. The Higgs Boson is the particle that mediates this interaction. You know how a hollow conductor can shield the space inside it from an external electric field?"

"Of course. It's because there are positive and negative charges and they adjust on the surface of a conductor to cancel out external fields. I have an idea where you're heading with this, but you can't cancel out a field unless you have positive and negative mobile carriers. There are no negative masses."

Andy smiled. "Oh, but there are."

"No, there're not." I was pretty emphatic. Like I said, I had a pretty good BS detector when it came to technical things. I did not want to waste my time tonight with some fake 'cold fusion' - mumbo-jumbo. At the first sign of being fed pseudoscience crap, I was prepared to get up and leave.

Andy must have picked up on my stubbornness. "I don't have time to give you the entire background, but consider this. How does an electron get from one potential well to another when the space between them has a potential barrier greater than zero?"

"Five minutes."

That damn clock was ticking down and I was caught up discussing quantum mechanics with a CEO. If he tried making stuff up, I thought I knew enough to catch him, but I had to get around to what this current crisis was really about. I answered with enough jargon to give him a hint not to try to bluff me. "The electron tunnels through the classically forbidden zone inside the barrier."

"Very good. We won't have to waste as much time, now. What our Dr. Flowers discovered was that when the electron is in the classically forbidden zone, it has negative mass."

He instantly brought back memories of my first quantum mechanics class in college. I had asked that same question. The equations said negative mass, but my professors had explained, it was non-physical, just ignore it.

"But that's crazy. Everyone knows that's non-physical. You can't have negative mass."

"Doesn't that sound like circular reasoning to you?" Andy raised his right eyebrow at me. He was being very patient for someone on the clock. "Now you begin to get a hint at how the pursuit of knowledge is manipulated. You learn a catechism in school that influences the way you think, the sort of questions you even ask."

"But just saying something doesn't make it so. It's all about evidence. That's what science is."

"You are right," Andy said. "But to start the process to look for something, you must first accept the possibility. That's the starting place to even design an experiment to measure it. That's what I did for my team. I allowed them the opportunity, and even encouraged them to think crazy ideas, as you put it, unrestricted by the catechism we are taught, and then the funding to search for proof."

I was willing to give him a little more rope to hear the end of the story. "So what did you find?" I was ready. My BS antenna was deployed and the gain was at full strength.

"Flowers found that if you drive enough electrons into the classically forbidden zone, they did indeed have negative mass. It was a tiny effect, but his initial measurements did show their negative mass shields the residual background Higgs field."

I still wasn't ready to believe this, but I was beginning to see the consequence, if it were true.

"Four minutes."

Andy continued, "Surround an object with negative mass electrons and the object's mass doesn't couple as much to the external Higgs field. It has less inertia in our space. We've developed materials that can shield about seventy percent of the Higgs field."

"Wait a minute. If anything you just said is really true, how come no has seen this before?"

"First, in conventional materials, it's a small effect. You'll never see it unless you are specifically looking for it. And second, no one is looking for it. The focus in particle physics today is on filling in the blank spaces in conventional wisdom. There's no way a scientist will get funding to pursue a crazy idea like this."

He shook his head, "While I have great respect for the physicists at CERN, they are working single mindedly on one task, confirming what is believed. Six thousand physicists worked on building the two massive detectors, ATLAS and CMS at CERN. Each is as complex as a five-story tall Swiss watch, a tour de force in engineering. They have no time to think about crazy, off-the-wall ideas."

"Flowers was sweating bullets when the Higg's boson was announced a few years ago. He thought it was just a matter of time before someone else thought about the possibility of negative mass. But like I said, there seems to be some subtle manipulation of what research is pursued. New, radical ideas are being suppressed."

I was silent, not sure what to believe.

"But this was just the beginning," Andy said. "When an electron travels in a magnetic field, it feels a force. The forces on the current and on the magnet are equal and opposite."

"Of course, that's the basis of all motors," I said. I was a little shell-shocked with these notions banging up against what I had so long been lead to believe, but wanted to re-engage in the discussion. I figured there were a few more shoes to drop before the clock ticked to zero. I wanted to hear them.

"Yes, a cornerstone of our conventional science. But, if the electrons in the wire have negative mass, when the magnet pushes on the wire, the wire pulls on the magnet. There is a net force."

"Impossible," I said involuntarily. My BS detector was just pushed into the red zone. "What is the current pushing against?"

"The Higgs field. It's non zero and permeates everywhere."

"All this is just a theory, and a crazy one at that. It flies in the face of conventional wisdom. You can't really make negative mass." I was beginning to see where he was leading me, but I still couldn't believe it. "Can you?" I added tentatively.

"Take a molecule with lots of conjugated bonds like polydiacetylene. It's got single and triple bonds down its length. Dope it with a little titanium and it's conductive. How do the electrons flow through the single bonds that act like barriers? They tunnel. And where they tunnel, they have negative mass.

"Coat a surface with a film of doped polydiacetylene, run a current through it and the object it coats has less inertia. Make a coil out of long wires of doped polydiacetylene, run a current through it in a strong magnetic field and you get a propulsion unit. An engine the size of a breadbox can generate a 5,000 pound force."

"Three minutes."

I wanted to ask a thousand questions, but that damn timer was ticking away. Before I could interrupt, he continued.

"Here's number three. While investigating the Higgs field, Flowers realized that the vacuum of space quite literally sucks. It has negative pressure. Pull two plates very slightly apart, but keep them really close and there is a pressure trying to push them back together. The static pressure of the quantum foam of empty space produces a potential difference between the inside and outside of the plates."

"The Casimir Effect," I said. "It's about zero point energy. People have talked about this for years. But it's an effect of only a few microvolts."

Andy's right eyebrow raised in surprise. "Good. I don't have to explain it to you. Yes, it's only a few microvolts per layer, but stack them a million layers high in series and you get a 10 volt battery. We wrap graphene nanolayers on a rotating mandrill, stamp out sections the size of a penny and bus alternate layers in parallel. A perfect application for nanotechnology."

"You're talking like you've done all this."

Andy smiled back, not the terse, nervous smile like before, but the grin of a proud father.

"Bryan, take a vessel, coat it with the Higgs field shield, add a few propulsion units and you suddenly have a vessel that can travel very fast. Add a battery powered by the Casimir Effect and you have a vessel that can travel very fast for a long time. Do you know what you get?"

He was pushing my limits. The more he talked, the less I was able to believe. Was this just to test my credibility? But I was in my consultant mode. My client asked me a question. I was working through my assessment when it suddenly struck me what he had just described.

"A space ship," I whispered in disbelief.

"I'm impressed," he said, smiling.

The wheels were turning in my head. Everything was fitting into place. It might really be possible. He had given me an almost convincing argument. My BS detector had pulled back slightly from the red zone. I couldn't immediately find the obvious flaw, yet. Of course, I wanted to see the proof, but if even a fraction of what he was telling me was true, this would change everything. Was I just being tested here? Why go through such an elaborate story if it was a hoax? While the kid inside me wanted desperately to believe everything he told me, my engineering discipline was holding my enthusiasm in check until I could see the evidence. I'd let him carry me along on this tale, but keep on my guard.

"Two minutes."

"Now comes the last problem we were working on. If you could travel anywhere in our solar system, what would be the most important question you would want to answer?"

I was at my limit. I was saturated with new revelations. Who needed a purpose to go into space? If I had a space ship that could take me anywhere in the solar system, I'd just want to go out there for the thrill of it. I shook my head slightly, a bit shell shocked, no idea how to answer.

"Is there life out there other than on Earth?" he answered for me.

He paused for my reaction. I nodded. Yeah, that was a really good question. I wanted to hear the answer to that one!

"Well," I asked to fill in the silence. I was a little numb to exotic, heretofore unreachable possibilities. "What's the answer? Have you found it? Is there life out there?"

"It's a lot more complicated an answer than any of us were hoping for. We only started our trips a few months ago, and today I think we got an unexpected and alarming answer." He paused again.

"What did you learn?" I prodded.

"Kathy is our resident astrophysicist and planetary astronomer. She's traveled farther in our solar system than any other person. On one of her first trips, she brought back samples from Europa, a moon of Jupiter. There was no life in the samples, exactly, but there were complex DNA fragments in some surface ice, but, surprisingly, not in the subsurface water. She had the brilliant idea that maybe the DNA fragments were from comets impacting the surface, just not penetrating under the thick ice layer."

"The first sample she brought back from a comet showed a complex mix of DNA fragments, some reptile, some bacterial, and some advanced segments, almost modern human. Michael, our mathematics expert, suggested we might be seeing DNA fragments from Earth, blasted out into space during meteorite impacts, contaminating our solar system."

"One minute."

"Kathy and Michael took two of our ships and mounted the last expedition to get samples from comets that were on their first pass through the solar system, far enough away that they could not have picked up contamination from Earth."

"They sampled one comet and were heading off for a second, near the orbit of Saturn. That's where they encountered..." He paused searching for what words to use.

"What?" I almost shouted. "What did they encounter?"

"I am not sure. They tracked four other space ships coming toward Earth. She and Michael followed them to Earth. When they got close to our orbit, Kathy said they veered off to the Moon. She and Michael split up. Michael followed them to the Moon. We haven't heard from him," Andy's voice broke as he said, "yet."

"Kathy says her ship was attacked before entering Earth's atmosphere and after she crash-landed, well, you know as well as anyone what happened next."

"So the attackers that I killed were..." I paused for an instant. I couldn't quite vocalize what was on my mind.

"Zero. Andy, you are due for your staff meeting now."

"Computer, set up the conference room. Tell the others to review Kathy's files until I get there. I need one more minute."

"Yes, Andy."

"Were what, Bryan?" He paused, waiting for me to finish my sentence, but I had no idea what I was going to say. As I ran through each alternative that came to mind, it was crazier than the last. Crazy ideas might effortlessly roll off Andy's tongue, but I was too much of a real-world engineer to have enough practice at this sort of thing to follow suit.

I just sat there like a newbie actor who's in front of an audience and forgets his lines. My mouth was open and nothing came out. I couldn't accept this reality yet. To say it, would be one step closer to believing it. I couldn't.

Andy said it for me, "It's likely the two men who attacked Kathy are somehow connected to another space faring group. Which is easier to believe: that this group is aliens from another advanced civilization, or that we are not the only shadow organization on Earth with sophisticated space craft? Regardless, their intentions are not good."

12

NO, NO, NO. I felt like the frog in the hot water. It had gradually gotten hotter and hotter and I hadn't noticed how I'd got to the point where I was cooking. I was brought along and sucked into Andy's fantasy, to this completely unbelievable conclusion.

"Time's up, Bryan. Now you know what we are up against."

"And I can't believe any of it. A secret company, working in the shadows, all these new discoveries, inertial shielding, propulsion units pushing against empty space, Casimir batteries...If any of this is true, it will completely change the world as we know it."

"I left out the advances we've made in information science and man-machine interfaces. Bryan," he quickly continued, "I've run out of time. My top priority is coming up with a plan to find Michael and bring him home safely. If you are going to help us, I need you engaged, not questioning every detail. I can tell from your comments, the proof for you will be in seeing the execution. This will happen in due course. Can you accept what I've told you for now and use this information? You have to decide to take the next step. Will you leave the shadows of your past and join us in the light?"

Andy stood up and reached over his desk holding out his hand. His eyes, his very serious, intense eyes, locked on mine. I felt each microsecond tick by. My brain was overwhelmed. They'd made space travel practical. This was my second chance, and if just a small fraction of what he'd told me was true, I'd been living in the shadows all my life. I felt like Dorothy when she opened the door to first view Oz. The world had gone suddenly from black and white to Technicolor.

It took me another microsecond to calculate the risk reward ratio in my head. At worst, they'd laugh at me for being gullible and believing all this science fiction. And, at best? If even a fraction of what he had told me was true, the reward was, quite literally, astronomical.

Realization hit. I suddenly saw the consequences of what Kathy had discovered, and the implication of the attack on her. I'd just been introduced to the possibility of a whole new reality that exceeded my wildest dreams. And some group of high-tech bullies wanted to take it away from us? I'd fight them tooth and claw, or for me, soldering iron and keyboard. My Ninjaneer mojo was twitching in anticipation to get my hands on these new technologies at Sciquest. I anticipated a whole new arsenal to bring against this threat.

I stood up, met his gaze, reached over, shook his hand to seal the deal and said, "I'm okay, assuming for now, you've been truthful. If I find you've been fooling me, I'll retroactively add a 300 percent hassle factor to my consulting fees."

He grinned and gripped my hand. "Welcome to the light, Bryan."

He instantly switched modes from selling to being a commanding CEO. "There is no time left and I have two last things to do before my staff meeting. First, I'd like that weapon. I want to get it to Flowers and his team to reverse engineer. Can I have it?"

He reached his hand half way across the desk for it. I guess the trust started here. Was all of this just a ruse to seduce the laser out of my hand? Surely, he could have come up with a shorter and simpler story, or just offered me money. I might have taken it.

But I had to commit. Giving up the laser was the ante for his game. I passed the laser to him, rounded hemisphere first, and he took it gingerly.

"There are three small indentations near the base," I said. "Push the two on the side, then the top pad fires the weapon. There seems to be about a half a second recharge period."

"Bryan, you're making the right decision." He started to move around his desk to leave his office but suddenly stopped and grabbed his glasses from his desk.

"And one more thing. You're coming to the staff meeting, which is a virtual meeting. You'll need a pair of these to join us." He opened the top drawer of his desk and pulled out an identical pair to the glasses he wore and handed them to me. "The only color I have right now is black. You can access your preference file at your convenience. For now, I'll set you up with my preferences."

I put the glasses on, expecting to be wowed, but it was like looking out of a pane of glass.

Andy walked over and stood at the door. "I asked Kathy to get you settled into the conference room. I'll be back in just thirty seconds."

He opened his office door. I heard footsteps coming down the corridor outside. It must be Kathy. He said softly, "Computer, activate Bryan's glasses. Use my preference settings and authorization codes," and the room suddenly changed. I vaguely heard him whisper as he slipped out the door, "you'll get used to it." In my first glimpse at this new augmented world in the light, I wasn't so sure.

The featureless room I had first entered was now anything but. The wall to my right was not a blank wall, it was a large picture window showing a scene of a meadow with trees around the edge and in the distance, a white capped mountain range. But it wasn't a painting. I could see the upper branches of the trees swaying in some hidden wind. A hawk or eagle was circling over the meadow, on the hunt for some rodent in the field.

I slowly rotated to my right, looking around the rest of the newly decorated office. On the far wall, directly across from Andy's desk was a van Gogh painting. It was Starry Starry Night, illuminated like in a gallery by a small spot light from beneath. This wasn't a print, this was an actual painting. From across the office, I could make out the texture of the thick layers of paint in van Gogh's style.

To its right was a huge grandfather clock with a pendulum slowly swinging back and forth. Over my racing heartbeat, I could pick up the faint tick, tick, tick as the pendulum came to the end of its swing, triggered the advance mechanism in the clock drive and caused the hand to advance an incremental amount. I heard a faint tick at each end of the arc. Then I noticed the other sound behind me. It was the sound of water trickling down from a fountain.

I spun around and the bookcase had changed. The wall behind his desk was still covered from floor to ceiling with the same books, but in the middle, a section was hollowed out and filled with an impossible water fountain.

Three large, smooth rocks floated in space about a foot apart, one on top of the other. A small stream of water appeared out of space and gently splashed on the top rock. The water flowed around it in a smooth sheet to coalesce on the bottom in another focused stream only to hit the next rock down and continue the process.

The water from the last rock just disappeared into space about three inches after it left the bottom surface.

As impossible as this suspended sculpture was, I could hear the distinct, but faint burbling of the water hitting each rock. I could pick up distinct impacts and see when the splash hit a specific rock. Each one made a slightly different sound and I could distinguish them from one another.

I didn't have to move my head to look around. Just moving my eyes changed the images. This wasn't a projection on the inside lenses of my glasses. This was an image projected directly on my retinas. They had to have sensors built into the nose piece to do retina tracking and modulated lasers to project the images based on where I was looking.

I could probably have developed a system like this, but it would have taken a helmet the size of a basketball and a refrigerator sized server for all the real time image processing. Plus a few years with a team of software engineers skilled in image processing and real time operating systems. My evaluation of Sciquest technology jumped more than a few notches.

Andy's desk was radically different in this virtual world than in the real world. It wasn't empty anymore. It was filled with stacks of folders, some with papers sticking out the edges. There were five piles haphazardly splayed over the desk. The center was empty and a standard keyboard was embedded in the surface of the desk.

Now I understood why he had a minimalist office. Who needed real decorations when you could synthesize anything you wanted, wherever you looked? Why have a computer or monitor on your desk when your screen could be your entire field of view? You could have a hundred different screens scattered 360 degrees around you. Your desktop could literally be a desktop with files separated into piles on top of it. A filing cabinet could literally be a filing cabinet for files.

This augmented reality would change everything. Spaceships would have an immediate impact on less than one percent of the population. But this seamless augmented realty would hit the remaining ninety-nine percent and possibly change life was we knew it. Now I realized why Kathy said some of these features wouldn't be released to the market for another five years.

I heard a click to my left, where the real door was. "Close your mouth or your brains are likely to fall out," Kathy said behind me. I must have looked like a five-year-old kid at his first Disneyland parade. Was she real or virtual? The rendering was so perfect, initially I couldn't tell. I lowered the glasses to my nose and peered over the frame. She was the real thing. This *was* going to take some getting used to.

"Sit down, we have work to do," she said.

13

"ANDY TOLD ME in the hallway you're officially onboard. You have a lot of catching up to do and not much time. I'm convinced our problems run deeper than I initially thought."

"We almost got killed, how many times out there? How much of a bigger problem can you have?"

She sat down and pulled out the chair next to her. "Sit," she said. "You'll see."

I was too much in awe to sit just yet. "This is so incredible. I have so many questions."

"They can wait. Your PDA can fill you in when you have a minute free. Ask for the orientation program."

"How do I talk to my PDA?" I asked, wondering where to start.

"You'll want to name your PDA. I call mine Fred. Michael thinks I did that because he says I have a thing about wanting to dominate and control men." She gave me a sly look: "You don't think that, do you?"

As naïve as I am, even I realized this was a trap. I ignored it and said. "Andy just calls his 'computer.'"

"He says he wants to remind himself that the PDA, however cool it may be, is just a computer. It really does help to have some sort of identifier. Then it knows when to respond. The default name is PDA, try that."

"Andy started me with his preference file."

"Huh," she said, her mouth twitching. "Then try 'Computer'."

"Computer," I said into the air, feeling a little foolish. I didn't want to waste time thinking of a clever name, so I just picked the name of the best admin I ever had. "Computer, change your identification to Sally. Respond also to Sal. Do you understand?"

"Yes, Bryan," The voice came through in an ear piece in the frame, which meant I also felt the voice against my skull. It was a bone conduction speaker, one on each side of the frames. "You can access my preferences file at any time and select the voice and sound level. Please speak quietly and I will respond."

"Kathy, did you hear any of that?"

"Communication with your PDA is private. If you want someone else to hear you or your PDA, just tell it. It's smart enough to find anyone through a cell phone network, the web or any other way possible. It's got a software-defined radio interface so can synthesize any signal needed to connect to any wireless network."

She gave me an impish smile. "I think I have a better option for your interface. Accept the incoming preference file." She waved her hands in front of her, the last motion sliding her hand toward me.

"Sally, accept the incoming preference file from Kathy," I said.

"Yes, Bryan," This time the voice was a lot younger, a slight sultry tone, not at all the matronly voice I had heard from the wall speakers. This was getting better and better. "Where are the processor and the memory?" I asked. So much capability and so little size.

"Quantum processor and holographic memory in the frames. The PDA periodically uploads a mirror image to the network server or ship when we're not local.

"Look, are you going to be asking me twenty questions all night? Figure it out. You seem pretty good at that." She looked over at me and smiled, an honest-to-goodness Duchenne smile. Cute, smart and an Andromeda Galaxy tattoo. And I felt like a toy-starved kid suddenly let loose at Macy's during a Christmas sale.

"Questions later. Got it. What do I do for the meeting?"

"Sit down. Sally, bring Bryan into the meeting when Fred starts in."

"Of course, Kathy."

I sat down to the right of Kathy. There was another chair at the head of the table for Andy when he came back.

"Here we go," she said.

In the next instant, I was teleported into a different room. The real-world room lights dimmed to make it easier to see the projected images.

With the glasses on and Sally controlling my view of the world, I was going to have problems distinguishing reality from virtual reality.

The oval table in front of me disappeared. In its place was a long, rectangular, dark, mahogany table. No windows in the room, just beautiful paintings on the walls, mostly Monets. There was a Renoir directly across from me, a still life of roses in a vase. In the painting, a few roses were scattered on a table. It was brilliantly clear. Like gallery paintings, each of these virtual paintings had a small spotlight shining from the bottom, highlighting the artwork.

In the dark, shiny surface of the conference table, I could see a reflected image of the Renoir. The wood grain of the conference table added even more texture to the tiny brush strokes of the rose petals. I was astonished at the processing power in my frames. Voice recognition and synthesis was one thing, this was real time complex image processing. The processor was rendering not just the paintings, but how their image was altered by reflection from the textured surface of the table, seamlessly in real time. What else could it do?

The room felt oddly claustrophobic. I looked around and I realized why; no windows, no door. I was sealed into a box. It was large, and it was tastefully decorated, but it was a box. What if they started collapsing inward? I felt trapped.

Adrenaline, and not the good kind, trickled back into my system. I was breathing faster, gripping the arm rests. I looked frantically around for an exit.

I don't do pain. I don't do violence. I don't do roller coaster rides, and, ever since being trapped in a collapsed root cellar during a tornado when I was a kid, I definitely don't do small, confined spaces with no exits. I made a mental note to have a chat with Sally about this and modify my preference file.

I forced myself to lower my glasses and peer at the real-world small office. In the very dim background light, I saw the door, the exit, comfortably within reach. I pushed the glasses back on my nose and entered the virtual world, struggling to stay in control. The meeting was starting.

Kathy gave me a quizzical look. She had changed positions. In the real room, she was on my left. In the virtual room, she was on my right. Pretty creepy! Jumping back and forth would take some getting used to.

I was about to make a comment to Kathy when the seam of a door materialized in the wall near the head of the table. It swung open and Andy walked through. Just as suddenly, the door closed and the frame melted back into the wall, now invisible. I lowered the glasses to the tip of my nose to look over the top and saw in the dimly lit real-world, Andy really was just now entering his office. I pushed the glasses back up my nose.

Maybe now I'd meet some of these cream-of-the-crop mad scientists who were turning my world Technicolor, or else exercise my 300 percent surcharge. I was really rooting for the Technicolor.

Andy came around to join us and took the chair at the head of the virtual table. As he sat down, three other people, a middle-aged black man, an elderly woman, and a college kid, materialized around the table. They looked surprised, even shocked, to see me.

Maybe I'd just end up with the extra cash after all.

14

"I'M SORRY TO gather you all so late on a Sunday night, but we have a crisis to deal with. I've brought Bryan onto our team. I know it's against the protocol I put in place, but given the state of affairs, I felt we had to accelerate his application. He's a tech-savvy problem solver. Kathy and I agreed his skills would be invaluable to us right now. You can review his file later."

The black man sitting just to Andy's right, across the table, nodded at me. "Your assessment is good enough for me, Andy," he said. He had that slow, comfortable drawl that hinted at growing up in a place like West Virginia or South Carolina, of someone who never appeared hurried.

Sally floated yellow words just above his head, 'Ron Owens, director of operations, headquartered in the San Jose Plant.' I was thinking I could really use these glasses at parties. I'd never have to remember a name again.

Ron looked to be in his late fifties, a seasoned operations manager. It's been my experience they usually have a keen sense of deadlines and will pay through the nose to not miss one. My kind of client. Ron may have seemed calm, but if he was like a typical operations manager, deep down he was a simmering cauldron of fury ready to be unleashed to protect his plan. I could probably work with him.

One down, two to go.

"As much as I trust your judgment, I must say this is a rather extraordinary step," said the grandmotherly woman with silver and grey French braids tightly wrapped around and bobby-pinned in the front of her head, sitting on Ron's right. "With all due respect to this young man," she looked over at me and smiled kindly, "what exactly leads you to believe we should bring him in as new member? Shouldn't we be vetting him more carefully?"

Well, that wasn't very inviting. She smiled at me brightly, and when her eyes met mine, I could tell there was a depth of intelligence to them. Her self-confidence made me doubt my presence there. I started to sweat. Proving myself to her might be the toughest thing I did tonight.

Sally labeled her: 'Millie Drexler, molecular biologist in charge of the DNA Analysis team, stationed out of the Prescott Lab.'

"If Bryan hadn't jumped in and acted as quickly and as bravely as he did, I'd be dead," Kathy interjected. "He has special skills and I think we need him."

I was rather pleased she jumped to my defense. I guess we were still a team. I smiled and started to crack a comment, but then I remembered Andy's comment; she thinks we're screwed even with me in the mix.

I saw the college aged kid roll his eyes at her comment.

"Okay," chimed in the kid. "So what makes him so special? What else has he done for us to deserve to be brought into our very exclusive, extraordinary group?" His voice seemed to break when he said this, but he fixed me with a flat, aggressive stare you usually see in bullies and troublemakers, despite the fact that he was so skinny that a good wind would knock him over.

I leaned forward for a better look at this kid. The label over his head said it all: 'Richard Rayburn, information systems assistant lead'. This punk kid was the CEO's son. He couldn't be more than twenty years old, tall, thin, wearing a white tee shirt that hung on him. He sat, kinda hunched and, when I stared back, he started fidgeting in his chair. What was he doing in this self-proclaimed, 'very exclusive, extraordinary group'?

Ron shook his head. "Son, if you're going to ask him 'what else have you done for us' after Kathy just told you he saved her life and has exceptional skills, your next word should be, 'Prometheus.'"

Richard shot Ron a dirty look. "I'm not your son," he shot back.

"Enough of this, Richard!" Andy said. "It's decided."

"And my opinions don't count," said Richard, glowering at him. "I'm just a coding nerd to you."

Andy frowned. "You'll get your turn, Richard," he said. "For now just listen and pay attention."

Richard slumped back into his chair, muttering to himself.

Andy pursed his lips and looked around the room. "Where's Dr. Flowers and the Whiz?"

Ron glanced down at his notebook. "Doctor Ozman is fishing, off the grid. I can send a drone to tell him to connect. Might take a few hours to find him."

"Make it happen. Find the Whiz," Andy said. "We need his input."

"We don't need him. I'm here," Richard said, in a loud voice. "While he's gone, he said I would be in charge of the information systems group." He gave his father a baleful look. I could see his shoulders trembling.

"Richard, the problem we face now is going to take everyone working together. Please let the senior staff handle this without interrupting." Andy's voice was clipped and cold.

Richard looked like he wanted to respond, but withered a bit under his father's glare. I got the impression this was not the first time Andy had to rein in his son. He sat back in his chair, suffering the rebuke with arms crossed, almost hugging himself.

I felt bewildered by his actions. By the way everybody studiously ignored him, they seemed used to his behavior.

"What about Doctor Flowers? Computer, ping David please."

A window opened up across the table from me like I was peering into an adjacent room, though I figured it was just part of this virtual world. Through the aperture, I saw a pretty crowded lab with three benches filled with stainless steel equipment. I could identify an Argon-ion laser, some vacuum systems, and maybe even a spectrometer system. The pick-up camera was mounted in some sort of shroud or tube giving a limited field of view. Put a lens cover on it and Flowers could control his invasion of privacy. Clever guy.

In the next instant, a face peered through the window. "I'm right in the middle of analyzing the laser weapon that Bryan delivered. Thank you, by the way. Fascinating device. No clue yet what it's made of or how it works. Obviously not ferrous. This is going to take a while."

"We haven't heard anything from Michael for about three hours," Andy said. "At last report, he told Kathy he was following the incoming fleet to the Moon and was going to go radio silent with his black screen on. I have my computer monitoring all communications channels for anything that might be a possible contact."

"Anyone else have any contact of any sort with Michael?" Andy looked around the room.

Doctor Flowers gave a curt response, "No, not me." He seemed to be only minimally engaged, more interested in playing with my laser on his lab bench.

"No," said Ron.

Millie shook her head. "It's not really that unusual for one of us to be out of touch for a few days. Andy, are you just a little too worried? Do we have any reason to believe Michael might be in danger?"

"I really believe he's in trouble," said Kathy. "Those ships we followed were heading to the Moon and Michael was following. And you know him. He wouldn't be able to resist knocking on their front door."

Millie leaned back in her chair. "Do we know anything more about these ships, where they're from, what group they're with?"

"I don't know who they are, but they shot me down," said Kathy. She looked a little agitated.

"Dear, were you really shot down?" My attention was drawn back to Millie. She sat with her hands folded in front of her, a picture of calm. "Could your ship just have had a malfunction or maybe a meteor hit like Apollo Thirteen?" She smiled at Kathy. "Are you sure this isn't another case of Europan Fever?"

Europan? Did I hear that right? What was that, like the black plague?

"I was really sick from that." Kathy pursed her lips.

"Yes, I know, dear," she said with surprising sincerity. "But it wasn't an alien space virus you picked up on Europa. It was just a normal H1N1 Earth virus you picked up from Valerie when she was servicing your ship before you left."

Finally, another skeptical voice. I felt a little relieved. Kathy might be my teammate, but I was going to have to reevaluate everything she'd told me so far. I could buy the shootout, the hand-held laser weapon, and the virtual conference. Still, other spaceships out by Saturn? More than a little hard to swallow without a whole lot more evidence.

"Millie, I wasn't sick this time. Michael was with me. We really did track four craft from beyond the orbit of Saturn. We even recorded transmissions from them. And one of them really did shoot out my communications antenna." Kathy's voice quavered.

"And I don't think mine was the first craft to be shot down. I think these ships have been flying around for at least twelve years and shot down the Columbia Space Shuttle. And if those thugs that tried to kidnap me are part of this group, and they have Michael, he may be in terrible danger. The whole earth could be in danger!" She slapped the table, her eyes a little wild.

"I don't doubt what you experienced," Millie said, "I'm just looking for alternative explanations."

"I was shot down! What more explanation do you need?"

"Kathy, relax," Andy said. "We can check your ship for evidence. Ron, what's the status of the recovery operation?"

Ron looked down at his notebook, moved his fingers along a page as though scrolling. "Max is on the scene. It looks like the wings show melting along the edges, all the polymer coatings are burned off, and significant damage to the dorsal region, right where the antenna is. An entire section of the fuselage is gone. I can't tell for sure until we bring her ship back in whether it was a meteor or . . ." He looked up at Kathy. "Some advanced weapon from one of these mystery ships."

A white flash saturated the camera image from Flower's lab simultaneous with a sharp blast like a firecracker in a small room. "What the hell!?" shouted Richard, hitting the floor. It was a strange reaction for someone who was supposed to be in a virtual meeting. The rest of us just gave a brief shudder at the sudden shock.

"That was me," shouted Flowers. "Looks like the laser is still working."

"A warning next time, David," Andy said.

"Holy Toledo," said Ron.

Millie merely shook her head slowly back and forth, I guess her way of showing displeasure at the rude interruption.

The image came back on in Flower's lab. He stood over one of the instruments in his lab, waving the smoke away with his hand, trying to read the screen. "I'm going to need a new spectrometer and microprobe analyzer. I got an initial read before it melted. What we have here is a relatively broadband UV laser, not using an emission line. Might be a free electron laser. I've got two more tests I can do here, but I can't do the microprobe analysis of the metal. Analyzer was in the beam's path."

"You've been bitching about that old spectrometer for months. I think you aimed for it on purpose hoping you could wrangle an upgrade," joked Kathy, making most everyone at the table chuckle. Except for Richard, who had settled back in his chair again, looking extremely put out.

Flowers whistled. "Looks like this beam can penetrate about a half an inch of stainless steel. I need to use the mass spectrometer in my Prescott lab. I'm going to finish up and head out."

"Doctor Flowers," Ron interjected, "if you can wait twenty minutes, Max can fly you down in one of the shuttles. You'll be there in less than an hour and a half."

Flowers grinned. "It's a deal. I'll take you up on your offer."

That didn't seem right. Prescott was about a thousand miles away, their shuttles would have to go about a thousand miles an hour. If they were trying to fool me, at least they were going to get an A for consistency.

"Ron, if you're sending a shuttle down here, can you pick up the comet sample and send it along?" asked Millie.

Ron looked down at his notebook, seemed to scroll along the side for a second and said, "Max recovered it. Looks intact. Cooling is still active. I'll have him bring it along."

Millie looked excited. "Kathy, if this comet sample is pristine, it could make your whole trip worthwhile."

"It won't be worth it if something happened to Michael," she shot back.

"Dear, Michael is a very capable and resourceful fellow. I'm sure he is fine."

"But we don't know that!"

This discussion was going around in circles and I wanted to learn more about what was really going on. I wanted to pry open the real story. Maybe throwing a match into this tinderbox would stir things up.

"Kathy, you said you thought you weren't the first to be shot down. What do you mean?" Maybe she was cute, but I was going to either help her make her case or hang herself.

"It was the Columbia Shuttle accident all over again."

She looked at me deadpan and then turned to Andy. "You've been telling us to be on the lookout for any evidence of tampering with the space program. On my violent reentry through the atmosphere, all I was thinking of was the Columbia and was I going to suffer their fate? Then I thought, maybe they suffered my fate."

"What do you mean?" Andy said, shaking his head. He was probably as much at a loss where she was going with this as I was.

Through my virtual interface, I could see the intensity in her eyes. "After I left your office, Andy, I had Fred do some digging. He found a comment buried in the transcripts of Columbia's last mission, twelve years ago. Three hours before they were scheduled for reentry, they were just stowing a high-resolution IR camera. This was a defense department program so the details were classified. That's why it was buried until Fred dug it up."

I made another mental note of the power of my new PDA. Any information, anywhere, even classified, instantly accessible. "They had an advanced IR spy telescope with motion tracking on board. Anderson, the mission specialist was running a calibration test, pointing off into space. He picked up a thermal transient, heading toward Earth."

Richard snorted but I was transfixed. "The camera's motion tracking was still on and they recorded about two-and-a-half seconds of tracked images at high resolution," Kathy continued.

"And?" said Andy.

"Anderson said he was viewing the images in real time and it looked like a distinctly extended object, slowing down before it entered Earth's atmosphere." She let that thought hang for a moment before adding: "Mission Control told him to stop talking over the open line and bring all the recordings back to base for review."

"And three hours later, the shuttle burned up in reentry," Andy said, finishing the story for her. "I assume the recordings burned with it."

I remembered the accident very clearly. It had set the space shuttle program back about ten years and it had never really recovered. But there was a yearlong study. I thought the report of foam insulation coming off the fuel tank knocking off some heat-shield tiles was pretty conclusive. Was this group just a little too paranoid?

"I saw the video," I jumped in. "It was pretty clear, pieces of tank insulation came off and shattered heatshield tiles. That's what brought the shuttle down."

Flowers looked back at me over his shoulder. "You saw doctored video. What came off the fuel tank was frost, not insulation. No way did it do any damage. Some of the data was faked." I saw him leaning over my laser, which was held on the optical bench with two clamps.

Richard got up and started walking in a little circle. "Here we go," he wailed to the ceiling. His father looked at him sharply but said nothing.

"How do you know they were doctored?"

"I got a first run copy from the master. There was a time stamp embedded in the frame header in the original on-board recordings. The images that showed insulation coming off and smashing the heat shield tiles didn't have an embedded time stamp. Everything before and after did. What you saw was inserted after the fact."

"Why would they do that?" I asked. He was criticizing my childhood heroes. NASA engineers could do no wrong.

Flowers walked over to the camera and stared back at us, his face filling the frame, very serious. "It never made sense to me, until now. It all fits. Maybe they were shot down by another space craft. I don't know for sure, but some executive level group on Earth, someone on the inside, high up, wanted to cover up what really happened to the Columbia. They just had to come up with a convincing cover story."

The boundaries of my real world and their fantasy world were blurring. Did I have to reevaluate every news report I'd read, or were these people all crazy?

"It doesn't mean Columbia was shot down, just that the official explanation NASA gave may not have been the real one," said Millie.

Richard just snorted. Kathy coughed. "It's the same thing that happened to me. The Columbia accidentally spotted another spacecraft. Whoever they were, they must have been monitoring Columbia's transmissions and shot them down so they wouldn't be discovered."

There was something in Kathy's earlier comment that was nagging at me, maybe something I could use to further test her story, look for inconsistencies. "Kathy, you said you encountered these ships near Saturn. Were they in orbit? What was their trajectory?"

She turned toward me and her gaze caught and held me. "Good question. I should have brought it up earlier," she said. "We picked up their emissions just outside the orbit of Saturn. We thought maybe the signals were from the New Horizon's Mission, or even Cassini. We had the ephemeris of every space mission and nothing was even close."

"Anything else?" prompted Andy.

"Then Michael plotted their course. They were decelerating, a lot. At their current speed, direction and deceleration, they'd be coming to rest near Earth." She was getting very excited, her voice rising in pitch. When she talked passionately about technical things, she looked even more attractive. Her eyes were having the same effect on me now as they had in the real world. Did she see anything special in mine?

"Do you know what that means?" she asked, directing her question right at me.

I was too focused on those green eyes and had to blink a few times to refocus.

"Oh, see! See?" howled Richard. He was standing in the corner now. "I told you that he wouldn't be any help."

I frowned. When it comes to engineering problems, I can do the easy ones on autopilot. My engineering forebrain had already processed her description. I knew what it meant in principle. It just took me another second to shift gears and put it in words.

I pictured it in my head. At Saturn, decelerating, coming to rest at Earth. That was a long way to decelerate. "They started their trip from really far away," I replied just as intently.

"Exactly!" She turned back to the group around the table and the moment passed.

Lucky for me. This was not a good time to be distracted. "If they had just gone through turn-around, and had accelerated at the same rate they were decelerating, they started somewhere between Pluto and the fringe of the Oort Cloud."

"Then it's not likely they came from Earth," Millie said, slowly.

Her statement hung in the air. No one else was brave enough to offer a follow on comment. Finally, Millie continued her thought. "We can't be talking about aliens, can we?"

Aliens.

There, someone finally said it.

I was with Millie. Are we really talking about real-life, out-of-this world aliens? There had to be a more rational explanation.

Andy rubbed his eyes. It was after ten at night and he looked tired. I had been prepared for an all-nighter, so I was good to go. "Either that," Andy said, "or another secret group from Earth. But what would they be doing beyond Pluto? And how are all these incidents connected?"

He turned to me. "Bryan, what's your assessment?"

Me? Talk about being put on the spot.

I still didn't believe ninety percent of what I was hearing in this room: aliens, space ships from beyond Pluto, a space battle above the Earth. That said, I'm a professional problem solver and my client just asked for my analysis.

I took a deep breath. Don't tell anyone, but I love this sort of challenge, being asked for my instant assessment of a situation. I can do two things really well, speculate and extrapolate. I have no problem suspending disbelief, speculating based on assumptions and extrapolating to a conclusion. I always have an opinion and never hesitate offering it when asked, and to the irritation of some, even when not asked.

I just didn't see the conclusion in this case. But the instant attention of the group kick-started the wheels in my head.

"If your interpretation of what happened to Kathy and the Colombia are true, we have a very secretive group with high level government connections that might have been around for at least a dozen years. And they don't hesitate to take lethal action to prevent discovery." I got up and, started pacing the room. I was making it up as I went along, but so far, so good.

"They tracked Kathy's reentry, and had enough resources locally on the ground to mount an attack in minutes of her landing. When they thought they could get away with it, they tried to capture her. When that failed, they tried to kill her and take out any witnesses, at whatever the cost. They didn't hesitate killing that one poor man and tried a dozen times to take us out before we got them."

The hair on the back of my neck went up, as I followed my line of logic. "They were going to capture her alive."

The last part came out as more of a whisper, and I stared off into space a second, feeling very creeped out. I realized what they intended.

Ron raised his hand. "Wait a minute, Bryan, if this was the same group that tried to shoot her down, why go to all the trouble of capturing her alive?"

"I'd say they thought they'd take advantage of this opportunity to find out where this phantom space craft came from, and if there were more."

"So what?" Richard broke in. "You still don't know who they are or where they're from."

"What Bryan is implying, Richard, is that if they are so interested in finding out about us, and Michael was really caught, there is a good chance he is still alive." Millie's gentle voice was tinged with sadness.

Kathy turned pale in the virtual room. "But how far would they go to find out about us? They could be . . . .torturing him."

Ron looked upset. "We have to talk about a rescue mission. We don't have the resources to penetrate some foreign base on the Moon, but the military does. I think it's time we call them in."

"No military," Flowers said. "Even if we could convince someone in the military, and they didn't get into a pissing contest to see which branch of the service got access to our technology, we don't know who to trust. We know this secret group has penetrated high levels of NASA. If they're the same group that's been suppressing our technology growth, they probably infiltrated the military and other government agencies as well."

He was adamant, and he was quickly dragging me kicking and screaming to his side. But I had an alternative idea. "Hang on, Dr. Flowers," I said. "I think I know a group that could help you on this."

"What's your recommendation, Bryan?" Andy asked.

"I know a group of former SEAL Teams, led by GD Steelanowski. He used to be the commander of SEAL Team 6, then the entire Special Forces operations. He has a private security consulting group now, OSS. I trust him absolutely."

"And who are you?" Richard broke in, "How do we know we can trust you?" I clearly had not won over Richard, and frankly, I didn't care at this moment.

"We don't need this kind of distraction right now," Kathy muttered, giving Andy a meaningful look.

"We're shooting in the dark about who we can trust and right now every minute counts." Andy said. I heard the voice of command. He wasn't making a suggestion. "Ron, get in touch with this former SEAL team and see how quickly they can help us. In the meantime, we have to learn everything we can about this secret group."

Richard was up again. "But we don't know anything else, Dad. Kathy's already told us everything she knows about them."

I couldn't believe Andy would have brought his son into this group unless he had good reasons, but right now, he seemed like he was losing control. Then I suddenly realized Richard brought up an important point. He was just wrong about it.

His comment triggered something Kathy mentioned earlier that had been nagging at me. "Kathy, the recordings. You said you were tracking their transmissions. What were they?"

"They're not decoded yet. I'm still waiting on the analysis so I don't have a lot of information to add about them. We recorded about three hours total over the two days coming in system. They shut down after we crossed Mars' orbit."

"And you haven't been able to make sense of any of the signals?" I prodded her.

"I'll decode them!" Richard was almost out of his seat, waving his arm like he had to pee real bad and desperately needed to be excused from the room. "Send me the files."

Kathy ignored him. "I hijacked the SETI@home project as soon as I left Andy's office and all two million PCs in the network have been working on decoding the signals."

"Where are you with that?" Andy asked.

"I'll check." Kathy was silent for a moment, staring off into the air.

"Good," she said, "They found a key." She was talking slow, like she was reading something and reporting as she learned it. "Looks like the signals have a high frequency modulation and a low frequency modulation."

"Sounds like image and audio tracks," I said.

"Right," She was distracted. I saw her hands moving in the space in front of her. She was mumbling something to Fred that I couldn't understand.

Then she gasped and pulled back in her seat. It almost looked like she had seen a creature out of a walking dead movie.

"What is it, Kathy?" I felt a burst of adrenaline. Kathy swept her hands in front of her, throwing the image out to the middle of the conference table. A flat screen, floated in the middle of the table, carrying a video image of a face. The loose flesh around the cheeks was pulled back like it was being hit by a gale force wind. Or was under four gees of acceleration.

It wasn't human. And the sound it was making didn't sound human, either.

But it was somehow very familiar. My eyes were drawn to the pronounced eye brow ridges, the bushy hair, and the mouth full of too many teeth. I was about to make a comment when Millie beat me to the punch line.

"Neanderthals. You were following Neanderthals."

It all clicked. But only partly. I could have more easily believed little green Martians, or even grey aliens with big triangular heads. I did not expect Neanderthals.

I looked around the room, at my new teammates. Everyone looked various shades of shocked. Even Flowers looked disturbed, though fascinated.

Except for Richard. Richard was smiling.

When he caught me looking at him, his expression went flat.

I shook my head. Had I imagined the smile? Because it had seemed a little . . . off. A little too smug.

"This guy looks kind of like the goons that attacked me tonight," Kathy said.

We all stared transfixed at the screen in front of us. The video image played as more of it was decoded in real time. In a few seconds, the image shifted to another face against a different background, probably in another ship.

But the second alien wasn't quite Neanderthal. He was almost a mix of human and Neanderthal. It might have been a half-breed. The forehead was pushed more forward, the eyebrow ridges flattened, the nose had a little more structure, the hair was shorter and his mouth had fewer teeth showing. In fact, he was missing two bottom teeth that were oversized canines in his Neanderthal brother.

I looked closer. I could see scarring around his forehead, eyebrows, and nose. Not a half-breed; just not a very good plastic surgery job.

"Yes!" Kathy shouted. "He's one of the thugs that grabbed me."

Neanderthals were one thing, but Neanderthals using a bad plastic surgeon, trying to pass as humans? What was going on here?

"I would say," Millie began, "these visitors of ours have figured out how to alter their appearance in an attempt to blend in. They may be in our midst as we speak. I can't be certain these two creatures are really Neanderthals without a DNA sample, but they look just like the typical reconstructions based on skull samples."

I was feeling a mixture of horror and excitement. "Millie," I said, "I might be able to arrange that DNA sample for you."

She raised an eyebrow. "How is that possible, young man?"

"One of the 'goons' who attacked Kathy tonight left a rather large smear of blood on the door frame of my Jeep. It's in your parking lot."

Her smile brightened. "How wonderful." She looked over at Andy and said to him, "I never doubted your judgment for a moment." She turned to Ron and said: "We need that sample. Can you send it down to me as soon as possible?"

Ron nodded back at Millie, made a note in his notebook and just said, "Done. It's arranged."

The video of the aliens had changed the mood in the room. Here was an even bigger puzzle, despite the danger.

"I hope they're not responsible for engineering the DNA fragments," Kathy said.

DNA fragments? Where did this come from? Yet another loose end I would definitely have to follow up on. This time, I whispered a note to Sally to remind me. That and the comet sample.

"I really was hoping for something more magical or transcendental, or at least more spiritual," said Kathy, sounding disappointed. "These Neanderthals are just so distasteful."

Millie tapped the table. "I think it is a little premature to be speculating about the DNA fragments until I've looked at this new pristine sample you brought back. But it does beg the question: where did these Neanderthals come from? They've been extinct on Earth for at least 50,000 years."

I was drawn to the video images in the screen. Half the frame showed the head and torso from the chest up, lying down in a conformal chair, sort of like a dentist's chair complete with headrest and a few tubes near the head. There seemed to be a faint blue glow coming from under the chair that leaked out around the edges.

But I was drawn to something I noticed in the background of the ship's cabin, against the wall. Its presence chilled me even more than the presence of Neanderthals.

I needed to analyze the video image in more detail. "Sally," I whispered, "Can you make me a notebook like Ron's?"

"Yes, Bryan." Instantly, on the table in front of me appeared a seven-by-nine inch leather-bound notebook with lined paper. A black and gold Cross fountain pen with that little white star on the top of the cap lay across the front cover.

I picked up the pen with my virtual fingers. Without tactile clues, I couldn't feel the pen, but it sure looked like I was holding it.

I opened the notebook and wrote on the front page, "Sally, can you read this and respond in writing?" My normally scratchy hand writing came out on the virtual page like school teacher script, clean and crisp.

On the left-hand, facing page, Sally wrote, "Yes Bryan." I drew a square with a slider bar under it, and asked Sally to play the video feed in the box, adding in a log sensitivity scale to the slider.

Instantly, the video played on my page.

I fiddled with the slider. There was a lot of interference or a decoding error, or the recording device was mounted poorly and their ship had a terrible vibration. Successive images were fuzzy from frame to frame. Maybe one out of five frames was clear.

As I feverishly reviewed the recording file, I heard Andy double back on Millie's comment.

"Computer," Andy said in exasperation, "Have we located the Whiz yet? Where is he?" This was loud enough for me to clearly hear in the real world. I didn't hear the reply, but Andy said to the group, "When Ozman links in, I'll have him set up a thorough search through all databases and camera feeds for any sign of these masquerading Neanderthals."

"Dad, I'll do it. I can put together the algorithm."

"I want the Whiz in on this project, Richard," said Andy. He was clearly losing patience. I didn't blame him.

"Ozman isn't here, I am."

Andy looked over at his son and pursed his lip. "Okay Richard, calm down. Go ahead and search all video and camera feeds from all public or posted cameras for similar images. Look for any evidence of these modified Neanderthals and any patterns in their movement. See if you can locate any other presence of these characters."

"I know, I know. Stop telling me what to do."

Something about the kid really set off my alarms. He was just off, like a behavioral version of the uncanny valley with robot features. I was trying to figure him out. He seemed almost like he might be on the Autism spectrum, except that wasn't quite it. He had some sort of obsessive personality, coupled with anger at his father and maybe the rest of the Sciquest team that went beyond all that.

Andy slammed his fist on the table. "Just follow my directions, Richard. This is not about you. This is serious! If you don't like it maybe you'd like to get your ass back to your boarding school and this time, apply yourself."

Richard shook his head, his eyes wide. "Mom wouldn't treat me like this."

"Well if your mother were alive she'd be ashamed of how you are acting! Grow up!"

You could have cut the tension with a proverbial knife. Ron busied himself with his notebook, Kathy looked aghast, Flowers turned his back on the camera to work on the bench, and Millie held her hand in front of her mouth.

The look on Richard's face was sheer anguish. He was pale before, but now he was white. I hadn't known him for even an hour, and didn't much like him. But the son, whether on purpose or not, had pushed the father beyond the breaking point.

"You'll be sorry, Dad," he said. "Not everyone thinks I'm incompetent."

Andy looked over at Richard in the virtual room. "Son, I didn't mean that. We're under the gun now. I'm sorry."

Richard flung back his chair and stood in the virtual conference room. "I know what I'm doing," he said. "You don't trust me, but I know more than you think I do."

"I'm sorry," said Andy. "Let's get back on track with what's important."

"I'm important," said Richard. There were tears on his face now. "You'll see."

At that, he pulled off his glasses and just melted into a grey mist, disappearing from the virtual conference room.

Andy rubbed his eyes. He turned to look at Ron and Millie. "I don't think Richard will do anything rash. Will he?"

Millie sighed. "Don't worry about it Andy. He's in a difficult position. Give him some space. He's conflicted trying to live up to your expectations and not sure what he really wants."

Andy looked about ten years older. I made a mental note not to have any kids. "Rough night," he said. "What's really important is Michael. Ron, any ideas?"

All during Richard's tirade, I was exploring the video feed, my alarm bells rising in pitch with each second. There was more than an hour of the feed decoded and available, almost half of the total recordings. Plenty to collect the images I needed.

When I saw the scene I wanted, I circled a region of the screen showing a round conical cylinder on its side, top half open, exposing what looked to be knobs, switches, and indicator lights. Three more cylinders, with only their bases visible, stood propped upright against the wall behind it. Even though it wasn't in very good focus, it looked very conventional, not at all alien.

There was writing on the cover, and I asked Sal to build a composite, higher-resolution image from all the frames in the video.

My anxiety was growing as yellow lettering crystallized in the reflection on the cabin floor below the cylinder. It was grossly distorted from the curved surface and the funny angle.

"Sal, take this reflection. Assume it came from the surface of a conical cylinder. Recreate the image on the cylinder."

My commands were instantly carried out. If this meeting was all a sham and I was going to collect my hassle factor payment, I'd be taking this PDA with me.

I was hoping it was a sham, but it was getting harder and harder to believe all this was staged for my benefit. As hard as the alternative was to accept, I was rapidly moving closer.

Sally had finished rendering the image I asked for. The notebook page stared back at me. I knew those letters. They were unusual, but they weren't alien. Their origin was very human. Just not in English.

They were Cyrillic.

"Guys," I interrupted Andy's comments to Ron about a rescue mission. "I think I've found something you'll want to see first."

I circled the letters and the one number, all written vertically in large, yellow block letters against the dark olive green background. "Sal, project this for the room, please."

The yellow letters hung suspended in the middle of the table, slowly rotating for everyone to see. Even Flowers was looking at us, paying attention to what he was seeing displayed inside the conference room.

"Those look like Russian letters," Millie said.

"Sally, translate this."

Oh damn, I thought, staring at the translation. I suddenly realized Kathy's comments had been an understatement. We were in really, really big trouble.

15

YOU COULD HAVE heard a pin drop.

On the screen floating in the middle of the conference table, the yellow Russian letters and one number were clearly visible on the rounded, almost cone shaped lid. Directly underneath was the English translation, also in block yellow letters, written vertically, "WARHEAD 3."

"Is that a nuclear warhead?" Millie asked. Her hands, flat on the table, trembled.

Andy looked dumfounded. "Are the Russians working with them?"

"These warheads are available on the black market," said Ron. "If some of these Neanderthals are altered to look like us, maybe they've been doing a little shopping."

"But they were headed toward Earth," Kathy threw out.

Flowers suddenly appeared sitting with us at the table, making me jump. He wasn't playing in his lab, half distracted anymore. It took a nuke to finally get his attention. "They were working out a way around the arming lockout," he said.

"Are you sure about this?" Andy asked.

"I should be. It was my team that reverse engineered the re-arming process for the DOD. I think the aliens took the nukes back to wherever their home is, armed them and now they're bringing 'em back."

"How many nukes are we talking about?" Andy asked.

"Sally, scan all the video feed and count the total number of unique warheads in all the views."

"Yes, Bryan."

The response came back in less than two seconds. I wished I was in a better place to enjoy this wonderful interface. A cold shudder went through me when I heard Sally's tally. "There are six unique warheads in three different vehicles."

"Six that we know of…" Flowers said, gloomily.

"I'm going back to my original questions," Ron asked calmly. "Who are these Neanderthals, where are they from, and what are they planning to do with presumably armed nukes?"

Andy held up his finger, and tilted his head, appearing to be listening to something. "We have an incoming message from Michael." He grinned.

"He's alive," Kathy cried. "I knew it."

"It's a recording. Coming in garbled. Computer, play it."

"Believe …hostile. They fired on … destroyed Kathy's ship. I am … to be dangerous.

"Have … silent and do not believe I have been detected yet. They … base on the Moon at coordinates 102.34.9 and 95.03.8. Seems to … three domes … I saw three ships come in and land, …, the fourth one…, two more …

"I've parked in shadow about one kilometer from the base. No .... detected me.... must not capture my ship....Will set the ship for automatic lift off in two hours ... burst transmission if not back. Am going out on foot .... the base. If you receive this, I didn't make it back. .... their intent to be hostile. Take all precautions."

"He would try to infiltrate the alien base on his own," said Andy. He sounded both annoyed and admiring.

"I hope we aren't too late," said Kathy, worry shadowing her beautiful eyes.

"It's not too late." I was pretty confident of my assessment.

"Why do you think that, Bryan?" Millie asked.

"We're still here," I said. "If Michael told them about Sciquest, they would have squashed this building like a bug. Look at what the team going after Kathy did when there was just a hint we were trapped in that building. They'll probably keep him alive until they learn what they can about us."

Kathy looked even more anxious. This Michael fellow was obviously important to her.

"Ron, what's the update on Bryan's contact, Steelanowski? Any luck?" Andy asked.

Ron's hand scrolled down his virtual notebook. He looked up at Andy, but it was not a very happy look. "Bad news, boss. The note back from OSS says Steelanowski and his team are out on a job and can't be reached for at least twenty-four hours."

"So, what do we do?" Andy threw out the question to the group.

I was teetering on the edge. I wanted so much to believe in this fantasy reality of a super high tech shadow company with working spaceships, but then, I'd have to carry along the baggage of a reality filled with alien Neanderthals with armed Russian nukes and probably ready to use them. If half of what I'd heard this evening was true, this team would need every bit of help they could get. Everything I lived for was at stake.

I was rapidly thinking through options, but all possible paths lead in only one direction. It looked like I'd finally get my wish. I just hoped I'd be alive long enough to enjoy it.

I jumped in. "With GD out of the loop for another twenty-four hours, there is only one option. Sometimes, the decisions we make are not the best ones, but the least bad ones." I stopped talking and took a depth breath. I disconnected my rational, thinking brain from my mouth.

"I have a plan," I said.

16

IT'S AMAZING HOW a person can feel scared and exhilarated, all at the same time. I was about to volunteer for something crazy. Everything had changed over the course of the night. Chalk one up for Neanderthals with armed Russian nuclear warheads and a penchant for kidnapping beautiful women off deserted streets. Now we humans were going to get up to bat.

"Like you said, Andy, we don't have a lot of time left. Our only advantage right now is that even with the little we know about these Neanderthals, we know more about them than they know about us. They don't know what sort of threat we might be, how many there are of us, or where we are. But this advantage may not last. Surprise is our only leverage."

I stopped talking, and took another depth breath. I realized I had just said 'we' and 'us' a lot. I was no longer on the fence. I'd unconsciously jumped over to their side. While the skeptical side of me would never accept anything as one hundred percent the truth, the rest of me was ready to fully embrace the whole fantasy tale I'd heard tonight. Time to make the pitch to my new teammates.

"I'm going to the moon. I'll sneak into their base, find Michael and bring him back."

Flowers looked like he'd been hit in the face with a two-by-four, Andy appeared unsurprised, and Kathy regarded me with maybe a mixture of a little relief and resentment. Ron and Millie looked skeptical.

As soon as the words were out of my mouth, I realized that was not a particularly carefully planned out rescue, but more a recipe for disaster.

In just a short few hours, I'd learned about a secret company I was now part of, with technology to drool over, and some space-faring Neanderthals about to take it all away. Not on my watch.

The thought of them suppressing our space program for the last fifteen years, and maybe other programs, made me more than a little angry. If Andy's conspiracy theories were even half true, I was ready to go to war. I saw this rescue mission to the Moon as the first skirmish.

I ignored the voice in my head that shouted, "Danger, danger Will Robinson."

Andy folded his arms. "I appreciate your enthusiasm, but we don't have a clue what you could be getting into. If Michael is a prisoner, it could be like a small piece of Hell barging in there."

Kathy snorted. "Michael would have stormed the Gates of Hell carrying a can of gasoline if it was one of us held prisoner."

Millie smiled politely at her. "Dear, I really think Michael would be much more clever and subtle if he were to storm the Gates of Hell. He would probably engage the Devil in a philosophical discussion and leave him twisted in a logical knot."

"I'm going with Bryan," said Kathy.

"It's too dangerous, Kathy," Andy said.

I tried not to smile. I was going, and Kathy didn't want to be left behind.

"What do you mean, Andy, too dangerous for a woman?" I could see the fire in her eyes. I made a mental note to not piss her off.

"No, Kathy. I meant too dangerous for an astrophysicist."

"I've been shot down and attacked and I still kicked one of these creatures in the balls and gave him a bloody nose. I think I can handle this. I'm not afraid."

"Well, you should be!" I blurted out. "Me, personally, I'm scared to death."

I could feel the look she was giving me. It wasn't the innocent, 'I'm scared, don't hurt me look' I had seen from her in my Jeep. This was a 'say one more word and I'll bite your head off' look.

Note to self, I thought, double star that previous note about never piss Kathy off.

"I guess it's settled then," I said, never wavering from her gaze. "Kathy and I will go." She smiled back at me in victory.

"Bryan's right," Flowers said. "Time is critical. We have to act now."

Millie shook her head. "Young man, please don't take offense, but what makes you think you have a mouse's chance in a cat convention of getting into this Moon base and bringing Michael back?"

I wanted to say, because I was a Ninjaneer. I wanted to say because I'd found a cause that mattered to me more than anything else in the world. But as I quickly ran them through in my head, I was afraid they would sound too corny. Instead, I looked at Millie, and Ron, and then Andy. "It would be great to send a team of Navy SEALS to storm this Moon base. That's what they do. But we don't have them available right now. And unless you have a shadow army to go along with your shadow company, it's probably up to us in this room to mount the rescue. They don't know we're coming, but this advantage may not last."

"Nice speech," said Kathy, her mind obviously set. "Like you said, we need to move, now."

"Bryan," Andy said, leaning over the table to look directly at me. "I can't ask you to go. Are you sure this is something you want to do?"

I can't say I've ever been in a more difficult position, but there'd never been so much at stake. Going up against these Neanderthals would be my biggest challenge and I had absolutely no idea what we would encounter. We'd basically be making it up as we went along. Sort of my specialty.

But everything was at stake. I don't know why the first thing that popped into my mind was that I would miss my little cabin in Bodega Bay. If we failed, no more quiet evenings and moments of tranquility escaping from Silicon Valley. Hell, probably no more Silicon Valley. If we succeeded, maybe I'd have a chance to share a sunset and glass of wine with Kathy, the beautiful astrophysicist with the Andromeda tattoo.

This image was energizing. But even with my confidence in my abilities, I gave myself less than a ten percent chance of coming out of this alive.

I nodded. "Absolutely." Then a disquieting thought occurred to me. "Andy, maybe you should evacuate all non-essential people from this building."

There was a palpable fear in the room, as though everyone suddenly realized the potential danger.

"Andy," Kathy said, "We can be ready to go in less than thirty minutes."

"What about weapons?" I asked.

"Why, you leave that little task to me," Ron said. "I know a few good 'ol boys I might be able to collect a favor or two from. Max is already out in the field. I'll re-direct him to make a slight detour on his way back."

Andy took one more sweep around the room. "Agreed. Do it."

We were dismissed. The virtual room disappeared and I was back in the real world, in Andy's office. I saw Andy sitting at the head of the table, holding his head in his hands. Kathy's glasses went transparent and I noticed her eyes were teary. "Come on Bryan," Kathy said quietly to me, pulling on my arm, heading me out the door, "we're going to the Moon."

"I got shotgun," I said and followed her out.

17

I WAS A little numb from having my life change at the speed of light. Finally, I was going into space, and to the Moon! I really didn't want this to be a one-way trip. I had just been given a second chance at living a life I had only dreamed about. I was so conflicted. Part of me was catching the paranoid fever everyone at Sciquest seemed to have, but I was too excited to be scared. My insecure half that usually visited me to shatter my confidence was running full speed to catch up and falling farther and farther behind. And I was determined to keep him that way.

Kathy led me to an elevator door in the main lobby, which I'd mistaken for a double door when I had passed it earlier. The access buttons were hidden from view by the large potted ficus tree. It occurred to me that so much of the world had apparently been hidden from my view when I had sat on that couch an hour earlier. This company, all of its technological progress, had all been hidden in the shadows to me.

I was still preoccupied when I entered the elevator. By habit, I moved to stand in front of the buttons. I hated confined spaces, and only feeling in control helped me overcome my claustrophobia. An easy choice, only two buttons. I glanced up to see the number one on the inside of the door frame and reached over to push the number two button. "Second floor?" I asked, looking across at Kathy. My hand paused next to the button when Kathy brushed my hand away.

"Scoot, you're in the way." She nudged me over and stepped in front of the control panel. But instead of pushing one of the floor buttons, she pressed the open and close door button simultaneously.

The elevator doors closed and the floor dropped out from under us as the car accelerated down. I grabbed the bar behind me and held on. My gaze darted around the small, tiny confined, closed-in cage. The trip was mercifully short. Just as soon as the car stopped accelerating down, it started decelerating and quickly lurched to a stop. "Hey! How about a warning next time the floor's about to drop from under me?"

"Oops," she said, but she didn't sound like she was sorry.

The rear elevator doors opened at the entrance to a long, poorly lit corridor that disappeared into the darkness. Only the region near the elevator was lit by one row of fluorescent lights in the middle of the ceiling.

"For a super high-tech company, you've got a pretty bland hangar bay down here," I said. My voice was a little shaky from that claustrophobic ride.

"It's just the walkway to the hangar," Kathy said, watching me with amusement. "The hangar's built under the manufacturing plant that's across the parking lot."

Two motor-driven walkways, like you'd find at an airport, extended into the distance. The walls of the corridor were painted a dull neutral grey. A wide hallway extended on the left side of the belts, wide enough for a large cart or even a small truck.

Kathy walked onto the belt and it started up automatically. I heard the click of the gears shoot down the corridor, disappearing into the darkness ahead, as successive regions of the walkway started in motion.

I ran to get on the moving belt and scrambled to pull up adjacent to her. I felt a faint breeze blowing from the far end of the corridor. It carried a vaguely familiar odor. It wasn't a burning smell and wasn't a food smell, but close. I took a few more tentative sniffs and then memory flooded in. It was the resin flux used in soldering components to circuit boards. Somewhere in the darkness ahead was an electronic assembly line and a ventilation system that wasn't entirely efficient.

She just leaned against the rail, waiting for me to catch up.

I said, a little anxious, "Shouldn't we be hurrying to where your spaceships are? Time's running out."

"Relax. There's nothing else we can be doing right now and it's only three minutes on the walkway to the hangar. I'm monitoring the status check list. Valerie has fifteen minutes to go on filling the water tanks and then another ten minutes to complete the preflight check list. And who knows how long it's going to take Max to get back with your weapons?"

I liked her attention to detail. "Then I have time to ask some questions."

She smiled back at me. "Ask away."

"The DNA fragments." I had asked Sally to prepare a list of follow-up questions, which floated as white text against the grey wall opposite me. The DNA fragments were at the top of the list.

This was just one of the dangling threads I wanted to weave back into the bigger tapestry.

"What about them?" Her smile brightened, though her eyes looked shadowed. She was teasing me now, forcing me to work for my answers, which I suspect was a way of distracting herself from worrying about Michael. Or maybe Michael's assessment was right and she liked to dominate men.

"What's this all about? Did you find DNA in space?"

"On my first mission after Europa, near Mars' orbit, I rendezvoused with a comet coming in-system. I was able to pick up a few bottles worth of dirty snow and brought them back. Millie evaluated the samples. In addition to a pre-biotic soup, Millie also found traces of DNA. And not just some random codons. There were sections with hundreds of codons."

"What did they code for?"

"They matched a lot of segments in our database. Unfortunately, the sample warmed up by the time I returned and some of it denatured. Millie mapped some of them to bacteria and what might have been a protein in reptiles like alligators. But, the fragments weren't large enough to really confirm anything absolutely. That's why Michael and I were out by Saturn, collecting fresh samples."

When she mentioned Michael, she looked sad. I felt a teensy bit jealous about her obvious feelings for him.

"Where did the DNA come from?"

Kathy stopped talking, shifted her head to the side in that look I'd learned meant she was listening in on a phone call on her PDA. "Go, and patch in Bryan."

It was Ron and his Southern drawl sounded agitated. "A major complication. You've got to speed up the launch and be gone in less than ten minutes."

"What? Why?" I asked.

"That God damn Foxconn spy was just spotted cruising around our plant in the foothills. We caught him driving by on one of the surveillance cameras. If he keeps to his past patterns, he'll be driving around here in another fifteen minutes."

"What's that got to do with us?" I asked.

"We can't afford to launch a ship out of the hangar with this guy driving around taking pictures of the plant. He counts cars in the parking lot to figure out how many shifts we're running and anything else he can tell about our production rates. We can't risk him catching a hint of a ship."

"An industrial spy, huh?" I mused.

"I've got Kathy's damaged ship on its way in. Should arrive in four minutes. Once it's in and you're out, all operations are going on hold until we're sure he clears out. Your launch window closes in eight minutes. If you miss this, you'll have to wait around for at least an hour, maybe two until he gives up and leaves the area."

I looked at Kathy, "Can we launch in eight minutes? I thought you said it would be another twenty-five minutes at least before we're ready?"

Kathy had turned pale, but kept her composure. "We don't have any choice. We don't need the water tanks full and we do the preflight on the way."

"On the way? I thought the whole idea of a preflight checklist was to do it before you took off?"

She pushed away from the railing and began jogging down the conveyor belt. "No time to waste. Come on." She was in pretty good shape for an astrophysicist. Even though I'd been staying in good condition from my Kendo class, I found her hard to keep up with. I was liking her more and more. "Then why even bother filling the water tanks? We can just grab a few bottles of water," I asked when I caught up with her.

"Air."

I thought maybe she was having problems breathing, we were both jogging at a good clip down the conveyer belt. "Are you okay?"

"For the ship." She looked at me like I was dimwit. "We use the water. For electrolysis." It was hard for her to talk and run. "We'll have three days of air. That's plenty."

That sounded ominously like famous last words.

As we ran down the belt, the lights overhead followed us. We left one section, the light behind us turned off and the light ahead turned on. It was like peristalsis, pacing us down the long corridor. I could see the big double doors at the end of the walkway, just catching the glow from our lights.

I was hoping for some more time to work on a plan. Now, I had to do it, literally, on the run. I was trying to think through what we would do once we got to the Moon and what we would need.

"Ron," I huffed out to Sally. "Weapons?"

"Max is still out foraging. He'll never make it back in time. You'll have to meet up with him."

"Space suits?"

"On the ship," Kathy said. I heard her voice next to me and echoing in my earpiece. She was tied into the link with Ron.

We reached the double doors and they opened automatically for us. Kathy kept moving into the hangar. I stopped at the entrance, taking in this incredible view. I just stood there, catching my breath, figuratively and literally.

I know it was a stupid idea, but I was expecting something like Cape Canaveral with rockets on launch pads. Instead, I saw a super-store-sized cavern, mostly empty. The ceiling was thirty meters above me. That put us at least nine stories underground.

In the center of the roof was a giant circular hatch, twenty meters in diameter, with two huge, half-moon doors. They were closed.

Racks along the sides of the walls were filled with equipment and boxes, with lab benches jutting out in U-shaped bays. I counted six different workstations. And nestled next to four of them were…jet planes. They were small Lear jets with engine pods near the tail. They were all painted a flat matte black, making them appear like three dimensional extensions of their shadows.

Kathy headed right to one of the planes and workstation bays situated just a dozen meters from the door, which looked like the only active area in the hangar. The jet sat with its side and rear stairs down, a faint red glow illuminating from its cabin. A young woman in a white jumpsuit and short cropped red hair, her back to us, was disconnecting one of the hoses attached to the starboard wing.

By the time I took in the view and turned to the plane, Kathy was already at the base of the cabin stairs. She paused and frowned at me. "Time to gawk later. Come on."

"Valerie, we're in a hurry," she said to the woman working on the plane. "How long to finish up?"

The woman, who couldn't have been over twenty, turned and gave Kathy a nod. "Just got the word from Ron. Suits are ready. Scrubbers cleaned and water topped off. Just balancing the wing tanks now. Three minutes and you're good to go."

Then the woman noticed me, still standing in the entranceway, and waved me over. I stopped my gawking and sheepishly walked that way. There were so many revelations with Sciquest that it was difficult to keep my mind focused on this crazy rescue we were about to undertake. Which was good, because if these were my last hours alive, at least they'd be exciting.

"You're Bryan. I'm Valerie." She didn't bother to shake my hand, engaged as she was with adjusting the hose coupling to the wing tank. "I heard what you're planning and we're all behind you. We love Michael. He's. . . " Her face looked pained as she searched for the words. "Simply the best of us. Anything we can do to help, we're there for you."

The best of us? I thought, feeling curious, but a little jealous of this person who I had not even met, but whose life I hoped I was about to save. I gave a little shrug. "Thanks Valerie. Weapons are the last item."

"I heard from Max. He said he's picking up a package for you. He should be ready by the time you launch. Ron'll figure out a pickup spot. And welcome to the team. Your ship will be ready in a jiffy. Even washed the windows for you." She grinned at me. I started to chuckle but then I realized that she was referring to the plane she was working on.

Aside from the paint job, it appeared to be a regular jet.

It certainly didn't look like anything I'd seen come out of NASA, an organization that I had long presumed was setting the benchmark for space travel.

"Kathy, these planes are the spaceships you've been talking about? You're kidding right?"

"Yes, these are our spaceships."

I started to sweat and rubbed my hand along the back of my neck, trying not to look nervous. "They're planes, not spaceships."

Kathy pursed her lips. "Bryan, these planes were designed to cruise at 45,000 feet. That's pretty close to vacuum. We just modified them slightly. Added inertial shields and propulsion pods. The main modification is for life support. We use on-board water to supply the oxygen and carbon nanofibers as CO_2 scrubbers. Why build something new when we have what works off the shelf?"

I heard what she said, but it was hard to take in. I gave the little jet a nervous look. "But they're just airplanes."

"Been flying these into space for almost five months," she said, looking at me like she dared me to question them. "Haven't had a problem with any of them, yet."

We were going to the Moon in this plane? This rescue mission was looking shakier and shakier.

"But integrating a whole new flight control system into an airframe is not a minor modification."

"Ron's team spent almost a year developing the propulsion units and flight control systems on practice pods, like those over there," she said, pointing to the rack of shelves on my right. They held three beach ball size spheres, also painted a matte black, which I wouldn't have noticed had she not pointed them out.

I walked over to get a closer look. Their surfaces were smooth, except for some small windows, which probably held camera ports, and a few recessed bars that looked like mounting points.

"We used to use them like drones to test out software, mostly feedback systems and navigation for the ships. They have cameras, propulsion units, radio transceivers and a mark 2 processor. They can push 5,000 pounds of force each. Now, we just use them for utility transport."

She was tapping her foot and, if she'd had a watch, she'd probably be pointing at it. But something she said raised a big red flag for me. "Ron, this spy of yours, does he park and sit in front of the plant or drive by periodically?"

"Bryan, quit stalling," said Kathy. "We need to button up the hatch and get out of here before it's too late."

"He usually drives by a few times," Ron replied. "Why?"

"Kathy, it's already too late. We missed the window."

"What are you talking about?" She narrowed her eyes at me.

"Ron, he's using a drone to do the surveillance. It's probably out there right now."

"How can you possibly know that?" Ron asked.

"Because that's what I would do. I'd fly my drone over the plant, check things out. Then hover around recording video and watch for personnel movement during a shift change. This way, I could leisurely count operators coming and going."

Kathy was pacing now and gave me a beseeching look. "Come on, Bryan. We can't leave Michael hanging like this."

"This is important," I said. "Typical battery life for most commercial drones is about thirty minutes. I'd recover the drone, maybe do a quick drive by to do an eyes-on survey at ground level while I charge up the drone, or maybe I'd have two and fly them in shifts."

"Holy crap. That's about the interval he drives by, every thirty minutes or so," said Ron. "Kathy, Bryan has a point. You can't take off until we're sure this guy is out of the area."

"That could be an hour or more. If Michael's been captured then the sooner we get to him, the better. He's not some Navy SEAL guy, used to withstanding torture for days. He's a scientist like us, or at least a mathematician." She looked agitated and her voice was raised. She seemed more upset than she'd been when we were dodging laser blasts earlier. She blew out a deep breath and added: "We need to risk it."

"No," I said, thinking through the beginnings of a plan. This situation was like a chess game. I had to anticipate what I would do if I were spying on this factory and how to counter it. And I had to think three or four moves ahead.

"No?" she asked, incredulous. "You don't understand. Michael is everything to us. We have to leave now!"

I looked over at the practice pods, the wheels in my head churning. "Relax. We'll be wheels up in a few minutes. But first, we're going hunting."

18

KATHY STILL APPEARED upset, but she looked at me with a mixture of curiosity and confidence, a look I'd savor, if I had more time. This wasn't the time, of course.

"Bryan, if there's a drone out there, I have to divert Kathy's ship," said Ron. "It's coming in right now, and Max needs my help securing the weapons. Can you handle finding this drone and neutralizing it?"

Before I could reply, Kathy broke in, "Yes, we can handle it. Do what you need to do."

"I'll check back. Out."

I let myself relax, just a smidgen. We were a team again. I wasn't an expert on industrial spying, but I was familiar with security systems, and how to defeat them. I'd picked up a few special skills working on my security systems gigs. I met Rusty, my SEAL buddy, on a consulting gig for a sensor company. I was the maker team, he was the breaker team. He taught me how to think like an intruder, to be tricky.

A scientist doesn't have to worry about nature being devious, just subtle. But a security systems expert has to assume his opponent is sly and devious, and be more devious to outsmart him.

"Okay, Bryan, what's the plan?" asked Kathy.

"We track the drone's emissions. Then jam it. Then go after the source. Do your practice pods have any sort of directional antenna?"

Kathy nodded. "Just isotropic, but if it helps, all of our transceivers have a software defined radio with a five gigahertz bandwidth."

"Good. Most drones use the 900 MHz channel for communications. It's an unlicensed FCC band. But we need to find it. We could just fly around, pick up the signal and see in which direction the signal gets stronger." I was thinking out loud. What would be the fastest way of finding the drone?

"I have a better idea," Kathy said. "We can use these three pods and set up a long baseline interferometer. 900 MHz is about a one foot wavelength. If we space them out a hundred feet, we can get the direction to better than a few degrees. It's the same algorithm Michael and I were using to search for the comet."

She seemed to have quickly regained her focus. I knew there was a reason I wanted her along. "How long for you to set up the algorithm for these three pods?"

"Less than two minutes. Fred can pull the code and download it into each pod's DSP receiver."

"Start working on it. Can I control these pods through Sally?"

"Get with the program, Bryan. Everything is networked and controllable through your interface. Everything."

"That's what I wanted to hear." The clock was ticking away in my head. I was thinking of move and counter move. We needed to find the spy's drone, neutralize it and then find our spy and neutralize him.

"Sally, can you give me control of one of these practice pods?"

I saw one of the spheres rise up from the shelf and move forward, just hovering in space in front of me. "Yes, Bryan," came her superfluous reply.

"Kathy, is that hatch the way to the surface?"

I glanced her way. She was standing at the top of the stairs, leaning against the fuselage, using a kinetic interface by moving her hands in the air. There was no training manual for this new virtual interface. I'd just have to pick everything up along the way.

"It's the bottom of a shaft that goes through the manufacturing and assembly plant above," she said, without stopping what she was doing. "There's another hatch in the roof that opens up. It's camouflaged. That's how we launch the ships."

I felt a twinge of worry. "How do you hide the shaft from the assembly operators?"

"It's inside a fenced-in region with a lot of high voltage 'keep out' signs. Don't worry, it's secure."

"Perfect." I looked back at the three pods in front of me. "Sally, designate these practice pods as pods one, two and three." I said the last pointing my finger at each drone in turn. I'd already learned that my fingers could be seamlessly integrated with the augmented reality view of my world. "Take these pods out through the hatch and hover a thousand feet above the plant. Orient them in a flat equilateral triangle, spaced fifty feet apart. Use the highest speed that is safe."

"Bryan, you have to learn to think in acceleration, not speed," Kathy said. I realized unless I specified otherwise, my comm link to Sally was an open mic to Kathy. This would be really efficient working as a team, but also potentially embarrassing if I wasn't careful. I made another note to have a chat with Sally about this.

"What's the maximum acceleration these pods can handle?"

"Their internal steel frames with the inertial shielding coating were designed for up to twenty-five gees."

"Sally, give me the maximum acceleration."

"Yes, Bryan."

I watched the black spheres rise to the ceiling and, in the blink of an eye, shoot over to the hatch and hover while the doors opened. I had to recalibrate my ideas of speed. At twenty-five gees acceleration, after one second, they would be going 250 meters per second. That was 500 miles per hour! They could be more than a little dangerous in this confined space. I decided to leverage this feature.

The semicircular doors slid back silently on their rails, opening just enough to let the pods slip through, then immediately closed.

"Sally, give me a view from pod one."

With a shift in perspective, I wasn't in the hangar bay anymore. All three pods were obviously hovering above the plant. With their visual feed patched into my glasses, it felt like I was floating in space. The feedback was so real that I had to stomp my feet on the ground to remind myself where I really was in time and space. "It's just an image," I muttered to myself, taking a deep breath.

I moved my head and the view tracked with my movement. I saw the plant and the parking lot sprawling below. Not many lights on in the parking lot between the two buildings.

"Sally, do the pods have low light level or IR sensitivity in the cameras?"

"They each have one IR camera. Switching now."

Much better. I could see the details of the parking lot. I tracked the path to the back of the main building and saw my Jeep near the entrance, right where I left it. Now I was oriented.

With the one IR camera in each pod and so much space to look through, I wasn't hopeful I'd be able to pick up one tiny drone. I'd have flown one that was painted matte black. An electric motor would not give off much heat. We needed to track its radio emissions.

"Kathy, how you coming with that radio interferometer?"

"Almost there."

I had the time. It was worth a try. "Sally, can you scan the visual field and look for any movement?" To Kathy, I added: "We might get lucky and pick up the drone from its motion."

"All changing pixels are highlighted in yellow."

As I moved my head, I could see small flashes of yellow, probably due to slight motion of the pod, but nothing that looked like our bogie. I spun around looking down for anything that might be a drone. No joy.

"Coming online now," Kathy said. "Picking up 900 MHz emissions. Let me take control, I need to change their spacing."

"Sally, let go and turn off the motion detector."

I still had the visual feed and watched the ground below shift as Kathy moved the pods to change the baseline.

"Images coming up. Painting the intensity with red shading."

"Sal, identify the location of the strongest emission." I was thinking that an orbiting drone, transmitting video would be the brightest source. Rarely did they have directional antennas, so it should be easy to spot.

Sure enough, immediately in front of my view, I saw a flashing green arrow pointing to my left, I swiveled my head, following the arrow leading me to a small but intense red splotch in the direction of the edge of the parking lot.

"Got him!"

"Sal, designate this source as target one." I circled the red dot with my finger and a small yellow circle appeared surrounding the red dot. "Move the pods in formation to hover ten meters above target one."

I was figuring the camera on the drone wouldn't detect something above it.

I looked down at my feet and now could see the drone floating below me, a dark shadow against the glow of the parking lot and street lights. It was a standard quad copter, about one meter in diameter with four, shrouded struts supporting the electric motor direct-drive rotors. It was painted black. At night, it would be silent and invisible unless it was right on top of you. Just like I would have done.

"Emissions are strong and steady," Kathy said. "It's FM encoded, 6 MHz side bands."

"Video," I said. But where was it broadcasting? If it was a high-end drone, it was probably flying in an autonomous mode. Once programmed, it could travel a pre-planned route and return to its start without any remote control. How to find the location of its pesky little owner?

"Sally, how many sources have you detected in the 900 MHz band?"

"Bryan, there are fifteen sources identified."

But which one was our guy? We needed to smoke him out.

"Kathy, if we jam these transmissions, will you still be able to scan for emissions?"

"If we modulate the jamming, I can gate the receiver and detect emissions in between bursts."

"When we jam this drone, I'm betting our spy is going to want to take back control and will light up. We pulse the jamming and search for new emissions. Ready?"

"Ready."

"Sally, on my mark broadcast random noise in the same band as the video emission and pulse it on and off synched with the receiver at ten hertz. Mark!"

I quickly pivoted around, looking for a new red dot which would be the emissions from the controller. Nothing. "Sally, any new emissions?"

"No Bryan. Sources in the 900 MHz band have been unchanged."

"He could be using a different channel to control his drone than the video emissions," Kathy said. "I'm widening the detection frequency band, 100 MHz on each side."

A second later, shouted, "There!" Got a source that just turned on. Check out this location." She was pointing, but Sally translated her motion in my virtual world as a green arrow pointing to the north. I swiveled around and saw a tiny pinpoint of red. It might be him. I couldn't see anything in the darkness in that direction, but the green circle was in the vicinity of a residential street. Just where I would have gone.

Like shooting fish in a barrel.

"Sal, designate this source as target two. Move pod one in the direction of target two, at maximum acceleration, but keep your speed below six hundred miles per hour. Stay at an altitude of one thousand feet."

I watched the view from pod one as the ground zipped by below. I crossed over the 101 freeway, then through the residential sections of Mountain View. In twenty seconds, I was hovering over a quiet street. I looked down at my feet. Every house on the block had a tree in front and a tiny fenced in backyard. There was a car parked either in the driveway or in front of each house. The street lights illuminated small patches of the street.

A thousand feet directly below me sat a dark-colored SUV with its moon roof open. It was parked almost equidistant between street lights, where the patches of light did not overlap.

Gotcha. The pieces were now positioned. Soon, it would be checkmate for our friend down there.

19

"NOW WHAT, BRYAN?"

I could tell all this cloak and dagger stuff was way outside Kathy's comfort zone. I had a feeling tonight was going to only get weirder for both of us. But I was looking forward to the challenge.

I grinned. "We take out the drone and neutralize this spy."

"I hope that's not a euphemism for kill," she said, frowning. "We don't do that sort of thing to people, even industrial spies."

"Sorry, no. I literally mean neutralize him. How much damage can these pods take and still fly?"

"Ron dropped one once from a five-story building when the Casimir battery wasn't connected to the propulsion unit. Most of the optics shattered, but the frame and propulsion system survived."

I did the quick calculation in my head. Five stories, twenty meters, about two seconds in free fall. That was twenty meters per second or forty miles an hour. Plenty fast for what I had in mind.

"Sally, what is the make and model of that SUV below us?"

"2014 Cadillac Escalade."

This might be outside my normal work, but it was sure fun with the high-tech toys I had at my fingertips. "Bring up the specs for this model." I saw the text appear in front of me, and used my fingers to scroll down just like I was sitting in front of a touch screen. On the next page, I saw what I was looking for. Perfect. It had OnStar.

"Kathy, can our PDAs override an OnStar interface?"

"I suppose so. We can hack into the OnStar database, find the control protocols and synthesize the signal."

"I'm going to need another pod. Can you send pod two over to my current location?"

I heard her give the command to Fred.

"Turn off the jamming. I want our friend down there a little distracted with the video feed trying to figure out what went wrong."

"Done. Pod three is still hovering ten meters above the drone. It's got some sort of route programmed in. Looks like it's heading right over the roof of the plant," she said, clearly peeved. "If we'd launched on schedule, the doors would be opening and we'd be on candid camera right now."

Finding our prey was easy. The hard part was going to be disabling it with the tools I had on hand and not really hurting the guy. "Sally, on my command, drop pod three on top of the drone and drive it to the ground at twenty miles an hour. Can you give me the address of the house this SUV is parked in front of?"

"The address is 23256 Cedar Park Way, Mountain View"

"What are you doing? Let's just take out the drone and get out of here," Kathy said, shooting me a we're-late look.

"I'm following Rusty's rule number 2."

"And what's that?"

"SEALS never leave a functional enemy behind them."

"Oh no," said Kathy. When I looked over at her, she'd closed her eyes briefly. It was going to be a long night.

"Sally, use pod one to dial 911 using the nearest cell tower and patch me in. When I give you the word, cut the connection."

I heard a familiar dial tone. It rang once and I heard the connection to the dispatcher. "911, what is your emergency?"

"Come quickly," I tried to sound panicked. "There's a crazy person driving up and down our street. He's either drunk or on drugs. He's driven up on a lawn already and took out a tree. I'm afraid for me and my children."

"What is your address, sir?"

"23256 Cedar Park Way, Mountain View."

"A patrol car is in on the way. What make and model car is he driving?"

"It looks like a black Cadillac Escalade. Oh no! He has a gun! He just pointed it one of the houses. I think I heard a gunshot!"

"Stay on the line with me, sir,"

"I have to go protect my children."

"Cut," I whispered to Sally.

I could see Kathy looking at me with surprise and a hint of amusement in her eyes. That was a good sign.

"Sally, splash the drone, NOW! Use pod one to monitor all the radio emissions from the SUV below. You will pick up a broadcast to the OnStar service, probably around 1.8 GHz in the PCS band. Decode it and extract the access code to the SUV. Bring pod two down and hit the front of the SUV, at twenty-five miles an hour. Then immediately lift pod two back up to 1000 feet. Execute."

It was like precision clockwork. The drone was taken out, squished like a bug. I was hoping our spy would be distracted with dead air from the drone. In my bird's eye view from the cameras in pod one, I saw the SUV jolt backwards when it was hit. That should have activated the air bags and the automatic crash alert to OnStar.

"Bryan, I have the OnStar access code to the SUV below."

"Sally, find the code that locks the doors and closes the moon roof and transmit it. There is an anti-theft code that will disable the car's electronics. When the moon roof is closed, broadcast this code to the SUV. Can you do this?"

"Yes, Bryan. All doors are locked. Local lockout code transmitted and acknowledgment received from the SUV onboard computer. Automatic stolen car report filed with the police."

I heard Kathy snicker and I gave her a grin.

"Sally, bring the three pods back to the hangar bay."

"Finally, we're safe to launch," Kathy said. She'd clearly been cheered by our success. I wanted to get our show on the road while she was distracted from worrying about Michael.

I took another look at the converted Lear jet I was about to take to the Moon.

"This does not look in the least bit safe," I muttered to myself, hoping Kathy didn't catch it.

Just then, Ron broke in through Sally's line. "Bryan, I've been monitoring what you've been up to. Kathy wasn't kidding when she said you were one sharp fellow."

"Kathy and I make a pretty good team." I leaned against the railing of the stairs, not quite ready to commit to entering the ship. From the entrance to the cabin, Kathy grinned at me. It felt good, but I knew better than to let myself get carried away just yet. I kept thinking of her line to Andy. She thought we were screwed even with me on the team. We'll see about that.

"Before you two leave, I need to bring Kathy's ship in. I had to park it in a nearby baseball field until the coast was clear. Then you need to head over to meet up with Max. I'll send you coordinates."

"Roger that," Kathy said.

I was momentarily distracted by the overhead hatch opening slightly. The three pods shot through and made their way over to us. Pod one was still pristine. Pod two, aka SUV killer, was really dinged up. It was going to need a lot of fixing before it was back to normal. Pod three, aka drone killer, had some dents on the bottom, but otherwise looked in good shape. I had Sally position them back on the racks.

Then I had another problem pop into my mind. "Kathy, Ron was worried about being spotted when you leave. Even with the black paint job, what do you do about radar? There must be five airports within twenty miles of us."

"This isn't just black paint." Kathy rubbed her hand over the side of the fuselage. "It's a ferrite-filled polymer paint that absorbs radar, like stealth planes. And then there's an LCD film over it with an electrical grid. When it's active, the pattern created on its surface is matched to what the cameras see on the other side. The army calls it Chameleon skin, for obvious reasons."

I gave her a wry smile. "Nice."

"And, we don't linger around the plant. When we take off, it's like a bat out of Hell to get to altitude. We aren't really in detection range for more than a few seconds."

I heard the gears of the hatch doors grinding open again, this time revealing a circular shaft. A plane slowly lowered through the opened hole, suspended from two of these one-meter diameter pods. Heavy canvas straps looped under the tail section and the aft fuselage. A sheet of some polymer film was flapping along the edges. Her ship had obviously been attacked; its tail section appeared to be held on with duct tape.

It came to rest in the adjacent bay.

I turned to her and raised my eyebrows. "You landed in that mess?"

She ran her hand through her hair. "I didn't realize just how bad the damage was. That's no meteor hit. Look how the edge of the breach in the top is smooth and shiny. It was sliced off with some beam weapon."

I tried to ignore the alarms going off in my head. "If their aim was that accurate, it's a good thing your antenna wasn't in the nose of the plane."

She looked up at her damaged plane and shuddered a little. I probably shouldn't have reminded her how much danger she'd been in. Well, that was nothing compared to where we were going.

She bit her lip and looked like she was muttering to herself, before shooting me a weak smile. "Okay, hot shot, Michael's waiting. Time to leave," she said and proceeded into the cabin.

I followed her up the stairs. At the top, Ron cut in.

"Kathy and Bryan, it looks like the best place to meet up with Max and pick up the weapons is the roof of the Foothills plant. Max is on his way over there. ETA about three minutes."

"You've got to be kidding me," Kathy said. "That's the safest place you could come up with? That's where those goons tried to grab me earlier tonight."

"It's the only place Max can get to quickly and we can have some control over your landing site." He sounded matter-of-fact, but I thought he could have added an apology.

I gave Kathy a reassuring nod. "It's okay, Ron. We'll be there in three minutes. But, I'm going to have one of these pods scout out the area before we get close. If it looks suspicious, we'll just have to come up with another plan, and quick."

"I understand. Patch in to Max when you're in position. He should be on the roof with your package about the time you arrive. Good luck! Out."

I took a deep breath. I was full-on with the team now and it was obvious that Kathy was going to let me drive the show. She knew she was out of her element, but was nevertheless a willing wingman. "Sal, re-designate pod one as Scout. Have Scout fly five meters off our port wing."

From my perch on the top of the stairs, I watched Scout leave the safety of the shelf with his buddies and make a beeline, hovering off our port wing. I noticed Valerie had finished her work and moved to the inside of the workstation bay. She stood off to the side watching us.

Before I turned into the cabin, I impulsively gave her a little wave. She waved back. I couldn't help noticing how young she looked. I smiled back to her wondering if she had an idea what we were really getting into. Not just Michael's future but her own depended on what we did in the next few hours.

I turned and got my first look inside the cabin, which was lit by a red night light. It took a few seconds for my eyes to adjust to the dimmer interior. The aft third of the cabin was sealed off by what looked like a submarine hatch. Three crinkly, sparkly, silver space suits hung on the port wall, opposite the cabin door. The circumference of their barrel-shaped chest pieces were lined with inverted, narrow cylinders, all polished to a mirror-like finish. The arms and legs sections hung limply from the brackets on the chest unit. They looked paper thin, almost like the material fire blankets were made from. They didn't cheer me up.

Filling the rest of the cabin were a few chairs bolted to the floor, a table between them, and a Murphy bed folded up on the opposite wall. Two overhead handrails were mounted in the ceiling, one on either side of the center line, leading to the front of the ship where the cockpit door hung open.

Kathy, who was already adjusting her seat belts in the port side, pilot's seat, turned and pointedly jerked her head toward the other seat.

I hesitated a moment, and she gave me a look, so I made my way to the cockpit and sat down. I wasn't convinced this was the smartest move I'd ever made, though I had no choice. I was excited about going to the Moon for sure, tempered only slightly by the ridiculously insane odds against us, but sitting in the cockpit of a Lear jet was not how I envisioned getting there. And those suits did not look NASA-approved.

Kathy was flipping buttons on the dashboard. I was thinking through scenarios. The suits bugged me for several reasons. "Kathy, I think we have a problem."

"What, only one? Which one are you worried about now?"

"These suits, they're shiny."

"That's to minimize the heat load from the Sun."

"If we're going to storm this Moon base wearing these suits, we could just as well be waving flags on our way in."

The pained look on her face made me feel like I had just peed on her favorite chair. "That's the only style we have," she said. "Not sure what we can do about it. And besides, we need to leave like right now."

"I have an idea. Your damaged plane, when it came in, it had a plastic film under it. Was that your chameleon skin?"

"Yes. Supported from pods like they were, it couldn't tolerate much altitude. The winds would be too strong. Max probably put a layer underneath so someone looking up wouldn't see a Lear jet a couple hundred feet above them."

"I have to talk to Ron about another idea."

"Make it snappy. We're airborne in less than a minute."

I stepped outside the cockpit for a moment and paced the cabin. No need to get Kathy all worked up. After a thirty-second conversation with Ron, we had a solution. The only problem was getting it to us in time to be useful. We decided to use pod 3, the least damaged of the remaining two practice pods. We'd do a mid-flight rendezvous, thirty minutes out. Ron thought we've be on the deceleration phase by then.

"What was that all about?" Kathy asked when I finished and sat back down.

"You'll see. I'm guessing that's an airlock, I said pointing to the aft hatch.

"The back third of the plane is the airlock. After liftoff, we close up the side door and go in and out through the aft stairs."

"Can a pod fit through the stairs into the airlock?"

Kathy paused, looking off to the side, probably querying Fred. "No, three inches too wide."

"Hmm, we'll have to figure it out."

"We're ready to seal up and head out."

I heard the whine of the stairs retracting and a vibration in the floor, I figured was the rear stairs rising up. Two faint thumps signaled the hatches closed and dogged, severing our last ties with the Earth.

Now I was really trapped in a small, confined space, no way out. I felt that too familiar panic starting in. I thought I might throw up. I closed my eyes and told myself, this was the least of my problems. Focus on the real danger. We were about to storm an alien base on the Moon filled with 300-pound, laser welding Neanderthals who wanted to torture information out of us. Yeah, that was cheering me up and getting my mind off of this trapped feeling.

"Buckle up," she said looking over at me and smiling grimly. "It's going to get rough."

This was getting better and better.

The inside cabin light came down. This allowed our eyes to adjust and get settled in the cockpit. Moments later, the cabin lights turned off completely. The only illumination came from the instrument panel.

"Fred, activate the chameleon screen and show us the view out the windows," Kathy said.

Through my glasses, the blacked out windows appeared transparent. I lowered my glasses just to check. The windows were opaque, but Sally filled in the view in my glasses.

I wondered why the windows were blacked out, then I smiled in admiration. Who needed transparent windows when you had strategic cameras and could synthesize a personalized augmented reality image that was just as clear as the real world?

I felt a jerk as Kathy lifted the ship a few feet off the ground, raised the landing gear, and floated us to the center of the hangar. The hangar overhead doors slid back, revealing the opening to the sky, more than forty meters above and through the shaft in the upper floor. The pitch black of the shaft contrasted with the deep blue of the late evening sky.

"Kathy and Bryan," I heard the voice of Andy from my frames. "Don't take unnecessary risks. We want you two, plus Michael, back safe and sound. We're doing everything we can to contact Steelanowski and hunt for these Neanderthals here on Earth. Good luck."

Kathy positioned the ship under the shaft in the center of the hangar. Just visible from the upper part of the synthesized window, the dark night sky at the top of the shaft beckoned.

"Acknowledged," Kathy said.

"Andy, I think this is just the first round. I intend to stick around to see this through to the end. We will come back," I said with as much confidence as I could muster. I was mostly trying to convince myself.

"Head back against the headrest," Kathy said.

I looked over at her and saw her tilting her head back against the back of the chair. Just in time, I did the same.

My weight doubled, then tripled, as we shot straight up, still oriented horizontal. The walls shot past. Without that warning, my head might have flopped forward to my chest under the high gee force and if it hadn't broken my neck, would have at least been sore for a week.

"Out of the exit well, 120 miles per hour," she said, straining to talk under the gee force. We were above the building and into the sky.

"Aerodynamic, going vertical. Hold on, we're going to rotate."

Hold on to what, I wondered. I just grabbed the arm rests tighter, not sure what to expect.

Still moving straight up, the ship rotated to point vertically so we were lying back in our seats, pushed back with at least two gees. The seats were incredibly uncomfortable at these gee forces, and hadn't been designed for this sort of acceleration.

Then I heard her say, "Now we can accelerate."

20

IT FELT LIKE someone was plastered on top of me. Not so bad that I couldn't breathe, but enough extra weight to make it hard to raise my hand.

Out the corner of my eye, I saw Kathy leaning back with her hands resting on the armrests. Who was flying the plane?

"Sal," I croaked, "Can you fly this plane?"

"Yes, Bryan." Good to know. I filed it for future reference.

This was like the worst amusement park ride ever. Times one hundred. I felt like I was going to hurl for real, except that there would be no place for it to go. *Focus on being caught and tortured*, I kept telling myself.

"How … much… longer?" I said to Kathy.

At just that moment, I felt the weight reducing.

"Relax Bryan, dropping acceleration now. At 600 miles per hour and passing through 30,000 feet. We need to get to altitude as quickly as possible. There's too much local air traffic around here."

"Sally, is Scout still with us?"

Kathy answered for her. "Yes, of course. We were only doing ten gees."

"It was pretty bad, but it didn't feel like that much."

"The inertial shielding. It's about seventy percent effective. It was less than three gees inside."

"These airframes weren't built for ten gees," I thought out loud. I was still nervous about flying into space in an airplane.

"Of course not. But all the structural elements are inside the inertial shielding."

"But what if the shielding were to fail or it peeled off in the slipstream?"

"Don't worry about it Bryan. Before you would feel the ten gees, the airframe would collapse and the plane would be instantly ripped apart in midair. You'd be squashed like a bug on a windshield, never feel a thing. Hasn't happened yet."

That was not a very comforting thought.

We had been cruising straight up 600 miles an hour. That was ten miles a minute. After thirty seconds, she said, "Beginning deceleration."

At least I got a warning this time. From comfortably leaning back in my chair at a normal one gee, it felt like I was held upside down and supported only by the seat belt straps. I had wrapped my legs around the base support of the chairs as soon as I felt that falling sensation. This feeling lasted a mercifully short time.

"Down to 150, switching to horizontal."

I felt the plane rotate again and I was in a normal one gee field.

"Where are we?"

"Leveled out, holding stationary at 60,000 feet over the Moffett Field plant. Time for you to get to work."

I sat there for a moment letting what she said sink in. There was something off. Then it hit me. Every time I'd been flying in a conventional jet, there was the dull roar of the engines. No matter how much Boeing tried to make the inside of airplanes quiet, they were just really loud. But inside this cockpit, it was too quiet. There was no engine noise, not even the whistle of wind going by.

I'd become so used to air travel that I was sensitive to small changes in the routine. When something changed at 60,000 feet, it was usually not a good thing.

This flight pattern was also disconcerting, unlike anything else I'd experienced. But, when you have a really strong engine and unlimited power, not constrained by flying by aerodynamics, I guess you had to rewrite the rules.

I wanted to process all this newness, but I had to concentrate on the task at hand. I'd have plenty of time to sweat the details on my next trip.

I hoped.

Sally, send scout down to the Foothills plant. Hover at 200 feet. Let's define the rules of engagement to always use the maximum acceleration but not exceed 600 miles per hour. Unless otherwise specified, use these standard conditions.

"Yes, Bryan."

"ETA for Scout to be in position?"

"One minute, six seconds."

"Plan a spiral search pattern from the plant to a five-mile radius. I want to scan the streets for any cars or any motion. Estimated time to complete the scan?"

"Two minutes, fifteen seconds."

"Execute."

I wasn't planning to just wait around. "Give me the view from Scout."

The cockpit dissolved away leaving me suspended in space. I saw the lights of Silicon Valley spread out below me. Lots of traffic still on 101. I was in a mad dive to the ground, falling a lot faster than terminal velocity. The Foothills plant was directly below me. In this view, I felt sure we were going to crash into the ground. The only thing keeping me from screaming was knowing it was just a movie. I could close my eyes and the image would disappear.

When I knew it was too late, I sensed Scout slowing down. From 600 miles an hour to a dead stop was about two seconds. The scale of what we could do with these vehicles was way beyond what my casual intuition was calibrated for. I would have to rely more on my engineering discipline and less on my gut feelings. Especially since my gut was unhappy with all these maneuvers.

"Scout, stay in this position for a moment."

"Okie dokie, Bryan."

I heard in a squeaky, little girl's voice.

"Sally, what's with the kid's voice?"

"As you addressed the pod directly, I assumed you would want to project a personality on it. I scaled the voice age to the relative size of the pod to the ship, assuming a ship age…"

"Enough. Okay, I get the idea. And Sally, adjust the profile to a thirteen-year-old girl. A kid is okay, just not a squeaky little kid."

I noticed a few cars in the parking lot of the Sciquest plant below us, to the west of the plant entrance. "Sal, identify the make of this car," I said, pointing to a low-slung, shiny black car that looked like it would be more suited for a racetrack than city streets.

"A Lamborghini Aventador."

"Any idea who it belongs to?"

"Max."

Interesting guy; can't wait to meet him. "Scout, execute the search pattern now."

"I am, like so on it, Bryan," I heard from Scout. I made a note to adjust Sally's personality file options first chance I got.

I wanted to close my eyes to the disorienting visual field, but I also wanted a heads up on what was going on nearby us. It was too much of a roller coaster ride, circling around and around at an unnatural speed.

About a mile away from the Sciquest plant, I saw a smoldering hulk. It was the car on its back, with the poor man from Carlyle Cleaning. It hadn't been discovered yet, hidden among the dark, deserted streets as it was. Right next to it was the pile of rubble that used to be the building with the parking garage.

"Scout, pause your search and hover over the smoking car below. Any signs it might have been discovered yet?"

"There's like sooo much dust in the street and no tracks. I'd say it's like totally undisturbed. Would you look at that? We have company."

"Show me," I said.

A flashing red arrow directed my gaze to the edge of the visual field. As I moved my head to look, the field shifted and I saw a police car patrolling the warehouse neighborhood. They were still at least a mile away. They just seemed to be driving up and down each street. "Scout. I want thirty second updates on the location of that police car, but for now continue your search."

"What a great idea. I am so there for you."

In a few seconds more in the search pattern, I was overflying the smoking hulk of the van we had left in the soybean field. It had not gone unnoticed. Next to it was a fire truck and police car with red and blue flashing lights. It was just at the edge of my five-mile radius limit.

"Hold here a second," I said, as Scout was starting to move away.

"Is that like a second in my time or a second in Bryan time?"

"Until I say otherwise." This was getting a little frustrating. Was this what being a father of a teenager was like?

"Scout, adjust your profile. The voice is okay, but use Sally's personality profile for now."

"Yes, Bryan," I heard with the same voice, but a better tone. If only kids could be adjusted so easily.

I looked all around at the scene of the wrecked van. From this altitude I could see distinct craters in the field where near-miss laser blasts had blown out large divots. Our tracks were very visible. I saw where they changed direction from heading into the field to heading out. I shuddered, reliving how close we came to being that burned-out hulk, sitting in that very spot not more than two hours ago. It was only a matter of time before it was discovered. For now, all attention was on what was left of the van.

So far, it looked like a normal crime scene. Uniformed men and woman taking their time walking around. More importantly, nothing hinted at an alien Neanderthal presence. They'd either have to use a helicopter, a drone or really expand their search area to discover the Jeep tracks. I probably had an hour before they picked up on this new evidence. I hoped to be long gone by then.

"Scout, continue the search pattern."

One more lap around at extreme range and Scout returned to the hover over the roof of the plant. Nothing else suspicious in the neighborhood; no other white panel vans or mysterious oval shaped saucers. She made a quick descent to the rooftop of the Sciquest plant. It was vacant.

"Kathy, I think it's okay to land."

"Heading down."

"Scout, get up to a one kilometer altitude and orbit around our current position at a radius of one kilometer and track any movement into this perimeter. Give me an update on that patrol car."

"Yes, Bryan." It was the young girl's voice, but a bit more subdued. Much better.

We rocked slightly when the wheels touched down. Kathy opened the side cabin door and the steps folded down. She stayed in the cabin as I walked down the stairs to wait for Max and collect our weapons.

Just as I set foot on the rough tar surface of the roof, the access door to the rooftop elevator opened. A tall, gangly kid came out, pushing a cart with two large duffle bags. As he got closer, I could see his beaming smile, the biggest one I'd seen all night.

Before he got four meters away, he said, "You must be Bryan. It is so cool to finally meet you. I've been following your adventures all night. That was cool how you trapped that Foxconn spy. All we've been doing is bitching about him for the last month. Ron wouldn't let me hack him. You actually did something."

"And you are Max." I held out my hand and we shook. He wouldn't let go of my hand, just kept pumping it and beaming that smile. I guess I had a fan here.

"Okay Max, good to meet you too, but we're on the clock here. Have you got some weapons for us?"

"You bet. I only had a couple of minutes at the hunting shop, so only grabbed a few things." He stooped down and unzipped the nearest duffle bag and pulled out a gun with the biggest barrel I'd ever seen.

"Behind door number one, we have your basic rapid fire assault shotgun with 12-cartridge capacity barrels topped off with the new explosive rounds. These are primed to explode ten milliseconds after contact. And to complement this, we have your basic H and K 416 assault rifle with underslung 40 mm grenade launcher, complete with the official Navy SEAL emblem."

He stood next to the cart, one rifle in each hand, one rifle butt resting on each knee, a huge smile still plastered on his face. He looked like an ad for a summer militia camp.

I expected a hunting rifle or two, maybe a revolver. "Where did you get this stuff? You don't find these sorts of weapons in a hunting store."

"Ron knows some guy that has a sporting goods store. The guy said he makes most of his profit from these sorts of weapons, not the low-end stuff."

"And he just let you waltz in the store, on a Sunday night, and let you pick up these guns from a rack?"

"I did smile and ask nicely. Well, and the $40,000 in cash helped a little. He even gave me these two duffle bags for free. They weren't on the rack, they were in a back room."

"What's in the other bag?"

"Oh, I picked up some more ammunition and a few handguns for you. There's even a little surprise for you in the bottom of the bag I think you'll like."

Before I could ask any more details, I heard Scout, "Perimeter alert. The police car is now at 998 meters and closing." I quickly calculated. We had less than two minutes before we were screwed.

"Who's that?" Max asked.

"I brought one of the practice pods with me as a scout."

"I like the voice, but it doesn't match the personality. Hmmm. I might try something like that. Genie, make a note." I looked over at Max briefly. I wasn't sure he understood just how much trouble we were all in. This just seemed like another thrilling adventure to him.

"Scout, project a map of the area and show me the track the police car has taken over the last five minutes."

The methodical up and down each street of the patrol changed in the last three minutes. They picked up the path we had taken, following the trail of damage that followed us on our mad dash through the deserted warehouse district. But, where we had turned right down a side street, they turned left and stopped, right in front of the parking lot where Kathy's damaged plane had crash landed.

In the bird's eye view I had, I saw the faint outline of a plane seared in the asphalt of the parking lot. It was like the plane's shadow had been stapled to the ground. I shouldn't have been so surprised. She had said her plane had come in hot. It left its mark. The cops had seen it too.

Our track led them to the remains of the upside-down car wreck and the totaled building. "Scout, how much time did they spend by the burned-out car? Can you make the width of their track proportional to the time they spent there?"

"Of course, Bryan."

Immediately, the scene below changed. Now I had a visual sense of their attention. The narrow yellow line meandering through the streets was now modulated. I saw a knob by the parking lot where they studied Kathy's landing site. At each of the damage sites from laser blasts, the track get wider.

This perspective made it clear something was off with this patrol car. They took notice of each encounter we had and followed them like breadcrumbs. But at the burned-out car, I would have expected the patrol car to stop and check it out in. At least they should have looked for bodies in the car. Instead, it slowed down as it passed by and continued its search for the next crumb.

"Scout, have you picked up any radio chatter from the police car?"

"None. The car is radio silent up to five gigahertz."

"What's the typical police band?"

Max overheard my question. "They use VHF and sometimes as high as 160 MHz, but never above one gigahertz."

"How come you happened to know this, Max?"

"It comes in handy when you want to stay one step ahead."

"What do you think? Is it normal for a patrol car to encounter a recent car accident and not stop to check it out?"

"They're clearly looking for something. The car accident is just a stepping stone to them."

"I agree. Look, they came to the torn fence at the edge of the field but didn't pursue it. There's no way they couldn't see the other cars and trucks in the middle of the field and they didn't call in this other set of tracks into the field."

"Definitely not behaving like any cops I know," Max said.

"Scout, where are they now?"

In real time, I saw the tip of the patrol car's trail growing, and heading right toward the Sciquest plant and us. They would be on the lookout for a plane and here we were on the roof, probably already in their sightline if we took off.

"Scout, still no radio traffic from this car?"

"Bryan, no transmissions picked up."

Kathy was monitoring my conversation with Max and the new developments with Scout. She stuck her head around the cabin door at the head of the stairs.

"Bryan, they saw the damage in the road from those laser blasts. They saw the burned up car wreck and how could they miss the scorch marks in the parking lot? Why haven't they called this in?"

"Hey, Kathy," Max said. "I didn't see you there." He waved up at her, that beaming smile that never really left him, got even bigger if that was possible. Kathy didn't even acknowledge his presence.

"Scout, maneuver to hover twenty meters above the police car and lead them by three meters. I want a view into the front seat."

Instantly, the ground shot by and the patrol car came into view. There was a glare off the front windshield. I could make out two people in the car, but not much else. They were less than a minute out.

"Scout, move around to modulate the glare. Build a composite picture of the front seat, subtracting off the glare." I had learned a valuable lesson in one of my signal processing classes. If you can't modulate the signal to pull it out of the noise, modulate the noise.

The new image was rendered quickly and I saw the driver. He was a big guy, but that's what most policemen were. It was the passenger that had me worried.

"Oh crap!" Kathy said. "That can't be what I think it is, can it?"

I sighed. "All the indications suggested they had penetrated other levels of the government. This is just another example."

The cop was apparently doing ride-alongs with Neanderthals. Or this was one ugly recruit. These two buddies were making a beeline to the Sciquest plant. This close to us, we'd be sitting ducks on the roof. If we took off, there was a chance they would see us and if this Neanderthal was armed with a laser weapon, we'd be a target. Even worse, Sciquest would be identified and our secret would be blown. We could put the entire company in jeopardy.

"Okay, hot shot, how you going to get us out of this one?"

The way Kathy said this sounded like she was making the incoming Neanderthal my fault. It may not be my fault, but as soon as I started on this rescue mission, I'd become responsible. Good thing I had the beginnings of a plan.

These guys were looking for something suspicious to go after. Maybe we should give them something.

"Bryan," Max said, "Can I come with you? If we leave now, we might be able to get away before they see us. I'd be a real help to you on this mission. I want to help rescue Michael, too."

"Max, I have something more important for you to do for us tonight. We need a distraction. That car of yours looks pretty fast. Want to take it for a spin?"

"Seriously? You want to give me an excuse to drive fast? Ron won't let me, but if you're telling me to, I'm there for you."

"You understand what you have to do? And they may be armed with a laser hand weapon, so don't take any chances."

"Bryan, I've made a few modifications to my car. It's all electric and I mounted a propulsion pod on the chassis. I could probably outrun a laser." I remembered when I was Max's age. I felt invincible, too. But I never faced Neanderthal aliens with advanced weapons.

"Like I said, no chances. Understood?" I gave him as serious an expression as I could muster, given his contagious enthusiasm radiating out and splashing on me.

"Patrol car is 400 meters and closing," Scout announced.

"Time's a wasting, Max. We're counting on you." I was worried about how long it would take him to get off the roof, over to the parking lot, and get his car in position. "You'll barely be able to make it down to your car before they arrive."

"I know a shortcut. Can I borrow Scout for a minute?" I nodded back. He whispered something in the air, presumably his glasses picked it up and, in the blink of an eye, Scout was descending in front of him, head height.

"Kathy, I guess I'll see you later. Gotta run. You make it back safe, okay?"

Kathy just stood at the top of the stairs. She looked down but hardly responded. I glared at her and nodded my head toward Max. I knew a crush when I saw one. With that little encouragement she gave a halfhearted smile, waved back, and just said, "See you on the return."

That little attention was all Max was waiting for. He grabbed hold of one of the struts built into Scout's frame and lifted off the ground. "Let's keep this part between you and me, okay Bryan? Ron doesn't like it when I let the pods fly me around."

"Mum's the word. You be careful playing cat and mouse. This cat has at least one very sharp and long claw."

"Piece of cake." His voice faded off the edge of the roof as Scout lifted him, dangling by one hand, to glide down and land him with a running start right next to his car. Scout immediately shot back into the black sky and disappeared from view.

I lugged the two duffle bags up the stairs and into the cabin. Kathy started securing them with bungee cords to one of the chairs. I moved into the cockpit and took my copilot's seat.

"Scout, show me the track of the police car and Max." I had my bird's eye view back. Max had driven out of the parking lot and waited in the middle of the street, one block away from the Sciquest plant. The police car was about to turn the corner to the street and see Max. He just sat there, a quiet shadow, a low profile black car, on a black street. What was he planning? He should have hightailed it out of there.

But when the patrol car had completed its turn and its headlights illuminated the black car, Max went into action. His car instantly became a brilliant beacon in the street.

The headlights turned on high beams, blue lights illuminated the under carriage, a thin line of white LEDs outlined the body, riding up and down the wheel well and making a complete circuit around the car. What was a silent electric car now exploded into the still night with the deafening sound of some heavy metal rock group. Even inside the cabin, more than a block away on the roof, I could hear the music booming from his car. I couldn't understand the words, but I felt the beat vibrating in my chest. I hoped Max had some sort of ear protection. He was a kid; probably not.

The police car slammed on its brakes. It just sat there for a few seconds. Neither car moving. The driver's side door opened and the police officer stepped out. It was more like he poured himself out. He was more than six feet tall, but definitely human from what I could see through Scout's cameras. He grabbed his night stick and put his hand on his sidearm. Then walked around to the front of his car and began approaching Max.

"Anytime now, Max," I whispered to myself.

"Almost time, almost time," Max whispered back to me. I forgot I had a live mic.

When the cop was halfway between the two cars, Max said, "Now!"

I expected his car to blast away from the spot and take off down the street like a bat out of hell. But instead, it lurched about one inch forward and stopped. The lights went off, the sound went off, and the car was back to a mere shadow in the street.

"Uh oh," Max said.

That was not encouraging. "Max, what's happening?"

"I just landed on a dead spot on the armature of one of the wheels. I routed power through the wheel for regenerative braking and…."

"I don't need the novel version. You have three seconds. What can I do to help?"

"I could use a teensy push."

"Scout. Get down there and give Max's car a push, then immediately pop up to 100 meters. Execute."

Two seconds.

"On it."

The cop was moving toward the driver side of Max's car when it lurched again, reengaging the light and sound show. It took the cop by surprise. He stepped back and pulled his gun. And Max shot down the street, this time like a bat out of hell.

He swerved around the stationary police car and stopped right after turning the corner.

The cop reacted. He tracked the car with his gun, but didn't fire. When Max stopped, he holstered his weapon, ran back to his car, slithered back in, but then the patrol car just sat there. I could just make out motion in the front seat from Scout's view. Arms were waving and one of them held a mirror smooth cylinder.

I held my breath. Would they shoot, take the bait, or continue to the Sciquest plant?

They decided to take the bait. The car executed a three-point turn in the middle of the street and, with screeching tires, shot back down to follow Max, who now pulled ahead to the end of the street. He must have been using his propulsion pod because he was accelerating at more than one gee and there were no tire marks in the road behind him. He would have no problem staying ahead of this car, providing no more dead zones.

The fact the patrol car kept its lights and sirens off, and never called in the report, suggested they thought Max really might be mixed up with the destruction of their kidnapping team.

"Max, remember your mission. Lead them away and whatever you do, do not get caught."

"Roger that, Bryan. Did you see my acceleration? I was up to 1.2 gees and not even close to my limit."

"Very nice, but I also saw you needed a push. Don't take any chances." I watched the chase. Max was toying with them, waiting around each corner before taking off so they would be sure to see what route he took. He was playing a very good mouse. I saw why

Sciquest latched on to a kid like Max. He had a lot of potential if it could be channeled. And if he didn't get himself killed.

"Hey, hot shot," Kathy nudged me in the ribs and got me back to the ground. "They're far enough away. It's safe for us now."

"You're right. Scout, you're with us. Stay three meters off the port wing. Let's go to the Moon."

I'd waited more than fifteen years to say those words.

21

"WE'RE SET UNTIL we get to the turnover point. I've adjusted our acceleration to keep a constant 1.3 gee field inside. It's about forty minutes accelerating, then a shorter time decelerating to lunar orbit. Once in lunar orbit, we decide where to go."

All throughout this passage out of the atmosphere, I watched Kathy manipulate the throttle controls, the yoke and a few other switches and joysticks. "How do you fly this ship?" I asked when she seemed to have her hands free.

"It's all fly by wire. I usually let Fred do the flying for me. He can interface to all the systems, but I wanted to do this take off."

"This switch," she continued, pointing to a series of rocker switches on the control panel, "selects the thrust axis. For long-distance travel, it's through the floor of the cabin. For local transport, it's down the length of the cabin. This switch selects constant altitude, terrain following. The yoke and pedals control the direction of the ship axes, just like a plane: yaw, roll, up, and down.

It's pretty simple and Fred is always watching over my shoulder to take over if I do something stupid."

"Sally," I said quietly, "can you also interface with the ship and fly it?"

"Yes, Bryan. I can also provide labels for you on all the cockpit controls if you wish to fly."

"Show me." As I stared at the cockpit controls, solid block letters grew under each button, switch and control surface to label thrust axis, vertical, horizontal, acceleration, and even cabin temperature. I realized again how augmented reality could change the world. I would never need directions or manuals again.

"Cool."

A thought suddenly hit me. "Kathy, the course we're taking, are we avoiding being silhouetted against the moon, viewed from Earth?"

"Of course. That's standard operating procedure. We always take precautions against being spotted from Earth and from any of the orbiting satellites. We have them all in our database."

"What about being spotted from the moon as a shadow against the earth or against the sun?"

"Oh damn, you're right," she said.

"Fred, move us out so we are outside the Earth's and the Sun's silhouette viewed from anywhere on the Moon."

The virtual view out the windows changed slightly as the Moon shifted farther to the right during our course correction. The motion attracted my gaze.

"The Moon is so clear!" I said

"You should see the Earth. Every trip I've made, I never tire of watching Her, especially on the homeward leg."

"I can't see it yet. It's below us," I said.

"Fred, have Sally make the hull transparent."

Instantly, I was dangling in space.

"AHHHHHHHHH!" I screamed. "Warn me next time you're going to scare the crap out of me."

"Oops," Kathy said, devoid of feeling. "No wimps allowed in space, Bryan," she said the last with a sideways smile. My hands, still sore from grabbing the armrest on the trip up, instinctively locked on the arm rests with a death grip again. It seemed to be the only thing keeping me anchored. It looked like I was sitting in space, no walls, no floors, no windows, just space above and the Earth, visibly receding, below.

And she was right. This was the easy, routine part of the trip.

The feedback from my hands and body that I was still in a chair helped pull me back. The illusion was perfect. I saw the Moon directly above my head. Below my feet, and stretching under most of where the floor used to be, the Earth. Most of America was still in darkness, but the city lights of New York, Washington, San Francisco, Los Angeles and Las Vegas were shimmering beacons. They seemed to be whispering to me, 'Hey, don't forget us'. The terminator line, in the middle of Europe, hinted at a new day coming. Would I be around to see it, I wondered?

"Okay, I'm sorry, I should have warned you. Happened to me my first few times."

"What a spectacular view," I said when I had calmed down. I lowered my glasses an inch to peer over my nose. There was the very dark cockpit, instrument panel lights nearly extinguished, windows completely black. The world existed only in my glasses.

"You get used to it after a few trips," Kathy said softly.

"I'm not sure I ever will," I responded. "I used to dream about going into space. I stopped dreaming years ago when I thought I never would. I was ready to give up. Now here I am."

"We have about thirty minutes until turn over. In less than an hour, we'll be at the moon. Then all we have to do is find the lunar base, figure out how we're going to sneak in, find Michael, bring him out and get back safely to the Earth." She paused and I looked over at her and saw, in my virtual view, that her hands were shaking on the arm rests.

"Okay, I'm feeling really scared again," Kathy admitted, her voice breaking with a slight quiver.

"Kathy," I said, turning to face her. I reached my hands across and placed a firm grip on her arm, steadying her. "Being scared is okay. It's even healthy. My friend Rusty, is a former Navy SEAL and the bravest man I know, but gets scared."

She looked at me gravely, her features pale.

"But he says 'courage is doing what you need to do even when you're scared.' And I think you are a very courageous woman. You've traveled through space, more than any other person in the world. You've actually stood on other planets. You've met foreign creatures, I even saw you kick the crap out of a really hairy one that outweighed you five to one!"

She smiled at that, but it was a little forced for my liking.

I smiled back at her. "I'm scared too, but that's not going to stop us from rescuing Michael and saving the world."

She laughed at my absurd boast. "You sound pretty confident in yourself." Then, more seriously, "Do you really think we're going to get out of this alive?"

I allowed myself that one moment of weakness earlier, trying to estimate the odds of our success. That was it. Now that I was committed, I could not allow myself one tiny ounce of doubt. Whatever we encountered, I absolutely knew we would deal with it. After all, I was a Ninjaneer.

"Bet on it," I replied.

"I am," she whispered back.

The moment passed and I let go of her arm. We still had about twenty minutes before turn around. I wanted to learn more about this astrophysicist with the Andromeda tattoo. "How did you ever get mixed up with this program?" I asked.

Kathy gave me wry, sidelong glance and shook her head. "I was actually in the process of being kicked off the faculty at Harvard when I got a call with a job offer from Michael. I had been rather vocal in my efforts to get NASA to fund and initiate some more planetary landing missions."

Kathy just stared ahead at the open, rich field of stars. I couldn't take my eyes off of Earth, visibly receding below us. I let her continue, uninterrupted.

"NASA didn't like the public pressure I was applying and someone high up talked to someone higher up, who talked to someone high up on the board of regents at Harvard who talked to someone lower down who finally talked to my tenure board. The party line was that I didn't have a large enough publications list and the imagination I demonstrated in those I had published, was not up to the standards at Harvard, blah, blah, blah."

She looked vulnerable and open now, as she got into telling her story.

"Michael didn't agree with that assessment. I had actually met him months earlier at a conference. At the time, he was setting up a research effort in Sciquest, something related to planetary astronomy. Rumor had it he was flush with money and looking for ways to spend it. So, he was doing the rounds. He seemed to know everyone. I knew he had a lot of influence so I introduced myself to him." She gave me another glance, this time sheepish. "He was very friendly. I used my five-minute window to plead with him for more robotic missions. He was polite and listened through my little speech. Then he just thanked me for my time and went off to another discussion."

"And that was that?"

She laughed. "That was the last I heard from him until five months later, when I got word from my tenure committee that I didn't make the first rounds. That night, my friend Sarah and I finished off the hundred-dollar bottle of Cabernet I was saving for a really special occasion. Somehow we found ourselves in Central Square and had another few drinks. Then she drags me into this tattoo parlor. Next thing I know, we're staggering out, me with what I thought at the time was an Andromeda tattoo. What did you call it?"

"A spider," I said innocently.

"Yeah, it sort of does look like a spider, too." She laughed.

"I was still pissed and shocked and angry and more than a little drunk when Michael called early the next morning. He wanted me to talk to his boss, Andy Rayburn. I don't remember exactly what I said, but he insisted I come to San Jose. He said they were looking to fund some planetary science R&D and 'did I want to propose a program.' Little did I know at the time!"

She paused, still just staring out the window, gaze lost in the stars. I decided not to interrupt her, to just let the words come out on their own.

"It was at the third meeting that I was brought into the group. That was almost a year ago. Ron's team had made a few test flights into orbit in the first modified plane and had an idea of the other modifications needed. It took another six months after I joined to get the infrastructure implemented for more than a day trip. It's handy having folks like Ron and his guys around. He's ex-NASA."

"Michael and I put together an exploration program, based on these converted planes. He is the last guy to want to go out in space. But me, I was thrilled to even imagine standing on a planet.

"I was the first explorer. Went out on my first trip to the Moon about five months ago. It was the scariest thing I had ever done in my life. I'm really just an astronomer, not an astronaut."

She turned and gave me a searching look.

"Can you imagine, Bryan? I was kicked off the Harvard Faculty, and now I'm doing field studies in planetary astronomy, on the planets!"

I just smiled back, sharing some of her thrill.

"With these ships, we can go just about anywhere in the solar system and back in less than a few weeks."

"How many trips have you taken?"

"Counting this last trip to Saturn, it's been six. I've been to all the inner planets, and to a few of the large moons. After my first trip to Mars, I decided we needed to find more astronomers and astronauts for the team. It was just too much for me on my own. It was taking about three months to reconfigure a commercial plane into a spaceship so we've been slowly building up a fleet."

"Sounds exciting," I offered.

"I feel a lot safer going out with two ships on a mission, just in case. Until this trip, we hadn't had any problems. Ron's teams have done a great job building in redundancy and a safety margin."

I looked around the cockpit with care, taking in some of the details of the instrument panel, control yokes, and LCD screens. It still looked like a regular jet, not a spaceship. But here we were, out in space.

"It's incredible that a small group can build spaceships and keep them going so well for so long and keep them quiet from the rest of the world."

"You'd be surprised how easy it is to convert a jet over," she said. "Space isn't that far away from their designed environment. We leverage our PDA mark 2 chips as nodes that run all the important functions and they all talk to a central mark 3 processor. Each subsystem is a self-contained module and has its own Casimir battery."

"Fascinating," I said, then mentally kicked myself for sounding like Spock.

She seemed not to notice. "All the software was created with a learning algorithm based on evolution. It keeps trying things and moves in the direction of better performance. It's constantly updating itself. The hard part was writing the first simulator to get each node started with what it was supposed to do."

I nodded. I would have done it this way, program in self-learning, especially if I didn't have a good algorithm to model the aerodynamics. A neural net algorithm would be the way to start.

"Once we had a barely functional ship, we flew it around a bit for it to experience more and learn how to control everything. I mean, how does a baby learn to walk? It watches adults and keeps trying things, until it can stand up without falling. Every staggering step it takes, it gets better."

"I hope our ship is out of its teenage years," I joked.

Kathy laughed. "It's at least twenty-four in human years, I think. That's what our neural nets do. The neural net algorithm moves quickly up the learning curve. We trained the ships how to lift off and fly and they get better and better each trip."

"That's a lot of work to do for each ship."

"They learn from each other. Every time we come back from a trip, all the Mark 3's in all the ships get rationalized together, so they all get better collectively. Each Mark 3 chip that goes into a new ship gets an initial download from the collective."

"Well, it sounds like a dangerous way of flying," I said. "I mean, it's like what they say, 'what doesn't kill me makes me stronger'. How do you prevent a ship from taking too big a chance?"

"We have fail safes. So far, the only ship we every lost was Michael's, blown up by these goddamn alien Neanderthals on the Moon." Kathy sat up straighter in the pilot's seat. Thinking of Michael had reignited her worry. "I just hope we're in time."

I saw the barest tremor in Kathy's lower lip. I wanted to keep her talking, draw her out, keep her mind occupied. "He's the other person you explore with?"

"Oh no, he's just one of the super geniuses that wanders around Sciquest doing whatever he wants. He actually hates space travel. He says he would rather wait until he can travel in space in a bit more style, or until we start converting cruise ships to serve as spaceships."

I heard the smile in her voice when she described Michael. I had to remember to reign in my interests. There was obviously a connection between them.

Kathy sat silently, eyes down. She seemed almost on the verge of tears.

"And he was out with you on this trip because of the DNA fragments?"

"These fragments, if they are real," I said, "would be extraordinary! Are they the origin of life on Earth? It would confirm the old panspermia notion that life came from outer space."

"Michael says that idea just kicks the can farther down the road. Where did that life come from?"

"So what's the alternative? What does he think?"

"He says, maybe if we can find meteorites on Earth that were knocked off of Mars and the Moon, maybe there are fragments of the Earth that were knocked off and are floating around in space.

Maybe Earth's life has contaminated our nearby space. A comet passing by could have picked up the contamination and that's what we saw."

"So you just happened to sample a region of a comet which just happened to encounter a fragment of a meteor, which just happened to be shot out from Earth by some other meteor hit, which just happened to have some pieces of Earth creatures with DNA on it, which you then collected?"

"And you think it more likely life originated from somewhere else other than Earth?"

"Well, they're both equally hard to believe ideas. How could you prove one or the other?"

"That's why we were out by Saturn. Michael had the idea that if we sampled a comet that had never come in to the inner planets, but was making its first run to the sun from the Oort cloud, it wouldn't have had a chance to pick up Earth contamination."

"But if he didn't like to travel into space, why was he out there with you?"

She paused a moment, looking down. Then spoke, not looking at me. "He said if it was just me out there collecting the sample, no one would believe the result. My competency would be questioned. He wanted to be part of the collection team to add credibility. He was out there to protect my reputation for me. And now look at the mess I got him into." She was shaking her head. This was not where I wanted the conversation to go.

"Well, if comets have original DNA in them, this could account for life as we know it on Earth. Evolution still happens, but instead of just random mutations, maybe life has a stacked deck to work from."

My last comment brought her back from the brink. She sat up and wiped her eyes. "Now you're catching our fever. This plays into Steven J. Gould's Punctuated Equilibrium theory."

"What's that?"

"He said, it looks like life has gone through long periods of stability punctuated by brief periods of rapid evolutionary change. He proposed it was either climate change or something in the environment that rapidly changed, forcing more severe natural selection forces to drive the periods of rapid evolution. What if it was really a comet fall that brought with it a few more options for life to try out?"

"But where did the new DNA come from?" I asked. "Are we just some weird alien kid's science fair project that escaped the kid's lab?" I was caught up in the possibilities.

"Yeah. If these fragments are real, where did they come from? That's the question. Were they designed and created by some intelligence, or did they evolve somehow in space?" She let this last statement linger.

Wow. Yesterday, around this time, I was trying to decide what toppings to get on my pizza. Now, here I was, in the middle of deep space, somewhere between the Earth and the Moon, debating the most profound question there is, and sitting with someone who may be close to actually finding the answer.

"How could they evolve in space?" I asked, prodding her on.

"These primordial comets out by the Oort cloud, they've been orbiting in interstellar space for billions of years. They were probably created when the solar system condensed out of the original dust cloud in our local space. And this cycle of solar system birth and death has repeated at least twice. Our original dust cloud definitely had remnants of previously evaporated solar systems and supernova explosions."

I looked at Kathy. I was captivated with those eyes. Up here, in space, between the Earth and the Moon, there literally were stars in her eyes. I could lose myself in them.

If she knew how infatuated I was becoming with her, she didn't show it. "Carl Sagan used to say, 'we are just star stuff.' Every element heavier than Lithium came from a supernova. So those comets in the Oort cloud which have all these organic molecules, have been passing through fragments and remnants of older solar systems for at least four billion years. With their surfaces at nearly three degrees Kelvin, anything that touches them condenses and sticks."

I whistled. "So, they've been acting like cosmic garbage collectors, sweeping up any molecules in their path?"

"Exactly. If the DNA is real, it could have evolved in another solar system. Or it could have evolved in interstellar space in a molecular gas cloud."

That last comment suddenly clicked for me. I'd read that story a long time ago. Now I remembered. "That's what Fred Hoyle's one and only science fiction book was about. *The Black Cloud*, about an interstellar gas cloud that was so large it was alive and sentient. If this turns out to be correct, I bet he'd be royally pissed if he was remembered for his science fiction and not his astrophysics."

"Royally pissed is very apt," Kathy said with a laugh. "He was after all, Knighted by the Queen and became Sir Fred Hoyle!"

"Look, our intuition is limited," she continued more soberly. "You have to have studied astronomy and astrophysics to have an appreciation for the true scale, not just of the universe but of the vastness of our local space. Some of the gas clouds in our neighborhood, from which our solar system evolved, have as much mass in the form of carbon monoxide, water, methane and ammonia, as a million earth masses, constantly being bombarded by ionizing radiation to make free radicals."

"And there's an equal mass of dust particles of carbon, silica and other minerals to provide surfaces for recombination. Let this soup of a million earths cook and percolate for thirteen billion years and it would be surprising if we didn't find something like DNA fragments."

"Is this the million monkeys banging on typewriters argument for the origin of life? Now you've burst my bubble. It would be so much more exciting if there was an alien intelligent designer."

"I'm sorry. I'm lecturing," she said.

"Not at all," I said. "I'm fascinated with the implications here."

"Well, like Michael says, this potential discovery of DNA fragments just kicks the can down the road. How were they created?"

"And if there was a creator, what else did they create?" I added. "Now we know we're not alone. This is another wrinkle. Who are these Neanderthals? I agree with you. I don't want to believe they created us. But maybe they came from the same source we did, or maybe they even came from Earth? And what else is out there?"

"I want to know where they came from and how they got to our solar system," Kathy said.

"And," I said, finishing her thought, "What they intend to do here."

22

JUDGING BY MY stomach, it was almost midnight and dinner was a long time ago. "All this talking is making me hungry," I said, "Do you have anything to eat on this ship?"

"I don't think so. We left in a bit of a hurry and didn't provision it for a long trip. There may be some snacks in the first aid kit." Kathy pointed to the pack hanging on the wall in the main cabin.

While our ship was accelerating ceiling-first to the moon, the 1.3 gee acceleration force inside the cabin made it a little awkward for me to walk around. I struggled to get up from my copilot's chair because it felt like I had on a fifty-pound backpack. Holding the rails along the side of the cabin for support and balance, I got to the first aid kit mounted at shoulder height.

I pawed through gauze bandages, an aspirin bottle, Kleenex, and flashlight. In the bottom of the bag I found a silver, vacuum-packed pouch.

"Did you find anything?" I heard from the cockpit.

"You guys are full of surprises. I found a pack of freeze dried ice cream, just like the astronauts eat. It's strawberry flavored."

"That's Max's little joke. He plants those things in every ship I take. I keep telling him I'm an astronomer, not an astronaut."

"I don't know. I picture an astronomer as someone who sits in the safety of a dark, cold observatory, staring out through a telescope. I think you're more of an astronaut than you are willing to admit."

I stared at the design on the pouch of an astronaut floating in his silver space suit, the Earth below him. I glanced down through the transparent cabin floor at the virtual image of the Earth, suspended in space at my feet, then back at the cover. They got it wrong, I thought. They left out the clouds.

I ripped the pouch open and saw small chalk-like cubes and a few freeze-dried pieces of strawberry, covered in the grey powder of the dried ice cream. I popped a piece of strawberry in my mouth where it dissolved, the intense rush of concentrated flavor exploding in my mouth. The faint, earthy aftertaste—maybe a hint of peat—mitigated the intense rush of the sweet strawberry. *Not a bad combination*, I thought.

"Oh, by the way," Kathy said from the cockpit, "Max always says, don't eat the dried strawberries. The packages are so old, most of the strawberry pieces have grown mold, but the rest of the ice cream is supposed to be pretty good."

I tried swallowing the little bit I was chewing. Suddenly, I wasn't hungry anymore.

A soft chime interrupted, followed by Sally's voice, "Time for turnover, ten second warning."

"Grab hold," Kathy announced. "Get ready for turnover."

"What do I do?" I asked nervously.

"Hold on."

"To what?" I asked, staggering back into the cockpit and strapping back into the seat. I gripped the arm rests just in time before I fell off a cliff, as acceleration stopped and we were in free fall. Our universe yawed around the center axis as the ship rolled 180 degrees. Before I could take a new breath I was back on the ground, with my thirty percent added weight. We began our decelerated leg on the way to the Moon.

"Isn't there an easier way of doing that?" I asked.

She looked at me, as though to say, 'wimp.'

"I guess I'll get used to that too," I answered myself.

I leaned back in my chair to watch the Earth through the now-transparent ceiling. To avoid being silhouetted, we had looped around the Earth so some of the day side was visible.

In the silence, we both stared up at the Earth, still receding away from us. I waited for Kathy to bring up the obvious question, but she was silent.

I asked it for her. "Okay, so where do you think the Neanderthals are from? Do you think they are roaming around our solar system from some other star system, or do you think they are from Earth?"

"I don't know, Bryan," she said softly into the stillness of the cockpit. "We all want to know those answers. I've certainly never found any evidence of them on any of the planets or moons I've visited. Their transmissions out by Saturn were the first hint of anything. But some organization has been influencing technological progress on Earth, and they're likely candidates." She let the last comment drift off into the silence.

I looked down at my feet. The moon was getting visibly bigger. Focus, I told myself. This wasn't some typical consulting gig I was heading into. This was potentially the first skirmish in the battle for Earth's future. This was cosmic in the literal sense.

Just earlier this evening, I was complaining how bored I was getting. This would teach me to be careful what I wished for.

I had a dumb question, but I knew I had to ask it.

"Kathy, why were you so quick to volunteer on this admittedly hair-brained rescue?"

Kathy sat up straighter in her chair, shoulders pulled back slightly. "Michael would have done it for me. He is the greatest man I have ever met. He respects me as a professional. Do you know how hard it is, as a woman in a man's profession, to be taken seriously? He would have done everything he could if our places were reversed. How can I do less!"

Interesting, I thought. Kathy was angry now, not scared.

She wiped her fingers through her hair, putting the two strands that had come loose back behind her glasses. "Sorry, I didn't mean to vent on you, I'm just really anxious about what's ahead. I really am just an astronomer, not some kind of warrior princess." She gave a faint laugh at the image she conjured, paused a moment and then asked, "What about you, why are you here? You didn't have to be so quick to volunteer."

Though I'd been known to do stupid things before to impress a woman, there was more to my motivation than just that. She'd just asked an important question. I hadn't really thought it through until right now. It had just been a feeling in my gut until I was put on the spot to articulate it. Why was I here, risking my neck on this admittedly risky rescue?

"I'm both scared and excited. I'm scared for the human race. I don't know what these Neanderthals have planned with the nukes they have, but it can't be good. I think they may be out to annihilate us, all of us. I'm afraid of what they can do, and I don't think we have much time."

"I'm excited because with Sciquest's technology we are on the verge of broaching our cosmic quarantine. I mean, this is what every kid that ever went into physics has dreamed of, and we are so close to moving through this doorway. I'm here because it looks like Sciquest holds the key to our future."

"And I think rescuing Michael is just the first of many battles we must fight and win if we, as a species, are to survive and expand into the universe

Just as soon as I'd given my big speech, I felt a little melodramatic, like I was giving some inspirational talk at toastmasters. I had to add, "I feel pretty silly when it comes out like that."

"Don't feel silly," Kathy said. "You've been on the team for just a few hours and you already feel what most of us have felt for years."

"There is another thing for me," I said. Now it was my turn to sit up straighter, to connect with my inner strength. "I don't like the idea of some alien race muscling in on us. I'm pissed that they might be pulling our strings, suppressing our technology. I don't tolerate bullies very well."

Our moment of serious reflection was interrupted by Sally. "Bryan, the third practice pod is approaching rendezvous."

"What's this all about?" Kathy asked.

"Ron came through for us. It's supposed to help us sneak into this alien base. I'm hoping there's a bag attached to this pod. We need to it bring inside the cabin. Any suggestions?"

"If you think it's that important, I'll have to go out there and get it. I'll suit up and we'll cut our acceleration."

It was all of two minutes for Kathy to assemble her suit around her. She entered the airlock in the rear of the cabin and we cut our acceleration. In less than one minute, she was back inside the cabin with another duffle bag. With the bag stowed with the others, we started our deceleration again.

"Sally, designate this other pod as Scout 2. Position Scout 2 three meters off our starboard wing."

"I'm here, Bryan," I heard, this time in the voice of a thirteen-year-old boy. Great, I thought, now we've got a couple of kids along with us.

In our deceleration, the Moon was below the cabin floor, visible getting larger as we watched. The Earth loomed above, looking dainty, just a small ball of oceans, clouds, and sprawling land. A storm swirled over the Mediterranean. The Arctic was a flat white cap to the brown of Europe and blue of the North Atlantic. This was our Earth. It was time to fight for it.

I clapped my hands to break the spell. "I think we're close enough to the Moon to start searching for Michael. Can we project the coordinates he sent us onto the Moon?"

"No can do right now," Kathy said. "It's just on the other side of the moon's horizon from us, near the North Pole."

"Do you have any magnification for the cameras?"

"Bryan," she gave me that irritating, patronizing smile again, like it was another dumb question, "this is one of the ships we use for planetary exploration. What do you think? Here's the moon at 10x. Want it at 50x?" She moved her hands in front of her, like she was selecting two different buttons and the Moon image dangling at my feet exploded in view.

I stared down at it, suddenly realizing how large the haystack was and how small a needle we had to find. And the clock was ticking down.

"Great!" I said, now feeling more than a little overwhelmed. "The problem is where do we look, and what do we look for?"

23

KATHY GAVE ME a smug smile. "I can get you started. I'm having Fred project Michael's reported coordinates on our image," she said. "They're just coming up over the horizon."

At least we were taking turns making things up as we went along. We made a pretty good team, each feeding off each other.

"Sal, what's the step size resolution of the coordinates we have from Michael?"

"Approximately 50 kilometers, Bryan."

"That's a bit discouraging," I said, "Even at best case, that's an error circle of almost 10,000 square kilometers. And every minute we spend looking is another minute into a precarious future."

"And Michael's in danger," Kathy added, the tension in the set of her shoulders clear as she scanned the moon's surface. "Bryan, how are we going to find him? It could take days!" At 50x, the surface of the moon visibly expanded below us as we decelerated to match orbits.

We'd just plucked all the low-hanging fruit and now we were both freaked out at the same time.

"We're never going to find Michael in time. It's hopeless. There's just too much land to check." I could hear in her voice a rising fear. She was looking to me for leadership, strength and, more importantly, a solution.

"We can do it, Kathy, just keep your eyes peeled. Look for a pattern that doesn't fit the rest of the landscape."

"What does that mean?"

"I bet we'll know it when we see it."

"Like that helps! We're going to have to slow down a lot if we have to inspect every square kilometer."

We had a difficult trade off now: how to move fast enough to cover a large area, but watch for the faint detail of an alien base that probably blended in with the surface? With just two pairs of eyes, there would be no guarantee we could pick up this moon base traveling at this extreme ground speed with so much to cover. Even if we were sharp now, in ten minutes, eye fatigue would set in. This really was beginning to look hopeless. We couldn't rely on luck. Too much was at stake.

Those familiar tendrils of insecurity were pulling on my confidence. I could feel the sweat beads starting on my forehead. There had to be a better way.

Leverage your strengths, I heard Rusty's voice shouting in my head.

I took a deep breath. I'm a professional problem solver; a master in identifying the problem and the unknowns, eliminating the unimportant, acquiring the important, analyzing it and finding a solution that worked. And I am especially skilled in computer automated monitor and control systems. I was itching to feel those slimy Neanderthal eyeballs squishing under my boot.

With every new feature I'd learned about my PDA glasses, I was blown away. What an incredibly powerful tool, with the combination of VR glasses, integrated earphone, microphone and cameras, radio link into a LAN, voice interface and neural net based AI agent tied into a powerful computing network. I already saw how powerful an image processing engine it could be and I was convinced there were far more problems that could be solved with this tool than were currently being exploited.

"All I see are mountains and craters and shadows," she said

"That gives me an idea. See those shadows?" I pointed at one large ridge we were about to pass over. "They have jagged edges. I'm willing to bet alien structures are going to be engineered smooth. Michael mentioned domes." A glimmer of an idea was forming. "We look for unnaturally smooth structures and we enlist some help."

I needed a way of quickly scanning multiple cameras for some sort of change in the pattern of the landscape. I didn't really know what the alien Moon base looked like, but I was willing to bet the features would stand out on the lunar landscape. It was a pattern analysis problem.

I broached the idea to Sally. "Sally, can you take the visual feed from the cameras and search the surface on the moon for anomalies?"

"Bryan, you must be more specific about what you mean by anomalies."

"I'm looking for smooth, rounded features among the jagged terrain. Here's a possible algorithm. Take a region of the surface as viewed in one image. Calculate a numerical description of the surface features, like a measure of the spatial power spectral density. Compare this to a moving average baseline in a few spatial bands. When a region of the surface falls outside the baseline value, identify it. As the terrain passes by can you highlight the location of the outlier? Is this possible?"

"Yes, Bryan. What feature size do you wish to search for? This will determine the optimum baseline area and sweep rate."

"Assume for now the anomaly is larger than ten meters across with smooth sides. Use a resolution of two meters."

"Optimal search conditions are six kilometer altitude and velocity less than two kilometers per second."

"Sally, using the destination coordinates Michael gave us as the center for highest probability, plot an optimized course that allows us to map out the surface within a 100-kilometer radius. Use the highest acceleration possible, while keeping the internal gee force to less than 1.5 and never place us between the Moon and the Sun or Earth's image. When this is plotted, give me an estimate of the search time."

Almost instantly, Sally responded, "Total search time will be 15.3 minutes, for a 95 percent probability of detection. We will be positioned to begin in 2.9 minutes from now."

I was starting to enjoy myself. Talk about a personal digital assistant. This is what computer interfaces were supposed to be like. Just give a concise command and have it implemented. The details of how to implement it and all the calculations that are just textbook algorithms should be completely transparent to the user. I was already dreaming of how I would run my own ship, if I ever got out of this.

"I could have come up with that algorithm," Kathy said, sounding defensive.

"I'm sure you could have."

"But not as fast as you did. But I still get credit for recognizing your value and pushing to get you on the team."

"If we survive the next few hours, remind me to thank you," I said.

"Okay, hot shot," Kathy said. "You've got the reins. I'm along for the ride now."

"Then buckle up. This is going to get a little rough."

"Where have I heard that before!"

I just couldn't resist the temptation. After setting up the command and settling into our seats, all I could think of saying was, "Engage."

In 2.9 minutes, we began the search pattern. In the initial spiral pattern, the ship kept up a tight turn radius. The lunar surface zipped by uncomfortably fast. The seat belts held us in place, but I was in an awkward position, leaning over to stare down below my seat. I grabbed hold of the arm rests to steady myself.

How bizarre we would look to an outside observer. A jet aircraft, flying through the vacuum of space, six kilometers above the lunar surface on this convoluted path.

The cockeyed internal acceleration field coupled with the lack of visual clues of any solid foundation gave the distinct impression of being spun off into space. But I didn't mind this rollercoaster ride so much. I had a view of the moon's surface like only a handful of humans had ever seen before.

Still, after the first thirty seconds of the search, I became nervous again. I felt helpless, just staring at the terrain flashing by. It wasn't that I couldn't see anything. I was seeing too much and couldn't tell what was relevant.

"Sally, can you overlay some measure of the degree of anomaly for the terrain below, in real time, without interfering with the search? I want to compare the actual features with the calculated value of how unusual the feature looks."

"Yes, Bryan. I will superimpose out of sync contours on the image. Each contour will represent one standard deviation from the moving average, based on the statistics of the last square kilometer."

Immediately, white contour plots augmented the view of the surface. It was rather bizarre to see contours that did not correspond to the actual terrain, but to some abstract calculated quantity. It required a mental shift to see the landscape and interpret the contours in terms of how unusual the feature was. What made it doubly difficult was the speed of travel. The view projected was the direct feed from the cameras. Our velocity was based on the rate at which the images could be acquired and processed. It was faster than I could really absorb. Recalling my experience in the virtual conference room, I decided to push the envelope.

"Sally, I want to be able to look around at the surface from a different altitude. Add a marker for Michael's original coordinates and circular grid lines every 10 klicks. Superimpose our search path and change my perspective to an altitude of fifty kilometers."

Instantly, it looked like I was moving straight up and away from a bull's eye pattern. I was surprised how quickly my order was implemented and at the smooth transition. Rather than a snap change in perspective, I was treated to a gradual change in altitude. Obviously, the VR processor algorithms had a feature that tried to minimize non-physical views.

What a ride. I just hoped we would find their base before they found us.

Most of the landscape below looked like how I imagined the Moon might be. This region of the Moon was illuminated directly by the sun at a low angle to the horizon. The shadows were sharp and long. The boundaries between bright and dark were distinct. This made the pattern recognition process easier.

I scanned the view from high altitude while Kathy quietly watched the lower, real-altitude view. Where I looked and there was no image recorded, I just saw black. Swatches of image were drawn into the black as the ship progressed through our search pattern. At this altitude, I probably couldn't see a small Moon base, but I could gain a perspective of how much land we had covered and the general pattern of anomalies. I was relying on Sally's search algorithm and Kathy's mark-one eyeballs.

"Fred, freeze view," Kathy said suddenly. "Now back up one kilometer. Bryan, this might be it. Fred, transfer this image to Bryan's view."

In my glasses, it looked as though the ship had stopped and had dropped back down to hover over a spot six kilometers from the surface. Below me, I saw contour lines highlighting three features in a straight line on the surface. It was too regular to be a natural lunar feature. The detail was obscured by the contour lines.

"Sally, label the linear pattern below as target one."

"Bryan, the pattern you refer to is not clear to me. Please point to it with your finger."

I moved my index finger into the field of view; it appeared as a small cross with a persistent tail. By moving my fingertip in a circle, I could draw a circle over the suspected image in VR space.

"Sal, zoom in on this feature." Displayed in both pairs of our glasses were the only smoothly curved surfaces on the Moon. There were three oval shadows. At the current real altitude and resolution limit of our cameras, we were already seeing the pixilation in the ovals.

"I'm glad you were paying attention, Kathy. This could be the base."

"The anomalous contours around the base caught my eye. I always knew spending a year looking through 4,000 old photographic plates of galaxies from the Harvard Smithsonian Center for Astrophysics would pay off."

"Sally, freeze search. Change ship's position to two kilometers away from target one, at an altitude of one kilometer. Circle target one at this radius and project a composite image of the terrain."

In thirty seconds, we were staring at an alien Moon base and a prickle of apprehension washed up the nape of my neck.

"Holy crap," said Kathy.

The base consisted of three domes, each about twenty meters in diameter, separated by only a few meters. There was a narrow corridor connecting each one. What materialized into view as a detailed image rendered and built up was a fleet of space craft parked near the domes The four smaller ones were identical, about five meters in diameter, scattered around the domes at roughly fifty-meter separations. The one large one was at least ten meters in diameter, parked closer to the domes. The whole base spanned less than a square kilometer.

In this 3D VR view, the five ships could be seen as flattened spheres, flying saucers. They each had a large spherical center, tapering to a thin disk at the periphery. At this resolution, the surfaces were smooth and featureless, but I could make out small stubby legs protruding from under the saucers. The larger one had a ramp extended to the Moon's surface.

"Sally, create a file with this image and precise location followed by the complete search history and our discussions. Also mark this spot as the location of where we'll park." I moved my cross hair finger to circle a small crater with a steep wall and deep shadows. The shadow of its cliffs would provide a perfect hiding spot. "Designate this location as 'parking lot'."

"Add the following note, 'our plan is to land and infiltrate the base on foot. This spot puts us less than three hundred meters from the first dome, designate dome one, followed by two and three. The square feature on the side of dome one looks like an entrance. We're going to check it out. Wish us luck.' End note."

I glanced over at Kathy. She looked positively spooked. "Cool with you?"

"Sounds like a plan," she said.

"Sally, place a copy of this file in Scout 2 and send it off to headquarters, maximum acceleration."

I looked over at Kathy. She nodded agreement.

I nodded back and said into the air, "Execute."

24

SCOUT 2 PEELED away from our left wing and shot off towards Earth.

I looked out the ship, searching for the receding sphere, but, of course, there was no sign.

"Sal, how long until it reaches San Jose?"

"Approximately eight minutes, Bryan."

"Okay Bryan, we need to get down to the surface. I can pilot us down to that crater you pointed out. Our chameleon screen is still on so we shouldn't be seen. I've had the rf and microwave antennas on full gain as we've been searching. No emissions from the domes, and we haven't been painted yet."

"Let's hope our luck lasts a little more time. Take us down."

The plane landed in shadows at the foothills of the crater wall. This was my first time experiencing the lower gravity of the Moon. I walked into the main cabin, holding on to handgrips in the ceiling to keep steady. This lower gravity threw off my balance. It was going to take me a while to recalibrate my reflexes.

I hadn't paid enough attention to the suits when Kathy had gotten into hers to pick up the package from Scout 2. When I examined them more closely now, I saw the three silver suits hanging on the racks had flexible, collapsed, clear plastic hoods, now folded back. Their torsos looked like they'd been salvaged from an old deep sea diving suit. Each suit had those long, skinny tanks mounted around the circumference along the chest plates.

I couldn't imagine slipping into these paper thin suits, straight out of a deep sea movie. Getting into this converted jet plane and taking it into deep space really hadn't prepared me for jumping off of this new cliff. But, it was too late to back out now.

"Where did you get these suits? They look awfully flimsy for space. Can you really trust them?"

"Actually, they came from NASA mostly like this," said Kathy, walking up beside me. "We only did a little modification."

"What was NASA doing developing these kinds of suits? They're nothing like the suits I've seen astronauts wear."

"You'd be surprised at the programs NASA engineers have worked on over the years that haven't made the light of day. Ron arranged to buy out NASA's entire stock and asked for a dozen more suits."

"Didn't the NASA folks get suspicious when a small high tech company comes along and wants two dozen space suits?"

"Oh, we didn't buy them directly. One of the Sciquest subsidiaries is a start-up building conventional space launch vehicles. They bought the suits. They said their engineers were going to use them in their walk-in vacuum chamber where they test the vehicle integration. With NASA's budget so tight, they loved the $100k they got per suit."

"I guess that start-up is going to be worth nothing when your ships become public."

"It's well worth the investment as a good cover."

Strapped next to the suits was the duffle bag with my last-minute request from Ron. I unzipped the bag and pulled out the hastily cut ponchos of Mylar covered with the antireflection polymer. There wasn't time to make them smart, so Ron just adjusted them with a black surface. It sure beat the silver space suits. They each had a hood that could be pulled over the helmet. But, it attached in the front and would cover our entire head.

"I just realized a problem with these ponchos," I said, holding one of them up. "If we cover our heads, how are we going to see through these black sheets?"

Kathy reached down and picked up one of the ponchos. She held it out in front of her and inspected it. "Trust Ron to think of everything."

I didn't get it. "What do you mean?"

"Each suit is fitted with six cameras, placed around the neck collar, at sixty degree intervals for a fifteen-degree overlapping field of view. Ron cut holes in the hoods with openings for the cameras."

Kathy held the poncho in front of her, showing off this feature. "Look, this is perfect! He made the hood fold back. He's got Velcro tabs to hold it in place."

Kathy helped me get into my suit. It was surprisingly easy. I put the leg unit on like a pair of pants using suspenders to hold them from my shoulders. The top of the pants ended in a stainless steel ring flange. The seat of the pants had a small rigid plate built in. I crouched down and slipped underneath the chest unit, hanging from the wall. It also had heavy padding inside to rest comfortably on my shoulders. This was the main structural piece and everything else snapped onto it.

My arms stuck out the chest unit, leaving my hands free to adjust the rest of the suit. The bottom of the chest unit ended in a matching round flange. After twisting the top of the pants ninety degrees, the flanges mated and I could rotate them to the front, hearing them click into place.

The last step assembling the suit was the arms. Each one was like a very long pair of gloves with rigid, rotating joints at wrist and elbow and a locking ring on the shoulder end. These rotated into the matching flanges on the chest unit at my shoulder. Suiting up took less than one minute.

I wiggled my fingers and checked my dexterity. The gloves were thinner than I expected. At least this relieved one of my worries. I knew I could pull a trigger through these gloves.

The lack of a helmet still worried me. All I had to cover my head was a clear, flexible, plastic cylindrical bubble. And it was sealed with a zipper.

"Kathy, don't these zippers leak like a sieve?"

"Trust me on this, Bryan. We've been using these suits for more than six months. The inside flap under the zipper has self-sealing silicone-coated surfaces. The pressure keeps them closed and the zipper teeth have a silicone gel coating. The combination makes a very effective seal."

"But it's just a thin layer of plastic between me and vacuum. What if it gets cut or torn?"

"You're such a worrier. I've been out for more than a hundred hours in them. The suits are three ply of twenty mil Kevlar fiber reinforced and the helmet is twenty mils thick transparent Kevlar."

I felt a little queasy. "I guess I don't have much choice right now."

"I think your suit ripping is the least of your worries," she said with a smile. "We're about to storm an alien Moon base, and they have laser guns." She had a point.

The plastic helmet zipped around the neck to the chest unit and the suit became rigid as it filled with air. I spun around and waved my arms in the tight cramped cabin and was amazed at how flexible and unencumbered I felt. The rigid chest unit lined with cylinders filled with water gave me a bit of a barrel shape, functional, not very elegant.

Finally, we lifted the ponchos over our heads and aligned the peep holes with the cameras. Then came the hood to seal in the front with Velcro. A belt pulled the sides in. I was surprised my hands didn't shake when I pulled everything together. Every blasted science fiction movie I'd ever seen was rattling through my head. I just had to have confidence in Kathy's judgement. If these suits worked for her, they should be good enough for me. At least we wouldn't be waving a flag to announce our entrance.

"I'm sold," I said, feeling slightly better. "You look like a shadow against the cabin wall with hands and feet sticking out and I can see perfectly with the external cameras."

"You can have Sally make my hood transparent, you know. There are cameras in the neck ring viewing inside the suit too."

With a simple command, the top of Kathy's poncho disappeared.

I scanned the cabin and spied the two canvas bags strapped with bungee cords to chairs in the back of the cabin.

"Can't leave without the weapons."

Sure enough, in the second bag, Max had stashed a few hand guns. I saw two 9mm Glocks and thought of Laura Croft. When I looked up at Kathy, the spell was broken. Neither of us would qualify as tomb raiders. But I selected the handgun for Kathy anyway. Whether Max had thought of it on purpose or the way they came, there was a holster in the bag that conveniently clipped on the belt holding her camouflage cape.

I chose the 44-magnum revolver for my right hip, also in a holster. I opened the barrel and saw six rounds in the chambers. I grabbed the other 9 mm for my other hip. Why not, I thought. You can't have too many guns when you are going up against lasers. But did we really stand a chance, bringing guns to a laser fight?

I decided on the assault shotgun as my main weapon. My first concern was being able to reach the trigger with my gloves. It was a tight fit, but both assault weapons were designed to be fired with gloves on.

Kathy carried a backpack with the extra suit in the event Michael would need one, and her go kit for surface exploration. I reached down and picked up the H&K416 and passed it over to Kathy. But she backed away from it.

In my opinion, now was not the time for this kind of squeamishness. "Take the weapon. We might need it."

"Bryan, it's hard enough for me to have this pistol on my hip. I don't think me with a big rifle I don't know how to use is going to be of much help."

She had a point. Worse than not having the rifle would be having it in the hands of an inexperienced, unsure shooter, standing at my back. I reluctantly left the automatic assault rifle in the bag.

"Okay, Kathy, not a problem," I said. "We'll make do with what we have."

I ruffled through the bottom of the second bag for some extra ammo and found a present from Max—two vintage World War II pineapple hand grenades. They'd probably been manufactured before my parents were born. Did grenades have an expiration date? But they wouldn't take up much room and they might come in handy. I added them to my belt.

"I'm good to go," I said, moving to the airlock. "Are you set, Kathy?"

"Ready as I'll ever be." But she stood there without moving.

I gave her an encouraging smile. She said, "Remember when I said I wasn't afraid? I lied. I'm about to enter an alien moon-base that may be filled with Neanderthal Monsters. And I'm 200,000 miles from the nearest help. What was I thinking?"

I walked back to her, and took her hands in my gloved ones. Even though we were each encapsulated in our hermetic suits, looking at each other in synthesized images created by our glasses and communicating through an encoded rf link, I thought this moment needed some piece of a human connection.

"Remember it's courage that helps us manage our fears. We are fighting for our very survival here, not only ours but our world's. And you are not alone. The two of us, we're a team, and a damn fine one if you ask me. Between the two of us, we can do anything. If you want to feel scared for someone, feel scared for the goddamn Neanderthals that get in our way!"

She was finally smiling back at me. I don't think she realized that little speech was actually for me. I probably needed it more than she did.

"Okay, hot shot, let's go kick some alien butt!" She chuckled and added, "I never in my life imagined I would ever say that line."

"Just remember," I added, as I spun the wheel on the airlock, "having said all that about courage, there's no substitute for caution."

We entered the airlock through the submarine hatch. She closed it behind us and the airlock cycled. A very faint red light from one LED illuminated the confined space. As the air was pumped out, all I could hear was the very faint purr of the air circulating fan in my suit. There were no other sounds in the vacuum of the airlock.

Kathy opened the back hatch and it silently lowered. The stairway unfolded onto the surface of the moon, stirring up a small cloud of lunar dust. I could feel a slight bump in the cabin floor through my boots when it made contact with the surface.

There was no turning back now.

I went first. Still unsteady in the lighter gravity, I held the shotgun in one hand and a tight grip on the handrail with the other. Before I stepped off the last stair, I paused. This was a momentous occasion. I was about to step foot on the Moon.

But Kathy had done this dozens of time, and on other worlds. She didn't bother to stop and savor the moment and ran smack into me.

So, rather than step onto the Moon, *a la* Neil Armstrong, saying something profound, I tripped onto it, nearly falling flat on my face.

I hoped this wasn't an omen.

But still, I was standing on the Moon. The Moon!

25

I STOOD LOOKING around at the shadows of the steep crater rim and our ship, visible only as a faint red lit open doorway. I held my breath. Absolute, complete silence.

A new problem struck me.

"Sally, hold all communications. Send a burst to Fred, lowest power, then go to radio silence."

"Yes Bryan."

"Sally, we need to keep radio communications hidden from detection. We don't know how sensitive the alien receivers are and our only advantage is surprise. Can you adjust your transmission strength to absolute minimum? We want local area communications with the suit cameras, between Kathy and me, and to the ship, but don't want much leakage."

"Yes Bryan, I can do that."

I thought for a moment, then added, "Better yet, can you encode the signal in white noise so it looks like residual background? Use a pseudo-random spread spectrum modulation."

"Yes Bryan. I can send the algorithm to Fred and the ship."

"Do it."

"I just got the word, Bryan," Kathy said in my ear. "Good idea. Michael and I never worried about suit-to-suit radio transmissions getting picked up, since we were always so far from any listening posts."

"Let's still try to keep the radio traffic to a minimum."

We verified the ponchos blended in with the shadows and all internal lights in the ship were turned off. Only my assault shotgun was visible, held against my chest. I tried to hold my arms under the poncho as much as possible. We left the rear door down and the airlock open to the vacuum so we could get into the ship in a hurry.

I heard Kathy take a deep breath and give the okay, "Lead on."

I began a slow, awkward walk in lower gravity, following the edge of the crater.

"Bryan, you have a flying suit, use it," said Kathy, sounding impatient and nervous. "Sit back on the seat. Sally can drive it for you."

"Why didn't you tell me?"

"I thought you knew. You're picking up everything else pretty fast."

"Next time, assume I don't know," I muttered, glancing around apprehensively. "How do I activate this flying suit?"

"There's a rigid bar against your butt. That's the seat. The thruster units are in the shoulders. If you just lean back you can sit. Tell Sally where you want to go."

"Sally, up half a meter." As my feet lifted off the ground, suspended by the propulsion pods mounted on my shoulders, I wiggled back on the built in seat. This wasn't so bad; it was like sitting on a swing.

Time to get moving. "Sally, project a map of the path from our position to dome one, taking us through shadows wherever possible."

Instantly in my field of view, I saw a dotted yellow line, a virtual "yellow brick road" to follow. The path led us around boulders along the rim of the crater. There was a gap we could pass through, like a small canyon, which opened into the wide open crater the base was in.

I looked over to the port wing but could not see Scout in the shadows. "Scout, you still with us?"

"Yes, Bryan. I am still three meters off the starboard wing,"

"Scout, move out on the trail. Keep three meters ahead of us."

"Sally, let's move out on the path at one meter a second, but be prepared to stop."

"Yes, Bryan."

As I started moving ahead, rocking gently from the shoulder harness, I realized it was like swings, but without the chains to hold. I cruised over the surface at a walking pace. There was too much to pay attention to. I was extremely concerned about foot patrols seeing us, even with our black ponchos. Would there even be any Neanderthals out on the surface?

"Sally, I want you to monitor any motion in the visual field and from Scout. Alert us at the first sign of motion. And highlight it in our glasses."

"Bryan, understood," was the reply in my ear.

Since I had addressed Kathy, Sally interpreted the context of the command and relayed it to Fred as well.

The three domes, each the light tan color of the lunar rock, were just visible through the gap in the crater wall. I stopped us and dropped to the surface to stand on my own feet. It was as quiet as a still life painting ahead.

I stared through the gap. There were scattered islands of sharply peaked boulders, but otherwise, it was a flat plain to the domes and five parked ships now visible in the crater floor. This was it.

"Ready, Kathy?" I said, looking behind me. I saw a distorted shadow with a clear helmet and the hint of silver hands and feet poking out.

"Michael's waiting," she whispered back.

I looked into the gap for movement, took a deep breath, gripped my shotgun for assurance, and walked through the narrow passage in the crater wall.

I hadn't gotten three steps before Sally broke into the silence, "Motion detected, 5 o'clock position."

A yellow flashing arrow pointed to the right in my visual field. I turned to see a small black box atop a tripod, which had been hidden from my line of sight earlier. I took one step toward it and a dull grey blur came out from the right.

I swung the rifle around, as fast as I could.

Unfortunately, it wasn't fast enough.

26

WHATEVER CAME AT me grabbed hold and pinned my arms to my side.

The creature was strong. I couldn't move my arms, which hurt like crazy from being squeezed up against the cylinders. My rifle, pinned against my chest, was useless. It just dug into my hands. I couldn't even release my grip on it.

Whatever got me was grey, fuzzy, and blocking my camera so I couldn't see. And it was obviously trying to crush me to death.

When I refused to immediately die, it squeezed me tighter, like a python. My solid chest plate was the only reason that I could still breathe. My adrenalin spiked, but a heck of a lot of good it did me. "Shoot! Kathy! Shoot!" I managed to gasp.

My cry provoked the thing on top of me. It lifted me off the surface and I found myself being shaken like a rag doll, my teeth clanging together until I tasted blood.

Holy crap. It was only a matter of time before my suit was ripped. I was a dead man, for sure.

In the near total darkness inside the suit, I could see the front surface of my flexible helmet being indented. The Neanderthal was banging his head into my helmet under the black hood. If it had been a solid piece, I bet it would have been cracked open like a soft boiled egg by now.

"Kathy! Help!" This time I managed to shout a little louder, a fat lot of good it did me.

I tried to think, to calm my shrieking brain.

There was nothing my technology could do. Or was there?

"Sally, up… one meter… now!"

I felt myself go up, dragging my assailant up with me.

"Sally, rotate with my back to the domes and hold us steady."

My inner ear told me I was moving. The Neanderthal was squeezing harder. Now that it too, was off the ground, it had more reason to hold me tight. My arms were going numb. Much more and I was sure they'd break.

"Kathy, you have to shoot him now! I can't last much longer." I wheezed under the pressure.

With the propulsion plates holding me suspended, I was relatively stable. The Neanderthal had no leverage to shake me or swing me around like before. I felt a small jerk and then another and another. But the grip hardly changed.

"It's bulletproof," cried Kathy. "I shot it three times, nothing. I'm afraid of hitting you. What do I do?"

"Keep shooting! Find a vulnerable spot!"

I felt three more small jerks but, if anything, the bear hug got stronger. I tried shaking from side to side, suspended by the shoulder pods. Nothing.

I had to think.

I noticed a pattern in the indentations in my helmet. When the Neanderthal pulled back to head butt me another time, it relaxed its bear hug slightly. I could almost feel my arms again.

But it was a stalemate. It couldn't do any damage to me while it held on, and I couldn't bring my assault shotgun around.

Suddenly, I heard a banging. With each bang, I could feel its arms readjust.

Kathy was shouting and yelling incoherently.

Then I realized what was going on.

She must be out of bullets and had resorted to banging against the Neanderthal's suit with her empty gun.

It was distracting him, but it wouldn't kill him.

But it gave me enough leeway to shift the shotgun. I couldn't see much, so I hoped its tip was pointed away from me and at my attacker. The next time the head pulled back, I was ready, but my plan was a gamble.

Would the armor-piercing shell have any impact on the Neanderthal's suit? Or would it just ricochet and hit me?

I didn't have any choice. With Kathy beating on him, he might go after her next.

Then the moment came. His head went back, his grip loosened. I closed my eyes, pushed the tip of the barrel away from me and pulled the trigger.

Everything happened at once. I felt a tremendous shock in my arms and chest. I was suddenly free of him. My camera came clear, just in time to see what was left of the headless Neanderthal fall to the Moon's surface. I watched, in morbid fascination, as it sprouted a small fountain of blood that froze almost instantly in the vacuum.

Then I heard the whistle of air escaping and my ears popped.

My heart sunk. That bulletproof transparent Kevlar wasn't designed for shrapnel from exploding alien space suit fragments.

"Bryan," I heard Sally's voice against my skull. "Your suit pressure is down fifty percent and falling."

"Tell me something useful. Increase the electrolysis. Can you make me more air?"

"The oxygen generator is at maximum production rate."

"Kathy. I punctured my suit somewhere. I only have seconds. What should I do?"

I sounded calmer than I felt. There was no time to make it back to the ship. This was not how I wanted to die. We had barely started our assault.

"Sally, lower Bryan to the surface. We have to find the tear."

When I hit the ground, I dropped my gun next to the dead goon.

"Air pressure down to twenty-five percent."

I tried to unclip the belt holding on my cape, but I couldn't figure out what I was doing. I felt another pair of fingers pushing mine out of the way and the belt fell away.

She was saying something to me, but I was fading fast. Finally, the hood was open and I could see with my real eyes.

I was weak. Even in the reduced lunar gravity, I couldn't stand up.

My knees buckled.

It was all I could do to breath as deep as I could and stay conscious. My vision was starting to tunnel. But I could at least look out the clear cylindrical helmet. In my narrowing tunnel vision, I saw two plumes of smoke shooting off from my head. I was like a little steam engine with two whistles blowing. Part of me giggled hysterically and said, "choo, choo."

I couldn't keep my eyes open.

I felt my hands being moved. My fingers were being pressed against the plumes of steam. I heard someone shouting to me.

"Press here. Do not move your hands. Do you understand? Cover the rips until I can repair them."

I didn't understand what the words meant, but when I tried to move my hands back down, they were slapped and pushed back into position. I guess it was important to hold my hands here, fingers stuck in the holes. I didn't want them slapped again.

"Air pressure stabilized."

The blackness all but took over my field of view. It was like looking through a soda straw. My arm was so tired. I had shoved my fingers into the rips in the helmet to hold my arm in position. I was too out of it to even worry about expanding the holes.

Later, I figured I probably looked like that Dutch kid with his fingers in the dike before the water was about to surge outward.

I was breathing hard, one ragged breath after another. My world was that tiny opening in the blackness, I concentrated on keeping those holes plugged.

Maybe the leak rate was reduced, but at this stabilize pressure level, I wouldn't last very long. It took everything I had to concentrate on breathing and not moving my arm. Deep breath. Exhale. Deep breath. Exhale.

Kathy was saying something to me. I had to refocus on her voice to understand the words. "When I tell you to, remove your fingers from the holes."

"Huh?" I mumbled. I heard the words, but couldn't parse their meaning.

I was fixated on that tiny, dwindling circle of light and it was shrinking as I watched.

I could feel Kathy crouched, leaning against me. At least I wouldn't feel like I was going to die here on the Moon's surface alone. She would be at my side.

"Move your God damn fingers," she shouted at me again.

"My air…it's gone." I tried to mumble my last words, but my mouth was too dry and I just didn't have enough breath to form the words.

"Just do it! Trust me," she said a little more gently.

I couldn't see her. In my head I had this vision of the woman with the green eyes and an Andromeda tattoo. We'd made a pretty good team so far. I was willing to take my last breath with her at my side. I pulled my hand away. My helmet deflated like a popped air mattress. But only for an instant.

My helmet popped out to its full shape and for the first time in what felt like a lifetime, I could feel my suit pressure rapidly rise.

As the air came back, the fog of near death began to clear. I shook my head to try to accelerate my recovery. I could see a strip of duct tape slapped over the holes. I looked up. Sure enough, there was another strip. They looked like two giant band aids covering a really bad bruise.

Who would have thought duct tape would work in a vacuum?

After a few moments, I felt suspicious. If the suit was really as safe as she said it was, why would she have a roll of duct tape with her?

"As long as we got all the holes, you should be in good shape. How's the air pressure?"

"Sally," I spoke with my new found voice, "how stable is my air pressure?"

"Suit integrity is restored. There are no leaks."

It looked like a piece of shrapnel had entered from the front and exited through the top of my helmet. Another centimeter lower, and it would have grazed my head and done a lot more damage. Another millimeter larger and I probably wouldn't have been able to plug the holes while Kathy grabbed the duct tape.

With air pressure and oxygen levels back to normal, my panic was subsiding. I looked over at Kathy and gave her a grim smile. "We're even!"

She looked at me, clearly relieved that I was still kicking. "We're both alive. Let's try to stay that way."

I couldn't agree more.

27

I LOOKED DOWN at the Neanderthal that had tried to take me out. It was about two meters tall, stockily built, with disproportionately long arms. That's how it was able to get such a strong grip. It wasn't quite headless. There was still some of the back of its head attached to the neck. The faceplate of the suit was gone, like it never existed.

With my boot, I rolled the alien over. There were a few scratches on the back of its suit from the 9mm. The bullets hadn't penetrated the suit. It looked like the shotgun had been enough to do the job, though. The shell had entered right at the neck joint and exploded inside the helmet, just like Max said it would. At least it could penetrate some parts of the suit. I wasn't so sure how it would do in a torso shot.

I looked around uneasily. So far, there was no other motion from the ships or the dome. I hoped the alarm had not been given and the skirmish had gone unnoticed. With luck, his buddies wouldn't come looking for him.

"We need to find a way in," I said to Kathy.

She nodded. We walked to a small rock mound twenty-five meters ahead. This brought us within the circle of alien ships, parked around the domes.

Only three of the five space craft were visible from our position; still no motion anywhere outside.

By my calculations, it had only been a few hours since these ships had landed at the base. It was a little past midnight in San Jose. Which made me wonder: had all the aliens come out of the ships since they landed?

I eyed the path to the first dome; it had less cover. We might be spotted out in the open.

Three craft each had ramps extended to the lunar surface. Looking closely, I saw the nearest craft also had a hatch opened at the top of the ramp. The waves of anxiety I felt were cresting into whitecaps. Our position was precarious. Approaching the domes would leave our backs to their ships. Who knew what would be coming down the ramps, or when?

We could easily be surrounded.

I stood there behind the last hiding place before the dome. I was thinking about Michael's chances. We were nearly killed by one of these Neanderthals on our approach. I hoped he'd had better success.

I turned to face dome one, steeled myself to move, and stepped around the rock shielding us from view, Kathy right behind me.

A warning from Sally made my fear spike. "Motion detected at eleven o'clock."

A blinking arrow in my glasses pointed left. I jerked my head in the arrow's direction to look at the closest spacecraft.

The arrow disappeared, replaced by a rapidly flashing red circle surrounding the alien craft's ramp. I saw the doorway outlined in my display and an alien in a suit emerging.

I swore. Just in case Kathy wasn't clued in, I nudged her arm with my elbow. She reached out and squeezed my arm.

We huddled back in the shadow of the rock barrier. "Scout, give us the view forward." I knew it would be handy having Scout along with us. She could be our eyes while we stayed hidden.

We watched as another figure came out the craft's doorway and down the ramp. The first one carried a small spherical bag by a strap. The two marched single file toward dome one. They were each armed with the now-familiar laser weapons hanging from their waist belts.

Though less than ten meters away, the aliens didn't bother to look for humans huddled in the shadows and Scout was a motionless dark shadow amongst other scattered shadows.

"This may be our ticket in," I whispered to Kathy. "We might be able to follow along and look for an opportunity to enter with them."

"But what about the ship? What if there are more alien's coming out of the ship? What about your rule number two?" Her voice shook.

I was as tense as I had ever felt. I wasn't sure if either of us were cut out for this cloak and dagger business. This was not a weekend warrior exercise. There would be no time out if I got tired or a next week to make up for points lost in this game. This was, quite literally, a sudden death playoff.

But the game was in motion, and we had to play it out.

I shrugged in answer and just watched the aliens through Scout's cameras. They appeared to be arguing with each other. The lead Neanderthal had stopped and shoved the second one, who gestured wildly. I had no idea what might be their problem; maybe they were talking about a missing buddy? If so, they might suspect some intruders were lurking. I hoped we hadn't given up the element of surprise just yet. It was our only advantage.

"Here's the plan, Kathy. You scoot over to the first ship, under the doorway by the ramp, and toss these two grenades into the open hatch. That should eliminate any resistance from this ship."

She nodded mutely.

"I'll follow these two and hold them once we find out how to get inside. Then you come join me." I pulled off the two grenades, which hung from my belt. I was going to thank Max for his little gift if I ever saw him again.

"I'm not sure I can do this, I'm scared."

"You can do this. I'm counting on you. Michael is counting on you."

"I've never used a grenade before. What do I do?"

"Well, I've never used one before either, but I think it's just like in the movies."

I was trying to lighten the moment, but the way she looked at me told me she was not amused.

"Hold this spoon compressed against the side. Pull this pin out and throw it. Three seconds later, make sure you're not around. Here you go." I pressed the grenades into her gloved hands, which were shaking, but she took them and moved to the left, staying in the cover of the rocks.

I cut across diagonally to intercept our targets. A large rock gave some cover from the advancing aliens. I held the assault shotgun, ready to fire. I watched to see Kathy get in position at the base of the nearest spacecraft, then forced my attention back to the figures approaching.

I was alone. It was silent. I was scared. Two aliens from a space traveling species, possibly far advanced from humans, with hostile intent, were meters away. What was I doing here, I asked myself. How could I expect fifty-year old grenades to work in the cold vacuum of space? I clutched the shotgun tighter in my hand for assurance. Would it even have an effect?

I glanced over again at Kathy, just below the open hatch of the craft. It was slightly more than one meter above her head. The ramp extended down at a thirty-degree angle. I saw her bending back so her cameras were able to give her a view of the open hatch. She stood.

Holding one grenade in each hand, she brought them together and pulled the pin of one and then the other. She stood rigid, two live grenades in her hands. "What if I mess this up?" she said in a frantic whisper.

I had to show courage I didn't really feel. I had to be the strong one right now. "You won't mess it up. Just toss the grenades into the doorway. It's just a meter above your head. It's easy, just gently lob them up."

My stomach churned. I knew she had it in her, but she needed to do it soon.

"I've never been so petrified."

I remembered her reactions during the virtual meeting. If I wanted to help her overcome her fear, I was going to have to piss her off, even if I had to make stuff up. "If these Neanderthals take over Earth, all women will be slaves. You'll be chained to kitchens, forced to wash dishes. Forget science. You'll never see a computer again. They hate women!"

"Not on my watch," she said. "I'm going to blast these Neanderthals back to the Stone Age where they belong."

"Atta girl!"

"Sexist pig."

"You pulled the pins. Now throw them," I whispered.

While I waited, my targets reached the dome. The lead pushed a spot on the side of the hemispherical front lobe that extended from the dome. Instantly, the surface rotated up ninety degrees and blended in with the circular entrance near the roof. It left a wide, clean opening. That was a really cool trick. The spherical entrance must have been made of some metamaterial that could dissolve on command.

"Come on," I said. "They're almost inside. Now's our only chance."

"Motion detected, ten o'clock," Sally alerted me.

I snapped my head toward the left, back toward Kathy, following the arrow until it ended in a red circle.

Another figure emerged from the spacecraft's doorway above Kathy's head.

Kathy still hadn't brought herself to lob the grenades. I was betting she couldn't see the alien above her.

I wondered if I should tell her. She had two live grenades in her hands. Would she freak out?

At that moment, one of the hulking aliens in front of the dome turned to face his partner coming out of the ship. Crap. If Kathy moved, this alien would see her. She was in a vulnerable position with no cover. If she stayed still, she was a shadow under the ship.

"Kathy!" I whispered, trying to keep my voice calm. "Don't move. There is an alien right above you at the hatch. One of my aliens is looking your way."

"Bryan, what do I do? I already pulled the pins!" She sounded panicked.

"Just stay put, but be ready to lob the grenades through the hatch. Do you think you can do that from where you're standing?"

"I don't know. I'll try." Then I heard her exhorting herself: "They're Goddamn Neanderthals and they have Michael."

Now both my aliens were hesitating at the doorway, looking toward the ship. Something about their posture was off. Had Kathy been spotted?

One of them pointed.

Crap.

"Throw the grenades!" I hollered. "And run for cover."

I watched the slow motion arc of first her right hand, up and over, and then her left, releasing the grenades at the top of the arcs. The two spoons went flying off at ninety degrees. It was a dead reckoning. The door opening being a big target was the only factor making this shot possible.

Both grenades made it through the open hatch, but everything seemed like it was going in slow motion. They rattled around in the airlock like a hockey puck shot into a goal net.

In the silence of the vacuum, the alien standing in the hatchway had no idea his fate was just sealed.

But I wasn't the only one who saw her move. I looked back at the two aliens standing by the dome. The one closest the ship reached to its side and pulled out its shining laser. Its arm swung up and pointed the tube in the general direction of the base of the ramp where she had taken cover. To my horror, Kathy's arms stood out silver against the shadows.

"Scout, move between Kathy and the last Neanderthal in the line. Fastest acceleration possible."

In the blink of an eye, a spherical shadow shot out in front of Kathy. The sudden appearance of this dark shadow apparently confused the armed Neanderthal and he fired.

Scout took a direct hit. Molten metal sparks erupted in a spray. The blast must have hit a vulnerable part. Maybe it was a Casimir battery, maybe one of the processor units. The reactive force of the ejecting shrapnel sent Scout skittering back from the alien's position, narrowly missing the ramp at the end of the saucer and rolling down the Lunar surface, disappearing as it headed to the crater rim.

"Scout!" I shouted. "Scout, respond."

Silence.

"Bryan, the communications link with Scout is down," Sally informed me.

For an instant, I felt a pang of remorse, but quickly reminded myself it was just a drone, not a little girl.

"Kathy, you okay?" I asked.

"Yeah," she breathed.

I felt relief. Flowers had said a little more than half an inch of steel could stop the beam. Scout had done good work. I had found myself thinking of the machine as a young girl, sacrificing herself to save one of the team. She was just a drone. But it was hard. This was a dangerous consequence of giving machines personalities. Easy to get attached.

With Scout gone, and Kathy exposed again, it was now or never time. I jumped around in front of the rock, a mere six meters from the aliens. No time for doubts. I just had time to react.

My assault shotgun came up. I pointed it at the alien holding the laser and pulled the trigger. This shotgun was probably effective at a range of no more than twenty meters. I was less than seven meters away. Hard to miss, even for me. The recoil knocked me back against the rock. It took me an instant to reacquire the target. When I did, I stared in shock. I guess the alien suits were not resistant to explosive shotgun shells. In fact, the shell was very effective.

The alien was literally blown apart. I watched the top half of the suit, with helmet still containing the head, sailing away in a slow arc.

It was rocket propelled. What was left of the guts were squirting out the bottom, instantly freezing into a disgusting jagged geyser of mangled Neanderthal insides.

The arm with hand still clutching the weapon, but disconnected from the torso, slowly drifted to the ground in the frail lunar gravity. The other Neanderthal next to the target was splattered with red gore, now crystallized in the vacuum. It was as stunned as I was.

But the alien standing in the doorway of the ship wasn't so impressed. It reacted fast, pulling its weapon free from its side.

"Bryan, get to cover. I could see your muzzle flash!" Kathy shouted.

Before I could move, the alien on the ship fired on me.

I was a hard target to make out in my black cape, but the gun stood out like a sore thumb. The barrel exploded in a shower of sparks. The laser blast hit the muzzle and melted the rock next to me.

I threw the now useless gun aside and dived behind the boulder.

At least I intended to dive.

The Moon's gravitational acceleration is one sixth that of Earth. It seemed to me that I merely drifted to the surface, the seconds seemed to tick by. It felt as though I was suspended in mid-leap. Actually, I don't know if it was the lunar acceleration, or the adrenaline, but it seemed to me that I had ample time to think about my potential miscalculation and meditate on how a second laser blast would vaporize my suit before I reached the cover of the rock.

Finally, I hit the ground, but the expected blast never came.

I poked my head up cautiously. The alien at the ship's airlock was in motion, but not under its own control. Its arms were limp at its side, back arched as it was jet propelled down the ramp by a dozen holes expelling suit gas and jets of instantly freezing blood.

Surprise! The antique grenades still worked, fifty years later, even in the cold vacuum of space.

There was still one live alien Neanderthal left to worry about, less than six meters away, and Kathy was still exposed. I stood up and pulled the .44 magnum from my hip holster. It was the most powerful weapon I had left. But could it penetrate one of their suits?

Leading with my gun, I jumped forward and pointed it at the last alien left alive.

I was surprised to find it standing there like an idiot. It apparently was having a hard time processing the series of disturbances on its quiet little moon base. I sympathized. First there had been a disturbance at its ship; then a flash to the side; then an explosion right next to it; then a flash at their ship. Its buddies were dead. And it was covered in red gore, including its faceplate.

I saw the alien reach up and wipe its helmet.

It seemed to collect itself. It turned toward me. I was a dark shadowy blob with silver arm and gun extended.

I waited for it to go for its laser weapon, but it didn't.

Instead, it glanced at what was left of its two companions and then warily across at me. Neanderthal and human faced each other on the surface of the Moon, neither of us moving. In just four seconds, the balance of power had momentarily shifted. Advantage, humans.

28

KATHY GLIDED OVER to stand next to me. I imagined that the remaining alien saw two ghost-like apparitions in front of it, spouting arms and weapons. For a full five seconds, we stood staring at each other.

"Kathy, grab its laser weapon, but don't get in my line of fire'"

"I don't want to go near him. You go," she said. Now that she'd killed her first alien, she was more herself.

"It's okay. If it moves, I'm going to shoot and it knows it."

"Fine," she said. Kathy moved forward, slow step by slow step. I could see the gaze of the Neanderthal following her vague shape, then darting back to me. My finger was tense on the trigger, but I did not move a muscle, even when Kathy reached over and pulled the laser hand weapon off the Neanderthal's belt.

It was smart enough to know it was outgunned. Though I was still a little nervous that more of its kind would be joining the party outside. I hoped the fact that their base seemed remote meant they weren't expecting visitors.

"It's the same kind of laser we picked up earlier tonight," Kathy noted, shoving it in her belt. Then her voice sounded a little horrified. "Do you realize what we've done? We just killed three aliens."

"Yeah, that makes five that I know of. But don't feel sorry for them. They've tried to kill us and would again. We'll need to get used to it, Kathy. This is war."

"No, I don't think I will ever get used to it."

I didn't respond. We didn't have time to get into discussion on the morality of killing when your back was against the wall and you were threatened. I wasn't even sure we'd find Michael alive, or if we'd still get out alive ourselves.

"Check out the airlock entrance. I'll stay here and cover this guy. Tell me what you see."

"The entranceway is clear. It's some kind of front room and then another door. This must be the airlock. There're a bunch of containers and cylinders in here. I'm moving over to the inner door."

"Watch yourself."

"I am. The airlock must be at least four meters long. They must expect to load in an army at a time."

There was silence for a moment, then she added: "There's a window in the inner door, but it's high up. It's over my head. I'm floating up to use the neck ring cameras."

"Don't let yourself be seen."

"I'm being as careful as I can, Bryan!" She sounded annoyed. Good. I needed her to be sharp.

I could hear her rapid breathing as she moved into view of the window. This was curious, as even the Neanderthals were not tall enough to peer through the window. Why did they design a window so high, I thought? All the while, I pinned our captive with the gun pointed dead center, neither of us moving as Kathy continued her inspection.

"Okay, I can just see in the window. It's an empty corridor. The corridor is awfully tall, maybe three meters and it's really bright. There are lights in the top corners of the ceiling and wall. Putting my astrophysicist hat on, I'd have to say that if these lights represent the native sun of these Neanderthals, they did not come from a G5 sun like ours. Their sun must be much hotter and brighter, maybe a G1 or F5."

"Any idea how to open the inner door?" I asked.

"We might be in luck. There's a panel next to the inside door. And it looks like this is a standard design feature. There's a similar panel near the outer door as well. I think we have our way in."

"We're coming in." I motioned toward the airlock entrance with my gun and the captive complied.

I kept my gun pointed at our prisoner and Kathy slapped the pad near the entrance. It quickly rotated back down and sealed with the floor. After it closed, the same intense lights out in the corridor came on in the airlock. We could now plainly hear the hiss of entering air and feel our suits deflate. When the suit was fully relaxed, Kathy tried the panel near the second door and it also opened.

We were in.

Slowly, our captive reached up to its helmet with its free hand and under my watchful eye, still pointing my gun, pushed a button on the side of its neck. The helmet quickly slid back into its suit. Just like the door, only in miniature. *A pretty neat trick*, I thought again.

Staring back at me was a very ugly specimen: stiff hair, recessed forehead, flat nose, protruding eyebrow ridges and more teeth than should fit in a mouth. Even being prepared, it was still a shock for me to be face to face with a creature that died off 50,000 years ago.

"Kathy, I'm willing to bet if our friend here can breathe the air, so can we. I'll go first. Cover him with your laser," I said over our radio link.

I unfastened the hood of the cape against the front of my suit and lifted it back. Then unzipped the clear plastic hood of my suit. The duct tape was still on and making a really good seal. I felt a little self-conscious. I didn't want this Neanderthal to think I picked up my suit from a secondhand-shop.

Our captive stood in silence, staring at the unveiling of who could have attacked its squad.

The alien looked bug-eyed when it finally got a good look at me. It took a step back, took a deep breath, and exploded in a deafening racket, its belly shaking with each convulsion.

I felt an instant rush of adrenaline and grabbed my gun, pointing at it with a shaking hand.

"Be quiet" I said, though I was pretty sure it didn't understand me.

The alien was oblivious and continued with its staccato roar. In seconds, with no follow-on threat, the initial rush of adrenaline faded and I realized, with irritation, what was going on.

The alien was laughing at me.

29

I COVERED IT with my gun while Kathy removed her hood and helmet. The alien immediately began speaking in the same cavernous, tonal language Kathy had played back from the transmissions between the ships.

She gave me a puzzled look and waved her hand in front of it to get it to shut up and pay attention to her. "Do you speak English?" Kathy asked, talking slowly and distinctly.

The response was the Neanderthal breaking out with its guttural laughter again.

This was our first face-to-face contact with a Neanderthal. We had just blown two of its partners away, in front of it, and a gun was pointed at the third and its reaction was to stand there openly laughing at us. I failed to see what was so funny.

"Humans," said the alien in barely understandable English, "Humans die soon. Go boom." Then it laughed again.

"Keep it down," I said, jabbing my gun toward it. "Or I'll shoot you to shut you up."

It stopped laughing but still looked highly entertained.

It would be good to get some basic answers, though I hadn't expected to be interrogating one. If you could call being laughed at an interrogation. "Why are you attacking us?"

"RocNor feast. KaBac life stones, mine!" the alien roared, clenching its fist in front for emphasis.

"What is RocNor or KaBac? What are life stones?" I asked.

Its response—stepping back and thumped its chest—made me jump. "KaBac," he stated, then laughed again. "You die. RocNor food. Life stones mine!"

Kathy had a look of supreme impatience on her face. "You are holding another human. Where is he?" she asked.

The captive glanced over at Kathy, looking her up and down and leered.

"I don't like the way it's looking at me," she said, stepping back toward the wall.

"Hey you!" I waved the gun at it and got its attention.

It snorted at Kathy and turned back to me.

"Where's the other human? Where are you holding him?" It folded its arms against its chest and stared back.

I pointed my 44 magnum at the alien's torso and pulled back the hammer, locking it in place. The click was the only sound in the airlock. The alien looked at the gun again. I repeated the command again, with as much threat as I could manage, "Show us! Or I'll shoot out your kneecaps."

The alien looked at me to see if I was bluffing.

I wasn't.

It blinked, lowered its arms, and turned to walk into the open corridor, still clutching the bag it had been carrying.

"Wait," I said to its back. It turned around and faced me.

"The bag," I motioned with my gun, "Show me what's in the bag."

"God, Bryan, we don't have time for this."

"I just want to make sure it's not something it can use against us."

"The bag," I said louder, sounding as mean and savage as I could. It was a stretch, but I could fake it.

"Mine! Not share. All mine."

I stared into its eyes and said, waving the gun in its face, "That will depend on how you behave in the next few minutes. Now show me what is in the bag."

It reached its other hand around and seemed to pull the strap apart. It opened into a circular hole, held rigid by a hoop that instantly snapped open. These aliens had some pretty advanced sealing technology. I made a note to try to take back a souvenir.

I got a quick look at the contents of the bag. "Holy crap," I said.

Kathy was standing behind me and I was blocking her view.

"What? What's in there?"

"Not what I expected at all. This doesn't make any sense. Why would they have these? What are they going to do with them?"

She shoved me aside to get a good look in the bag. The Neanderthal tried to pull the bag away from her, but one jerk of my gun barrel and it let go. I covered the alien while she did a little rummaging.

She reached into the bag and pulled out a handful to get a closer look.

"I don't understand. Some of these gems are worth a fortune. This looks like a diamond, a ruby and an emerald. But some of these are just common quartz crystals, a little raw and uncut, but you can find them in any thrift shop."

"And look," she pulled out a bowl-shaped rock that fit snuggly in her hand. "This is a geode that's been smashed open. It's filled with amethyst crystals. These creatures don't have any sense of value."

"Or we don't see the same value they do. KaBac," I said in my sternest command voice, "What are these for? Why do you have these gems and crystals?"

"Mine. My life stones. Mine."

"Tell me what you are doing with them and I will let you keep them." Kathy stepped to the side so as not to get in my line of fire.

The KaBac, willing to assert its ownership again, pulled the side handles of the bag together and the bag sealed up again as quickly as it opened. "Still raw. Sort later. Power life generator. Keep RocNor food fresh. Keep KaBac strong in ship. Heal battle scars."

"Kathy. Does any of this make sense to you?"

"It sounds too much like New Age talk of crystals having healing power."

"Maybe with a life generator, crystals do some kind of healing. Maybe all the new age crap about the power of crystals got started from something leaking out of some crystals. I don't even want to think about the part about keeping RocNor food fresh. Didn't this guy say something about RocNor feasting on humans?"

Kathy turned pale. "Let's figure this out after we get Michael."

I felt like we needed to know more, but a man's life was at stake. There would be time for more answers later. "Agreed. KaBac, lead us to the human prisoner you are holding."

"Sally, track our path and build a composite map. Keep the motion sensor alert active," I whispered. My black hood was flapping over my back and the rest of the poncho rested low enough that the six cameras around my neck ring had an unobstructed view. The clear helmet, loosely speaking, with its duct tape band aide, was unzipped and collapsed behind my neck. We cautiously walked down this alien corridor, the Neanderthal, at gunpoint, leading the way.

I didn't trust the alien. My alarm bells were ringing, but no better solution showed up. We followed the alien down the corridor. Our captive led us around two turns. At four meter intervals, doors were built into the walls; doors to what we had no idea and not enough time to investigate. I shivered. What were we leaving behind us?

This corridor ended in another door. To the right of this door was a small panel, five feet above the floor. The Neanderthal slowly reached up and pressed it. The door slid open and it casually walked in.

Two aliens, one armed with a laser dangling at its side, the other in animated conversation with the prisoner, stood at the foot of a table in the center of the large, open room. Strapped to it was a half-naked man, wrists bolted at his side.

Michael, I presumed.

I caught the tail end of the Neanderthal's last words. In very passible English, it was saying, "… retake what is our birthright." He pounded his balled fist against his chest.

Kathy stood frozen in shock. "No," she shouted.

The aliens looked over at us standing there.

The man rolled his head to his side to see the commotion in the doorway and groaned. But, in my split-second analysis, it wasn't so much in pain as disappointment.

His groan galvanized Kathy. In one instant, she had moved around me, into the room, running fast.

"Kathy, stay back. It's a trap," I shouted, reaching out to grab her.

She slipped through my fingers.

30

EVERYTHING EXPLODED. Our captive moved next, running to the side, shouting to its comrades.

I pulled the trigger of the .44 Magnum twice, as fast as I could, blasting twin holes in its back, even through its space suit. *Good to know.*

Blood and gore splattered the wall. The alien rocketed forward, falling face down and skidding along the floor. It didn't get up.

In my peripheral vision, I caught the motion of one of the aliens reaching for its laser. I swung my gun around and locked eyes with it as it began to raise the laser. It started to say something that sounded taunting in its tongue.

I didn't wait for it to finish. I pulled the trigger.

The gun clicked, but didn't fire.

Wait. That was only two shots. There were six in the barrel!

I pulled the trigger again and again, but only got clicks. The alien grinned and aimed his laser as I threw the worthless gun spun to my right, narrowly avoiding the laser blast that hit the wall behind me.

In the lighter gravity of the moon, it felt like I was going in slow motion. If all these lasers worked the same, I had a half a second before the recharge. Still twisting in midair, I drew the Glock from my left holster, reached out over my head, and, neck bent all the way back against the folded helmet, roughly aimed and pulled the trigger three times. Two blasts and two bullets, each one hitting the Neanderthal in the chest.

Its laser dropped to the floor.

All during this battle that lasted, in real time, no more than three seconds, the other alien Neanderthal, the one that spoke English so well, reached to the counter next to it and pulled out a small rectangular box with a knob on the outside. It twisted it over. Now Michael's scream was unmistakably from pain.

Around his neck was a solid metal rod bent in a perfect circle. It had two small orange balls positioned on opposite sides. They glowed faintly as Michael rocked his head from side to side.

Kathy was by Michael's side. The last standing Neanderthal looked at me, crouched as I was on the floor. I pointed my Glock at it. Its hand was poised over the knob, about ready to twist it, staring directly at me. It said in very clear English. "Stop, or I kill human."

"You stop, or I kill you!"

Its hand was now on the knob and moved slightly. Michael screamed. Then the alien turned the knob back and the screaming died to a moan. That was the demonstration. The alien's hand never left the knob.

I wondered if I could take him out before he twisted the knob again. I decided to distract him. "Why are you doing this! What do you want from us?"

"You die. All humans die. Then RocNor own you. KaBac," it said standing straighter. "Get everything. Life stones all ours."

"Who are the RocNor?"

"Masters of all. They feast on you. No more on KaBac." It paused, looking at me intently. "YonLen. They bring you here?"

"Who are the YonLen?"

"Not with you? Good!" And it rotated the knob again. Michael screamed.

It looked at me, looked at the dead colleague next to it laying in a spreading pool of blood and at the laser hand weapon fallen next to it on the floor.

"Let him go!" Kathy shouted at the alien.

The alien laughed. Damn things had a sick sense of humor. We locked eyes and I blinked. So, I pulled the trigger of my Glock. All I got was a click, all three times. Both guns had jammed after firing only a few rounds. In the back of my mind, I had been worried the cold vacuum of space might cause the gun lubricant to evaporate. My worst fear had come true. We faced our last standing adversary and we were out of weapons. And the alien knew it. It twisted the knob again. Judging from the groans and screams Michael was producing, the alien must have hit the excruciating pain setting. It was a feint; the alien lobbed the control box at me, and threw itself down to the floor to retrieve the laser from its dead companion.

With Michael's screams filling my ears, I watched the box coming at me in the light gravity. The alien floated to the floor, its hand reaching out for the laser. Did time slow down, or was it the low gravity?

I threw my useless Glock at the alien. It passed the control box, still in midair, and bounced harmlessly off the alien's side.

The box was almost to me. If I went after the alien, Michael would surely die. If I stayed in place, I might be able to grab the box and turn it off, before I was taken out by a laser blast surely to follow.

 It would be close.

I had to make a split second decision. Michael was screaming, his deep voice, echoing inside the smooth walls of the cell. My heart won the debate. I reached for the box and plucked it out of the air. The alien reached the floor and the fallen weapon.

I just had time to rotate the knob in the opposite direction. I felt it reach a stop, but I kept up the pressure. Then it clicked. The screaming stopped and I saw the dull orange glow fade as the collar separated at the small spheres.

My momentary relief was instantly overshadowed by a new fear. This was the fourth time in just about as many hours that I stared down the wide open barrel of one of a high power laser. I just saw the alien's curling lip and that mass of teeth when I was blinded by a flash.

"Take that, you bastard," Kathy shouted.

I blinked, surprised to be alive. She was holding the laser weapon she had taken from the first captive, still pointing at the alien she'd just drilled a hole through.

I'd high-five her later. Right now, I had to breathe.

Kathy leaned over Michael, gripping his shoulders. His eyes were closed but he was alive.

"Michael, Michael, are you alright? Can you move? We've come to rescue you. Let's get you home."

I rushed over to the table to see if I could help, but stopped short when I had a clear look at him. The guy Kathy seemed so attached to looked eighty years old, with bushy, silver eyebrows, wrinkled skin and gray, thinning, hair. Had the alien torture device somehow aged him?

Kathy, to her credit, seemed to overlook all that, because she was gazing at him with obvious affection. I had to give her credit for being such a strong woman. She was unfazed at his shocking appearance.

I looked around the room for something we could cart Michael out on. Who knew when the next wave of captors would come?

Michael took one more deep breath and opened his eyes to stare up at Kathy, giving me another start. "You shouldn't be here. It's not safe at all for you."

"We just shot our way past a half dozen Neanderthals. Of course it's not safe," said Kathy, handing me the laser while she talked. "But we made it this far to rescue you." She sounded kind of petulant, at that last bit, like she was trying to score extra credit and had been denied.

"You don't understand," said Michael. "If they capture you, it will not be pleasant."

I snorted. Like we didn't know that.

He looked over at me. "I don't know who you are, but you will not let her be captured. Do you hear me? You will do whatever it takes to protect her." It wasn't a request. It wasn't a suggestion, it was an order given by someone who didn't question his own authority.

I had to admire the guy, he was lying helpless, strapped down on the table, half naked, having been prematurely aged, and he was giving orders. Plus he clearly had Kathy's best interests at heart. He continued, "If she is captured by these creatures, she will suffer a fate far worse than death. Do you understand, young man?"

She's done pretty well for herself so far, I wanted to say, but it didn't feel like the time to make jokes. Sometimes, when I'm nervous, I make jokes. And I was past hysterically afraid by now. And we needed to get out of here. Besides, this guy had an intensity and a presence that affected me. So I said, "Yes, I understand. I promise; you have my word."

He visibly relaxed, a new smile spread, flowing along well-worn laugh lines permanently sketched by the wrinkles around his mouth and eyes. He was recovering well from torture, I noted.

Kathy reached down and hugged him. His arms were still bolted to his side so he was unable to return it. He could just lay there as Kathy sobbed in relief over his chest.

He glanced over at me. "I don't recognize you, but thank you for watching over my dear friend." Still looking right at me, he added. "And I will hold you to your promise."

We needed to move, but he was giving a speech, and I felt obligated to play along. I motioned to the dead alien on the floor and said, "She didn't need that much watching over if you ask me."

"Yes, she can be a handful now and then. Let this be a lesson for you young man, you don't want to be on her bad side." Michael winked at me, and Kathy pulled back up and smiled down at him.

"You must be feeling okay, you old fossil!"

Well, I thought, she really cut to the chase.

"I could use some assistance. This is a bit of an undignified position for a professor emeritus! You won't ever tell any of my students about this will you?"

With sense of embarrassment, I realized Michael had aged the old fashion way; no torture needed.

I walked to the doorway and glanced out into the corridor, then paced back to the table. "Can we move this along?" I said.

Kathy was fiddling with the devices that strapped Michael to the table. "Give me a moment," she said.

While Kathy worked on his bonds, the old man rattled on: "I am remarkably okay. The pain is completely gone. Their device seems to be some sort of neural pain stimulator. I feel absolutely no after affects, but my gosh, did it hurt when it was on. I haven't been in such pain since I published my second paper and had to retract it a year later…two simple arithmetic mistakes."

"We can catch up in the ship," I said.

"Let's get you out of there," Kathy said gently, finally figuring out how to spring the latches.

"I've got this," he said, and swung his legs off the table. His knees buckled. I caught him by the arm and helped him stand.

"Okay," I said, back in command. "We have to get out of here as fast as we can. Michael, are you going to be able to walk out of here?"

Michael grimaced when he put even his feeble Moon gravity weight on his right leg. "You obviously haven't been in the program very long, have you, my boy? A man my age doesn't have to walk when he can ride, if you can find me my suit."

"Michael, this is Bryan. He just joined Sciquest a few hours ago."

"Indeed." He looked me up and down. I felt embarrassed being evaluated so directly. "These must be extraordinary times, or you must be an extraordinary young man. Considering where you are standing, I suspect a little of both, perhaps." One of those bushy eyebrows raised up a good inch as he looked over at me, some measure of respect showing in his eyes.

"It's a long story," I said. "I can tell you on the way home. First we have to get back to the ship."

"My suit is in the corner. Can you retrieve it, Bryan? And my glasses, I see, are still in one piece."

I followed the pointing arm and even before I reached it, realized the suit was worthless. I held it up, showing off the slits torn in the arms and legs.

"Oh my. This presents a bit of a problem," Michael said, with one glance.

"Murphy's Law, old man," Kathy said. "We brought back-up." She twisted around and pulled the spare suit out of her backpack.

I handed over the glasses. They had been tossed on top of the suit. The aliens apparently never suspected their true function.

Michael put the glasses back on and smiled as he looked at Kathy and me. "I'm so delighted to have James back. Did you miss me too, James?"

We couldn't hear the response but it clearly was positive as Michael chuckled to himself.

He stepped into the legs and then the torso unit of the new suit. He paused and said, "Bryan, we can't let my old suit fall into their hands. It has too much of our technology in it."

"I'll take care of it. You finish getting suited up, then we're out of here."

I was feeling jittery, wondering when we'd have company. I reached down and grabbed the second laser weapon from beneath the dead alien. Holding one in each hand, I practiced reaching the buttons with one hand, then proceeded to turn the suit into molten fragments as it lay in the corner. I aimed for the shoulder thruster pods and the front console that held the Casimir batteries. It also left me confident that I could fire these weapons without hesitation. Might as well take some souvenirs.

"Where are the reinforcements?" I asked. "They've had five minutes to check out the commotion in this cell."

"They are probably in the other domes. After they caught me, they pulled me in this room, stripped off my suit and tied me to the table. There were at least seven of them here. The one holding the box, the master torturer, had a shouting match with the others and pushed them out. I guess he wanted all the fun for himself."

"What did they want?" Kathy asked.

"Why of course, they wanted to know how I got to the Moon. I was a bit of a surprise to them. I don't think they are used to human visitors. I had to stall them as long as I could, while I learned as much as I could from my interrogation."

"You mean their interrogation," I said.

He looked at me a moment, his head cocked at a slight angle. I couldn't tell if he was pausing for dramatic effect or was trying to think about what he would say.

"You can own any interrogation if you know how to manipulate the conversation. And I am a master. In the first minute I learned they are arrogant, egotistical, and incredibly insecure. It was a simple matter of feeding them what they wanted to hear, leading them on and letting them fill in the rest for me." He closed his eyes and drew in a deep breath. "And the picture I have about our visitors is not a very pleasant one. But we must hurry. There is much to pass along to headquarters and plan how we will extricate ourselves from their growing stranglehold."

Michael struggled with the seals of the new suit. I watched him for a moment, wanting to help but knowing my help wasn't welcome. "What did you tell them?" I finally asked.

"About what?"

"About how you got to the moon. What explanation did you give them to stall them and get information from them?"

"Have you ever read Cyrano de Bergerac?"

I shook my head. I saw Kathy just smile, then release a brief laugh. She apparently had and realized what was coming.

Michael finished putting his suit on, reaching around to make sure the clear hood was positioned for easy access. "It's a famous play by Rostand, a masterful 19th century French playwright. Cyrano was faced with this same dilemma once. He jumped down from a tree he was hiding in and had to stall a rival suitor to give his friend some additional time in which to marry a certain young maiden. The man asked him where he had come from. He said, the Moon. The man said how could you possibly have been to the Moon?"

Michael checked all the joints in the suit. He was now ready, except for the helmet. He smiled over at me. I really just wanted to leave the confines of the cell.

"Can you think of six ways?" Michael asked, in full professor mode.

"Michael, I'll have to stay in suspense until we get to the ship. Time to leave Dodge," I responded, and gently nudged Michael ahead. He sat back on his seat and floated a foot off the ground.

With Michael floating behind me and Kathy taking up the rear, I led our group of humans down the corridor, following the yellow path Sally painted for me.

We almost made it to the airlock undetected.

31

THE INNER DOOR of the airlock was closed. This could only mean the outer door was letting someone else in. We were in the middle of a featureless, brightly lit corridor, with nowhere to hide.

"Quick, back around the corner. We have visitors coming in."

I was pushing the group from the rear. Before we turned the corridor, I pointed my laser weapon at the ceiling and shot out the overhead lights running up and down the hallway, darkening the corridor.

I peered around the corner to see the inner door open and two Neanderthals walk in. The leading one had its laser weapon drawn; the trailing alien carried one of those bags in each hand. More life stones, I figured.

It was going to be like shooting fish in a barrel and, after our experiences tonight, I wasn't feeling guilty at all about taking every advantage I could. I aimed the laser around the corner and pushed the top button with my thumb. My other two fingers were wrapped tightly around the barrel, barely reaching the two arming buttons on the side.

The high-pitched blast echoed down the corridor, channeled by the smooth walls. I saw the bright flash, the spray of sparks from the front of the space suit as the lead alien exploded. Maybe the front of their suits was less shielded than the back, or the beam was too weak to penetrate the back of the suit.

Regardless, the laser beam penetrated the suit and vaporized the Neanderthal in a cloud of guts and gore, superheating it into a plasma cloud that burst out the front hole, the neck ring, the gloves and every other weak link in the suit. The shock wave built up inside the confines of the suit echoed up and down the length of the alien, turning all soft tissue to liquid. This sort of squirted out the suit in every direction, splattering the walls with red and black vapor. If I wasn't so pissed at these aliens maybe I'd feel sorry for what I had done, but I only felt an instant of disgust, followed by relief. One less bad guy. But the second Neanderthal was left standing, literally holding the bags.

I jumped around the corridor and shouted: "Stop, don't move!"

The alien looked down at its companion, around the walls at what was left of its guts, then at me. While it held the bags, it couldn't very easily reach for a weapon. It had the sense not to laugh.

"It's okay, I have it under control, come on out."

"What do we do with it?" Kathy said.

"I'm betting it came from one of the ships and it may just be our ticket out of here."

"I don't think a hostage will really be of much value to us," Michael offered. "They don't seem terribly compassionate about each other, from what little I could tell."

"That's not exactly what I had in mind," I said.

"What do you have in mind?" Kathy asked.

"We need a diversion so we can get out of here and not be followed, and he's going to provide it."

"You're still not making sense," she replied.

"We're running out of time. Kathy, you and the professor are going to make a beeline back to the ship, staying in the shadows. He's going to be wearing my cape. Our friend here and I are going for a little ride. Now, let's move out."

With a protesting Kathy behind me, I motioned the alien ahead and back into the airlock. "Wait," Michael said, "this is a golden opportunity. Don't you want to know what he has in his bags?"

"We know. Gems and crystals," I said.

"That fits. The KaBac have some sort of generator that produces a distortion field from crystals. Some crystals seem to store some sort of energy that is released by this distortion field. They use it to heal wounds, eliminate pain and seemingly prolong life."

"Any crystals?"

"From what I got from the KaBac working on me, every crystal has some of this stored energy. But some more than others. The longer they took to form, the more the stored energy. I was hoping to trade it a twelve-inch diameter, three meter long single-crystal silicon boule, but they said if it was grown in less than a thousand years, it was worthless."

"You really did learn a lot."

"My boy, this was just part of the good news. There is far worse."

"Later. Time to leave before more of these guys arrive."

"Maybe I should take one of these bags with me?" Kathy said.

When she moved to grab a bag from the Neanderthal's hand and it was obvious her intent, the alien, still under our guard, gave a mournful groan, sort of like a tiger's bellow, high pitches, going to low pitches. It pulled its arms closer to its side as though to protect its bags. It was clearly agitated.

"On second thought, hold off. Our friend here is concerned."

Kathy backed off and I let the alien hold the bags. I had Kathy reach down to the dead Neanderthal and grab his laser weapon. Now there were two lasers trained on our hostage from opposite sides of the corridor.

"I recommend we let him open one of the bags for us, just to check. I think it will be alright," Michael said.

"At the slightest risk we shoot him," I said.

"No! No!" the alien bellowed out.

"So you do understand us," I said

"No shoot. Mine. Mine."

"Open it. Show us. If you threaten us, we will kill you," I said.

The alien lowered both bags to the floor. It picked up one bag with both hands and hugged it to its chest, repeating, "Mine! Mine!"

"Open it. Now!"

Slowly, the alien grabbed the bag from the two handles on top and did something to them. The handle twisted, rotating and a seam appeared in the top of the otherwise smooth surface. The alien gripped the two edges and opened it wide.

"Oh my, how lovely," Michael said from his vantage point, closest to the bag. "We seem to have a jewelry thief in our mists."

"Move back, against the wall," I motioned with my laser for emphasis to the alien. I walked over and peered into the bag. I reached in and pulled out a handful of rings, bracelets, necklaces, and individual stones. It was a pirate's treasure, a king's ransom, a fortune in precious stones and jewelry.

As I dipped my hand in the bag, the alien, pinned against the wall with the threat of Kathy's laser, just gave that mournful cry again. "Lifestones. Mine!" it said again.

"I'm not going to take your lifestones. I'll let you keep them, if you take me for a ride. If you won't, I'll turn them back into their native elements and melt them into a slag heap. Then I'll burn your arms and legs off and leave you here for your friends to find. Which shall it be?"

That mournful cry again, then the alien said in a low voice, "Ride."

"Pick up your bags and lead me to your ship."

"Bryan, what are you doing, you can't go back to earth with this alien. They'll follow you in the other ships and blow you out of the sky."

"That's the idea. But don't worry. I don't plan to be around when it happens."

32

MICHAEL RAISED HIS eyebrows but he didn't argue with me. He gently tugged Kathy by the arm. "Come along, Kathy. Bryan is going to create a diversion for us. Do please send along rendezvous instructions when you have a clear idea. You've come this far, we wouldn't want you to miss your ride home."

Kathy looked at me with a quizzical expression on her face. "Kathy, you and Michael head back to the ship, get out of here. Stay low to the surface. I'll have Sally send you coordinates when I'm ready. Get at least two hundred klicks away and stay hidden in the shadows somewhere. Now get your helmets zipped up and get out of here!"

I reached one handed to grab the zipper on my neck seal, when Kathy said, "Wait!" She shrugged off Michael's grip and stepped over to me and looked at me with those eyes, those wide open, innocent green eyes. Then she reached up and kissed me on the lips. I just stood there in shock, alien laser weapon in one hand, while the Neanderthal and Michael watched.

She pulled away and said, "Don't you dare screw this up! You're coming back with us." As Michael walked by, he winked at me. I was pleasantly shocked.

With a touch of a button on the side of its neck, the alien's helmet was in place. The outer door opened and we were back on the surface of the Moon. With their black ponchos on, Kathy and Michael looked like two shimmering blobs with silver feet sticking out the bottom, floating a foot above the ground. They shot out across the plains to the closest rock formation and disappeared among the jagged shadows of the craters. They were gone.

The alien stood in front of me, clutching its bags tight to its chest with both arms. I none-too-gently jabbed it in the back with my laser, prodding it forward. We followed the trail the first aliens took, passing the remains of the two dead ones still lying along the path. But then the alien turned to the left, to the second ship that had a ramp extended.

Sally said there was motion behind me, so I paused. The outer airlock door closed by itself; company coming. I turned and fired a shot at where I had seen the touch panel that had opened the outer airlock, hoping to damage the mechanism and slow down the pursuit. My shot hit the outside of the dome surface but had no visible effect. There was a faint splash of sparks, but no residual mark. Whatever the dome was made of, it was pretty impervious to these lasers.

I prodded my hostage in the back to hurry along. We rushed to the other ship, up the ramp and into the ship's airlock. I could look in the window of the inner door. I saw a one-room cabin, with two chairs in front of a console and four chairs arrayed in a square behind. Otherwise, it was empty. This could have been one of the interiors shown in the video Kathy had recorded on her trip back to Earth.

The KaBac and I easily fit in the airlock. The alien, still tightly clutching its bags, pushed a side panel with its elbow and the outer door closed. I felt my suit deflate and the inner door opened. I was inside the alien ship. The alien placed the bags in a small bin to the side of the airlock and pushed a patch on the side of its helmet. The helmet folded back seamlessly into the neck ring.

I unzipped my helmet and folded it back so I could communicate. I was feeling a little self-conscious of the duct tape. Here was this gross, massive, uncivilized Neanderthal with this advanced helmet that instantly appeared from the neck collar and then disappeared with an invisible seal and I had a plastic cap for a helmet held together with duct tape.

The alien took the first seat, I settled in the second chair. They were very similar to the chairs in the video feed, only now they were in a vertical position, sitting upright. It was big for me. As the alien began to fasten its straps, I shouted at him to stop. I figured if the alien wasn't belted in, it might act as a governor on how rough a ride I had ahead. I glanced at the overly long straps and decided to just tie the waist belt with a knot, rather than try to figure out the latching mechanism, one handed.

Now what? The front screens were blank. I had no idea what was going on outside the ship. I sat with the laser weapon leaning on the arm rest, pointed at the alien. My left hand held the barrel, my right hand on the trigger buttons. The alien pilot glanced over, waiting.

"Turn on the screens. I want to see outside the ship." The alien stared back, unmoving. I bounced the laser against the arm rest for emphasis and pointed to the three black screens, each a meter on a side above the control panel. The alien adjusted a button on the arm rest and all three came alive. It was like a transparent window, but the views were not contiguous. In the screen on the right, I could see the dome's airlock and the door now opening up again. The other screens showed the lunar landscape with four vessels visible ahead, still on the ground.

"Raise the ship, slowly, then move it ahead. Go slow or I will blow your arms off."

I watched carefully as the alien touched a depression on the side of the chair and a stick popped up on the end of the arm rest. Of course, I thought, under acceleration, it would be difficult to reach the control panel, so all the flight controls must be in easy reach of hands resting on the arm rest.

I watched as the alien manipulated two buttons and then the stick. The scene outside showed the ground dropping away. I could feel the acceleration. A flick of the stick and the alien craft moved ahead, the ground shifting by in the screen above.

The alien glanced over at me, then pushed the lever forward, a lot. The ship accelerated, a lot. I was pushed back into my seat with a crushing weight. My left hand still held the laser by the barrel, leaning it against the arm rest, but my right hand, hovering over the trigger buttons, was jerked off the laser and pinned against my side. My fingers were only inches away from the trigger buttons, but it could as well have been a mile. Nearing five gees, my hand felt like it weighed more than a hundred pounds. I had fallen for the oldest trick in the book. Easy pickings.

33

EVEN THOUGH THE alien was also straining under the acceleration, it was a lot stronger than I was. It was using the acceleration to its advantage, keeping me immobile in my seat so it could reach the barrel of the laser. Its long arm reached across the two chairs. Inches separated it from the front of the barrel. I was grunting with the strain, my breathing labored. I had to move my right hand to the trigger buttons. My eyes flitted up to the screen. We were still close to the ground, and there was a mountain range coming at us. We weren't going to clear it, unless the alien took back the laser and shot me. One way or another, I was screwed.

The fingers on my right hand slowly crawled their way over my chest plate, dragging the impossible weight of my arm. I was using the ridges of the narrow water tanks lining my chest plate as finger holds. My hand felt like it was encased in a hundred-pound lead glove. I crunched my teeth and dug deep down for every inch.

The alien's hand was almost touching the barrel. I jerked it back a few precious inches.

This gained me maybe a few more seconds, but more importantly, brought my right hand in contact with the barrel. I inched my right hand up the end, one more inch. Finally, I was there; my right fingers were over the trigger buttons. Only the tip of the laser was resting on the arm rest. The tail end was pushing into the chest plate of my suit. I couldn't leverage it up to point at the alien.

The mountains at the lip of this crater were getting closer, faster. With only seconds left, I pushed the trigger, firing at whatever I could hit.

The blast shot a fountain of sparks into the cabin, and a basketball size region of the cabin wall to the left of the monitors turned white hot. A cloud of black smoke billowed outward, obscuring the impact spot. Before it could spread very far, the smoke was sucked backward, out through a pinhole hole created when the very center of the molten hull metal ruptured into space. The cabin air howled out as it rushed through that tiny hole.

The blast affected our acceleration and trajectory. Both slackened slightly and now we were pointed near the peaks of the crater, not so much dead center to the mountain wall. With lower acceleration, the alien was able to reach up and grip the end of the barrel. The race for each inch of the laser ended in a tie. Now it was a tug of war.

He won, pulling the laser free from my right hand. My left hand still gripped it tenuously.

My breath came in ragged jerks, the air thinning, the strain catching up with me. My gaze darted between the rushing mountain peaks and laser barrel being dragged through my left hand. As hard as I gripped it, the alien's pull was relentless. I was breathing harder. The pressure was getting dangerously low. We were almost at the mountains. The ridgeline was separating into individual peaks. I was panting, tunnel vision was limiting my view. All I saw were the jagged edges of the crater rim wall. We were going to impact any second. The trigger buttons were slipping through the fingers of my left hand.

I gulped one last breath and held it, straining to move the fingers of my left hand ever so slightly. As the alien pulled the remaining inches of the laser out of my grip, the trigger buttons were pulled under my fingers and the laser fired.

The alien's shoulder was immediately vaporized by the laser blast. Its arm, with hand still gripping the laser, was thrown to the back of the cabin by the four gees of acceleration. Blood shot out of the stump where the shoulder ended, the high acceleration acting like a pump to squirt it full force. The alien bled to death in less than a second.

The throttle was free. As quickly as the acceleration had turned on, it completely stopped. I felt only the light tug of the lunar gravity as the ship continued to shoot along the surface, a second away from the mountain peak that now filled the central monitor.

I felt my eyes bulging out in the near vacuum. It was a race. Which would kill me first, the lack of air, or the impending collision with the crater rim? I was leaning toward the rim. Gasping for what might be my last breath, I reached to the side of the chair and felt for the button I had seen the Neanderthal touch. I pressed the control button on my arm rest and a stick popped up. I was close enough to the jagged ridge of the crater wall to see individual rocks resting precariously on a ledge.

One of the buttons on the side controlled vertical motion. Which one was it? I slid my finger along the side of the arm rest and felt a depression. I pushed it and felt the ship lurch lower. I was about to skim the rocks below. Immediately, I probed higher and found the other depression. Pressing it, I felt a stronger gravity and saw the lunar landscape fall away beneath him. I stabbed it again and again, trying to go up faster. I wasn't going to make it over the crater rim ahead.

I grabbed the stick and pulled back slowly, feeling myself pushing against the strap across my stomach. There was a gap in the mountains to the right. I tried moving the stick to the right and the view out the front window shifted. It was like threading a needle. All I saw now was the gap. Flashing stars obscured my vision everywhere else. Was it really a gap or the last of my vision fading?

Accelerating up and decelerating forward as fast as I could stand was giving me just that extra edge to clumsily steer through the gap in the mountain range. I was through!

Suddenly, there was an intense ringing in my ears. Either it was a lot louder than the whistling of the cabin air, or the air was finally gone, too tenuous to carry the sound. I couldn't breathe anymore, the lights in the cabin around me were off. Now the pounding in my head and the needles of pain in my eyes and ears took center stage.

I let go the controls and reached back to grab the hood of my helmet and pulled it up and over. I could feel the air blowing in from the hose vent under my chin. The electrolysis engine was probably going full blast. It helped. I fumbled with the zipper through my gloves. *The zipper!*

I had to fasten the zipper.

I felt around the right side of my neck. I couldn't grab the tab. But there was a cord hanging down, for just such an emergency. I gripped it and with my last ounce of strength pulled it across my neck, like slitting my own throat.

My suit immediately puffed up and the pain in my ears quieted down. I could hear the life-giving oxygen flow back in. My head was clearing, the adrenaline was slowly dissipating. My vision cleared and I took stock of the cabin.

I experimented with the knobs and stick and pieced together the up-down, left-right, accelerate-decelerate controls. Now to get on with the mission.

With the limp form of the dead alien hanging in the seat next to me, I headed back to the lunar base, coming in from an altitude of at least five kilometers. The four ships I had seen around the airlock were now hovering off the lunar surface, slowly moving, apparently searching for the intruders, me. I came down fast, decelerating too slowly and hitting the dome. I felt the vibration through the chair as the bottom of my saucer crashed down. I was violently jarred around, but the improvised seat belt kept me from bouncing out of the chair.

I accelerated up and headed toward the nearest ship. My antics were attracting attention. I saw the pattern of motion of all four ships change. They all converged on me. I headed right for the nearest ship, accelerating as fast as I could stand. It tried to veer out of the way, but I compensated.

It was almost enough.

As I shot by, I felt another jarring concussion in the chair and was thrown to the right. I was getting tired of this game of bumper-cars, and wasn't sure how much more my hijacked ship could withstand.

The ship I had just hit apparently did not take kindly to this tap. I saw in the center screen a saucer with a dent in the side pull back and a black square appear in the very top. A squat tube at least a meter and a half long and possibly a meter in diameter popped out of the hole and pointed in my direction. I pushed the button to accelerate up just as I saw a brief glow from the tube.

The right side of my ship exploded, taking the last bit of cabin atmosphere with it.

I wasn't sure my adrenaline could get any more jacked up. I looked over. The hole was almost two meters in diameter. The edge was cooling, fading from white to yellow to red as I watched. It didn't melt, it just evaporated, leaving a sharp-edged gash. The lunar surface came into focus through the hole, dropping off below and in the distance.

I pushed the stick forward and shot away from the four saucers, heading in the opposite direction from where I told Kathy to meet up with me. These Neanderthals were a lot better at flying than I was.

I was skimming the surface of the Moon, popping up to get over the next mountain range. But the other four caught up and flew formation, matching my jogs. I looked across at them. Now I had four barrels pointing at me.

They hadn't fired again; they were probably still trying to figure out what was going on, or maybe they knew about the bags of lifestones and wanted to collect them. Maybe I could use this. *Time for an exit plan*, I told myself.

When I estimated I had traveled ten klicks from the base, I popped the ship straight up, with the highest acceleration I could stand. For ten seconds, I grunted with the pressure, forcing my chest to expand out and take another breath. Then I pulled the stick back to neutral and coasted. I was weightless, in free fall. By rotating the stick, I could rotate the ship. I swung it around so I could see the other four ships in the central view screen.

These high gee maneuvers were not my idea of fun. I don't like roller coaster rides, whether as passenger or as pilot. I definitely did not have fighter jock genes in me.

The enemy ships were pinpricks against the surface, but coming at me, visibly getting larger.

Turning the alien craft upside down, I headed back toward the onrushing pursuers and adjusted the stick to give what felt like about a quarter of a gee of acceleration.

Accelerating toward the four alien ships, with a collision imminent, I untied the belt holding me in the chair and used it to steady myself on the deck. The two bags had rolled to the side of the cabin, near the airlock. I hopped over and picked them up by the handles. I saw the square pad near the side of the airlock door and pressed it.

Nothing happened.

Crap. The inside airlock door wouldn't open. Either I wasn't doing something right or it was damaged. I was stuck in the cabin, rushing toward the surface and toward four alien craft in pursuit.

There was only one option.

Using the chairs as handholds, I danced around to the side of the cabin next to the razor sharp hole. I tried to stay away from the edges, fearful of it ripping my suit, however easy it was to repair.

I opened the first bag and grabbed handfuls of the gems and bracelets and threw them out the gap. I saw the four ships zip by me. I shook the whole bag against the bottom of the hole, emptying it. I grabbed the second one, opened it and just stuck it out the hole, shaking its contents into space. I left a king's ransom worth of gems in my wake.

I looked down through the hole in the cabin and saw three of the ships break formation and trail after the gems. Partial success.

The forth one, with the dent, stayed after me.

We both accelerated straight down to the lunar surface. I was doing the mental math for the impact time, then kicked myself and just shouted, "Sally, estimated time to impact?"

"Bryan, ship will impact in four seconds."

I was cutting it too close. My stomach and inner ear disagreed about where up and down were. I tried to use my eyes to cast the dissenting vote, but the price of nausea was too great, and only closing my eyes kept my late dinner down. I knew my feet were pointed toward space, and my head was toward the on rushing lunar surface. I saw the stars below my boots. This wasn't a synthesized image. I looked up. Big mistake. The ground was coming up fast. Two seconds.

I couldn't tell which way I was going to fall when I jumped, but I knew I was going to fall. I had to open my eyes. I couldn't risk an accidental rip in my suit from the sharp edge of the exposed hull. Just beyond the toes of my boots, the icy bright diamonds of stars glittered across the velvety black of space.

I gripped the edge carefully and inched my boots to hang over the gap, into space. I had already run out of time, I had to jump. Even the pure oxygen I was breathing wasn't enough to keep me from hyperventilating. This was why I hated flying. It wasn't the flying, it was the thought of falling and going splat.

I had to jump. I had to let go. Kathy, and Michael and my future were waiting for me. I had to get back home to save the Earth. Each breath brought the ground and the alien ship closer.

I took a deep breath, held it, then I pushed out of the hole.

The ship continued accelerating away from me, toward the surface.

I was left in free fall, but that asymmetric launch now had me spinning. The universe rotated around me; the stars, the surface, the sun, the stars, the surface… I had to shut my eyes again to hold off the nausea.

"Sally, stabilize me, quickly. Stop my descent."

"Yes Bryan."

I felt a few tugs, like someone holding onto my shoulders and spinning me around. Then a much stronger tug on my shoulders and I was pulled violently upward by the swing I found myself dangling from. If my butt hadn't been in the built-in seat, I'd have been singing soprano. It sort of felt what I imaged a parachute opening would feel like.

When I cracked my eyes open, the horizon was mercifully steady. I was almost at the surface, but steadily decelerating. I was going to hit. I felt a stronger pull upward from the shoulder-mounted propulsion pods and my feet touched the surface with an impact I could absorb through my knees.

In that instant of contact, I felt the ground shudder and saw a billowing cloud of dust slowly rising from the surface, less than a kilometer away. The first ship I commanded was history. I saw the other ship circling the impact crater.

"Sally, move me away from this spot and into the shadows, now!"

Pulled along by my shoulder thruster pods, I was now moving horizontal. At the very limit to my visibility, I saw the other three ships, as small dots, join their companion, abandoning the vigil over the crash site and head back to the lunar base. I waited for them to move out of sight.

I sat back in the built in seat and let Sally do the driving. I had confidence in her abilities. I caught myself and smiled. It was "her" abilities, now. With the aliens gone from the scene, it was time to rendezvous with my teammates.

"Sally, plot me a course to Kathy and Michael's ship, shortest distance that keeps me in shadows and far away from the alien base. I want to stay two meters off the ground and keep my speed under ten meters per second."

"Bryan, plot is completed. Ready to execute."

"Send an encoded message to Kathy, I'm on my way, leave the light on. Engage."

34

IN A LITTLE over an hour, all three of us were safely on our way back home to Earth, already at turn over.

"Okay, I give," I said at last. The adrenaline had worn off, I was sitting comfortably in one of the seats in the main cabin, across from Michael. Kathy was in the cockpit, door open, chair swiveled around to face us. We were all sipping from bottles of water taken from the emergency supplies. We were past turn-over, so the cabin floor was facing Earth and the Moon was above us. So far, our getaway had been unobserved. It looked like smooth sailing until we landed in San Jose.

"About what, my boy?" Michael said. He leaned back in his chair, one arm loosely resting on the arm rest, the other, holding the bottle, which he waved in friendly acknowledgment to me.

"How did you stall them about how you had gotten to the moon? You said you told them six possible ways."

"An old colleague of mine, a physics professor at MIT, used to say, any physicist can come up with an explanation for something, but a really good physicist should be able to come up with at least three possible explanations."

"Rostand, the author of Cyrano de Bergerac, was both an extraordinary man of science and a man of letters. I suppose he felt obligated to come up with three explanations from each of his worlds, for a total of six possible explanations."

"Okay, so what were they?"

Michael looked at me, then at Kathy. We were both waiting for him. He smiled, the crinkles around his lips and eyes announcing how happy he was in his element; a classroom of attentive students hanging on his every word.

"Understand now, I was merely plagiarizing Cyrano. He is the one with these lines. I told them, first, I had anointed myself with the morning dew and when the sun came up and the moon was setting, when the dew rose in the air, I rose with it, to the moon."

"It seemed to puzzle them. They heard the words, but I don't think they understood what I was talking about. They must have thought they lost something in the translation. The one that held the torture box when you came in, he was the one doing the questioning. He told me if I did not answer their questions, he would torture me. I was shackled to the table. He got very close to me, I could smell his fetid breath. I believed he meant it. I did not think I would do well with torture. It was a very effective job of intimidation. But I've been through worse."

"You have?" I asked.

Michael smiled at me. "You've never been to a faculty meeting with 300 prima donnas, all intent to be correct and to have the other 299 know it, have you? At least I thought this interrogation would be mercifully short, compared to a five-hour, drawn-out faculty meeting." He chuckled.

"So then what happened?" I prompted.

"I gave them the second way. To quote Cyrano, 'To generate wind--for my impetus--To rarefy air, in a cedar case, by mirrors placed icosahedrons-wise.'"

I just stared back, waiting for the explanation. When Michael continued to stare back, clearly finished, I finally said, "What the hell does that mean?"

"I haven't the foggiest, but it sounds so good. This had them puzzling for a good five minutes. They talked back and forth among themselves. That's when they obviously came to a decision."

"There was a bag in the corner of the room, one of them had brought in after I was tied up. It was filled with those collars. They seemed to have a few different sizes. The first one they pulled out, I could see was much too large for me. Then they pulled out a smaller one.

"I don't believe I was the first human to have worn one of these torture collars. It had me wondering just how long they have been in our midst and what their plans may include."

"One of them slipped the collar around my neck and gave me a demonstration of the ring. The pain I felt was like a burn inside my head. It seemed to do no permanent damage and I was not harmed physically. As a torture device, it was very effective."

"You poor dear. I am so sorry we weren't able to get to you sooner," Kathy said.

He paused and seemed to be unsure of what to say. Finally, almost apologetically, he said, "I don't mean to sound at all ungrateful but if you had waited just a few more minutes I might have been able to find out exactly what they were planning."

We both stared back dumbfounded. I wanted to say something about taking him back if he wanted to finish his conversation, when Kathy, taking the lead, said the right thing.

"Spill the beans. What did you learn?"

"They really are Neanderthals, our Neanderthals. They were picked up from Earth 50,000 years ago by another race of creatures. My captor wouldn't say much but I gather this other race are the real masters."

"Yes, it's the RocNor. They eat KaBac," I added.

"Indeed." Michael raised one eyebrow at me in combination of what I took to be surprise and respect. I was going to practice that raised eye brow thing, though mine were not nearly as impressive as his.

He continued, "That seems to be one of the motivations for the KaBac to attack us. The RocNor are quite aggressive and, uh, are usually hungry, and uh, developed a taste for KaBac. And they only eat their food while its alive."

"Oh my God," Kathy said. Sitting in the pilot chair swiveled around to the cabin, she wrapped her arms around herself and shivered.

"We got some hints of this from some of the other KaBac we met," I filled in. "But what are they doing here and now?" I wanted to move this along to the important stuff.

"There is a third race, even more powerful, that has restrained the RocNor from conquering a civilized race."

"Is that the YonLen? Your torturer ask me if I was with the YonLen. For an instant, it seemed very worried."

"Yes, they could be the ones. I never got the name." Michael took another sip from his water bottle. "Then there is their interest in crystals. The KaBac call them lifestones. I think they are very valuable. There is something that gets incorporated into any crystal if formed over a long period of time. We will have to discuss this with Doctor Flowers when we see him. Maybe there is something useful for us to do with crystals as well."

"It is still an incomplete picture, but now you know what I know," Michael said. He paused and looked at Kathy.

"Kathy, you and your friend here did extraordinarily well, I would say. I was only captive for a few hours. You both should feel proud of your feat of bravery. Who else could have stormed the gates of an alien base, on the Moon, no less, to rescue me?"

"My Navy SEAL friend, GD Stellanowski," I broke in.

"Then if I should ever meet this friend of yours, I shall tell him of your daring raid and he will be green with envy."

I was a bit saturated with new realizations and the far-reaching implications of what this meant. There were whole civilizations out there, with their own politics. And the most unsavory of these apparently had plans for Earth. We each sat for a moment in silent contemplation.

Michael, broke the silence. "Would you like to hear the other excuses I used?"

"What?" I said, a bit confused.

"The other methods I told my captor I used to get to the Moon?"

He was back to being the professor with his tiny classroom of two.

"What were the other methods?" I responded.

"Now, the third method I told them was that I was mechanically inclined and I built a pair of mechanical grasshopper legs which allowed me to achieve a higher height with each jump. I merely jumped and jumped and jumped until the last jump enabled me to reach the moon."

"They didn't like this one either. However, I was able to proceed at length on a discourse on mechanical design and springs, before I got the orange light."

"Then as number four, I said it was all done with hot air balloons. I charged a globe with fumes and the fumes rose up into the air, carrying me to the Moon. This also didn't go over so well, but I could pontificate on density variations and buoyant forces. I don't think they understood more than every fifth word, but were not yet willing to think that the confusion was all due to me. I still got the orange light."

"For number five, I told them I had anointed myself with the marrow from a bull, and as Taurus, the bull, was the lowest figure in the Zodiac, so close to the horizon, and that Phoebus seemed to pull Taurus along the Zodiac, that Phoebus had drawn me up, thinking I was a bull."

"This allowed me to go on about the stars, the moons of Mars and bulls and Minotaurs, for quite some time. They seemed to take a keen interest in my account of Minotaurs extracting the marrow from the cracked bones of poor victims. They mentioned 'RocNor' a number of times in discussions among themselves. This was when I learned about the RocNor. I shudder now, knowing why they showed such keen interest in that story."

"Ok, so that was five. What was the sixth explanation?" I prompted.

"Finally, the sixth explanation that Cyrano had offered." He looked at Kathy, then at me. "Can you guess?" We each shook our heads, waiting for the explanation, both of us rather drained with the night's adrenaline rush.

"Why, I told them I sat myself down on an iron bench with a very strong magnet. Then I threw the magnet up in the air, and the bench was attracted to it. As the bench was pulled up to the magnet, I grabbed the magnet and again threw it up in the air again, and continued this operation until I reached the moon."

"This seemed to really get their attention. They actually seemed to understand what I was talking about, even though I was just making up gibberish. They wanted to know what powered the magnet, the type of bench and how I was able to overcome some effect, which had no translation, but seemed to refer to gravity interacting with magnetic forces. I was able to keep them busy for a good half an hour."

"Shortly before you arrived, I started pushing them on their intent. I used the phrase that humans had dominion over all living things, that the Earth was ours. That's when I learned they were originally from Earth and considered it theirs and were going to take it back. I was just starting to get the details when you arrived. Not that I'm complaining, mind you," he added rather hastily.

"Now you know the full story."

"Sir, if you don't mind me saying so, and please take this as a compliment, but you are probably the greatest BS-er I have ever met." I could not hold back any longer. "I mean, I thought I was pretty good. I can go on for a minute, maybe, before I crack up, but you had them going for hours! My hat's off to you, Professor."

Michael beamed back at me. "Indeed, I take it as a compliment. But you have to understand, I have been a professor for almost fifty years, at the most respected academic institution in the world. I have had years to hone my skill and have studied hogwash, to use a more polite term, from the masters."

"You see," he said, puffing his chest ever so slightly, and sweeping his arm holding the water bottle for emphasis, "I think it one of my most important duties to teach my students how to tell the difference between what is real and what is hogwash. In all modesty, I consider myself a master. I say to my students, to tell the difference, you must first study nonsense. I have studied balderdash, hogwash, crackpot theories, astrology, and pseudoscience for so long, I am fluent in its many dialects. I confess I never thought I would need this skill to save my life, but one uses the resources at one's command."

"Now," Michael said, finally breaking his spell, "I believe we should be getting close enough to send a burst communication to Andy and our friends in San Jose."

"Right," Kathy said from the cockpit, "I'm on it."

I got up and walked into the cockpit to join Kathy for the landing. She was looking at the console, with a perplexed look on her face. "What's the matter?" I asked. "You look puzzled."

"I'm not getting a response back on the transponder. I'm using the right codes, and I should be getting an automatic acknowledgement. Something must be wrong."

I could see out the cockpit window, through Sally, that the dawn terminus was just on the East Coast of America. This made it about 4 a.m. in San Jose. The lights of the West Coast cities were shining bright. I never thought I would welcome all that light pollution, but I looked at the tiny blot of yellow sodium lights of Silicon Valley with longing.

We decelerated to subsonic speed while outside the atmosphere. With unlimited power and thrust, there was no need for us to use air braking and leave a plasma trail. We could float down at a leisurely rate. We were making our way slowly down to the airspace over San Jose, when I saw an alarming sight.

"Oh my God, there are clouds of smoke around headquarters," Kathy said, exhaling sharply.

I felt shocked, too, but forced myself to remain calm. "And looks like strobes and blue lights. I think there was an accident. Maybe this is why we can't pick up anything."

Kathy nodded, but her hands were gripping the seat rests.

"Sally, can you tap into the TV grid and see if you can find any announcements about explosions at the Sciquest factory?" I asked.

"Bryan, I have a live feed now."

"Play it for all of us."

"…repeating. Two massive explosions at the Sciquest factory in San Jose have leveled the office headquarters and the factory next door. Windows were blown out in a two-block radius. Reports of dead and injured are mounting. So far, more than twenty bodies have been recovered. Investigators are calling this an industrial accident. Volatile chemicals used for manufacturing mixed with sparks from high voltage source seemed to have created the two explosions. Stay tuned for more news on this channel."

I felt Michael leaning over me, peering at the screen; he'd come up from the back of the cabin.

"Impossible," he said.

35

MICHAEL'S PRONOUNCEMENT DIDN'T seem to make Kathy feel better. She started taking deep shuddering breaths. "We have to get down there as quick as we can. We have to find out what happened and ... and..." Her voice broke and she started wiping her eyes. "Oh, God," she said.

Michael paced around the cabin, muttering into his glasses frame. I leaned over and put my arm on Kathy's shoulder. I held her as she sobbed. "I'm sure everyone got out safe before the accident," I said, trying my best to sound soothing while I looked at Michael beseechingly. "Can't we search for the rest of the team remotely? I mean, what about the communications net. Can you raise anyone?"

Michael held up his hand to me to indicate that he needed a moment. Kathy muttered thanks and pulled away from me, still sniffing "Until we know what really happened, it's too dangerous to go down to the site," I added.

"I've been trying to raise the Prescott and New Mexico facilities, but they won't respond either. And we're out of range for the LANs if anyone's on the ground."

"Actually, Bryan, Kathy is right. We have to get down to the base as quickly as possible. If there are some of our people off site, we can connect up through the LAN in our glasses, if we get close enough, and if their glasses are still functioning. Given the severity of the circumstances, the other facilities are probably in a lockdown state," he added.

He stood up straight, still favoring his right foot, standing behind Kathy and me. His voice was low and quiet, the joviality completely gone.

"Some time ago, we anticipated the possibility of a government raid. We have a protocol to sever all connections and responses between sites for forty-eight hours. We assumed this would isolate the potential of a domino effect of one raid taking down all our bases. The other facilities are obligated to not respond to our summons. We are basically on our own."

Michael walked back to his chair in the main cabin, his shoulders slumped. He held his head down, and said more to himself, "We always thought the threat was from within. We worried about discovery, not about destruction!"

Kathy was still sniffling, so I pulled out my handkerchief and offered it to her.

"And Bryan," Michael said.

I turned to look at him. He looked sad and his chin trembled. "Be assured, this was no accident. There are no volatile chemicals or gasses used in our assembly operations. The buildings were deliberately blown up."

This night was just getting better and better. "That's why it's even more important to find out what happened. We have to get a better idea of what we are up against. Isn't there any other source of information we can tap?"

Michael was silent for a moment, staring off into space, before he answered. "There is a remote mirror server," Michael said. There was just a hint of hope in his voice now. "It's stored at the edge of the San Jose plant. It has a fiber optic link which is supposed to be explosively severed in case of a lockdown. This keeps it completely isolated and off the grid. We have to enter the vault room at the edge of the parking lot, in person, to access it."

"Then let's get to it," I said.

He sighed. "There is a catch. It requires two executive level authorizations to access, and both in person. I have authorization, but neither of you two do."

"Sally, when you were activated, what was my authorization?"

"Bryan, Andy gave you his personal user preference file."

"Does this include server vault access?"

"No, Bryan.

"Well that rules out that option," Kathy said.

"Not so fast. Sally, what do I need to access the server?"

"You must enter an executive level user name and password at the same time Michael does."

"Sally, when Andy gave me my PDA he said for you to start with his user profile and authorization codes, correct?"

"Yes, Bryan."

"Well, does this include his user ID and password?"

"Yes, Bryan."

"Sally, can I used these, with Michael, to access the server?"

"Yes, Bryan."

"Okay, Michael, you're on."

"We still have another problem," Kathy said. "Where do we land and not be seen? It's way too crowded with all the emergency vehicles around headquarters. Our stealth screen is good, but it will never stand up to close scrutiny."

"Yes indeed," Michael said. He looked at each of us with one bushy eyebrow raised, the professor again. I definitely was going to practice that move. "Where do we hide a plane, even a shadow of a plane, in plain sight?"

Kathy gave him a grim look. Apparently she wasn't in the mood for professorial riddles. "Of course," I said, for both of us. "The airport. There's a private plane airport on the south end of the San Jose Airport. I've seen lots of strange-looking Lear jets there in the past."

"Kathy, while we go to the mirror site, I think you should stay here with the ship. We may need you to pick us up in a hurry," Michael said.

"I want to search for survivors. I have to go to the site and see if I can link up with anyone," she responded.

"Kathy, I agree with Michael. Until we know what's going on, you should stay here with the ship. It's dangerous enough that we are going into the hornet's nest. We need you here for backup."

All I got in response was The Look, but I was really only following Michael's lead this time.

"Kathy, take us down to the airport, then monitor our communications," Michael said, immune to her protests. "When we access the server, we will relay what we can to the ship's mark 3 processor. You can monitor the feed. Then we decide what we do."

She looked very unhappy. I understood. She may have lost friends and colleagues. Michael added, more gently. "You may be the only hope we have of getting this important information to Prescott and the rest of the organization."

"Yes, Michael," was her reluctant reply.

I wanted to connect with her, to tell her that I thought she should come with us to the vault, but I trusted Michael's judgment. She just regarded me steadily and turned away.

At just past 4 a.m., the private plane section of the airport was deserted. Our camouflaged, converted Lear Jet was just one of a number of oddly painted planes. It fit in between the solid pink jet with pig ears and curly tail and the one painted like a purple cow. Once on the ground, Kathy turned the active LCD off and it just looked like a very black, Goth Lear jet.

We were all quiet. The possibility that the Neanderthals had done something to headquarters hung in the air, but nobody seemed to want to talk about it openly. I desperately wanted to talk about a plan, but nobody seemed like they were in the mood, so I quietly ran possible scenarios and solutions through my mind.

The cabin's side door opened and Michael and I set foot once again on solid Earth. I could smell the smoke from the headquarters drifting down here, a few miles away.

"It's been so long since I was back at headquarters," Michael said, "I completely forgot about how we're going to get to the factory from here. I suppose we could try to get a cab, but it's so early."

"I've been thinking about that, Michael. I'd say these desperate times justify desperate measures."

"Just what does that mean?" Michael asked with some hesitation, right eyebrow raised. His tone was none too encouraging.

"I think we need to borrow a vehicle."

"And how were you intending to start it? Or is 'car thief' on your prodigious resume? I am afraid that is one area I have never explored."

"I have an idea, if I can find the right car." I led him to the parking lot adjacent to the stall where we'd left our jet.

I scanned the parking lot, found my mark and grabbed Michael's arm, leading him through the parked cars to my target.

He gave me a wry smile. "You couldn't pick a small, discrete Honda? You want this huge, black Hummer?"

"I'm thinking this might be our ride." I walked around the vehicle, trying each of the doors, just in case, but no such luck. I glanced in through the driver's window. Inspecting the dash, then looked through the windshield near the driver's side.

As I did this silent tour, Michael patiently watched, then asked, "And how do you intend to get in and start it?"

"Watch. Sally, you can synthesize any radio signal with your transmitter, right?

"Yes, Bryan. All PDAs are equipped with a software based radio transceiver system."

"Sally, can you read the VIN number?"

"Yes, Bryan."

"I noticed this car is equipped with On-Star. We just need to figure a way to send the right coded signal to unlock the doors and start the engine."

Michael looked amused.

"If I had access to a computer and a high speed line, I could probably hack in," I added. "Maybe Sally can find a vulnerability and get in."

"Young man, you obviously are new to Sciquest," said Michael. "I'm going to let you in on a little secret, but you can't spread this around."

Michael leaned against the Hummer for support and looked right at me. "There are no secrets from us. When Andy established the foundations for Sciquest, he read way too much about Howard Hughes and picked up a bit of his paranoia. From the very early days, we have been watching the watchers."

I stared back, mouth slightly open, waiting for the next shoe to drop.

"You know how our ships learned to fly?" he raised his bushy right eyebrow.

"Kathy told me—by using AI learning programs."

"Yes, well, they were developed by Will Ozman, our computer whiz kid. In addition to his AI space craft modules, he developed AI network agents. Their mission was to proliferate through the web and penetrate every port, to scan for and report back anything that might relate to Sciquest."

"I thought that's what we had the NSA for: spying on Americans," I said.

"Please believe me when I tell you we have been doing this with the utmost respect for privacy. We only want to know if we might be under suspicion."

"And then what?"

"And then we can conduct very subtle damage control. It has been remarkably successful over the years. As you can see, we have been undetected. Well, until now, that is."

"Michael, why are you telling me this now?"

"Yes, well, you see, our agents have gotten very good at proliferating through the net. We can teach Google a thing or two about web crawling. Our agents have learned how to get through absolutely every barrier and firewall created. With each one they encounter, they all get smarter."

I gave him a quizzical look, wondering where this was going. Michael looked down at his feet, as though embarrassed by what he was about to say. He spoke softly, a mumbled whisper, "If you wish to get access to the On-Star database, you need only ask your PDA."

"Okay, Professor. Next time you've got an important piece of information I urgently need, just come out and say it, don't bother with the novel version."

He nodded. "This was important for you to know, but also to know how sensitive this information is."

"Noted."

"Sally, can you tie into the internet from here, access the On-Star database, use this VIN number and locate the electronic code to activate this Hummer?"

"Yes Bryan."

"Please execute, and unlock the doors and start the engine as soon as you can."

I turned back toward Michael and was about to ask him if there were any other important secrets I should know about, when I heard the distinctive click of the doors unlocking, followed immediately by the soft rumble of the powerful V12 engine starting up.

36

THIS INSTANT ACCESS to all information everywhere at any time was going to take a little getting used to. It could be intoxicating.

As Michael walked around the passenger side to get in, I heard him, still mumbling to himself. What was that all about?

We got in the car and Michael reached over to my arm and held it, preventing me from engaging the transmission into drive. "Dear boy, I mean this in the nicest way, but I must emphasize to you the most important core value of Sciquest." He paused, and locked eyes, then spoke slowly and distinctly.

"We have tremendous power, but we can never abuse this power. We must each follow the moral compass we have and as the comic book heroes say, only use our power for good, never to oppress or take from others."

I did not blink. I just stared back, as solemn as Michael.

"You do understand this don't you, Bryan?"

I understood how serious Michael was. I also understood that I was being entrusted with the family jewels, with very little background checking.

I gave him a small smile. "I understand Michael. I think I have a very strong moral compass. However, I hope you have no problem with the fact that any moral obligations I may have do not extend to our alien visitors or their human collaborators.

"You should know," I added, "I do not tolerate bullies and all the indications are these Neanderthals are coming back into our solar system with bad intentions toward us. I love the world my eyes have recently been opened up to. I love the future I have glimpsed for me and for us. I will fight with tooth and claw and every other tool I can to save this world. As far as I'm concerned, cheating is allowed."

"Granted, but we must avoid at any cost 'collateral damage,' so to speak. If we do not treat all people with respect, then we are no better than our enemies. The ends do not always justify the means."

"Agreed," I nodded in acknowledgement, then broke the serious spell.

"Well, are you okay about us borrowing this car?"

Michael gave a dismissive wave of his hand. "I took the liberty of discretely wiring $85,000 into the bank account of the owner of this vehicle. I don't think they will be disappointed with the slight inconvenience. So, my boy, you may feel free to do with this vehicle as you wish. It's a company car now."

Michael gave my arm a last squeeze and I put the car in gear and started off to the freeway entrance, feeling anxiety in the pit of my stomach. The factory was less than five miles away, but it seemed like it was going to take forever to get there.

Even before we got off the freeway, we could see the red and blue lights of the emergency response crews reflected in the smoke still hovering over what remained of the Sciquest factory.

I got onto the frontage road and said, "Let's do a brief drive-by of the area and then head to the server farm. Where did you say it is?"

"James, please have Sally show a map for Bryan."

"Of course," I said, "I should have thought of that. I see it off to the southeast side."

"Bryan," I heard Kathy's voice from my glasses' frame, "what's happening at the site? I can't get a good look from your visual feed."

We were close enough to see the action. "Kathy, it looks like a huge bite was taken out of the main building. The fires are out but there are still five fire engines with ladders and hoses out around it. It looks like the tunnel collapsed. I can see its outline in the parking lot, with broken up asphalt over it."

I hesitated at that point. What I said next would upset her.

"What else?" she said.

I took a deep breath. "The factory complex is in ruins. It looks like the front was blown out and then the whole middle fell through and collapsed onto the hangar deck."

"I see," she said. Her voice sounded calm but I knew that she must have been going crazy, stuck on the ship, being out of the action.

"I'll keep you posted," I said.

"Sure." Her last comment was not very encouraging.

I drove the Hummer slowly around the edge of the property, on the frontage road, inspecting the damage. A steady stream of ambulances came and went through the main gate. There was a small crowd of people held back behind a police line. Some of them had police next to them, obviously being interrogated. Others were just wandering and looking. A few camera flashes were going off.

"Do you notice the pattern to the collapse?" Michael said, craning his head to rubberneck. "The front of the headquarters and the entire factory got the brunt of the explosion."

"What about the crowd?" Kathy interjected. "Michael, do you see any of our people in the crowd?"

"Dear, I'm sorry. I can't make out any of the faces from here. James has been probing for other PDA interfaces, but so far, has not heard from anyone. I'm sure the authorities have helped all the people they can. They have it under as best control as possible. The most important thing for us to do is reach the remote server and find out what really happened."

"I'm coming to meet you. I have to see if Andy made it. I checked the hospital records. I can't find any of the senior staff among the dead or hospitalized."

"Kathy," Bryan said, "I know Millie and Dave were going to leave right after us to go to Prescott. I'm sure they are safe there."

"But what about Andy!" she insisted.

"We'll find out more when we reach the server, Kathy. Do not leave, we need you at the ship for backup," Michael repeated.

"I heard you," she replied. But she didn't sound happy.

Michael frowned. I was relieved that not even he could stay in her good graces. It wasn't just me.

37

I LOOKED FOR a spot to pull the car in, without getting stopped by the police and firefighters on the scene. "She's right, you know," I said. "Where is the senior staff? I think even Richard was in the main building when we left."

"We'll soon see," Michael said, voice low and solemn.

I regarded the damage, feeling a sense of fatigue creep in. If this was the work of the Neanderthals, then this was just a small taste of things to come. "I see what you were saying about the buildings. I'm no expert on explosions, but it sure looks like at least three blasts, one in the front entrance of the main building, and one deep inside the factory. Something erupted inside the connecting tunnel and fractured the ceiling and then it collapsed. Do you know of anything that we had that could have blown up like that?"

"Sciquest had nothing to do with this. It could only have been somehow related to the Neanderthal presence."

The elephant was being named, but something else in the parking lot had caught my attention. "Damn!"

"What is it, Bryan?"

I hit my fists on the steering wheel. "My jeep. I left it in the parking lot when I brought Kathy in. There it is on its side. It probably rolled a half a dozen times. Now it's totaled. And look at all the glass scattered across the parking lot around it."

I surveyed it solemnly.

"Doesn't look so good," said Michael.

I nodded. "The explosion had to have been inside the building to get the glass so far out. Oh, no."

"What else?" Michael asked.

"That mess on its side looks like Max's Lamborghini. I guess the good news is he evaded the patrol car and made it back to headquarters. He was supposed to take one of the planes to Prescott." I paused, a terrible thought hit me. "At least I hope he evaded them. I can't believe he would have, even unknowingly, let the patrol car follow him to the plant."

"What patrol car?"

"It's a long story. Just before we left the foothills plant, we encountered a police car with a uniformed officer and a Neanderthal dressed like a gangster. Max led them on a rabbit hunt and was supposed to take them far away from us."

"Then I wouldn't worry. While my young friend Max is reckless, has no sense of his mortality and would rather break into a room than enter through the front door, he is intensely loyal to Sciquest. We are his family. He would never do anything to endanger us. It was not he who pointed the way to us."

I was reassured, but we had not gotten any closer to the truth. We drove in shocked silence around the perimeter of the facility until we reached the back entrance of the fence. This was more than a half mile from the main factory. If anyone saw us, we were far enough out, I couldn't image they would think we were associated with the Sciquest plant.

Michael got us through the chain with the combination lock and instructed me to drive to the server vault at the far end of the property fence. It was just a small steel shed, not much bigger than a single car garage, that looked old and abandoned. I circled once to make sure we were alone and parked the Hummer behind the small shed, using it to shield our vehicle from the crowd of emergency vehicles.

I got out and approached the front door, which faced the main building complex. There was no door handle, just a numeric key pad and hand scanner.

Michael punched in the numbers 1 3 7, placed his palm on the scanner, and the door opened. Inside, faintly illuminated by the distant dawn and flashing emergency lights, I could make out a nearly featureless, tiny room. Dead in the center was a spiral stair case with a stainless steel handrailing leading down into a pit. As soon as I was inside, Michael closed the door and a dim light came on inside.

"You guys think of everything, don't you?" I said.

"Apparently, not everything," he said.

Michael led the way down the stairs. As he stepped on the first stair, the lights in the staircase came on and I could see a large, dimly lit room below.

We walked down the stairs, the soft clank, clank, clank of our shoes on the steel steps the only sound to echo against the bare walls. When we reached the floor level, I could look around. Against the wall in front of us was a glass-enclosed closet with racks of servers. On each rack, two red LEDs glowed back, like devil's eyes. Reflected back to me in the glass wall was the image of the bare forty-watt bulb hanging from a cord attached to the ceiling. In front of the server closet was a table with two large flat-panel displays. I turned around to look at the rest of the room, but other than the bare light bulb, the walls were featureless. There were no signs of life or activity.

"Now, the moment of truth," Michael said. "James activate the interface display."

In front of us, the two screens came alive. There was no keyboard. Instead, the screens lit up with a standard login screen, asking for user name and password, identical on the two screens.

"Bryan, you must enter the user name and password Andy has in his file. We must enter each character simultaneously."

"But there is no keyboard to type out the letters."

"Sally, please supcrimpose the keyboard for Bryan."

Instantly, a keyboard appeared on the table in front of me and my screen. What a perfect encryption, I thought. Not only is there a first level defense of password, but the very method of inputting the information was encrypted by the radio transmission code from our PDA interfaces.

As Michael tapped in each character, I typed in the user name and password Sally reported to me from Andy's profile, user name SUNFIRE and password "R1ChArD."

With the last keystroke on the table top, the bare bulb turned off and the room switched to total darkness. It was like a blink; in the next instant, a virtual world opened up in my glasses. Michael and I were standing at the top of a theater room built like a cliff. A floor-to-ceiling screen, like an IMAX screen, was in front of us. It was segmented into at least thirty, six-foot square screens. Of course it was all just a synthesized image, I told myself.

Each screen held a different still image, mostly scenes from security cameras inside and outside the buildings.

"We're in," Michael said. "James, arrange to download the last twenty-four hours of stored data to the ship's holographic memory. How long will this take?"

I did not hear the response, but Michael said, "Bryan, ask Sally to connect you with Kathy."

I tried, but was unsuccessful. "I can't get through. Is there a problem?"

"No problem. I should have thought of this. It's the shielding. While we're down here, we're on our own. This facility is completely off the grid and shielded. We will have to record what we can into our glasses and then transfer to the ship's mark 3 processor when we surface from the vault.

"We'll take fifteen minutes, then return. Let's use this time to find some answers. James, please start the display from the time Bryan and Kathy left. Bryan, please take the screens on the left, I'll take the ones on the right."

"What am I looking for?"

"I don't know, but I think you will know it when you see it."

The images began to roll, mostly pretty boring. There was Dave Flowers and three others moving down the corridor to the hangar deck. They entered the same ship. Ron followed a moment later. He and Max walked up the steps of the last ship. Valerie unhooked the last hose, walked up the stairs and closed the cabin door. It was a full plane. I was glad to see Andy took my warning seriously about an evacuation. I saw it lift off.

I was glad to see Max made it safely back to Headquarters. I hoped he and the others were safe, somewhere.

I had Sally speed up the feed to five times faster than real time. I watched two ships take off. There was just Kathy's damaged ship and one other left in the hangar bay.

"Interesting," Michael said.

"What did you see?"

"Richard. He was in his office, for about forty-five minutes after your staff briefing, obviously accessing some database feeds, then he got up and walked out the front door to his car and drove off in quite a hurry," said Michael.

"Why is that unusual?"

"The note I read in Andy's log, posted after your meeting, suggested the urgent nature of everyone's attention. He feared the possibility of aliens among us, and humans working with them," Michael said. "He reiterated that there was nothing more important than uncovering the alien presence and noted that he left instructions for Richard to focus on the search through all camera feeds and access portals."

So why did Richard leave in such a hurry if conducting this search was his top priority?

"In the staff briefing, Richard made a fuss about wanting to do this search himself. Then he stormed out when he didn't get his way. What's with him? Is he as much of a spoiled brat as he appears?"

Michael sighed. "He is in a difficult position. He is very bright, but I don't think he would be on the team if not for his father's position. He is forever trying to prove to his father he is good enough, and must compete with super achievers. You can imagine this eternal struggle."

As Michael talked, I absently scanned the images flashing by at 5x normal speed. Something didn't look right. "Michael, look at this image. It's time stamped an hour ago, if I am reading this right. There is Andy in his office, and only two other people in the main building, with twenty-five people in the factory. Look at the parking lot. There is a large sedan pulling in."

Michael whistled. "James, freeze frame. Please identify the license plate of this car and tell me the owner."

I heard in my ear the voice of James, relayed by Sally. James had a distinctive English accent. It was very much the voice of a stiff, formal, English butler.

"This car is registered to a French company, D 'Auric Enterpris. Their local office is a building at Pier 54 in San Francisco."

"What is it doing visiting Sciquest at after three in the morning?" I asked.

"Watch. The first person out the door is a big guy. But look at the second person."

"Richard!"

"Indeed, but, do you see what I see around his neck. I know that sort of collar intimately. There's a third person coming out of the car. Another rather large person I might add. From the back, they do look a little familiar, don't you think?"

"He's leading them into the building!" I said. "What are they carrying? They look like small duffle bags."

Michael whistled. "I fear the worse. As soon as the front doors close, we lose the feed in most of the internal cameras. Look here, two vans that were outside the gate; they come into the parking lot. One goes to the main building, one goes to the factory."

"Those vans are just like the one that was after Kathy. Where was our security all this time?"

"Remember, you said Kathy's PDA link was disrupted by the alien jammer? As soon as the white vans approach, we lose the feed from the nearest cameras. All we have is this view from outside the lobby and in the foyer. That big person with one of the duffle bags, he goes into the elevator that leads down to the tunnel to the factory, but comes out of the elevator without the bag. He must have known about the secret code to descend. I bet he had the bombs in the bag. He left them in the corridor and maybe sent a few down to the hangar deck."

"I've seen one of their bombs. A small sphere the size of a softball. It flattened an entire building. A few of those could have done all the damage we see here."

"It was Richard. He sold us out. It can only be him," I said.

Michael put a hand on my arm. "Not so fast, we don't know enough yet. If they tortured him with that collar, he is not to blame."

"You didn't seem to have any problems not revealing information with a collar around your neck."

"I have had many more years than Richard to hone my misdirection skills. Richard just has some maturing to do."

"If you don't mind, I'll hold off accepting excuses for him until after I talk to him myself."

Michael pursed his lips and gave me a sad smile, but said nothing more.

"Look at these screens. After the two vans pull up, most of the video feed on my cameras is just snow," I said.

Michael interpreted his screen. "The outside camera is hardwired. It's legacy from our original installation. The jammer didn't work on it."

"Is that Andy walking out in front of the aliens? The time stamp says ten minutes after the sedan entered the parking lot."

"And it appears we have Richard with his father," Michael added. From the window of the lobby, we could see Andy get in the white panel van with one captor but the other one was leading Richard to the sedan.

Two minutes later, the cameras come back on. "Sally, look, there. Do you see any of the white panel vans on any feed at this time stamp?"

"Bryan, there is one white panel van parked approximately one hundred yards down the frontage road."

"They're just sitting there," I said. "Waiting."

Michael rubbed his eyes. They looked bloodshot. "After the cameras come back on, it's like still images. There is no motion in any of the frames."

"James, scan all frames from all cameras after the vehicle leaves. Is there anyone moving in any image?"

I heard James' voice relayed through Sally. "No, sir, I fear not."

"Michael, look at these images of the hangar. All the lights are out. On the factory floor, the night shift, they all collapsed on the floor or over their benches. It looks like they were gassed, or zapped with something. It's like they collapsed right in the middle of their work."

The next instant, all screens showed a flash and went dead.

"That's the end of that."

I took a deep breath and paced. "So, Richard brought them back, they picked up Andy, and set off explosives that blew up the buildings. And then they stuck around to watch their fireworks."

"Why would they take that risk?" Michael asked.

I shrugged. I could only guess.

"Oh yes," he answered himself. "They want to make sure there are no witnesses."

"And they kept Richard with them so he could finger them."

"Bryan, don't be too hasty. We don't really know the role Richard played."

I wanted to pin the little punk down and see why the heck he was colluding with the Neanderthals. I'd give him one chance to explain his actions. But then I thought about Andy and the high price he'd paid for having trusted his son. I merely nodded.

Michael looked deeply troubled. "I think we've seen enough. We need to pass this along to Prescott and plan our next steps."

I turned to face the real Michael, though I saw a virtual image in his place, in the dimly-lit room.

"What are our next steps?"

"We need to uncover how deep the Neanderthal presence has penetrated our world and what their true intent is."

"Whatever it is," I said for both of us, "it's looking worse and worse for us."

And I wondered if the CEO of Sciquest had long to live.

38

AS MICHAEL LEAD the way up the stairs to the surface, I spoke my mind. "Andy told me he would never leave a man behind. He said that to Kathy when she wouldn't let go of the possibility you were still alive on the moon. We have to go after Andy, if there is a chance he is still alive."

With his hand on the handle of the door to the outside, Michael turned to me. "Dear boy, I would do anything I could to rescue Andy, but I am an old man and you are just one engineer. What can one engineer do against this Neanderthal invasion? We need to get the resources of the rest of Sciquest behind us. We go to the Prescott base and assess the next step."

With the last comment, Michael pushed open the door and walked out on the tarmac. I saw that the flashing red and blue lights from the emergency vehicles were still going. They would be there for a long time, I thought glumly. I half wished they could help us out, but I knew we were on our own. I didn't know who to trust and, anyway, they were just firefighters and police officers. We needed Navy SEALs.

We were back on line. "Kathy, we have some disturbing news," I said immediately.

There was no response. I got a twinge of worry.

"Kathy," I said again.

Silence.

I stopped walking and Michael turned to look at me.

"Kathy, can you hear me?" I repeated.

"What's going on?" he asked, putting a hand on my shoulder.

I tried to keep my voice calm. "Michael, try to raise Kathy!"

"Kathy, dear, are you there?" he said.

Still no response. My heart started racing. "Sally, where is Kathy?"

"Unknown at this time, Bryan."

"What do you mean? Scan every camera feed on the ship and find where she was last known to be."

"She left the ship in a car from the parking lot shortly after you did. The last recorded feed from her PDA was transmitted to the ship approximately six minutes ago. She was standing in the parking lot of the Sciquest headquarters when her communications with the ship stopped."

I reflexively looked up at the distant parking lot, to where I hoped I could catch a glimpse of her, though I knew I was too distant to make out any details.

"James, play back what Kathy saw for the last thirty seconds before communications was lost."

"Of course, sir," James said in both our ear pieces.

With the image of the distant emergency lights and residual smoke as the dim backdrop, I saw the close up view from the PDA frame mounted cameras on Kathy's glasses. Superimposed were the sounds of the cleanup crews, hoses being pulled over rubble, the squawks of police radios, and fragments from scattered voices. Her head swung from side to side, scanning the scene.

Then the cameras locked on someone, tall and thin, from behind.

The image bounced as Kathy hurriedly stepped toward the figure, who stood, slouching, gazing at the destroyed building.

I suspected who it was.

"No," I said, as though I could stop what had transpired ten minutes in the past.

She reached the figure, grabbed his shoulder, and spun him around. He looked sadly at Kathy. The jacket collar pulled up around his neck did not fully hide the metal ring with two slightly glowing orange balls on opposite sides.

Kathy shouted in relief: "Richard, we were so worried!"

This was all she was able to get out before a big, hairy hand came around from behind her and engulfed the right-hand camera. The frames were ripped from her head and the image tumbled. Just before the image turned to black, an upside down face flashed in the frame. The hair was bushy, but cut short. The nose was flat, the forehead broad and there seemed to be a few too many teeth in that mouth. The bottom of its worn boot expanded to fill the frame, followed by instant blackness and the snowy white noise of dead air.

39

"MICHAEL, THEY'VE TAKEN her." The image from my glasses faded, and I was restored to the real world, I tried to pierce the distance and spot Kathy, but the events I just viewed were separated by more than half a mile and by ten minutes of precious time.

I grabbed Michael's arm and tried to drag him around the building to our Hummer.

He balked, holding me back. "Bryan, let's not rush into this. It's just the two of us against the entire Neanderthal presence. We have to get help."

I felt sick with desperation and I must have given Michael a look of disbelief. "You know what she said about you when we learned you were captured on the Moon? She said you would storm the gates of hell carrying a can of gasoline to get her back if she was the one held captive."

I had to admire his cool. "Bryan," he said, reaching to lower his glasses to make his point absolutely clear, the old fashion way.

"Never doubt that my desire to rescue Kathy is as strong as yours. I know even more than you the danger she is in. I didn't want to mention it in front of Kathy. Remember, I made you promise to guarantee she would not get caught?"

"Yes. What are you hiding? Why is she in even more danger?"

He had a pained expression on his face. "The KaBac plan to replace themselves on the RocNor menu with humans. But only human males. They have a fondness for human women. Neanderthal woman have been bred to be passive. The KaBac like their females to put up a fight. For the last fifteen years, the KaBac have been secretly kidnapping human females and keeping them as slaves. That is not a life either of us would wish for Kathy."

No, no, no! This was my worst nightmare. I didn't want to imagine what might be ahead for Kathy, the beautiful astrophysicist with the Andromeda tattoo, the girl with the green eyes, my partner. I'd only known her for less than twelve hours and I felt more connected to her than any other woman I had ever met. And now she was on her way to become a sex slave to Neanderthal monsters?

"All the more reason we have to go after her. I promised to you I would protect her. Whether you come with me or not, I'm going after her."

"Hold on, son." He held my arm in a loose grip and spoke softly but urgently. "Sometimes there is more than one right answer. I am sure we can find a strategy for rescuing Kathy with a higher chance of success that is not so prone to inviting disaster. We are gifted with intelligence. Let us use this to overcome our lizard forebrain. We are uniquely subtle; let's find a way to leverage this asset."

I took a deep breath to steady myself. "That's what Millie said you would do—be more subtle."

Michael was right. What could the two of us do against the entire Neanderthal presence? Now it was all becoming clear. They must have penetrated high levels of our government, maybe others. I saw one of them with a policeman earlier tonight. They had a fleet of cars and vans, openly driving around the streets. There could be hundreds or even thousands of them on Earth, or even just in the Silicon Valley area. We were just two people.

But my new world was now intimately threatened. The CEO of the company who had already revolutionized my world view was in danger. And my dream of space travel had just been handed to me; I wasn't about to let it be snatched away. And then there was Kathy.

Those hardwired hormones coursed through my veins. My world was in danger. It was personal; my woman was in danger. Yeah, we were just an old man and one engineer, but Michael was one clever old man, and I was one sharp engineer, a deadline junkie, a skilled Ninjaneer.

"Michael, you're right. We are just two people, but our friends need us, our world needs us. We don't have the time to get to the other base, rally the troops, and mount a rescue. They took Andy more than an hour ago. He's probably at their headquarters by now, wherever that is, and they could be torturing him."

"And now they have Kathy." I didn't mention that she'd likely be at their headquarters soon, maybe to be shipped off to the Moon or beyond. Now I gripped the side of Michael's arm.

"Michael, it's up to the two of us, just us, to save them. I can't do it alone. I need your help. Are you with me?"

Michael's expression lightened and he regarded me thoughtfully. "Son, I've learned over the years that passion is the most valuable trump card to hold in your hand. It can beat a full house of strength any time. And you've got enough passion going for the both of us."

I held his gaze, not flinching.

He nodded. "The only lead we have is the car registration. Pier 54. We'll develop a plan while we fly up there. Shouldn't take more than fifteen minutes."

Our mission settled, we started to walk around the shed to our parked car. Just before we rounded the corner, Michael stopped to take a last glance back at the rubble of the Sciquest plant. "If Richard is working with them and they have Kathy, they may know about the shed here."

I held his arm gently and urged him around the corner. I was pumped full of adrenalin, the good kind, after our pep talk. "It doesn't matter. Nothing will stop us now..." was all I was able to get out. When we turned the corner of the shed, and the main complex disappeared behind the side of the vault building, we were intercepted by a large, bald man.

I halted in my tracks. I noticed two important qualities. The first gave me a wave of relief: he was clearly a human confronting us, not a Neanderthal. He was tall, at least six foot, maybe in his forties, and broad shouldered, almost like a wrestler. His light grey suit hung over his shoulders with plenty of room for easy movement. His head was completely shaved. With his mouth slightly open, it was obvious he did not have all his teeth. One in front and two off to the side were missing.

Upon second glance, the relief vanished. This human was pointing a very earthlike 9mm gun at us.

40

"HOLD IT RIGHT there, yous twos," the man said. "Hands up. Come forward slowly." He gestured with his gun, around the back of the shed where the cars were, out of view from the emergency vehicles.

"What do you want with us, we didn't steal anything. We were just looking around," I said, rapidly flipping through one scenario after another in my head.

"I got my instructions. You guys snooping around, my boss, he wants to check you out." He sounded like a New York gangster.

I walked slowly forward, Michael quietly following. I needed time to think. "Where is your boss? We'll tell him we didn't have anything to do with this explosion. We were just looking around."

"You always go snooping around at four in the morning with your grandpa? Yous two are coming for a ride."

The last thing I was going to do was get in a car with this baldheaded gangster. As we approached him, the stranger backed up. I saw our Hummer and to the other side of it, a black sedan with tinted windows. The gunman was backing up to his car. He was parked right behind our Hummer.

"Michael, make a distraction," I mumbled under my breath. I hoped Sally would understand and transmit the message to Michael through James.

Michael slid out from behind me and stood still, clutching his chest and moaning. "It's my heart. I'm having a heart attack, you're killing me." He crumpled to his knees and began the death scene from Macbeth. The gunman did not take the bait, but stayed rooted in the same spot, using his gun to cover Michael. I used this time to speak very softly to Sally.

I heard the equally faint "Yes, Bryan," from my frames. In the next instant, the Hummer started up with a deep rumble. The sudden noise startled the gunman and he swung his gun over to point at the driver he imagined to be in the Hummer.

I hesitated, waiting for the right moment, but the gunman, not seeing a target in the car, swung the gun back on me, standing less than three meters away.

The engine sounded a little off and the exhaust was a thick, smelly, black. The gunman shifted his gun back and forth between me and Michael, who was now on his side on the ground, moaning and mumbling about his life flashing past and the pain of it all. The gun arm swung back and forth, as the greasy smoke billowed out of the exhaust. Then it settled on me. "I don't know how you're doing that but stop it now or I put one in your arm."

"Hey, it's not me, I'm not doing anything. I've had problems with that car since the day I got it. It's haunted, like it has a mind of its own. It just starts up like that by itself sometimes. It's got some defect in the timing."

"Not the answer I was looking for, bozo." The gunman shifted his aim to my left arm and a thunderous blast echoed off the back wall of the shed, rattling the aluminum siding against its frame. The gunman was engulfed in the fireball created when the fuel rich exhaust was ignited by the backfire of the car. He was thrown five feet to the side, his gun flying ten feet away.

I was expecting the shock, but was still surprised how effective it was. I glanced at Michael to see him still on the ground, shaken but okay. I ran to the scattered gun and walked over to the disarmed gunman who lay moaning on the ground, one side of his grey suit and exposed face covered with black soot.

I kicked him, turning him over on his stomach. I held the gun on him. "Michael, are you alright?"

"Other than a bruised ego from my unconvincing act, I think I have survived my second encounter with death today."

"Good. Check out the back of the Hummer and this guy's car to find something to tie him up. I threw Michael the keys I found in the man's pocket. I placed the gun on the back of the head of the man. "If you breathe too hard, I will blow your head off."

"Don't shoot. I was just following orders," the man said, fear, pain and exhaustion in his voice. Michael came back with two sets of jumper cables and I hogtied him.

I knelt beside the prisoner and held the gun against his neck, using it to push the man's face into the asphalt tarmac. "We want some answers, so start talking. Who do you work for?"

"They'll kill me if I tell you."

"Correction, I will kill you. You have to the count of three then I shoot. And I don't count so good, so I may miss a number or two. One."

"Bryan, you can't kill this man." Michael put his hand on my shoulder and spoke in all seriousness.

I looked up a Michael, gritting my teeth and shaking my head at him, hoping the man below couldn't see. Michael shook his head back.

"Okay. You get a reprieve. I won't kill you." I shifted the gun to rest against the back of the man's ankle, grinding it in. "We'll play one foot, two foot. Here are the rules. I ask a question. You give me an answer I don't like, I shoot one foot. Give me another answer I don't like, I shoot the second foot. Then I work my way up to your knee caps. When I run out of feet and knees, I go for what's in between. Understand how we play this game?"

"No, I can't tell you anything, they'll kill me. If they find out I'm talking they'll torture me to death."

"I don't like that answer." I pulled back the hammer of the gun. The audible click startled the man.

"They're French. The company's got some frog name. I don't remember it."

"Where in France are they from?"

"They said they are from some French colony in Africa."

"What are they doing here?"

"I can't tell you anything more, they'll kill me."

"Say hello to a cane."

"Bryan!" Michael shouted before I could do anything.

"Well, now you know who the good cop is. Don't go anywhere, I'll be right back."

I grabbed Michael by the elbow and walked him ten feet away.

"Michael, you can't interfere, we have a short period of time to get information. We need to know what this man knows and we need to know it now!"

"The ends do not justify the means. We don't know to what degree this man is guilty. We cannot punish him merely for his associations. Find another way."

I took Michael's words seriously, though I debated with myself how I would feel if Michael wasn't here with me. The way I felt now about rescuing Kathy and Andy, the ends did justify the means. This hired gun was mixed up with the aliens somehow, and that made him guilty. I walked back to the man tied up on the ground, rethinking my strategy, in deference to Michael.

"It's your lucky day. I decided I'm not going to blow your foot away. We're going to start over again and I'm going to ask you real nice and you are going to answer real nice."

"Where were you going to take us?"

"Headquarters."

"And where is that?"

"Downtown."

"What town?"

"San Francisco, it's some Pier, something like 50. I don't remember."

"Bryan, I have the address here from James."

I saw a map and satellite image from the web in my glasses. Pier 54, one of the converted wharves built on pillars over the Bay, now a modern five-story office building sitting on the Bay.

I continued the interrogation. "There was a woman your people picked up ten minutes ago. Where is she?"

The man flinched. "I can't tell you."

"Why have you taken her?"

"Please give me a break. They have these collars." His face was white and he was sweating.

"You don't like pain, I'll show you pain."

I was enraged. They had Kathy, time was short, this bully was standing in my way.

I pulled back the gun to swing it at the man's head.

"Bryan, find another way," Michael said sternly.

I took a deep breath, debating which battle I wanted to fight. Okay, I had another way. I knelt next to the man and felt on his back under his shoulder blades, feeling way too much muscle. I felt around with my fingers for the right spot. I moved my fingers over the big guy's back. The prisoner groaned then screamed out in pain.

"Found it," I said. I pushed harder and the man screamed again.

Michael leaned down and pulled me away from him. "Bryan, what are you doing! You can't torture this man."

I got up from the guy's back and walked Michael of earshot. "Michael, I'm not torturing this man. I am giving him what I usually pay 120 dollars an hour for. All I'm doing is helping to massage some of the knots out of his back. This is exactly what Norma, my massage therapist, does to me, and I pay to have it done. Sure, it's going to hurt him, but you can't call it torture."

"Yes, I see your point." Michael hesitated, clearly debating with himself. Then he nodded. "This is an acceptable alternative."

"Michael, you have to trust me from now on. Time is running out."

"Yes, of course. This is a new regime for me. Please continue." Michael waved me back to my task.

Back in position, I moved my fingers around and found the right spot again and pressed. The scream gave me confirmation.

"What are you doing with her?"

The man shook his head. I rubbed around slightly, found the center of the knot and pushed, hard.

The man screamed and I pushed again, for once in my life, thankful for what Norma had taught me about torture.

"Slave. They take women as slaves. I think they ship them back to Africa! Stop! I told you what you want to know. Now they'll kill me." The man shouted out through clenched teeth.

I relaxed the pressure. "Where are they going to hold her?"

When the man hesitated, I moved my hand back to the knot on his back. I'd trained him well. Before I could press, he shouted, "I'll talk. I'll tell ya."

"They have this big warehouse, office building. It's one of the piers. That's where they have all their equipment and they take people there."

"What do they do there?"

"They got some operation going. I don't know the details, I'm just a hired gun. I just do odd jobs for them. I just drive them around and sometimes I pick up people for them, and sometimes I pick up goods for them."

"What sort of goods?"

"I don't know. I think it's jewelry. I saw one of the briefcases open once. It was sparkling, like diamonds and rubies and things, gems and necklaces. Sometimes it's these funny egg-shaped rocks. That's all I know. Honest."

"Who are they?"

"I told you, I don't know. They must be from Africa somewhere. Some of them are real ugly. And they're big. They don't talk French. When they're together, they talk some other language, I don't know, maybe it's African or Arabic."

"Why do you work for them?"

"What do you mean? They pay us in gold. They got suitcases full of it. I'm gonna retire in a year from what they're paying me. We're just taking their money."

"You stupid, ignorant bastard."

"Hey, I'm the one taking their money."

"They're not from France, they're Neanderthals from space. They're planning some sort of invasion." As soon as it came out of my mouth, I knew it sounded crazy. As I listened to myself, even I didn't believe it. Neanderthals from space?

The man on the ground laughed. "Who's the stupid one here, buster? Like I really believe they're aliens, what, like from Mars? Are you telling me, I've been working for Martians?"

I realized I wasn't going to get anywhere trying to convince this guy, and I didn't need to. All I needed right now was some hook, some hint of a plan to rescue Andy and Kathy. Michael beat me to it.

"Bryan, here's a pop quiz for you: who is able to walk anywhere in a large populated building and you never really see him even when he is right next to you?"

I didn't want to work for the answer, but Michael was the consummate professor, wanting his student to figure it out for himself, maybe with a hint or two. My brain was turbocharged on adrenaline, churning possible answers and factoring in how it could be turned into a plan.

Of course! That was Michael's idea. I could share Michael's smile now as I said, "Okay, way subtle. But to make this work, every second counts. We have to risk bringing the ship to the parking lot."

"Agreed."

"Sally, bring the ship over here to pick us up. Activate the stealth screen. We need a fast ride."

Turning back to the man on the ground, I asked him, "Tell me about the janitorial service in this building on the pier."

41

THE SHIP ARRIVED with full camouflage turned on, following my instructions. It had taken off vertically from the San Jose airport and shot up to altitude, then traveled the five miles to the Sciquest facility, now in rubble, and descended from 50,000 feet to rest next to the Hummer behind the shed. There was little chance of discovery from the emergency vehicles half a mile away.

We left the hired gunman tied up in the back seat of his car, with no radio and all four tires shot out. He would be found eventually, but long after our plan either worked or we were captured or killed. In any case, it wouldn't matter then.

"Every second counts," I said after we got in the cockpit. "We have to get there ahead of the car with Kathy. I figure with little traffic this time of the morning, we have maybe forty minutes at best before it arrives. Sally, take us up and get us to Pier 54 as fast as you can."

"Yes, Bryan."

"And Sally," Michael interjected, "please steer us over the middle of the Bay and stay out of registered flight patterns."

"Of course, Michael."

It was less than three minutes for us to travel the fifty miles to Pier 54, just enough time for Sally to dig up the information I requested. The alien headquarters building lay below, shining with the street lights of San Francisco. I looked in my glasses through the transparent cabin floor to the building, hardly noticeable, jutting out on the water, hoping for some clue to confirm my new boss was still alive below us. As our half-baked plan faced reality, I was beginning to realize how fragile it was.

Do the unexpected, Rusty used to tell me. The Neanderthals could not possibly expect us to attack their headquarters. If we had more time, I could have brought Rusty in on this. But we couldn't wait for him to get back on the grid. We were on our own.

"Sally, ring the number." I heard two rings in my frames and then an old man's gravely, deep voice came on the line.

"Hello, Myron Novellus speaking. May I help you?"

"Mr. Novellus, this is special agent in charge Bryan Postman, with the FBI. I got your name and number from your company. Are you still working at the D'Auric building?"

"Why yes I am, sir, I have two more floors to finish and then take the trash out. What can I do for you, special agent in charge, sir?"

I saw the file photo of Myron Novellus hanging in midair in front of me. He was a black man, late sixties, grey hair cut short. It said he had one son and three grandchildren as of last year. I was acutely aware of Michael's previous comment and felt intense responsibility to not allow Novellus to end up as collateral damage. But we needed one small favor.

"Mr. Novellus, I must tell you some important information. Are you where you can talk?"

"Wait a minute, I'm close to my supply closet. But how do I know you are the FBI? I never have talked to the FBI before."

"Of course, sir. When you are in a secure location, call me back on the number appearing on your phone and you will reach FBI headquarters in San Francisco. Ask for me. I will await your call."

"Give me a minute here, son, I move slow at my age. I'll call you right back."

I looked across at Michael, sitting in the copilot chair. At our altitude, and in the clear sky, we could see the beginnings of dawn peeking over the horizon to the east. The black night sky was turning to blue. It would be light in a little over an hour. As we counted each heartbeat, waiting for the callback, I wondered if we would live to see the dawn.

I also wondered just how many dawns mankind had left to see if we failed.

"If we don't make it, we should prepare a message to warn the world." Michael was obviously thinking the same thing.

"Thanks for the vote of confidence! But I agree. While I'm out, why don't you do it. Only the crazies on late-night talk radio will believe us, but we have to do it just the same. Maybe someone else in Sciquest might have a chance to do something."

We were interrupted with a phone call. Sally picked up and said in her synthesized voice, "FBI, San Francisco branch office, how may I direct your call?" Sally had hijacked the official FBI number, She used it as the sending number and monitored calls into it and then routed them for pickup.

We listened in on the incoming call from Novellus. "Do you have a Bryan Postman working for you?"

"Yes sir. He is a special agent in charge, but he is tied up right now, may I be of assistance?"

I was nervous, unsure if Sally could handle her role in this charade. I had absolute confidence in her ability to intercept and control the communications channels, but could she fool a human on the other end of the phone and ad lib a delicate lie? I just realized I had put her up to a Turing Test. Was her programming up to it?

There was that 'her' again. Was she anything other than just a fast processor with a sophisticated GUI, or was there really a 'her' there? At some point, did it matter? I got attached to my first car, a '65 Chevy Nova. Yet another item I put on my 'to be explored' list, if I ever got out of this immediate crisis.

"I got a call from this special agent in charge and I just wanted to check if he was legit. Can you describe him to me?"

"Could I have your name, sir? We do not give out personal information about our agents."

"Well now, he made the first move to me. My name is Myron Novellus and I'm a law-abiding citizen, retired Navy chief petty officer, been doing my part and paying taxes for more than fifty years. He calls me and wants me to help him. Least as you can do is give me some personal information about him so's I can recognize him if I see him."

"Yes, of course, sir. Special agent in charge Postman is expecting your call. I can tell you he's about five-foot-eight, brown hair, brown eyes, thirty-one years old and has just the hint of a little dimple on his chin. Bryan is one of our most valued agents, and a very kind fellow. I do appreciate your patience, sir. His line is now clear; can I connect you?"

"Thirty-one is a might young for a special agent in charge. How long has he been with the FBI?"

I was sweating in the cockpit, listening in. What would Sally say? I had only given her the single command to intercept the call and get Myron to believe I was an FBI agent.

"Yes, he is one of our youngest agents. He started just a few years ago, but is the smartest, most talented and bravest agent we have." The synthesized voice lowered to just above a conspiratorial whisper. "Please, sir, if you can, please help him. We have placed him in a very dangerous position against some very bad people. Can I connect you to him now?"

"Thank you ma'am, please do."

I was amazed. Here I was literally right next to the computer performing this dialog, knowing it was a software program, and I was convinced. There was the fake ring. I picked up, "Postman."

"Sir, this is Myron Novellus. I'm in my supply closet. Now what's goin' on here?"

"Mr. Novellus, the building you are in will be raided by the FBI shortly. We need your help in order to minimize casualties, and we need to get you out of there. Here's what I'd like you to do..."

42

FROM OUR VANTAGE at a thousand feet over the Bay, I had a good view of our objective. Pier 54 was a throwback from the days when it was a real pier and was used to load and unload freighters. It jutted out into the Bay a good forty meters, with deep waters on either side. The nearest adjacent pier was at least fifty meters away with deep, cold waters between them. Around the north side of the pier was a narrow walkway with an iron railing, ending in a small lookout at the end of the pier. My challenge was finding a way to get from where we were to that walkway, leading to the side door entrance.

"Michael, you have any suggestions on where we can land?"

With Sally driving the plane, we were both in the cabin. He was sitting on the couch, strapped in with a seat belt. He was looking around through the cabin floor, surveying the scene, probably using a telescopic view.

"The process of elimination, I'm afraid, leaves only one option."

"I was hoping you were going to see some brilliant and clever solution."

"Sometimes our choices are not the best, but the least worse. There is too much traffic out front. The only option is the walkway along the rear."

That's how I found myself hanging on the edge of the lowered stairs, hovering about twenty feet over the dark, cold, churning waters of the Bay, the cold summertime winds of San Francisco biting through my thin shirt. I rolled the sleeves down to give just a little extra protection from the cold. There were a few splotches of mud still left from my first encounter with this Neanderthal threat just about ten hours ago. Was it just that short a time ago that I lived in blissful ignorance?

I was stalling. I was running on adrenaline. The damn clock was ticking away in my head. In the best case, I had maybe fifteen minutes to get in position before their car arrived.

The side door that opened on the walkway was about ten meters back from the edge. Getting down to the walkway was presenting a challenge for me.

The camouflage skin fluttered with the fake image of ocean waves lapping at the pier. I hung onto the hand rail of the pull down stairs, standing on the last step, looking across that three-foot gap to the cast iron railing along the cement landing. Given the width of our tail and the proximity of the building, I couldn't maneuver us any closer to the relatively narrow cement ledge.

Underneath me was a twenty-foot drop to the freezing waters. I could hear the waves splashing against the pilings of the pier supports, but I just couldn't get close enough.

My hands were damp, so I tightened my grip on the handrail. It wasn't fair. I had just crossed a half a million miles to save the planet, and now I was held back by a three-foot gap!

Even with the cold breeze, I was sweating. I had to force myself to not look down. I was too high. The water below was calling me. If I miscalculated, if I slipped, if the wind picked up, it would all end.

I did some quick calculations in my head. "Michael, take us up about two feet."

"Are you sure? That will make it a more dangerous jump."

"It's high school physics. I need a longer hang time to make it across the gap."

"Good luck, Bryan."

"Yeah, thanks."

I was going to need more than luck. Jumping this gap was probably going to be the easy part.

This was it. I took one final deep breath, thinking of Kathy on the other side. I had to do this to save her. I crouched down and shot into the air. Before I hit, I knew I wasn't going to make it. That second in the air dragged into two heartbeats. I was going to miss the landing. The extra time to fall the two feet got me just close enough to reach out and grab the top bar of the iron railing.

My arms felt like they were yanked out of their sockets, the shock of contact echoing through my shoulders as they took up my weight. My body slammed against the side of the platform. My feet dangled twenty feet above the water lapping against the pilings holding up the pier.

I held on for three breaths.

My fingers were already numb from the cold iron and getting tired. I couldn't stay like this for long and as much as I scrambled, I couldn't get my feet level with the ledge under the railing.

I tightened my grip and thought about Kathy turned into a slave, or worse, in the hands of aliens. I had to find the strength. I'd come too far and suffered too much to let go now.

I swung my legs, rocking side to side. With each swing my legs got higher and higher until I was able to get my right foot up and braced on the cement ledge.

Holding the rail, I pulled myself up and literally rolled over the railing to land on my side in the alley. I was once again on solid ground.

It was not the most elegant entrance, and I was glad no one was around to see me. I kept telling himself there were no extra points for grace. Getting Andy and then Kathy was all that mattered.

I stood up and brushed off the dirt picked up from the ground. My hands were raw from the rough steel railing. The middle of my back was sore where I had rolled over on top of the bald headed man's gun, now shoved into the back of my belt. It rested uncomfortably under my shirt. I waved off Michael to get the ship repositioned and headed to the side door where Myron had agreed to meet me.

There was one last step. I bid farewell to Sally and took my glasses off. I folded them and placed them in my front shirt pocket. These aliens already knew about our glasses from Richard; the first thing the alien did to Kathy was grab her glasses. If I wore them into their base, it would eliminate any possible advantage of surprise or bluff I might have. They would still be available when I needed them.

The door opened as I approached. Even though I expected it, I jumped at the click of the door and was about to reach for my gun when a grey head popped out and a kindly old face regarded mine.

"Hello there special agent in charge Bryan Postman. Myron Novellus, at your service." He held out his hand. "Where's your team and your car?"

"I'm here to set things up. The rest of my team is standing off. We don't want to alert the bad guys here."

Myron looked me up and down. "Ain't ya kind of short and scrawny and underdressed for a special agent in charge FBI agent? I thought you all were football players who wore dark suits and ties?"

I ignored the comments. "We're a little short of time here, Mr. Novellus. Did you bring the uniform?"

"Right here. Come on inside. No one's in the garage right now."

I followed him through a door that opened into a large, extended garage. It took up most of the ground floor, extending under the entire building. This used to be the storage area for shipping containers to be loaded onto ships. Now, it was just a service area for cars. This was where they hid their fleet of vehicles. I was half-expecting a spaceship or two. No such luck.

I glanced around. The ceiling was at least seven meters, and took up the first two stories of the building. There were two large black sedans and three white panel trucks in the garage, with room for at least an equal number more. Supporting the vehicles was a small, fully equipped repair facility with a portable hydraulic jack, racks of tools, a small gas pump, and a gravity-fed gasoline reservoir. Near one wall were rows of waist-high red and silver toolboxes on wheels. I saw another door at the rear of the garage on the Bay side with a small window in it. The lights of Oakland, across the bay, were fading in the coming dawn.

"Like I said," Novellus began while I put on the blue workman's jumpsuit over my jeans and white shirt. "Basement's always been off limits to me. I clean the garage here and the second and third floors. Second floor has the supply closet. Across the garage is the elevator. Stairs are right next to it."

"What do they do in the basement? Isn't that awfully close to the water?"

"Don't know, never been down there. I see mostly the big hairy French ones going down there. Sometimes one or two of the local suits. Lot of activity happened just an hour ago. Probably three or four of them down there now. Maybe five, six men in the building as of half an hour ago."

He looked me over, now dressed like a janitor. "Are you sure you're FBI?"

"You called my office didn't you?"

"Yup," the black man said, looking me up and down again. "Talked to your receptionist and everything. She described you pretty good. You watch out for her son, I think she might have a little thing for you," he said with a wink.

I didn't have time to think about the implications. "Mr. Novellus, you've been very helpful. Thank you for all you have done. Now, things are going to get very dangerous around here, so you be sure to get out and as far away as quick as you can."

He looked at me with pursed lips, then nodded. "One other thing, young man. You'll need this key card to access the doors." He handed me a card attached to the end of a retractable chain that clipped to the collar of my jumpsuit.

"Never did trust these fellers. Not very nice to me, you know what I mean? Don't smile, or say hello when I pass by. Just sort of ignore me, like I don't exist. Some of these guys are pretty scary looking too. Always thought they might be up to no good. Can you tell me what they've done?"

I looked back at the old black man. He stood slightly stooped. His eyes were clear and shiny, but surrounded by wrinkles. He smiled back at me, as though slightly amused at something.

I decided to take a chance. "They've kidnapped one man and we think they are holding him in this building." I paused, then continued, "And we think they've kidnapped a woman and bringing her here. They're due to arrive in less than fifteen minutes."

Myron stood up a little straighter. "And you aim to rescue them?"

"Yes, me and my team." I felt those eyes piercing mine. The old man smiled and nodded slightly to me, then reached over and grasped my shoulder.

"You take care of yourself, special agent in charge Bryan Postman." I nodded back and walked across the garage floor to the elevator on the opposite side of the floor.

I listened for any sounds of motion. It was deserted, as Myron said. Behind me, I saw Myron heading to the front of the garage where a small door, to the right of the large overhead door, led to the front street.

I faced two doors. One with a red exit sign probably lead to stairs and the other was the elevator door. I took a deep breath and pressed the elevator call button. It opened immediately. I stepped inside and pressed the button for the second floor.

I was in the lion's den.

43

THE DOOR OPENED to an empty floor. I went to the left, following the old janitor's directions and passed the small kitchen, and then the supply closet. Inside was what I expected for a janitor's closet: shelves of toilet paper, cleaning supplies, brooms, mops, and a bucket on wheels. I selected the bucket and large mop as a prop and was about to leave the closet when I saw two one-gallon tins of paint remover on the shelf, the universal solvent for cleaning gum off floors. They gave me an idea.

One way or another I had maybe ten minutes left before my time was going to run out. *Might as well plan on going out with a bang.* I grabbed the tins and threw them in the bucket, and then left the closet, pushing the bucket ahead of me with the mop.

I went back around the corner to the small kitchenette. As I expected there was an electric stove. I placed each tin on a heating element, opened the lids and turned the hot plates on low, then went back to the hallway.

Coming down the hallway were two men, dressed in loose-fitting suits. A requirement for working here seemed to be pushing at least 300 pounds and being over six feet tall. These two could have passed as professional football players, but at least they were clearly human.

I kept my head down, looking at the floor, shuffling my feet and pushing the mop around the floor. Out of the corner of my eye, I watched the two men pass me without a glance, ignoring me, just as Myron said.

I still sweated each of their steps. If they went to the kitchen, they'd immediately suspect me. But they stopped at the elevator and quickly entered the car. I saw one of them slide a security card into the slot in the panel and push the down button. The doors closed and I rushed over to listen. I heard a click as the elevator car passed through the garage level and then a louder click as it came to a stop at the basement level. I waited one breath and punched the recall button.

Once inside the elevator, I used Myron's card and selected the basement. I hardly breathed during the ten-second journey into the alien stronghold.

When the doors opened, I stuck my head out and looked up and down the corridor. It was empty, but I could hear noises down the hallway to the left. I pushed the bucket ahead with the mop and walked toward the voices.

I got fifteen feet down the hallway before a door opened behind me and I heard the footsteps of two men in the hallway. I dared not look behind me. Instead, I took the mop out of the bucket and began mopping the floor. A deep voice behind said, "Hey you, you're not supposed to be down here. What are you doing?"

I kept my head down, slowly pushing the mop back and forth, trying to look as subservient as I knew how.

"Myron tell me to mop the floors. I mopping the floors."

I heard the two sets of footsteps approach me. They split up coming on either side of me.

I was thinking about reaching for my gun. Then a rush of adrenaline-induced fear cascaded through me from head to foot. I realized how stupid I was. I could feel the reassuring, hard, angular shape of the gun pressed into my back, but it was under my jump suit. What a stupid, newbie mistake. I didn't have the skills for this cloak and dagger stuff. No way was I going to be able to get to it.

I needed some leverage.

As the two men came around to stand in front of me, I stopped mopping, but stayed hunched over. One stood directly in front, the other off to the side. This was a confrontation style they were obviously familiar with. "Who are you? Where's that old black man that usually cleans up here?"

"I'm Philippe. Myron, he went home sick, ask me to finish for him. I do good work."

"You'll do your work on the other floors. You don't come down here. They were closer, their presence supposed to intimidate me backward to the elevator. I rested my foot on the end of the mop and slowly, casually, twisted the handle, unscrewing the end. The noises at the far end of the corridor were louder. There was a scream, a man's scream, muffled by the intervening doors. I reflexively looked up.

The second guy, quiet up until now, saw the flash in my eyes and reached into his inside jacket and pulled out his gun. He pointed it at me and said, "Game's over. You're no janitor."

44

ANOTHER SCREAM ECHOED down the hall. Both guards looked behind them, momentarily distracted.

I gave the handle one last turn and the mop head came free. I swung the handle up and hit the guard's extended hand, knocking his gun into the air and away to the side. At the same time, I kicked the bucket across the floor at the second gunman. The fight was on.

Five months ago, at the urging of Rusty, my Navy SEAL buddy, I had walked into a dojo and signed up for a Kendo class. In the last five months, I had been transformed from novice to rank beginner. I found Kendo to be part stretching, part dance, and part dueling, all while holding a six-foot-long stick. My Sensei kept telling me the stick was an extension of my body, I was to be at one with the stick, the stick part of me. The one or two times I was in the zone—I could feel it, but it took a lot of imagination. I could never figure out how to recreate the feeling. It just happened when I let my reflexes take over.

Now I imagined my sphere of influence to extend to the tip of my mop handle. I owned this space. It was mine. And this sphere now encompassed the two guards out to kill me.

The guy on the right was caught by surprise when the bucket slammed into his knees. He jumped back to avoid the bucket and thudded against the wall. The guy on the left, now disarmed, was hurt and pissed off. He outweighed me by at least a 150 pounds. He lunged at me.

Seeing him out the corner of my eye, I whipped the metal tip of the handle around and punched the guy in the pit of his stomach. He was winded, but still grabbed the end of the handle in his stomach and tried to twist it out of my grip. I stepped to the side, crouched down and jabbed up. The grip of the man helped to aim the metal tip right at his jaw. I jabbed it forward. The blow was thwarted from full force, but it was enough to loosen his grip.

I saw the second man launch himself off the wall opposite me. There wasn't time to swing the stick around. Instead, I pivoted with my back to him, and pushed the stick as hard as I could behind me. I connected. I spun around, stick spinning in my hand, arm spread for balance and leverage, looking for the next opportunity.

Both gunmen had felt the sting of the stick. They were more cautious now. The gunman on my left rushed me. I deflected his leg kicks and following jab with my stick. This was like racquetball, the analytical engineer in me thought. Anticipate, move, position, and parry. Again.

But this left me exposed to the second man. He had recovered from his stomach blow and delivered a vicious kick to my ribs. This sent me crashing into the first gunman, which knocked the wind out of him.

There was no time to recover. The second man came at me. I drew in ragged breaths, my side in agony from the kick. I rolled to my knees and swung the stick like a baseball bat to deliver a side blow to his head. The mop pole broke against his skull, leaving a three-foot stick in my hand.

My sphere of influence had now shrunk in half.

The gunman shook off the blow and jumped me. I barely had time to swing what was left of the stick to make sure the narrow, sharp tip was the first thing the gunman hit. My raw hands hurt, but I held on tight and visualized.

In my Kendo class just the previous evening, we had practiced focusing on our chi. In pairs, we had held our sticks lengthwise between us and tried to push each other over. I always lost my balance first. I thought it was about strength. My sensei said it was about chi. So, he had kept me after class for remedial training in finding my chi.

Everyone had left the dojo. We had faced each other, kneeling on the mat. He is eighty-four years old, Japanese. The bio on his website said he'd lived in the states since after World War II, but he still carried a very heavy accent. He had said to me, "I don't understand why you not fall over all the time."

"Excuse me, Sensei?" I asked. I was very polite. He's eight-four years old.

"You so top heavy. You always live in here," he said tapping my forehead. "You never in here," a jab to my heart, "Or here," a jab to my stomach.

He kind of had a point. I'm a geek. But I couldn't say anything in response. Even I picked up he was asking a rhetorical question.

"I show you. I am 101 pounds of proud Japanese man. All my 101 pounds, here," he said, patting his tummy. "My chi so strong, when I wish it I have 1001 pounds of chi right here." He patted his tummy again.

"My chi is my anchor. You physicist. My chi stronger than your physics. I prove to you." I was surprised he remembered. When we introduced ourselves in class six months ago, I mentioned I had degrees in physics. We were a room of thirty-five beginners. Now we were down to fifteen amateurs.

"You try push me over. You cannot push over 1001 pounds of Japanese chi in me."

We had gripped each other's forearms. I was reluctant to hold on very tight for fear of breaking him. I tried pushing. I had pretty good leverage. He didn't move.

"You hold like girl. Grip hard. Grip tight. You can't move 1001 pounds of Japanese chi if you hold so light."

I tried again. I didn't hold back. I pushed. I felt him push back. Maybe I was moving him a little. Then I saw his face relax. He closed his eyes, breathing slowly. He sat up just a little taller and held firm. But as hard as I pushed, I could feel him deflecting my force to the point I got off balance and fell over, again.

"That better. You feel my chi now. I am mountain. You are still pebble. Feel what it is to be mountain. I push you now. You feel your chi in your stomach. You try become small boulder. Work up to mountain."

We had knelt there, battling back and forth for balance for a good thirty minutes. He'd been telling the class for the last five months we needed to get in touch with our chi, but never really said how. In feeling him through his skinny arms pushing back, I was feeling how his strength flowed from his body into his arms, and through to me. I felt the subtle shifting of his balance, compensating for my leverage an instant before I applied it. He was anticipating me and staying just slightly ahead, directing my strength to where he wanted it.

It was not his strength, but his intuition to anticipate and respond in advance that kept me so off balance. There was not an ounce of doubt in his 101 pounds that he would not feel my moves and keep me off balance. The harder I pushed, the faster he had me toppling over.

A tiny fraction of his muscle memory was flowing to my muscles, feeling him anticipate my motion before I even knew what I was going to do.

The fact remained, he was only 101 pounds and I had more than 50 pounds and more than 50 years of youth on him, yet, could never push him over.

He pushed me back and made me topple over for maybe the fiftieth time and said, "You getting better. You may be stone now, not pebble. You try practice think from here." He patted my stomach again. "Think mountain. Then you are mountain. You are just stone now, you be mountain someday. Not need to gain weight."

In the half a second while the 300-pound gunman fell towards me, I pictured myself a mountain. I was the Rock of Gibraltar. No, I was Mt Everest. No, I was Olympus Mons on Mars, the largest mountain in the solar system. I felt the energy flow from my arms.

The gunman fell on top of the stick, jolting my arms, but I held fast. Tired and shaking, I held the dead weight of the impaled gunman for a moment before I was able to shift to the side and he dropped to the floor. Dead before he landed. What was left of my mop looked like a toothpick sticking through the bacon wrapped around a scallop. Except for the growing red stain in the white shirt wrapping the scallop.

I rolled to my side. The first gunman was shaking off his daze. I was defenseless, sore, and tired. I desperately looked around for the dropped gun. I spied it a good fifteen feet up the corridor. I crawled toward it.

I'd almost reached it when I felt a grip on my ankle. I was turned over and yanked back. The gunman was pulling himself up off the floor, reaching for my other foot.

I waited just a moment and then kicked him in the head.

He let go. I rolled back on my stomach, wincing at the sharp pain in my side. I scrambled up the corridor and reached out with my hand for the gun just as I felt that hand on my foot again. My fingers touched the handgrip and I felt myself pulled back by the ankle. But the gun slid along the floor with me.

The grip on my foot tightened. This guy didn't know when to give up. My fingers walked their way up the handle of the gun, sliding it along the floor with me. A second hand took a firm grip on my other ankle. I felt myself pulled violently backward. My hand came around with the gun.

I tried to ignore the sharp, hot ice pick of pain in my side. I was sure I had a few broken ribs.

With my last breath, I tried to vent the pain in my side, the rawness of my hands and the frustration of coming so far yet being stopped by this wrestler almost on top of me. I let loose one piercing scream and twisted around just enough to point the gun at his head. I pulled the trigger.

The explosion of the gun was the exclamation point at the end of my scream. As its echoes faded, my panting was the only sound left in the hallway.

Before the ringing in my ears eased off, I heard the click of the doorknob ahead in the corridor. The same door from which the other screams had come just minutes before, was opening. A head, with bushy buffalo fur and a thick-ridged forehead, pushed out to see the commotion.

Still breathing hard, in agony from the kick in my side, and my lower body pinned by the dead body of the guard, I lifted my head and looked over my shoulder, making eye contact with the Neanderthal alien. I saw the alien's eyes widen in surprise. Before I could bring my gun up, the alien pushed farther into the corridor, bringing a laser hand weapon dangling from his belt up and around, targeting me.

There wasn't time and the pain was too great for me to swing my left arm around and shoot the alien. I saw the alien's fingers tighten. I knew the blast was coming now. My whole lower body was pinned like a frog on a dissecting board. I watched the alien's lips twitch upward and expose his crooked teeth, his fingers clamping down on the trigger buttons.

I thought of Kathy. I was her last hope. I might be all that stood between the Earth and these aliens. Aliens.

I saw the fingers twitch.

"Wait," I said. "The YonLen are upstairs. They're on their way down. Shoot me and they will hunt you down."

This bought me a momentary reprieve.

Using my last bit of strength, I rolled as far as I could to the left, feet still pinned, just as the laser fired.

I no longer felt the pain in my side. The searing agony on my shoulder and leg distracted me. I screamed again and with the next inhaled breath, smelled the acrid sweet aroma of burnt meat. I was too afraid to look at my shoulder. I knew I had less than a half second before the laser was recharged and I would be finished off. I had nowhere to go.

I brought my left arm and the gun around, fighting to stay conscious. I forced my left arm to move, swing around, target the alien, aim higher, higher, now. Pull the trigger, once, twice, a third time.

I collapsed on my back, each breath painful, and barely heard the thud of the alien falling, the higher pitch clatter of the laser weapon hitting the floor, washing over me like a wave of relief. I allowed myself three breaths. The smell of barbeque was too overpowering. I had to know how bad it was. I rotated my head to the right and forced myself to look at my shoulder.

My shirt was still smoldering and there was a black gash four inches long down my upper arm. The beam that grazed my arm cauterized the skin so it wasn't bleeding. I looked further down my right side and saw the jagged edge of a six inch gash in the right side of my jeans still smoking. As I focused attention on each of these new wounds, I felt the intense stabs of pain, like hundreds of embedded fishhooks being pulled out of my skin.

I had gotten only a splash from the outer edge of the beam. The full brunt of the beam had hit the guard, still pinning my feet, in his upper body. There was a two-inch diameter hole going clear through him from shoulder to hip. A blacken, charred mark on the floor was visible at the end of the hole.

I actually felt a little better in comparison, knowing how bad it could have been. The pain was still there, but I knew none of my injuries were fatal. The faint moans coming from the opened door drew my attention away from myself. I still had a world to save.

45

I KICKED THE lifeless mass of the gunman off my feet, rolled to my side and pushed myself up off the floor. Still clutching the captured 9 mm Glock in my left hand, I leaned against the wall to keep my balance. I walked to the dead alien and reached down and retrieved its laser hand weapon. This I was familiar with.

Leading with my gun, I poked my head through the doorway of the room. In a quick glance, he saw Andy tied to a chair in the middle, his head rolling slowly from side to side, moaning. With no other threats visible, I rushed in.

"Andy! Andy! Can you hear me? You're going to be okay. We're getting you out of here."

His head came up and I saw the two orange, glowing spheres on either side of the collar. Andy's eyes were glazed over in pain. They looked at me, but did not focus. I looked around the room for the control unit. There was a table pushed against the wall, with a console, papers, a briefcase and the contents of Andy's pockets scattered about. On the chair, behind the table, was the same small box with a light and a dial I had seen on the Moon just a few hours earlier. I ran to it and cranked the dial full counterclockwise, heard a click and saw the light go out on the collar. It snapped open.

There was immediate relief from Andy as the constant pain relaxed. Now he raised his head on his own and looked at me. He smiled and said in a weak voice, "What took you so long?"

"Don't take this personally Andy, but I really came to rescue Kathy. You were an unexpected bonus."

Andy immediately got serious. "Is Kathy here? We have to get to her." He fought against his constraints.

"Easy Andy, let me get you out of there first. Kathy's on her way. We have less than five minutes before she's supposed to arrive. Sally's had the ship broadcasting a message to her for the last fifteen minutes. I just hope she can hear it through her subcutaneous ear pieces." As I spoke, I was rifling through the contents on the table, considering using the piece of broken glass from what was left of Andy's glasses, until I found a pen knife. I was able to cut the straps holding Andy's arms and legs to the chair.

Andy rubbed his wrists and then his neck, then grabbed my arm and pulled me close. "Bryan, no matter what, you have to promise me you will save Kathy. You cannot let her stay a prisoner. They will torture her until she tells them everything she knows and then torture her some more just for the fun of it. I've learned that they have been kidnapping women for at least the last five years and taking them off planet. You cannot let her go through that. Promise me!"

"I already made the same promise to Michael. Why do you think I risked coming into this hellhole? I came to rescue Kathy, and now you. We will get out of here," I said, staring back into Andy's intense eyes, "all three of us, or we will die trying. Now, let's get positioned."

Andy grabbed my arm as I eased him up out of his chair onto his wobbly legs.

"Michael. Did you find him, is he safe?"

"He's as safe as can be expected. He's at about 30,000 feet right above us. We saw the recordings in the server vault. We saw what happened to the plant."

"What happened? I was pulled out of my office, my glasses removed, and a hood placed over my head. They put this collar around my neck and the next thing I knew I felt the most excruciating pain in my life. I must have passed out and came to in this chair. This one Neanderthal has been grilling me for what felt like an hour. He already knew about Sciquest and our ships."

I decided not to cushion the blow. "Andy, we saw Richard lead the aliens into the headquarters building. The whole complex is gone, the main building and the factory were both blown up. Richard opened the door for them. I don't know what sort of deal he made, but he sold us out to them!"

"It's not his fault. He was with the first round of Neanderthals when they entered the building and grabbed me. He told me he found them when he did an image search. He tracked their traffic to this pier. He said he came here to talk to them. He thought he could reason with them, maybe make a deal," Andy said, grimacing.

"When they got an inkling of who he was, where he was from, they put a torture ring on him and have been controlling him. He's really a good kid. He's not responsible for what he's done. The torture was too much for him. And once they had me, he followed their orders so I wouldn't be hurt."

"Well, that didn't seem to work out very well for either of you, now did it?"

"Bryan," Andy said, gripping my arm, "we have to break him free."

"I think he's in the same car as Kathy. When it arrives, we'll get him out. Then we can get to the bottom of why he sold us out."

"There's more. You have to get word back, to everyone. Earth is in danger."

"I've got Sally in my pocket," I said. "She'll broadcast to the ship." I reached into my inside shirt pocket to retrieve my glasses. I was able to fish out my glasses, or what was left of them. At some point in my rolling around, I crushed them. Having 300 pounds of wrestler land on top of them didn't help either. The lenses had shattered into chunks and the nose piece was cracked and held together with only two remaining wires. The frame dangled on one side by wires that still remained attached.

With little hope, I put the mangled glasses on, wishing I had some tape to put across the nose piece at least, which would surely complete the image of me as a geek engineer.

"Sally? Sally? Respond."

There was no sound out of the ear piece and there was no image in my eyes.

"Andy, Sally's down. It's up to us to get the message out. What else did you learn?"

"They call themselves the KaBac. They kept asking me about two other races."

"Yeah, Michael learned about this on the Moon. It's the RocNor and the YonLen. The RocNor are the badasses out there. I think we might be on their menu. They eat the KaBac. The YonLen might be cops or at least sympathetic. Did you learn where they come from?"

"It's not our solar system. They have some sort of space station locally."

"You mean on the Moon?"

"No, I think they were hinting it is somewhere out beyond Pluto. They kept asking me if I knew where it was, and whether we had been as far out as Pluto."

"What are they doing here? Are they planning on invading Earth?"

Andy walked gingerly across the floor. "It's not an invasion they want, it's the destruction of human civilization they're after, followed by raping and pillaging what's left. And then their clan takes over what he called their rightful place ruling Earth and us weak humans."

"This one that was questioning me," Andy kicked the side of the KaBac, sprawled dead in the doorway, with three bullet holes, "bragged they were close to the final stage of their plan. He was going to accelerate their time schedule since he thought we were going to tell the world about them. They've been working on this for almost twenty years. Our early moon missions got their attention."

"But why the secrecy? Why not just attack and destroy our defenses?"

"The YonLen wouldn't let them touch a space-faring civilization. But if they can get us to bomb ourselves back into the stone age, we'd be fair game again.

"How are they going to do that?"

"They're going to start World War Three."

46

CAREFULLY SIDESTEPPING THE dead bodies along the way, we limped down the corridor, supporting each other around our various injuries. Between the two of us, we didn't have the strength to climb the stairs, so we took the elevator, opening into the garage just as the large rolling front door began to open. But this time both Andy and I were armed and ready.

We crouched behind one of the red portable tool cabinets that paralleled the wall, waiting in ambush. If Kathy had gotten the messages, she was expecting something and should be ready.

The large black sedan, just like the other two already in the garage, pulled in through the open door. Even before the overhead door finished closing, the front passenger door opened and a hairy, wide KaBac got out. He wore jeans and a massive leather jacket that was still too short at the arms. He held a control box and barked something to the backseat. The side door opened and Richard stepped out. The two spheres on either side of his neck were glowing orange and he was clearly in pain.

Andy started to rise from behind our hiding place, but I grabbed his arm and pulled him down. "Not yet," I whispered. Kathy followed Richard out of the passenger side door, her neck also decorated by two glowing orange balls. She looked around expectantly.

A human driver got out and came around. The KaBac said something and handed him the control box. Now was our chance. The human driver and the KaBac were on our side of the car, exposed.

I grabbed hold of the top of the tool box to pull myself up. I was too weak from the last fight and my wounds. I held the laser weapon level and Andy, standing next to me, leveled the 9 mm Glock.

"Hold it right there you two." I froze. That was going to be my line. No! We were so close. I didn't bother turning around. From the position of the voice, which sounded all too human, I thought he must be standing in the door to the stairwell.

"Drop your guns." We were in a stalemate. I might get a shot off and maybe kill the KaBac, but I would surely get a bullet in my back and we would all still be captives. We lowered our guns to the floor.

"Don't you know they are aliens," I pleaded with the gunman behind us. "From another planet. They're going to destroy the Earth and kill humans. How can you let them do that?"

"They're not going to destroy the Earth, buddy boy, just re-organize the power structure. Who do you think is going to come out on top when the dust clears? We supply them with what they want now and we become the new kings later. People like you think you're so smart. This is the end of the line for you guys, now move." The traitor shoved us ahead.

"Swell rescue, hot shot," Kathy greeted me as I approached. "Oh, what happened to you, you poor thing," she immediately changed her tone, once she got a good look at my torn shirt, limp, and burns.

Richard's string-bean thin frame was hunched over, shoulders rounded. He looked up and saw his father for the first time. He tried to move toward him, but the driver, holding the control box, got his attention with a small twist of the control knob and a brief shout, "Hey!"

Richard just stood slumped at the shoulders. "Dad, I didn't mean for this to happen! I tried to stop them." Andy made a move toward his son, but the driver shouted at him and the orange balls around Richard's neck brightened. He screamed.

"Enough!" Andy shouted and backed off. The torture collar around Richard's neck was just as effective at controlling his father.

"It's okay, Richard. There was nothing you could have done."

The KaBac laughed in its deep guttural, belly rocking laugh. "I take the younger one," it said, pointing to Richard. "Might last longer with RocNor." Then, looking over at me and Andy, said, "I studied some human language. You are, what you call, walking dead. You will soon know it." And it laughed again.

The traitor with the gun, standing behind me asked, "What do you want done with these two?"

"You," it said, pointing to the human driver, "come with me. We prepare the slaves and lifestones for the ship. It arrives." Then turning to the human traitor behind us, it said, "Take the female and young male with us. Kill the other two."

"Wait," I shouted. "Lifestones. I can get you more lifestones" I was desperately searching for some way to stall.

"Stupid humans. You have most valuable possession in ten planets and it is decoration for slave women. I will get all the lifestones I want after humans die."

"Is that why you are attacking us? For our jewelry?" I asked, incredulous.

"No." the KaBac paused, looking directly at me, staring me down with deep set, black eyes. "We take female slaves for us and RocNor eat males. Better humans than KaBac. Ha ha ha!"

Without a further glance our way, the KaBac, with the driver in tow, headed off down the stairs. The control box was handed to the human traitor. Now one hand held the gun, the other the control box.

"I will kill you quickly," the human guard said to Andy. "You," he said, pointing the gun at me, "I kill slowly, piece by piece. I saw what you did to Joey downstairs. He was my cousin. He got me this job. You shouldn't have done that to Joey. I'm going to pay you back with interest. Then, I'm gonna kill you." He smiled in anticipation.

While he was distracted, Richard was watching him closely, waiting for his chance. With the guard's attention on me, he lunged for the gun. But he wasn't fast enough.

47

THE SHOT WAS muffled when Richard fell on the gun, the bullet killing him before he hit the ground. I stood there in shock. There wasn't time for anyone to react. Things felt hopeless. Beyond hopeless. Now they were killing us off. The traitor effortlessly pushed Richard's lifeless body away from the gun to the floor, ready to cover any one of the three of us who might decide to try again.

"Richard, no!" Andy ran to his son and, oblivious of the gun trained on him, knelt down to the floor, and cradled Richard in his arms. "I should never have gotten you involved in this. You could have been in any one of a dozen other companies. I'm so sorry to have agreed to let you in."

He sat there, gently rocking his now-dead son.

The guard looked at Andy. "Now you take his place. The KaBac can't tell us apart very well. For where you'll end up, one human is as good as another. Put his collar on."

I watched in horror as the gunman turned one of the knobs to the click. The wire rings around Richard's neck broke apart at the orange balls.

"I won't. Just shoot me now and be done with it," Andy shouted.

"No, I won't shoot you. I need you alive. I'll just torture your girlfriend here until you do what I say." His thumb moved and Kathy, who had stood there, broke the silence with an ear-piercing scream and clutched at her collar, now glowing more brightly. She fell to her knees in agony. Andy had no choice. "Stop, damn you. I'll do it."

I stood there, my mind racing, trying to put the adrenalin rush I was feeling to good use. I needed a plan. More than ever.

The guard moved his thumb again and Kathy collapsed on the ground, unconscious from the neuron-stimulator. Just her shallow breaths broke the sudden silence. "You see what you made me do? I'm not very good at this stuff one handed, and it's my weak hand too. Now put the damn collar on," he shouted. "A few more notches and she dies."

Andy looked at me and I nodded. With shaking hands, he placed the collar around his neck and touched the ends of the rings to the balls. I looked around; all around me were tools and potential weapons, but they were all outside of my reach. I felt so helpless.

"You caused me way too much trouble. How about a little of this?" And his thumb moved again. This time, Andy clutched at the collar, screaming, his face contorting, every muscle contracting. One more touch of the traitor's thumb and Andy passed out from the pain.

The traitor turned his attention back to me and smiled. "Now it's just you and me pretty boy. Time for a little payback." My stomach churned and I couldn't seem to catch my breath. Me against 300 pounds of ex-football player wasn't going to be a happy ending for me.

The human traitor placed the control box on the hood of the car behind him and shoved the gun in his belt. He walked over to me and let swing a sudden right hook. I wasn't expecting it and didn't react in time. I took it full on my cheek and eye. The fist rocked my whole body around, dazing me. I was staggering, able to see out of only my right eye. I was looking for something, anything to use as a weapon or leverage against this guy.

I shuffled back to stay out of his reach, but I missed the clue. He punched me in the stomach with enough force to lift me off the ground.

I tried warding more blows off with my arms, but I was too weak and they were just batted out of the way. The pain of my broken ribs grinding over each other left me nearly immobilized. I fell on my hands and knees, moaning, unable to catch my breath.

Get up, get up! I told myself. If you don't get up, everyone's going to die.

I knew it was up to me; and I wasn't going to make it. I looked up with my one good eye and saw the huge man towering over me. He kicked me in the side, forcing me to fall over on my back.

I slowly rolled over onto my hands and knees. The pain was terrible. Blood dripped to the cement floor from my broken cheek and nose. The simple attempt at shaking my head to clear my vision caused me to almost black out again. I knew I was quickly loosing strength. I had to fight back.

With what? I was out of options. Out of breath. Out of strength. Out of karma.

"Come on college boy, get up and be a man for once in your life. I want you awake when I smash your head in. I want you to see me when you die, so you can remember what payback feels like."

I tried to let the rage wash over me. It fueled me back to my hands and knees. I staggered up on one leg. I just couldn't make it all the way up.

That was just what he was waiting for. With my head at waist level, he pulled back and took another swing at my face. In my daze, I reached up to ward off the blow, only to have my arm batted aside. If it took any of the force out of the blow to my nose and cheek, I couldn't tell.

I ended up on my back again. The pain was too much, every part of me ached, my breathing was ragged. With every panting breath, I thought I could hear broken ribs grinding. I tried to mumble something, anything, but there was too much blood in my mouth.

This was not supposed to be the way it ended.

Lying there, in the most pain I had ever experienced, I realized Michael was wrong. Passion did not always trump strength. Sometimes you did need more strength than the bad guys. I really was just an engineer, not a warrior. I found myself back in the situation I'd been trying to avoid the last twenty years. In my foggy vision, I could almost see the shattered pieces of my space shuttle on the ground next to me.

The traitor knelt down beside me on the garage floor. Out of the blurred vision of my right eye, I saw the faint smile on his face. That huge, massive arm slowly pulled back. It was aimed straight for me. I made a feeble attempt to kick out with my leg, but I could hardly get it off the ground, I was so weak and in such pain. All I could do was watch that fist swing back, preparing to land the last blow.

A new hand entered my field of view, tapping the shoulder of the human traitor. *Tap, tap, tap.* It was surely a mirage. It was hard to see, dark in color against the darkness of the garage. This was how it would end, I thought, seeing phantoms.

"Mind if I step in?" the deep voice said. Now I was hearing things. But, obviously, so had the traitor, who twisted around from his crouched position on the floor. Before he was fully turned around, a right hook connected with the side of his face that sent him spinning off his knees and flat on his ass, ending up five feet away.

A large black shadow stood where the traitor had been, moments before. I must be hallucinating. Maybe I was already dead. Is this what the angel of death looked like?

Then the angel spoke: "What sort of sissy-ass fighting were you doing, special agent in charge Bryan Postman? If that's how they teach you to fight in FBI school, my hard-earned tax dollars are being wasted."

I stared through the slit that was left of my right eye, through blurred vision, at Myron. An angel of a different sort. I tried a feeble smile that probably looked like a contorted grimace.

The traitor pushed himself off the floor, shook his head and got a good look at Myron, who must have been twice his age and half his size. Then he lit up, obviously having recognized him.

"Why you piece of crap. You're just the janitor. I'll take you apart in two seconds."

Oh, crap. I was completely out of commission and now I was going to have to watch this thug take Myron apart. I didn't want to see another good guy taken out.

"Myron, you need to get out now," I croaked, spraying blood on the floor. I spit out another glob of blood to give Myron my last piece of advice. "These guys are bad news."

Myron grinned but he didn't take his eye off the traitor. "Let me give you a few pointers, special agent in charge Bryan Postman. I teach boxing at the Y to the young kids so they aren't afraid of the older, bigger punks in their neighborhood. And that's all they are, big, dumb punks, like this guy here."

"I'll show you who's dumb," said the thug. He started toward Myron, but after he had taken two steps, he stopped and remembered his gun. He reached for it in his belt and pulled it out.

Myron flipped his left hand out, slashing down quickly. A crack echoed in the garage as a thin steel antenna slashed the traitor's hand. He hollered and dropped the gun, clutching his wrist. "You crazy old man."

Myron nodded in acknowledgement and smiled thinly. "First lesson, Special Agent in Charge, is disarm your opponent," Myron said calmly. "At the first sign of trouble, you rip off the nearest aerial car antenna, or find a stick and you carry it along with you."

The traitor cradled his right hand in his other hand, blood from the long gash dripped through his fingers to the floor, looking at Myron in shock.

Myron continued his lecture. "I tell my boys, sometimes it's not a question of looking like a fool or not, sometimes it's a question of what kind of fool you want to look like. Better to apologize for a damaged car and pay the price, than to be in the hospital, or worse. Now, this antenna is nice for disarming your opponent, but you can inflict a lot more damage with two free hands." He tossed the aerial aside, just as the traitor launched the remaining five feet to tackle Myron to the ground.

But Myron wasn't there.

I was having a hard time following everything through my pain and my one barely-open eye, but I'd say things were looking up. If I didn't hurt so much, I would be enjoying this.

I thought that maybe I'd find that gun that the thug had dropped, but it had gone skittering across the floor, under a toolbox. I tried to crawling to it, but the pain in my side and arms and legs and head froze me in place. It was all I could do to not join Kathy and Andy in blessed, pain-free unconsciousness.

"Five lessons, special agent in charge Bryan Postman. Second lesson, always keep moving." As he spoke, Myron shuffled his feet, moving backward, rotating as the traitor repositioned.

"Third lesson, defense." And he raised his fist in the traditional boxing pose. "In this position, you can protect your sphere."

The other guy tried a few jabs, but Myron's arm was always there to push them aside. "Defense is not about strength, it's about deflection. Always watch your opponent. Keep your eyes on him. His eyes tell you everything you need to know. You use your opponent's strength against him. The stronger your opponent, the stronger your defense."

Myron's opponent was frustrated in not being able to land a blow. He made a few feints.

"Come on Donny, try to hit me again. I got to show special agent in charge Bryan Postman here how to properly defend himself against punks like you."

Just for a second, the thug stopped short.

"Yeah, you look so surprised. I know your name. I been watching you punks for six months. That's all you are, big, musclebound punks."

"Screw you old man," said Donny. "I'm going to rip you apart."

"Okay, time for lesson number four: offense."

Myron took a step closer, feinted with his left and followed through with his right, into the side of Donny's head. Then, before he could react, it was a left into his stomach.

"Remember when I said defense is not about strength? Well, offense is. When you hit, hit as hard as you can. A scrawny kid like you needs to work out some more, build up some muscle. There is no substitute for strength and no excuse for not being prepared."

Donny was breathing hard now and staggering backwards, bent over. I knew how he felt, but I can't say I was sympathetic.

"And remember the most important rule about defending yourself," Myron looked down at me and winked. "There is no substitute for a good offense. Even if you have a perfect defense, the other guy will just wear you down. It's a strong offense that wins battles. Gain the higher ground and never give it up. When someone attacks you, they lose any right to fairness. And I almost forgot, the most important lesson, number five. Never, ever leave a conscious enemy at your back."

Myron stepped over to Donny and preceded to delivery one blow after another, into his stomach, into his face, and finally swung his right hand up into his lower chin, lifting Donny off the ground momentarily with the force of the blow. Donny ended up motionless, flat on his back on the cement floor of the garage.

I lay my head back down on the floor and looked at the ceiling. I was still alive. Things were definitely looking up.

48

AFTER A FEW moments, Myron's face swam into view just above mine. "You okay there, special agent in charge Bryan Postman?"

"Help me up," I said.

"You might pass out," he said.

"Don't care," I said.

He shrugged and lent me a hand. He was really strong for someone his age. I struggled to my feet, feeling my ribs grinding against each other. It was not a pleasant feeling. I leaned heavily on Myron. "Where did you come from, not that I'm complaining?"

"When I heard that girl's scream, I thought to myself, Man, I tell ya, that young man has gone and screwed up his rescue. And that nice young receptionist asked me to help you out, so I figured I better not waste any time."

"Why did you have to wait until I was beaten to a pulp?"

"I think you'll remember my lessons now that you know the consequences. Now let's help your friends."

I wasn't in a position to complain. I asked Myron to hand me the control on the hood of the car. Myron looked at me curiously, but complied. I leaned heavily on the hood of the car and grabbed the control box. I rotated the two dials counterclockwise until they clicked and both collars fell off.

"What's with the collars?" asked Myron.

"Big trouble," I said. "Now I need your phone."

Myron fixed me a look but merely nodded and handed it over. Andy and Kathy were still unconscious, but for the moment, they were free. We needed to get out of here before the guys downstairs were on to us. I didn't know if our friend Donny was supposed to check in. I used Myron's cellphone to call Sally who was monitoring the FBI line. Her mirrored image now resided in the ship's computer network.

"Michael," I slurred out through swollen lips, "we need transport. Back the plane into the lowest level of the building, and be careful of the second floor." I found I had to lean heavily on the car, and felt my ribs grinding with each breath. Any motion brought a wave of pain.

A few seconds later, the Bay side door of the garage was crushed in by the tail of the jet, taking a good part of the bay sidewall with it. The back stairway dropped down and Michael's head peeked out.

"Myron," I gasped, "we'll fill you in later. This is Michael. Michael, could you help get Kathy inside. Myron, you take Andy. I'll follow."

Michael came down the steps, looking as unruffled as ever, like he was merely late for his lecture. "Myron, so good of you to assist. Bryan, dear boy, you look terrible. Are you sure you can make it?"

"You should see the other guy. Kathy and Andy need more help than I do right now," I said, motioning my head toward them. By the way they were stirring, it appeared they were just beginning to regain consciousness. "Get them aboard. I'll follow," I barely managed to get the words out, blood dripping down my chin. I reached up with trembling arm and used my shirtsleeve to wipe it off before it dripped to the floor.

"I'm awake," groaned Andy. "But I don't think I can stand on my own." He looked around, blinking his eyes, clearly surprised but pleased to see Michael. He looked at the thug, laying on the ground. "You got him," he said, surprised.

"He was a punk," Myron said.

"He killed my son," said Andy. As they walked by the inert figure, Andy mustered enough strength to kick him. Nobody said anything.

"Richard. We have to bring his body with us," Andy mumbled.

"We have to get all of us out of here," I said. "We'll come back for Richard, I promise."

Kathy was awake too, though barely conscious, and needed to be supported by Michael.

"We really need to get this show on the road," I said, nervously, looking at the back of the garage, waiting for the alien reinforcements to arrive.

With help, Andy and Kathy crawled up the plane's rear stairwell with Michael and Myron assisting. I took a moment to collect the laser weapon I had relinquished earlier. I thought for a moment about grabbing the collars with the orange balls and giving them a closer look, but I was in pain and I never wanted to see them again. Technology was usually exciting to me, but these things were evil.

I staggered to the extended stairs, one hand holding the laser, the other firmly grasping the railing. Standing on that first step, heavily leaning on the railing, through the fog of pain cascading from the tips of my toes to the throbbing in my head, I felt a wave of relief. I was finally safe.

Just then, a shot rang out and I felt my right leg collapse. And then the tsunami of pain shot up my leg, into my spine, and cascaded over my already oversaturated brain. I screamed out. If I hadn't been holding the rail, I would have fallen to the garage floor. As it was, I collapsed on the bottom stair, a sitting duck.

"Sally," I shouted through my raging pain, "move us out, now!"

The plane pulled away from the hole in the wall. Plaster and pieces of sheet rock rained down on me. Multiple shots fired. I could hear them ricocheting off the stairwell and the plane fuselage. I crouched helpless on the stairs, no cover anywhere. I was gonna have to pay it forward to my karma bank after this.

I was looking down, through the stairs, as we moved out over the water. I saw the ocean surface twenty feet below me. And just beneath the surface there was the outline of a silvery sphere, at least as large in diameter as the plane I was on. It was slowly moving toward the building we were just leaving, a barely perceptible bulge on the water's surface confirming its presence.

The detached engineer part of my brain suddenly realized how the KaBac were able to move back and forth from space to our cities undetected. They landed at sea far away from anyone able to spot them and traveled the rest of the way underwater to their bases at ports.

The gunfire had stopped, but it was only a matter of time before the shooter loaded a new clip or got word to other gunmen in the building. I was in pain from every part of my body, my leg was throbbing. It was as though I could feel the blood pumping out of the bullet hole with each heartbeat, but there was one more thing I had to do. Myron's rule number five was Rusty's rule number two. I couldn't get it out of my head.

The wind from the bay, cooled by the fifty degree waters, chilled me, which might have helped numb some of my pains.

While we were less than thirty meters from the warehouse, I reached out with the captured laser weapon and leaned it against the stair to steady my aim. I was going to break my promise to Andy, but this was more important.

Struggling to keep a grip on the stairwell and aim the laser at the same time, using my one partially-opened eye, I fired into the second-floor window. And hoped for one last piece of luck.

The cans of paint thinner I had left on the stove had all evaporated. The toluene vapors had mixed with the air, dispersing throughout the hallway. When the laser passed through the window, it hit the wall in three places, which immediately turned white hot. The fuel-air mixture ignited from three different points, exploded outward, first blowing out every window on the second floor, and then finding a weak spot into the garage below.

The weak spot was where the gasoline reservoir was mounted to the inside wall. The tank ruptured, spraying gasoline throughout the garage. With the flames from the second floor shooting down every crack that had just opened up in the garage's ceiling, the gasoline-air mixture in the garage, with a much higher energy density than the toluene and air mixture, exploded.

The shock wave front hit the plane a half a second after the second floor blast. Even the stabilization routine that kept the ship horizontal, struggled to compensate and the plane was battered about, rotating ninety degrees, broadside to the blast. This was the only thing that saved me from even worse damage, as only my arm was exposed to the heat wave from the secondary, much larger blast.

Still, the explosion burned the hairs off my arm and left me with second-degree burns. The second shockwave hit a half a second later, lifting the plane more than a hundred feet in the air. No amount of compensation could keep it from being battered about like a leaf in a hurricane. But, once the shock fronts passed, the ship gained stability again.

Every structural support pillar in the garage was pulverized in the blast, almost as though the first floor of the building vanished, leaving a vacuum in its place. Through the slit in my remaining eye, I watched the rest of the building collapse, one floor after another. The pillars holding the garage above the Bay were weakened by the explosion. Finally, the unevenly distributed weight of the rest of the building, crashing down on the already weakened garage floor, brought down the rest of the structure.

I was only dimly aware of Myron's helping hand, pulling me back into the plane. By the time the stairs were pulled up and the jet safely away, I had mercifully passed out.

49

A FIERY ICEPICK of pain stabbed into my calf, rudely forcing me back to consciousness. I felt myself dropped onto a mattress, the jostling instantly exciting all my other pains. The pain in my leg was shouted down by the hundreds of barbs of electrical fire in my shoulder, which took up the song, keeping time with the throbbing beat in my head. The nearly imperceptible comfort of the soft mattress provided an important clue; it couldn't be hell, where surely I had ended up.

The rest of the world slowly coalesced through the fog of pain. Entering on the left, a high pitched clanking of stainless steel instruments scattering on a metal pan; on my right, the nearby murmur of two voices, an old man and an old woman. The growing light against my closed eyes was interrupted by the passing of a shadow.

I opened the eye that was not swollen shut, but closed it immediately against the bright light. The effort caused me to jerk my head. Big mistake. The throbbing turned to explosions. I inadvertently rolled onto my left ear, rubbing my raw flesh. I moaned.

"He's awake," I heard in the background. I opened my good eye, or at least my less damaged eye, mostly swollen shut, squinting against the light.

"What... where..." I croaked the words out. A shape leaned toward me.

"It's okay, Bryan." The familiar voice was Michael's. The recent memory ebbed back. I felt comforted.

Slowly, forcing each word in a separate shallow breath, I eked out, "Where...are...we?"

"You're in the infirmary. We made it to our Prescott base."

"Kathy? Did she...?" Fear and anxiety washed over me. I was afraid to hear the answer and I couldn't even choke out the rest of the question.

"Oh yes, she's okay. And Andy. They rushed to the emergency briefing just after we landed. Now that you're settled, I have to go too."

"I should...go...too." I said, my chest hurting with the effort. Each word required its own breath and with each breath, I could feel the sharp stabs of ribs grinding against each other.

"You're not going anywhere, young man," the older woman said in her Mom voice. I couldn't turn my head but I could picture the face associated with her. Millie.

"Nothing...wrong....feel...fine." I croaked.

Millie sighed, "Let's see, you have a bullet still in your leg. Michael did a terrible job binding it and you lost a bit of blood. You got a laser burn on your shoulder, and another close hit on your other leg. You have superficial bruising to your left eye and left ear. I'm afraid your nose may be broken There are burns on your arm, some gashes from broken glass on your arms and face; you might end up with a Heidelberg scar, and I think a few broken ribs, on both sides."

As her kind voice rattled off the list, I followed along, cataloging the aches and pains from the inside. She had missed the possible concussion and Mount Vesuvius headache.

"You'll be fine, Bryan," Michael said, "Millie will patch you back together. I have to leave for the briefing. I'll leave you in her capable hands."

"Millie," I said as a one-word sentence. "She's… biochemist." The effort to stay conscious was draining my energy.

I heard the rustle of the plastic wrapping as the IV bag was opened and attached to the pole. It rattled as she tested its mount to the improvised hospital bed. "Actually, Bryan," Millie responded gently, her old voice steady and strong, "I'm a bacterial geneticist. But, you know, bacteria, people, you're all the same to me; just bags of protoplasm under the control of DNA." I could hear the reassuring smile in her voice.

I felt my left arm being held and positioned. The slight prick of the IV was almost lost in the background noise of my other pains.

She patted my arm, and continued, "Don't worry. I used to be a clinical surgeon. Haven't lost a patient yet."

Don't worry. Those words were troubling me. There was something I had to do.

Michael's leathery hand took mine and gave it a brief squeeze. "I have to go, Bryan. For a geek engineer, you did extraordinarily well. You're safe now. Rest."

Maybe it was the drugs flowing into my arm. Maybe it was just the extra fluids diluting my blood that made me feel light headed. I was losing the battle again for consciousness. I felt myself slipping below the surface. I had to hang on. Just one more sentence.

I marshaled my remaining strength and gripped the hand in mine. It squeezed back, channeling a small boost of strength. "No, not safe...maybe only days...must contact him, he can...help."

"Who's that, Bryan?" Michael's face swam into focus.

"Steelanowski...Navy SEAL...find...him. Trust...him. He can help. Tell him... underwater...ships dock under pier..."

I felt my hand loosen its grip and Michael's hand slipped away. "Yes, that explains a lot. Good lead. I'll call him right after the briefing. I have to go now."

I felt Michael's comforting hand patting the top of my arm. "Don't worry, you're safe now," echoed in my head as I floated half in, half out of consciousness.

Had I just used those same words last night? We could never feel safe, ever again. Twelve hours ago, my world was so safe it was boring.

How I wished for boring now.

That was it, I thought, that's what started all this. Be careful what you wish for. Yes, that shooting star, my wish, it had changed my world forever.

The last words I heard, as I sank below the surface into blessed unconsciousness, was Millie telling me, "Bryan, I thought you'd want to know. We ran the comet samples Kathy brought back. They are real. The DNA fragments are real. And there's a much larger variety of fragments in these samples. Life has proliferated. How exciting to imagine what new life forms we may find out there."

Her voice sounded faint to me. As my hand slipped from Michael's grip, I mumbled, "Michael...we're going to need a bigger boat."

If you enjoyed this book, please write a review on Amazon.com
and tell all your friends to read this book.

Don't miss book 2 in the Sciquest Legacy Series,

S is for Space.

Visit our web sites for more information:

www.AddieRosePress.com
www.EricBogatin.com
www.LoriDeBoer.net
www.BoulderWritersWorkshop.org

Eric Bogatin, Eric@EricBogatin.com , Longmont, CO
Lori DeBoer, LoriDeBoer@RocketMail.com , Boulder, CO

ABOUT THE AUTHORS

Eric Bogatin is a physicist, writer, and educator. After receiving his BS in Physics from MIT, he went on to finish an MS and PhD also in physics from the University of Arizona, in Tucson, specializing in cosmology, lasers and quantum optics. For the last 35 years, he has focused on signal integrity, a specialized field in electrical engineering related to how signals interact in interconnects. It's basically applied Maxwell's Equations. In this field he has written seven technical books and lectures on this topic around the world. He is also on the adjunct faculty at the University of Colorado, Boulder, where he teaches graduate classes in electrical engineering. This is his first science fiction book, but won't be his last. His signal integrity web site is www.BeTheSignal.com. His personal web site is www.EricBogatin.com.

Lori DeBoer (www.LoriDeBoer.net) is the founder of the Boulder Writers' Workshop and works as an independent writing teacher and coach. She is a contributing editor for *Short Story Writer* and her essays on writing have been published in *Mamaphonic: Balancing Motherhood and Other Creative Acts, Keep It Real: Everything You've Wanted to Know About Research and Writing Creative Nonfiction* and *A Million Little Choices: The ABCs of CNF*. She has had more than a thousand articles and essays published in newspapers, magazines and literary journals, including *The Bellevue Literary Review, The New York Times, Arizona Highways, Pithead Chapel, Working Woman, America West Airlines Magazine, Black Enterprise, Gloom Cupboard, PHOENIX* Magazine and more. One of her stories was top-25 finalist for a Glimmer Train Fiction Open Contest and another was shortlisted for the Bellevue Literary Prize, judged by Jane Smiley. She also works as a writing coach.

She lives with her husband Michael and son Max in Boulder, Colorado, where they own and operate The French Twist Food Truck.

www.ingramcontent.com/pod-product-compliance
Lightning Source LLC
Chambersburg PA
CBHW061308170626
46817CB00001B/95